Uncertain Paths

by

Lita Marinetti

authorHOUSE®

AuthorHouse™
1663 Liberty Drive, Suite 200
Bloomington, IN 47403
www.authorhouse.com
Phone: 1-800-839-8640

First published by AuthorHouse 12/18/2007

ISBN: 978-1-4343-1791-9 (sc)

Printed in the United States of America
Bloomington, Indiana

This book is printed on acid-free paper.

With my heartfelt thanks for their invaluable help

To

Walter Marinetti, whose fine artistry created the cover design

And who provided indispensable technical know-how

And to

Camille Marinetti, who gave generously of her time and considerable

expertise in editing and copy reading my manuscript

Chapter 1

Fred Waverley's skin had cooled at last. Washed and dressed by his daughter, a square of linen dampened with vinegar covering his face, he lay on the sagging rope bed he'd sworn at for thirty years. Now, on this mild October day of 1791, that bed bothered him not one bit. Nor did the open cabin door, wide-open to any intruder.

Honey sat on the only chair, its canes sagging like the ropes on the bed. She rested one bony elbow on each knee and her chin on her fists. She and Mrs. McNair, their only close neighbor, had tried for nine long days and nights to keep her papa on that bed and cool his burning body. Now the fierce fever was gone and the fighting muscles lay slack. She'd tried with all her might, but she hadn't been able to save Papa.

When she was little she used to stuff her blanket in her mouth, up in the loft at night, to keep from screaming out her fear when Papa and One-Ear yelled and cursed at each other in the room below. But in time she got used to the way men would get mad and even into fights when they sat around the whiskey jug at night.

Now pictures from those past times came rushing back into her head.

She hadn't never stopped being scared of One-Ear, because he was a Redskin. But he just came to trade, didn't he? Naught but a red piece of skin hung on one side of his head where the ear should rightly be and his eyes was all yellow where they ought to be white, but he never did nothing worse than kick the chair or the dogs. Papa complained a heap about Indians. Everybody did. How they surprise poor settlers and split the heads of babes with their tomahawks and tear the scalps off people's heads and carry off men to their camps and stick little twigs in their bellies and set them on fire.

But that was <u>other</u> Redskins. Besides, Papa said the English was the real devils. The War was supposed to be over. We'd got our own country now, but them English was still siccing the Indians on us. She remembered ten years ago--she wasn't as high as the spinning wheel--when Papa, and Mama too, was so happy about the end of the War. Papa was swearing to everybody at the Corners that he was going all the way to Yorktown to see that haughty General Cornwallis lay down his sword meekly in the dirt. He never did go, of course. Mama cried and said that place was so far away from these mountains he would never get back.

And now it wasn't the English, it wasn't wild Indians, it wasn't far journeying. It was One-Ear that took Papa off forever. And poor little Josh, and Dan too.

It didn't seem right that she couldn't save Papa. Here she'd been with Granny Harriet way over on the other side of Hemlock Peaks for nigh on two years and helped the old woman with just about every chore: herb-gathering and root-digging and boiling and bottling. She'd go with Granny on her rounds and fetch and mix and watch and try hard to store up every bit in her head, because she liked doctoring sick people better than anything.

But all that went for naught with Papa. They'd sent for her, and she and Sarah had set out right directly. They was strong walkers, but it took them two full days and when they got home Sarah's feet was so bad blistered she needed doctoring too. Just as well the boys was already in the ground, though she would have dearly loved to see their faces just one more time.

Seeing Papa as he was then made her insides go cold as spring water. The belly wound was angry red, shot with vomit-yellow puss, and sent out streaks of pink like the spokes of a wheel. The leg wound was already mortifying, a swampy green all round the gash. For both they made poultices of slippery elm bark, bruising and boiling it, dipping linen pads in it and tying them right firm round Papa's hips and leg. Mrs. McNair had a good store of bark, of course, but Granny Harriet had sent along tincture of arnica that Honey used to wash out them wounds just as soon as she walked in that cabin door and took one look at her papa. But he sweated and shook and raved way out of his head. Someone was always running to the well, night and day, to keep him bathed in coolness every single minute. But all to no avail.

"Death is deaf and hears no denials." That's what Granny Harriet always did say.

A patch of yellow appeared suddenly on the packed dirt of the cabin floor. So the sun had decided to show itself once, anyhow, this day. It lit up a room tidy enough for visitors. After she'd finished washing Papa, Honey had swept every speck of ash and crumb out the door, and dusted off table, chest and chair, the only furniture left besides the bed. Papa looked fair decent, too. Not too many moth holes in the boughten suit they'd found at the bottom of the cedar chest. Honey had seen him wear it only once, when Mama died. He'd been married in it, of course, and worn it to bury his first two babes. After that there hadn't been any weddings or burials for a good long time. Until now. She could hear the hammer ringing outside, first a weak little bang, then five or six louder ones, then a long silence before the next set. It wouldn't be much of a coffin. Mrs. McNair's boy hadn't ever made one afore, but there wasn't nobody else at hand. Mrs. McNair was out there with the vittles she'd brought. And Sarah too, most likely. Sarah was too scared to come near Papa, sick or dead.

Come to think on it, she herself had never felt so peaceful when Papa was alive. And close by. You had to be ready to jump, with Papa. You never knew what he'd do next. He was a lively one, he was, and he liked to play jokes. You had to be careful not to make him mad, too, especially when he'd had a dram or two.

She could see by the patch of sunshine, now near the legs of her chair, that the afternoon was wearing on. Nigh on time to set out for Fox Bald, the small level clearing farther up the mountain where her family buried their dead. Would no one else come at all? It was true that some folks didn't much like Papa. They envied him, him being

3

the best shot in the whole country, and powerful sharp, too, when it came to driving a bargain. But that wasn't no excuse for not paying your respects to the dead. Still, it had been midmorning by the time Jem, Mrs. McNair's husband, set off for the Carsons' place, to tell them about Papa's passing, afore he went up to Fox Bald with his spade to dig the hole. So mayhap it was still too early to expect anyone.

At that very moment the voice of Tom Carson reached her, loud and grindy like a rusty saw.

"So the Devil got him at last, Mrs. McNair. Like you always said."

"The Devil got him long afore this, Tom. It's the fires of Hell has gotten him now," went the tight little twang of Mrs. McNair.

Then Tom Carson's lanky frame was filling the doorway, and he was nodding to her with a big smile like it didn't much matter that Papa was lying there with two knife wounds in him, and a little one in his neck so as they'd had to pull his shirt collar way up to his chin. But Tom and his boy Will, who tramped in right behind him, did pull off their caps when she lifted the cloth from Papa's face. They went and stood frowning down on poor Papa who looked so small in that old suit that hung loose over his wasted shoulders and chest. How could he have shrunk so much in just nine days?

"He sure does look natural like, don't he, Will?" (Folks always said that.) "Mrs. said to tell you she's mighty sorry she can't come. She's taken so bad with the bloody flux that the girls can't leave either. This here with your pa is sorry business, Honey Girl. I reckon you'll be biding back home now your pa's gone."

"Much obliged for your coming, Mr. Carson." Besides the McNairs, the Carsons was the only family less than twenty miles away, so she had to be grateful at least two of them came. She'd heard that the womenfolk had come to see her brothers when they was laid out. Everybody was surely sorry about <u>them</u>.

"What you been doing over yonder all this time? Must be nigh on three years now. We ain't heard hide nor hair of you."

"Yes, sir. I worked a while on a fair-sized place where the mama was sick. And ever since then Sarah and me, we bided with Granny Harriet, the herb doctor." She hoped he wouldn't ask more. Thank the Lord it looked like no news of her had got back home. Enough shame stuck to her skirt from before she left.

She kept her gaze bent to the dirt floor, but she could feel Will's frogeyes staring at her like she was the first sinner he'd ever had the luck to see. He'd growed big enough in three years to shame a girl with his eyes.

She was glad when the both of them hurried out to eat some of Mrs. NcNair's fish stew and greens and corn cakes. They would pass round the bottle of spirits, too, but not too much, she hoped, until after the burying. She stuck her fingers in her ears to shut out the words that came in all too clear, but soon her arms got to aching, so she had to let loose.

"I thought that gal would have filled out by now," Tom Carson was saying. "She's still skin and bones. Looks like Sarah here is aiming to be bigger than her big sister afore long. Now don't you go hiding yourself, girl. How are the boys going to see how pretty you are lessen you show yourself?"

"Let the child be, Tom. Beauty don't make the pot boil."

"Well, a God-fearing woman like you sure does make it boil good, ma'am. I admired your Mulligan stew when we buried them two poor youngsters, and I knowed I'd be back for more soon, with Fred Waverley cut up so bad."

"Me and Honey had a hard time of it, I can tell you, with him kicking and cursing and screaming for his gun. Why, he kicked poor Honey so hard when she was trying to hold him in bed that her poor little legs is black and blue all over."

"God's will be done. Mayhap it'll take some of the Devil out of that girl. I heard she didn't behave no better over yonder, wherever she went." That was Jem McNair's voice, back from his grave-digging task up on Fox Bald. Honey's throat knotted up tight. So somebody had brought evil tales of her after all.

"Hush your mouth in front of the child, Jem," shushed Mrs. McNair. "Be a good girl, Sarah, and go pick us some posies to put on your pa's grave."

"Do you reckon they'll catch that Redskin, Pa?" asked the McNair boy.

"Not if he don't come back this way, boy. He's a fool if he does, and One-Ear ain't no fool. He's off on the other side of the mountains by now, and when he's ready to trade again there's a heap of other folks farther north where they'll never hear of this killing. Besides, who's to say Fred didn't bring it on himself? Didn't I keep telling him to do his trading with the rascal and be done with it, like the rest of us? But he had to always keep the bastard all night and get him liquored up--said he could drive a harder bargain that way. But of course he would get just as crazy drunk and you know he hated Indians near as much as sheriffs and tax men."

"Aye, but the boys, Jem. They sure didn't deserve to get their throats cut like hogs. Why, Josh was bare fourteen. Thank the good Lord they went fast and was in the Lord's bosom afore I ever got here. My, but didn't they make as pretty corpses as you ever seen?"

"How do you know they wasn't drinking, too, and jumped into the scrap? Dan was turning just as ornery as his pa."

By now the sun was sending a golden plank of dancing dust from the doorway over to Honey's chair, reaching up her legs and almost to her waist. She snatched off her thin worsted shawl and waved it over Papa's face where two fat flies were circling closer and closer to the rough gray skin. She carefully replaced the vinegar cloth. How could she make them folks outside stop their mean talk? She'd just have to go out there. She dreaded letting anybody look at her, for fear her sinful anger would show. But they hadn't ought to say such things about the dead, especially about young Josh and Dan that she hadn't even got there in time to bury. She hadn't had time to cry for them either, straining as hard as she could to hold on to Papa and help him fight to stay here in this world and get his revenge on One-Ear like he kept moaning he would do. Though she knew that wasn't right, for vengeance is mine, saith the Lord. Well, she'd have to go outside now and try to eat something because with her there they'd surely hold their spiteful tongues.

But thankfully, no sooner had she choked down two spoonfuls of stew and a bite of corn cake than the others were ready for the trek up the rocky hillside, the two men and two boys taking their turns carrying the rough-hewn pine box with Papa inside. Only two could carry it at a time on that narrow path. It was steep, so Honey heard a heap of grunting and cursing until at last they came out on the open place at the edge of Shanda's Cliff, where a new hole gaped in the red clay next to the five other graves: Mama's and the babes' flat and overgrown with scraggly weeds, and the two boys' still humped with naked earth.

The sky had cleared completely now, and hung, blueberry-blue, behind the black firs that rose and dipped along the top edge of the hills. All down the slopes spilled the reds and yellows of turning leaves, and the greens of them that didn't turn. The powerful crimson of the sumacs always made her think of the burning bush the Bible told of. This time of year was her favorite. It was sad because things was dying and you knew frostbite and chilblains was on the way, but it was a kind of gentle sad, with colors soft, to comfort you. She and Josh and Dan used to like to come here picking berries, or gathering chestnuts, most particularly on a cold fall day, because the minute you came out of the shivery dark of the woods the sun poured down free and friendly on you and the laurels and the spicebushes and all the grasses that growed on the Bald.

Now the sun had just about set, but the air was still mild. The softer light showed off the purple of the ironweeds and the white of the asters. Once the coffin was in the ground and covered, she and Sarah added a bunch of these to the flowers Sarah had brought from below. They made a pretty coverlet for the little hills of the new grave and the recent ones. It comforted Honey that Papa had a gentle evening for his burial.

Mrs. McNair led them in the Lord's Prayer and then she, Honey, managed to say a few words about how famous Papa had been for his sharpshooting and how he'd fought so bravely with the Regulators against them thieving tax men from back east. And how he was a true hero at the Battle of King's Mountain when he helped Colonel Shelby beat the Loyalists and make Cornwallis get out of Charlotte.

When she stopped she suddenly realized that she'd never said so many words all at one time to anyone in all her eighteen years. And that in front of five people who surely didn't appreciate her being so forward. (She didn't count Sarah who she knew was glad.) She could feel herself flush all hot from forehead to fingers. But who else would speak up for Papa? Wasn't it her place? They'd told her that the preacher had been out this way only weeks ago. So he wouldn't be back for five or six months, mayhap longer. They would have a funeral for Papa and the boys then, as was only decent, but she couldn't be here to make sure the preacher found out something good to say about Papa.

Afterward the men sat passing around Brown Betty, as they called the liquor bottle they had of course brought along. They claimed they needed to rest a spell after all that climbing and shoveling.

"What's Sarah and you gonna do here alone until your big brother as is out in Kentucky Territory comes back? Or do you think maybe he'll send for you to go out there?" Tom Carson asked. She hadn't seen James for more than five years, when he'd lit out with some folks going west and never sent a word back himself. But word had come to them that he'd made it to Kentucky. Ever since then Papa had champed at the bit to go out there too, because the end of the War had brought settlers swarming like bees into these parts. He would chew his lips in anger when he told of how these woods used to fairly burst with deer and turkeys and muskrats and otters. Coons and beaver and rabbits, too, of course. You'd bare set out before you'd trudge back, bent over with game slung on both shoulders. Now your dog and you had to track hard for hours to shoot your fill. But somehow Papa never found the right moment to set out for the West.

"I surely hope James will come, Mr. Carson, and get a few things Mr. McNair is keeping for him. But me and Sarah can't bide here waiting for him." She hated to say more because she knew they'd have their own word to put in and end by faulting Papa even more than before.

"You surely ain't going back yonder and fetch and scrub for strangers now you got yourself a place to lay your head and your pa ain't here no more to throw you out."

"But we got to go to Papa's folks in Virginia. Papa said so. He made me promise."

"Well I'll be a skinned polecat! Your pa has kin in Virginia? That's the first I ever heard tell of it." Mr. Carson scratched his hairy ear and Will did the same to his bare one.

"Well, that's where Papa came from. It's a place where they've got little baby hills, not tall mountains like here in Carolina. Papa was brung up there. His pa and this gentleman's pa had bad blood between them, even though they was brothers. But that's long ago and both of them is dead and buried. Papa never wanted to know naught about the son, name of Matthew Waverley, who's rightly his cousin. But he'd hear somewhat of him when he took the hogs and skins to market. That was when Mama was alive and they kept a few animals and even a cow. Appears this Mr. Waverley is a mighty rich man."

"I told her she was daft to even think of going so far, two little slips of gals as has never been further than Green Hollow." This was Mr. McNair talking. He'd just spilled liquor into his beard and was wiping it with his finger and then licking that. "Even if they get there, do you reckon them swells with their stuck-up ways want to see two shabby gals walking up their path and asking for bed and vittles? Gals that growed up in these here mountains and don't hardly know to write their own names? And wait 'til you see all them Nigras, gal. They'll scare Sarah out of a year's growth."

Sarah's eyes popped wide open and so did Will's and Tim McNair's. And for sure, now that Mr. McNair had got on the subject of scaring, and it working so good, he couldn't hardly stop there.

"Did you all hear that owl hoot whilst we was packing in the last of the dirt? You know trouble's coming when an owl hoots in broad day."

"Don't you worry none about that, Jem," said Mrs. McNair. She was sitting a little apart, on a big rock, and carefully fitting some loose gray hairs into the tightly stretched strands that led back into the bun at her neck. She kept a stern eye on her husband, surely counting every swig he took from the brown bottle that now had to be tipped high to yield any liquid. "I aim to turn Fred Waverley's shoes upside down as soon as we get back to the cabin. Anybody's shoes will do, but a dead man's has double strength. And what's more, I already made sure the clock was stopped. We don't want Fred's ghost walking the woods at night or whispering in the chimney."

"You ain't going to stop a mulish spirit like Fred's from walking. He's got a chore to finish. He's got to shoot that murdering Cherokee and he'll get him right between the eyes. Just you wait and see."

There was more of the same kind of talk, but Honey didn't stay to hear it. She took hold of Sarah's clammy hand and said they'd go on down ahead. She didn't want Sarah to catch a chill in the night air, right before they had to set out on such a long journey.

By next morning Honey had repented many times over her anger at the McNairs. They had truly been their brothers' keepers in what they had done for all the Waverleys. Hadn't Mrs. McNair saved her life

Major
Market

845 S. MAIN STREET
FALLBROOK, CA 92028
(760) 723-0857

Store #2   Checker Name: VERONICA

	Sale
RINGL-S RT CRSP ORG	0.99 F
SH GRND SIRLOIN	3.84 F
LOOSE MUSHROOMS	1.19 F
0.34 lb @ $3.49/lb	

Number of Items :   3

SUBTOTAL $6.02
TOTAL $6.02

CASH $20.10
CHANGE $14.08-

SALE SAVINGS $0.80
ALL SAVINGS $0.80

WELCOME TO MAJOR MARKET
EXPERIENCE THE DIFFERENCE!

Tran #26178   Lane #8   Chkr #1B
Date: 04/18/08   Time: 06:39:32

that terrible night she was bleeding so bad and couldn't stop it? Mrs. McNair's words was harsh oftentimes, and she worshipped the Lord a different way from Preacher Morris. Back where the McNairs came from the preacher was a man of book learning who called himself a Presbyterian, and their ways was stern. But they was still God-fearing people.

Honey was glad only Mrs. McNair came to help her and Sarah get ready for their journey. Sarah was smiling and eager to leave. Her feet was healed now and of course she didn't remember much about Papa or their life here. She'd taken to the dogs, though, and would go out to romp with them in between cleaning and packing. She looked so pretty with her long brown hair flipping all about her shoulders.

It was Friday, a bad-luck day, but Honey just could not bide another minute in that cabin. She had finally let herself be talked into taking old Dasher, Papa's gray gelding. James ought by rights to have him, but who knowed if James would come at all? Poor Dasher had no idea what it meant to dash anymore, but he surely would be a help in toting the things they needed, and Sarah too when she got tuckered out.

They would wear the boys' leggings and shirts, so as to look, leastways from afar, like boys. There was oftentimes drunken men on the paths at night. She would take Papa's rifle, too, the old Pennsylvania one that by sheer good luck he'd given Mr. McNair to repair the very day before he got stabbed. She hadn't touched one in the years since she left home, but Papa had taught her how to shoot.

"You'd best take along a skirt and petticoat, each," advised the older woman, who didn't much like the idea of their dressing like boys. "You can quick put them on when you're nigh on your kinfolks' place. Else what will they think of you? It's a shame you don't have no real shoes. Folks don't wear moccasins back east, my girl."

But Honey's thoughts were far off in the past as she dragged her eyes painfully over every inch of the one room that had been home to her and Sarah until they'd sneaked off one night near three years ago.

<u>Not thrown out by Papa</u>, like Tom Carson thought.

She and Sarah had made the room as clean as could be, had even brushed away all the cobwebs high up in the corners. But there was cracks aplenty in the mud that chinked the walls, and the room, once so crowded, looked mighty bare now. Spinning wheel and loom was gone. Used for easy kindling, of course. Only one pot still hung on a peg next the hearth, and only three pewter bowls and a few spoons was left in the cupboard. Above the fireplace the horn brackets that held guns and hatchet and knives was all empty. One-Ear had made off with them, for sure. A wonder the Redskin hadn't taken the pewter bowls, so treasured by Mama. She'd leave them for James, and the almanac. But she couldn't bear to leave the Bible. It was the only other thing left of Mama's. Mama couldn't read or write, but Papa would write in the names when there was births and deaths.

She hadn't been able to do anything about the outside. Weeds and brush choked the vegetable garden and you could hardly find the corn patch anymore. The cowshed was mostly gone for firewood, but the smokehouse was sound, and the hams and side of bacon hanging there would be left for the McNairs. They'd had to kill the chickens to make broth for Papa. The racks for stretching hides, and the staking-board for rubbing them down still stood just outside the door.

"Honey, stop your woolgathering and tell me what more you're aiming to take."

"I'm fixing to take Mama's Bible, ma'am," and she placed it in Sarah's outstretched hand, a hand almost as big as her own. And the child not yet twelve! Sarah favored Mama, who'd been a tall, full-figured woman before she took sick. "Roll it up good in my petticoat. That's a girl."

"You got that bag of apples we picked, child," asked Mrs. McNair, "and the other one of chestnuts you brought? Take these here journeycakes I made, as well. None of this will give you strength, though, and won't last long, and what will you do then? I still say you oughtn't to pay mind to what your pa said when he was out of his head with the fever. Did he even know to tell you how to get there?"

"He was mighty clear when he made me promise, ma'am. He said it's on the Solway, not far above Petersburg. Just keep going east and north and asking folk the way, he said. It's called Laurel Hill. Ain't that pretty? But we can't take all them apples, ma'am. We daren't make Dasher tote so much. Maybe half of them, and the chestnuts. Sarah and me gathered them after a windstorm. We're much obliged for the journeycakes. You've been so good to Papa and us. We'll find berries and more nuts on the way. October's a good month for traveling."

"That might well be, but today's a bad day. Them clouds to the west denote rain. As for your Dasher, your pa said he can't hardly go three mile without he stop and rest. Did you know that?"

"It don't matter. Directly he's winded, we'll let him rest."

Mrs. McNair let out a mighty sigh.

"Listen, Honey. I'm going to tell you something maybe I hadn't ought to. But it just might make you change your mind about dragging Sarah way yonder."

She remembered Sarah then, who was combing out that thick brown hair of hers that was so pretty.

"Sarah sweetie, run out and throw some sticks for them dogs you've taken such a shine to."

Sarah ambled out the door with not a sign of curiosity. But then, Sarah was not a curious kind of girl.

Mrs. McNair took hold of Honey's wrist and pulled her over to the chair where she herself sat down, cautiously, because she was a stoutish woman and never trusted that worn-out little chair. She kept tight hold of Honey's wrist, making her stand there with her knees pressed against those of the older woman.

"You know, child, your pa grumbled to me heaps of times about that Mr. Matthew Waverley that is his cousin. He pure hated that fella 'cause he wouldn't help your pa none when he ran afoul of that sheriff and had to run off. That Mr. Waverley wouldn't even hide your pa for a spell. One time just a couple of days ago when you was fetching water and he was halfway clear in his head, he told me he was going to make you promise to take Sarah and go to that Mr. Waverley's place, so as to be two big loads on his back, and a shame to yourselves as well. He was cackling away about you being in pure misery there. 'Serve the slut right for running off on me,' he said. I'm sorry to say that nasty word, but that was a nasty idea of his, and I don't see as how you need to keep a promise to such a mean man, I surely don't."

Mrs. McNair peered straight into Honey's eyes, anxious furrows cutting deep across her forehead. She meant well, of course, but still, she hadn't ought to talk like that about Papa who was just barely laid in the ground.

"I just got to do what I promised Papa, ma'am. He didn't really mean those things he said. That was his fever talking."

Mrs. McNair heaved another great sigh. "Well, I writ a word on this paper to my oldest girl, Mary. You just follow the creek 'til you get to the Yadkin, and ask for Mary Sikes. She'll find a body going east who'll take you part of the way. Maybe even her own William. He's a large, likely man, and wouldn't let harm come to you. Now don't you be ketched out alone at night! Go knock at a door where you see a petticoat hanging on a line, or youngsters about. Lord, child, I do dread hearing hereafter that someone found two girls starved and frozen solid in the woods. Or maybe kilt by a bear or Redskins or God knows what."

Honey had never seen the tough old woman look almost teary-eyed before. And she herself had to squeeze her eyes shut for a moment. Mrs. McNair was the closest thing she'd had to a mother since she was ten. But she had to be strong right this moment, or for sure, she would never leave. Of course she knew all about the dangers. She might not be pretty or strong, but she had a head on her. Even Papa used to admit that.

"Please don't you fret yourself, ma'am. If need be, me and Sarah can get us food and lodging. We've got the two fine deer skins Papa already grained real good, and I've rubbed them nice and soft. They'll fetch a dollar each, and then I've got sang aplenty, and you know that's worth a good deal." She pulled a pouch filled with ginseng roots from inside her brother's shirt. "Only I'm aiming to keep the skins and as much of the sang as I can as presents for Mr. Waverley. I'd be shamed to walk up to his door empty-handed."

As she and Sarah set out, she thought on what Mrs. McNair had said about Papa. She already knew the story of Papa's feud with those Virginia Waverleys. Her papa's father, her grandfather that was already dead when she was born, was the black sheep of that family on account of him marrying his indentured girl. Then when her papa had to leave home because he'd had to kill a rascally lawman, even his kin treated him bad. So he just scraped the mud of Virginia off his shoes and made off for free air, as he told it. And when Papa, on his deathbed, made her promise to go back to Virginia, it was to "tear a chunk of his birthright out of their foul flesh." Didn't she know well enough that her and Sarah was going to them as the beggared children of a man they'd sure and certain been glad to be rid of? And as if her and Sarah's poorness wasn't enough to make them scorned by those rich and school-learned folks, wouldn't they see right through her to her own worse shame and disgrace? Their only hope might lie in Sarah, whom Honey had managed somehow to keep good and pure through everything. Sarah was such a pretty thing. Maybe even those mighty Waverleys would take to her.

In that doubtful hope she turned her eyes for one last look westward toward Fox Bald. The mist of morning had lifted and the furry hills crouched fearfully under the pale sky. Beyond them the mountains rose slate gray in the distance. Eastward, where Honey and Sarah were headed, thin streaks of milky cloud stretched all the way across a soft blue sky. Somehow, Honey began to hope that God would help them, and even, if she tried very, very hard to do His will, would forgive her for what happened to Papa.

Chapter 2

Six weeks later Matthew Waverley, into whose hands would soon be tossed the reins to guide his young cousins' future, was sitting in the taproom of the Red Heron in Richmond, quite unaware of the girls' existence. He wouldn't have paid it much heed in any case as he sat sipping from a saucer of coffee and listening with half an ear to the familiar complaints of Colonel Meachem, a neighbor of his back in Solway County. His gaze swung repeatedly from the courtyard outside the window, where hostlers sauntered nonchalantly through their task of replacing a wheel of the Petersburg stage, to the hall stairway where he hoped to see his younger brother appear.

The only one in his family who concerned him just now was his wife. Charlotte's lying-in was almost at hand. Her last confinement had brought her close to death. This time he had absolutely insisted that the Negro midwife not touch her mistress. The doctor from Petersburg must attend her. But he was also determined to be there himself. Never again, whatever happened, would he return home to find that Charlotte had been moaning in delirium for days, calling his name and he not there to take her hand and press his cheek against her burning forehead.

Yet duty and reputation called almost as urgently as his wife. They had held him fast by the coattails at this special session of the Virginia Assembly while his fellow delegates argued on and on about those amendments to the new Constitution, a Bill of Rights, as they were calling it, dragging out the session beyond all reason. The weather was blustery, the sky leaden, threatening snow. That would impede, if not prevent altogether, his journey home.

"Colonel Meachem, sir! Up at this ungodly hour? Your fellow delegates will surely not be gathered on the Hill before midday." A rotund little man, who entered the taproom with these words to the

Colonel, also nodded a greeting to Matthew. "Now my stepson here insists he must be off home before the final vote is taken. But you will surely stay the course, Colonel."

"Good morning to you, Mr. Levier. Yes, I'd sooner let you cut off my leg than budge three paces from this wretched town. Until I know, anyhow, that we have at least a modicum of security against those grasping moneymen from the North. These amendments are not all they should be, but they're better than nothing. What we really should do is send those rascals in Philadelphia a remonstrance like the one we wrote on that cursed Assumption Bill."

"Oh yes indeed, Colonel. The one about those northern gentlemen 'conniving to prostrate agriculture at the feet of the large monied interest,'" laughed the little man whose circle of wiry gray hair surrounded a ridiculous knitted cap that covered the spacious bald dome within.

"Well may you laugh, Mr. Levier, with your newspaper selling like small beer, but it's no joke to those of us who supplied General Washington's army and our Virginia militias during the fight for our freedom, and accepted those paper certificates as payment. Then, when the war is over, what do we find? Our paper is worth less every blessed day, until we are obliged to sell it at one-fourth its original value. Just to scrape together enough to pay our mortgages. And now that all our certificates are in the hands of Yankee speculators, that damnable Hamilton and his New York and Massachusetts friends in the Congress ram down our throats a bill obliging the federal government to pay them at par value."

"But sir," said Matthew's stepfather, "there is the question of national honor. National solvency. We must be known to honor our obligations. Some are owed abroad, you know."

"National honor? Hogwash! My country is Virginia, sir, and her honor alone is of concern to me. Everyone knows that Virginia has paid her war debts already. That Assumption Bill requires us to pay off the debts of all the other states. The money the Congress extracts from us in levies will go to pay off the obligations of those northern states that have been sitting on their hands waiting for us Southerners to come to their aid. I tell you we were fools to make this Union in the first place. It will be a narrow squeak just to get these paltry amendments passed. 'Milk and water amendments,' someone has justly named them."

"Indeed, sir," said Matthew, hoping to bring some meeting of minds into the discussion, "they are not all that many men hoped for. Yet you will agree that it is a fine thing to protect our freedom of speech and worship. And of the press. That appears vital to me."

"Speech and the press be damned! I'd sooner protect the freedom of Virginians to make our own laws. And the freedom of my strongbox from the grasping hands of those Federalists in Philadelphia! The best of all those proposed amendments was to refuse to the Congress the right to tax us. But curse me if that one wasn't tossed aside!"

Mr. Levier's response to this was surprisingly mild. "Allow me to express my hope, Colonel, that you and the other gentlemen up on Shockoe Hill will be inspired by the noble architecture of Mr. Jefferson, and decide most wisely." Matthew winced, as he had earlier at the remark about staying the course, because he knew the vote was an important one. Virginia's was the last vote needed to confirm this Bill of Rights and make it part of the law of this nation so new, so untried in governing its fourteen self-interested states. His good repute, he was sure, depended on his participating. Yet how could he live with himself, or live at all, if Charlotte . . .

"Noble architecture, Devil take it. But now there's this fool quarrel I must attend to."

"Col. Meachem is up betimes," Matthew explained, "because of a delicate duty to perform at Miller's Field."

"Ah?" exclaimed Mr. Levier, disdain evident in the pout of his lips. Still an outsider despite nearly thirty years in Virginia, he decried all violence, that of the field of honor more than any other. To him nothing was more foolish than risking life and limb because of an impulsive insult, or something taken as one. In this respect, the second husband that Matthew's mother had accepted betrayed his Philadelphia Quaker background.

"It's that young fool Stuart Ludwell, you know," said the Colonel, "my wife's cousin once removed. He's got himself smitten with Hannah Finch. You know of her, of course, as who does not. A wanton wench and the subject of that charming ditty: 'Round and pink and soft Miss Finch, the wench whose bum we love to pinch.' Unfortunately, Mr. Faircloth has laid serious claim to her, serious in terms of lodging and baubles, that is, so a meeting between him and young Ludwell was inevitable. I was to join the boy here, as his second, and he's already late. I hope the young whelp will not cry off. He was rather fainty in heart last night when he came to me. Whimpering like a spaniel."

"Oh, I doubt that signifies anything," interposed Matthew. "He was sodden drunk, I'm sure, but will have regained his spirit this morning." Matthew was defending the son of his late neighbor and friend, Mr. Ludwell, buried only six months ago. And here again he was remiss in his duty. Small as was his regard for the wastrel son, he should be present in the field to ensure a fair fight.

"Heaven be praised, here's the scoundrel, and with your brother," said the Colonel, brightening at the sight of two men at the hall doorway. The taller one, a sturdy chap with dark, tousled hair and large features, had his arm around the shoulder of the smaller, whose drooping head and slow feet betrayed a somewhat dazed desire to be somewhere, <u>anywhere</u>, else.

Stuart Ludwell's manservant, a burly Negro named Titus, appeared from a back room and took over the support of his young master. Col. Meachem raised a hand in salute to Matthew and his stepfather, and then led master and servant out the front door of the inn. Miles (for that was the name of the taller man who had just been relieved of his burden) nodded to his older brother and to his stepfather. He pulled up a chair, yelled for the innkeeper, and launched into one of his favorite sports (when deprived of any more physically active), that of joshing his stepfather.

"Zounds, sir. How did you ever slosh here through the mud and keep your boots so clean? Surely you risked no mounting on a nag? Such courage so early in the morning could be asked of no man."

Everyone knew Patrick Levier's custom of keeping three yards' distance between himself and all equine creatures, and since he did not keep even a dogcart in Richmond, his legs were his means of conveyance while there.

Now nothing amused Mr. Levier more (when cut off from more significant debate) than parrying the thrusts of his younger stepson, and aiming some of his own.

"I walk on air, my boy, so mighty are the momentous affairs that fill my head and uplift me. Or, to regard the subject on a more mundane level, the mud on the square is quite safely frozen this morning. But you, of course, would have no notion of the world outside. I wonder you are upright at all, with fermented juice of the apple sloshing about in your belly and your ears no doubt still ringing with the din of last night's dice boxes."

"Ah, but I've been abed these five hours, sir. Snoring heartily, so one of my bedfellows groaned in my ear as I extricated myself from his ponderous leg. As for dice boxes, that's the music that lulls me to sleep. But tell me, sir," looking meaningfully at the seat of his stepfather's chair, "do you sit on air, too? I seem to remember that the seated position does not please you well."

Matthew knew that fear of horses was not the only reason that Patrick Levier avoided riding them. He suffered from piles, among numerous other bodily complaints. High spirits and raillery were all very well, but Miles pushed his privilege as his stepfather's favorite too far. Wasn't he old enough to show a little restraint?

But then Miles quite unsuspectingly laid himself open to Mr.

Levier's revenge by inquiring about Matthew's brother-in-law, Geoffrey Burnham.

"How is Mr. Burnham's lawsuit progressing? You have your ear so close to the ground for any whisper of news for your rag. What hope of success for our erstwhile Tory?"

Geoffrey Burnham had fled from Norfolk with Governor Dunmore at the beginning of hostilities, and spent the war years in England. He hoped to regain at least a portion of the estate near Norfolk that he had been managing for his uncle, Lord Ashton. The land had been left him at the death of his uncle, but he had to convince Virginians, in a court of law, that he had done nothing to aid the English during the War. Matthew had undertaken his brother-in-law's case, and was gathering affidavits from both sides of the Atlantic. Of course those for which he had sent to England would take months to arrive.

Here was opportunity for Mr. Levier's revenge on his teasing stepson. "No, I've heard nary a word. The North Star is due in Norfolk in three or four days, and perhaps she bears evidence in her mailbags. However," and here the stepfather allowed himself a broad smirk, "I do hear that Mr. Burnham is having considerable success in another quarter. The fair Lucinda..."

"And what of the fair Lucinda? Miss Ludwell, that is." Matthew noticed the momentary tightening of his brother's grip on the arms of his chair, before he relaxed again into his nonchalant sprawl and gave a mighty yawn.

"They say she looks with favor on Mr. Burnham's many graces and talents. By Heaven, if he's successful there, and I've observed him doing everything advancive of that end, he will not be rich--the girl's portion is modest, so I'm told--but he'll have the wherewithal to settle cozily right here in Solway County, even if he should lose his lawsuit. How pleasant for Mrs. Charlotte to have her brother within visiting distance. And for you, dear Miles, who have such affection for the little Ludwell lass. It appears you forge ahead with your intent to buy the

Humbolt place?"

Matthew feared that this thrust penetrated deeper than their stepfather intended. Everyone knew that Miles was especially fond of Lucinda Ludwell, a lovely girl of twenty. She was sister to that worthless profligate, Stuart Ludwell. Ever since he was a roughneck lad of twelve and she already a charmer of two or three, Miles had made a pet of her, bringing her birds' eggs and colored pebbles. And since he, more than most, scorned the delicate tastes and disdain of man's work that characterized Geoffrey Burnham, he would naturally regret seeing Lucy fall prey to his appeal. But Matthew suspected (or rather, his wife Charlotte suspected, and he always had full faith in her view in matters such as this) that Miles' regard for the girl was far more tender than he revealed to anyone.

Fortunately Gionelli, the innkeeper, hurried into the room at this moment, finally responding to Miles' call. He bowed low in apology as he wiped bloody hands on his apron and muttered curses at some potboy whose absence was clearly both a felony and a sin.

"Pardon, gentlemen. My boy and a new dunce who doesn't know hock from fatback were slaughtering a hog and my attendance was sorely needed."

Miles waved the apologies aside and ordered half a side of bacon, half a dozen pieces of toast, a bowl of hominy, and a large mug of chocolate.

"Mind you lace it well with rum," he added.

"And pray light some lamps, my man," said Mr. Levier. "It's as dim as a root cellar in here." Indeed, as the sky darkened outside, the inn's smoke-blackened oak walls absorbed what meager light still entered.

Gionelli bowed again, but Matthew caught his look of vexation. He would doubtless try to satisfy them with an extra candle or two. Oil was too dear to be used in the daytime.

As soon as the innkeeper left, Matthew reproached Miles for refusing their brother-in-law's offer of lodging in his house, only two miles from

Richmond, where he himself always stayed at Assembly times. He received the same old reply, which he could not understand.

"The inn is far more jolly, old fellow. I defy you to claim that anyone offers as good a mutton chop or small beer as Gionelli presented me with last night."

"That's as may be, but at least my bedfellow was a known gentleman, the bed was free of vermin, and we heard only the song of crickets from midnight on. Not to mention that Mildred was quite put out with you." Their sister Mildred was mistress of the house near Richmond.

"Well, if she'd leave off being so persnickety, I might go there. She gives me the willies with her incessant fussing about. Besides, crickets don't sing. They rasp. Evenings at our brother-in-law's are infernally dull. Not a fiddle nor a card after eleven." Miles shrugged his robust shoulders and heaved a sigh as he surveyed his elder brother with an air of commiseration. Gone were the days, thought Matthew, when he was an object of admiration to Miles. No doubt the younger man, now well inured to life in the West, thought him overly delicate. Indeed, he did appreciate Mildred's attentiveness. Striving so hard to please was surely not a fault.

A planter of all three men's acquaintance strolled into the room at that moment. Mr. Appleby was a small man of sinewy movements and a thin voice like the mew of a cat.

"The coachman assures me the stage will leave shortly, gentlemen, but I don't like the look of the sky. I shall stay on here another day at least, and I'd advise you both to do the same. And Mr. Miles Waverley, if you please, I'd like a word with you about that Kentucky acreage you told me of." Miles had done extensive surveying in the Ohio Valley, in addition to developing a farm of his own there on land their father had left him. He and Matthew worked together in procuring land for those who wished it, with Matthew doing the legal work in Richmond. The newcomer pulled a chair up close to Miles, and Mr. Levier drew his own closer to Matthew.

"Mr. Appleby is right, Matthew. Frozen in a snowdrift at the side of the road, what possible use could you be to your dear wife?"

"Permit me to say that you exaggerate, sir. A few flurries is all we have to fear, and with water in the ruts frozen hard, we can expect a smooth ride." Matthew considered himself a reasonable man. Where Charlotte was concerned, however, he sometimes chose to believe whatever would delay his leaving her or hasten his return. He had some inkling of this, but would not have admitted it to a living soul.

Now he was up and moving toward the stairway, calling up to his man Stove to bring down his portmanteau and writing box. He turned to his stepfather.

"You won't forget to send an order for the model of the new threshing machine when you're next in Yorktown, will you? I must have mine built by summer. You'll be sure to specify the Meikle model, the drum and beater kind. I'll be much obliged." These instructions had been carefully gone over twice already. Matthew knew himself to be a fussbudget, but could not stop.

Your brother says you are bent on leaving today, Mr. Waverley," said Mr. Appleby as he followed Matthew into the hall. "Even on taking Dauntless with you. And I thought you so careful of that revered, but ancient creature."

"Dauntless is not so old as all that, sir. You forget that he is the great grandson of Old Fearnought. I assure you he has plenty of mettle in him yet. Besides, my man Stove will be on his back the greater part of the way, and Stove sits light in the saddle as a dove on her roost." Matthew did take special care of his fine old stallion, had not raced him in years. But he disliked hearing the animal's stamina impugned.

"What ails that good fellow, your brother? I've never before seen him low in spirits. Could he have taken something ill in what I offered for the land? Or perhaps," with a laugh, "he lost heavily at Faro last night?"

"Neither the one nor the other, I assure you. You mistake him, I rather imagine. But excuse me, sir. I must look to my baggage." Matthew then busied himself with quizzing Stove, a small Negro with smooth, pecan skin who stood waiting patiently by the hall door.

"Portmanteau?"

"Yes sir, stowed in the boot."

"And the things for the ladies: Persian cotton, silk thread, packthread stays? How about the pearl buttons for my new waistcoat?"

"Yes, Mr. Matthew, all in the portmanteau."

"And let's see...trunk key, knife, pistol, all in my pocket. But you forgot my book."

"No sir! In the writing box." Stove grinned broadly. He knew his master's habits well, and never forgot anything, but he enjoyed being given the opportunity of showing just how perfectly he performed his duties.

Meanwhile Miles was pacing impatiently by the side of the coach, his one small trunk already thrown carelessly, by his own hands, onto the top of the vehicle.

Miles and Matthew were the only people boarding the empty stage, as the first tiny mist of snow began to fall. Gionelli shook his head and Mr. Levier shivered in spite of his thick wool cloak, while the coachman, with reins already in one hand, downed his last tot of grog and one of the hostlers blew a final warning blast on the horn.

"The gentleman's lady is in circumstances, you know, and her time is nigh. You won't see him tarry for an avalanche of snow, if he won't tarry to vote on those blasted amendments," said Mr. Appleby as he and Patrick Levier reentered the taproom.

"Ah well, sir. Perhaps they will make it to Petersburg before the road becomes impassible, and will stop at Ferguson's for the night." This was the sanguine opinion of Gionelli, who wished good business to all innkeepers, with the exception of his rivals in Richmond, whose beds (he would tell you in confidence) teemed with lice and whose fare wasn't fit feed for hogs.

As the coach slowly bumped its way down Shockoe Hill both brothers turned for a last look at the new Capitol, rising loftily above the river, yet forlorn this day on its mound of hardened mud beneath a pewter sky streaked with snow.

"Hardly an inspiring sight at the present moment," sighed Matthew, "but in spring with new grass and trees in fresh leaf, it will surely be proclaimed the finest building in the country. Nothing, even in Philadelphia, to rival it. At first I questioned Mr. Jefferson's idea as too grandiose. Copying a Greek temple, of all things. But why should we not, we in America, have fine public buildings? To be sure, it will look more elegant once it is clothed in white plaster. Brick looks so ordinary."

"God's red britches, Matthew! You're still one of them. A lover of pomp and kings. A Federalist, in short. I see no wrong in plain red brick. I suppose you approve the President riding through the streets of Philadelphia in a fine coach with six horses and four footmen, like an English lord?"

"No, but I see no great harm in it. General Washington has surely proved by now that he has no aspirations to kingship. All that is mere decoration. Let Mr. Adams and the others play with grandeur to instill awe in the city rabble."

"It's more than play, I vow. There's danger in it. Why our own senator, Mr. Richard Lee, who becomes more of a Federalist by the hour, supported a proposal to address Mr. Washington as 'His Highness the President.' I agree with those who say that titles and high living are an insidious way of making an already-too-powerful government even more so."

"No, no, Miles. You and those gentlemen give too free rein to your imaginations. However, I do fear this new breed of men, of whom there are many in New York, Boston, and Philadelphia. Land is nothing to them. Attachment to it, responsibility for it and those it supports, and all those round about. It gratifies me immeasurably that you will soon have land of your own in the county, after so many years."

Miles felt the warmth of his brother's smile. He knew that Matthew, so much older, loved him like a son, and had missed him sorely these last few years that he had spent almost entirely in the West, proving himself and improving his fortune. He had scarcely spent above a month at a time at the home plantation since he ran off to join the Continental troops at the age of fifteen, eager to escape the excessively paternal eye of his elder brother. The only eyes he had missed were the lovely ones of--but he willed himself not to think of that just now. Back to the manly subject at hand.

"Indeed, you're exactly right. About the moneymen and the proposals of Highhanded Hamilton. We need more men of <u>our</u> stamp, planters from the South, in Congress, which is what Mr. Jefferson is working to achieve. Have you subscribed to his new semiweekly, the <u>National Gazette</u>? A bloody fine idea, if only our High Federalist postmaster, Mr. Pickering, doesn't manage to 'lose' many copies in the mail. We do need a counterweight to that Tory rag, the <u>Gazette of the United States</u>."

Matthew smiled again, but wryly this time. "Yes, to be sure I've subscribed, but I despise all this talk of the 'republican interest,' this talk of Tories. Are we to go the route of the English, with factions governing us, rather than we governing ourselves? A government riddled with favoritism, corruption, and shameful sinecures? In short, all the evils of the government of Sir Robert Walpole, so notorious that in England herself his very name suggests them? I shudder to think it."

"That's stretching things, Old Fellow. Surely..."

But Matthew raised a weary hand. "Excuse me. Doubtless you have good arguments, but my head is throbbing. I must rest my eyes." Miles pressed his lips together in vexation. He, like his stepfather, hated to abandon what promised to be a good argument. Yet his brother did look pained. And <u>old</u>. How he used to envy Matthew's aristocratic grace and regular features. Now, near forty, he looked worn. Fine lines etched the corners of his eyes and ran from cheek to chin. He did not close his eyes, but instead fastened them anxiously upon the thickening snow that clicked against the coach windows. Miles knew well what his brother feared, and that there could be no relief for him until he was by his wife's side.

No help for it. He might as well let his thoughts stray, in silence, to his own worries. Yet why should he let the foolishness of a mere chit of a girl interfere with the firm course he had set for himself? He had now, at not yet thirty, the wherewithal to acquire a good piece of land in his home county which lay in the most prosperous part of Virginia, now that tidewater land was worn out from too many years of tobacco crops. By hard work and taking well thought-out risks in land speculation he had tripled the modest inheritance of a younger son. The unfortunate Mr. Humbolt, whose health was fast declining and who had no heir, had pretty well agreed to sell his estate. Miles had political ambitions, and he knew that Matthew was weary of service in the Assembly and that family repute as well as his own abilities gave him, Miles, an excellent chance at becoming Matthew's successor. He was ready to marry. The life of a bachelor, though taken good advantage of, had long since begun to pall. There were one or two quite respectable girls in the West who would not hesitate to accept him. Yet when he conjured up, in his mind's eye, their faces, their manner, their voices, Lucy Ludwell's conquered them with scarcely a skirmish, though that word was hardly appropriate because no face was more mild, no manner more sweet, no voice more gentle, than hers. But for those other girls it could be said that they knew a real man when they saw one. They would never look at a milksop like Geoffrey Burnham!

"Can you see my man?" Matthew was shouting to the coachman, trying to be heard above the wind, and getting a shake of the head as answer. He turned to Miles.

"Do you think the fellow has had the sense to dismount and lead Dauntless? Since we're going at less than a walking pace ourselves. That injury to his right foreleg is not completely healed, and if he should break through ice and stumble..."

But Matthew soon forgot the horse in his impatience to get home. "Great God! At this pace we'll not even see Petersburg before nightfall."

Miles resigned himself to the role of reassuring cushion for his brother's anxiety. Not unwillingly, in truth. Better that than to droop like a whipped hound because a girl chose to forget him.

Darkness was indeed closing in on the roofs of Petersburg as the coach horses slipped and strained over the snow-covered cobblestones in the courtyard of the Fighting Cock. Then Matthew paced the wet boards of the Inn's parlor for half an hour before Stove led a soaked, but still soundly-walking Dauntless into view. Yet such comfort counted for nothing when he finally tracked down the servant who was to have met them with horses and wagon for the final stage of the journey to Laurel Hill. Or rather, Stove tracked him down, goodness knows where. The man was trembling when he was dragged into the gentlemen's parlor. Only recently brought from fieldwork on a distant plantation to stable service at the home place, he'd had as yet no direct contact with his master. And quite evidently, Stove had done nothing to allay his fears. Matthew had to do that, forcing himself into calm words said in a calm tone before he could get anything out of the fellow.

The man had been sent out in haste that very morning to summon the doctor here in Petersburg--Mistress being sore in labor and snow beginning to fall--and when he got here, with snow already up to the fetlocks, no doctor! He had left on an urgent call to a farmer with his head kicked in by a horse, and could of a certainty not be expected back that day in such a storm as this.

Even worse than that, there were no fresh horses to be had anywhere, none whose owners would lend or hire them out with darkness falling and wind and snow increasing by the minute. Nothing for it but to stay the night in Petersburg, and hope for better weather in the morning. But whatever nature might bring on the morrow, Matthew would certainly set out at dawn, on his precious Dauntless, if necessary.

The horse would be well fed and rested. The fortunate animal knew nothing of the anxiety that so gripped his master's stomach that he could barely touch his food, or catch more than fitful moments of sleep.

Chapter 3

"Merciful God!" cried Charlotte as the pain welled up out of the pit of her belly and spread in waves up, up, and out until she didn't know whether she would puke first, or faint. Then she shrieked, really shrieked at the top of her lungs. And the pain began to subside.

She lay in the big ground-floor chamber, hers and Matthew's, and still little Edward's, whose crib had been shoved into a far corner along with the birthing stool. They'd had her on that wretched stool for hours--must have been hours--until she made them help her onto the bed, too tired to sit up, even with support. The bed had been stripped of its curtains and coverlet so as not to be stained with her blood. The wooden planks of the floor had been bared of their Turkey carpet. She cursed that infernal bed. If ever she got off it alive, she would never lie on it again. It had brought her to this, had it not?

Had she said that aloud? Thank God the old woman wasn't there. Pious, stern-faced Mrs. Levier, her mother-in-law, had certainly been too firm in her Quaker stoicism even to groan, much less curse, when she was delivered of her many children. All grown to healthy adulthood, damn them!

She opened her eyes...and quickly closed them again. Three faces, two black and one white, were staring down at her in helpless anxiety. Even old Nancy, the midwife who had seen her through how many births? Five. And now, because Matthew had forbidden the woman to touch her, had left strict orders that they call in the Petersburg doctor at the first signs of labor, Nancy, idiot that she was, was afraid to come nearer than five feet of her mistress. Charlotte had had a wretched time with her last lying-in, when poor little Edward was born. Ever since she'd discovered that she was again with child, she had dreaded, truly dreaded, this day, sure that this babe would cost her her life. Had not her cousin in Williamsburg died only days after the birth of her sixth child? It was a common fate. You lost your children--she'd lost three of hers--and then you yourself were lost.

Then came another onslaught of pain, worse than before, surely splitting her in two, and she sank into a gray mist, far from caring what indecencies came out of her mouth.

"Where in God's name is Kate?" she heard herself screaming as the pain lifted and the cloud in her head began to clear. Kate Nelson lived on the plantation nearest theirs. No use even thinking of that Petersburg doctor getting here before she expired, not with the snow deepening by the hour. She must not have been screaming after all because her woman, Joan, was leaning her black ear close to Charlotte's mouth to catch her words.

"Big Moses gone to fetch her, Mistress, nigh on three hours ago. But the snow...it's so thick you can't never see your hand before your face."

"How long have I been here, Joan? Brought to bed, I mean?" and the tears broke from her eyes. <u>She</u>. Crying before the servants.

She didn't hear the answer because the pain hit again, but in between the next few sieges, not tears, but rage against Matthew surged up in her throat and jaws. She would have bitten him if he were there and she had the strength. How could he go off to his foolish politicking and leave her to a doctor who wouldn't come and a midwife forbidden to help? What's more, he'd allowed his mother to go off to attend her own daughter's first labor. Who was left to aid and comfort his wife, whom he claimed, the lying bastard, to love so dearly? His Aunt Abigail, a doddering old woman who could scarce remember her own name, was hovering over the bed at that very moment, dabbing Charlotte's neck with some foul-smelling rag.

"It just won't come. And she's too tuckered out to push any more," she heard someone say. Serve them right if she died, and the monster inside who killed her turned out to be the great, lusty boy Matthew so longed for. And he would strangle himself in his navel cord, for so he deserved for killing her.

"What if we let the stranger girl come in? She say she know to birth babies. Couldn't do no harm now."

"And Massa find out we let some ragamuffin in to touch Missus, when he done forbid <u>me</u>?"

"Then <u>she'd</u> be to blame. Besides, she's kin, so she say."

Charlotte was beyond caring what those words meant. But later, in brief moments of relief, she caught glimpses of a new face above her, that of a young girl. The face was calm, and the voice that came with it was firm. She couldn't grasp the words, but the voice spread over her like a stream of cool water, lifting her and easing her strained muscles. Then hands were moving over her swollen belly and reaching deep inside her. Knowing hands were touching her at last. Then she could hear no more. When she next came to, they were lifting her onto the birthing stool. Then the young girl was clasping Charlotte's hand and bending over that hideous mound of her belly. The voice, in which Charlotte felt herself enfolded, was telling her to push. Hard. She was a giant fish about to explode and sink in its cloud of blood to the bottom. An end she fervently wished for. At last it came: the creature inside ripped her open. It was over.

The fires of Hell were licking at Honey's hair and burning her forehead and cheek. The smell of smoke filled her nostrils and throat with every breath. Coughing, she tried to open her eyes, then quickly squeezed them shut again against the roaring flames, but not before she spied a black face looming over her shoulder. She must submit meekly to God's angry judgment.

But she couldn't help struggling to escape Hell's terrible fire. She rolled away from it and slowly, fearfully, opened her eyes. She truly was in God's eternal Hell. Not God, but a black devil stood over her, and not far away another one was stirring a huge iron caldron that spewed out clouds of evil-smelling smoke. Honey trembled, and turned away her face, hiding it in the dirty shawl that covered her.

Something touched her shoulder and she gave a small cry.

"Missy, Missy, don't make no trouble, please. Don't you stop here. If Mistress know you here all the night, we all catch it, for sure."

At the first words Honey realized that the thin, old-woman voice couldn't belong to a devil, nor the words either. She turned her head and opened her eyes once more. A stooped, gray-haired woman with black, black skin stood over her, looking mighty cross. As Honey struggled to sit up, the old woman hobbled, muttering and leaning on a stick, over to the other black creature next to the caldron, and Honey saw that it was only a black child scrubbing pots with lye soap.

She was in a kitchen twice as big as Papa's whole cabin at home. It had to be a kitchen, since it was filled with big tables laden with food--another Negro girl was plucking a goose at the end of one of them--and the wall on either side of the huge fireplace was hung with more pans and pots and ladles and tongs than Honey had ever seen in all her life.

33

In two of the corners there were cupboards that went all the way up the wall and looked to be full of platters, bowls, and utensils of every sort.

Honey now remembered how she'd helped with a birthing, but everything else that had happened since she and Sarah finally got to this place was blurry in her mind like early morning on Fox Bald. An old lady had let them in a side door--they hadn't dared go up the steps to the fancy porch in front--and led them through a quiet house, then up many long, dark steps to a cold room where they'd been left huddling in a corner to keep from freezing.

Later the old lady came back, babbling excitedly and hard to comprehend, but saying over and over: "Oh dear, oh dear, poor dear, the baby won't come." Honey of course begged to be allowed to help, saying she'd birthed many a babe, but the lady went away and did not come back. Sarah had found a blanket in a chest, and the two of them curled up in it on the bed and went to sleep.

It was much later, after screams from far below began to rise through the darkness and woke them up, that a brown—skinned woman (not black like the people here in this kitchen) had come and taken Honey by the arm and pulled her right out of that bed and out of that room and down those many stairs to where a lady was lying all wet with sweat and limp with misery. The baby was in a breech position, but Honey had seen that before and had even been useful to Granny Harriet because of her small, narrow hand that could slip in easy. There was plenty of good hot water and lye soap to wash her arm right up to the elbow, and then Honey was able to reach in and turn the little bottom away and let the head come into place. After the mother--Mrs. Waverley, Honey supposed, though no one thought to tell her--was delivered of a boy, weak and battered from the long birthing but breathing regularly, Honey suddenly had to pee, and bad. And more, too. So she managed somehow to get out of that house and through deep snow to a thicket away from all the little cabins that she could barely make out in the dark.

But after she'd done her business, how was she to find her way back to that cold little room where she and Sarah had been put? The whole house was dark: not a candle showing from any window. But then she had seen a little gleam of light coming from this kitchen, and had crept in. There was embers still glowing on the hearth, and no one was about, so she had curled up close to that little bit of warmth. That was all she remembered.

But the old black woman was standing over her again with a big frypan in her hand. "You got to go, Missy, and I got to fry the folk's bacon and toast their bread. You is in my way."

Honey was used to obedience, so she got up like the old woman said, and moved uncertainly toward the only open door. That led into a small room where another Negro stared up at her from a steaming tub where she was scrubbing stains from sheets, no doubt the bloody ones from the birthing.

"Well there you are!" Honey turned to see a white girl standing in the bright sunlight of an open doorway, stamping her booted feet and laughing to see the snow shower the threshold. The old black woman hobbled over to close the door.

"Where you been, Missy? We done looked for you all over yesterday for long after sundown to give you your supper. And your poor Mama near 'bout to meet her Maker."

"That's for me to know and you to find out, old Sukey," answered the child. For Honey could see now that she was only a child, skinny and almost as tall as Honey, but that didn't say much, since Honey was so small.

"Are you really my cousin? Two or three times removed? Is your name Waverley too? What's your first name? Mine's Molly....So yours is Caroline? But Honey for short. I'll wager it's because you're sweet. Well, I'm not sweet, and Mama isn't either. And Grandmama, she's as sour as persimmons before they're ripe. Mama's not sour, but she's tempery."

"Child, child!" said the old cook. "Your tongue do wag us to death. Take this lady to the house, and Jillie will bring her and the other one some hominy directly."

Honey shivered in the outside air, bitingly cold though the sun was shining so bright she had to squint. Close to two feet of snow was piled up on either side of the narrow path to the house, and all about as far as she could see was pure, shining whiteness that near blinded you to look at it.

"Lordy, lordy, whatever happened to your face?" asked Molly as she turned at the back door of the house to see if Honey was following her. Honey slowly raised a hand to her cheek. It felt right rough to her fingers and sore to the touch. She must look even worse than she feared.

"Just a touch of the frostbite," she managed to say. But that was a lie. She knew it came from crying, near to every day on the long trip here, with the cold November wind whipping across her wet cheeks. Way back when she was a little, little girl, and cried over some little-girl pain, Mama would rock her in her arms and tell her: "Cry all your tears out now, child. Once you're a woman, there won't be no time for tears."

But there was time, all that long walking from her mountains to this place. That was when the misery of what happened to Papa and the boys came over her strong. She felt worst about Josh, who was such a cheerful little cricket, only eleven two years ago when she left home, just about the size of this child ahead of her on the stairs, and a chatterbox like her. "I am my brother's keeper," the Bible said, and those words kept worrying Honey like a bellyache that don't never quite go away. She knew in her heart that if she hadn't left home, and taken Sarah, Josh would be alive today, bright and chattery as ever. And Papa and Daniel too. Mrs. McNair had near to said as much. She said Papa's drinking had gotten much worse and Daniel was drinking just like him, and getting mean, too. After all, One-Ear had been coming for years, drinking and quarreling with Papa, but in the morning the Indian would be gone and Papa sleeping and snoring late into the day.

What devil had got into her to leave? Didn't Jesus say the meek would inherit the earth? Didn't He say to turn the other cheek? And Papa didn't even beat her. A slap now and then was all. When she did something wrong and needed it. As for that "playing house" he liked when all the other children was asleep, that didn't hurt her one bit. She'd been wicked to leave Papa forlorn and her brothers deserted.

She tripped on a step of the dark stairs they were climbing and scraped her hands on the rough wall to get her balance. She couldn't see, more from tears than from darkness. For the whole weight of her wickedness fell over her once again like one of those slides of rocks that would of a sudden sweep down the hillside back home. She'd truly been the death of Papa and the boys. Merciful Jesus! Papa had rightly prophesied when he told her, those few times when she balked at his bidding, that she would be the death of him. God would never forgive her for that.

"Come on now," cried Molly, running halfway back down the flight of steps to where Honey had stopped, and taking her by the hand. "It's at the next landing." And in a few moments Sarah, the one safe, familiar creature left in Honey's world, was clinging to her neck and weeping. "Why didn't you come back?" she gasped, and could say no more.

Honey stroked the thick, dark hair that fell almost to Sarah's waist. Such a soft, trusting girl, already beginning to fill out into a pretty woman. Honey felt a little of her courage return. She had no time to give way to grief, or even guilt. She'd got her and Sarah to this place, as ordered by Papa. The wish of a dying man had to be obeyed. They was inside Mr. Waverley's house now, but neither master nor mistress had been there to welcome them. Papa had ordered her to force these people to take them in. She could scarce fathom what Papa had meant by saying such a thing. But she must do her best to make herself useful somehow, so as how they'd be allowed to stay.

The child named Molly was still babbling on, as she doubtless had been all the while that Honey's memories of Papa and Daniel and little Josh had swarmed around her like angry hornets.

"You see? I made them build a fire. It was cold as hoarfrost when I came looking for you. And your sister not even in the bed, but curled up on top of it in that mangy blanket. The one Silky, our spaniel, used to sleep on, for goodness sake!"

Little wonder Sarah was afraid to get inside the bed. Such a fine one they had never seen, with carving on the posts and <u>sheets</u> clearly in view above the woven coverlet. And at the head, a long pillow with a baby sheet on it! Even Papa hadn't slept on sheets at home. The one they had found in the chest, along with his boughten suit, had been used to lay him out on. And bury him in.

Here there was a hearty fire blazing on two fancy bars of iron, nicely braided rugs on the floor, a small table with two small chairs, and a trundle bed in the corner.

Honey noticed that Sarah was watching her and trying to get her to look at the window. Oh my! There was glass in it! Neither of them had ever been in a house with glass in the windows, though they'd seen them from the outside whilst on their journey.

The goose-plucking black girl appeared with hominy, ham, and tea, and Molly insisted they sit right down to eat at the little table.

The brown-skinned woman who had come to fetch Honey for the birthing came in to see if they'd got their victuals, and to order a tub and hot water brought to them. She was carrying a little white boy on her hip. He looked to be about two, was very thin and had dark hollows under his eyes that seemed sunk into his head. The woman, whose name was Joan, told them to keep very quiet because Mistress was still sleeping deep and needed her rest. The visitors could now refresh themselves with a bath, and she would come fetch them when

Mistress was awake.

"And the babe?" Honey ventured to ask, in her meekest voice.

"He's sleeping just fine, too, Missy." Her voice was not friendly, Honey thought, and she suddenly realized that her hands and arms and gown was spattered with blood and smeared with soot from the hearth. Small wonder they talked of washing.

"That was Edward, my brother," said Molly as soon as the woman and little boy left. "He's sickly, as you can plainly see. He's been sick ever since he was born. He won't live to be a man. He's always with Mama or Joan or Grandmama. Won't let anyone else touch him. And with Grandmama he's always whiny. As who would not be? Her hands are so cold and rough. Aren't you going to eat any more? You'll never grow big eating like a bird. That's what they keep telling me. But I suppose you're already grown now and won't ever get bigger. Have you got your sixteen years yet?...Eighteen? Well! I'd have never known it. Here's Joe and May with your tub and water, and the water's good and warm. Better let Sarah go first. She's not near as dirty as you. Give me your gowns and I'll get May to wash them. Whew! I never knew people-birthing was so bloody."

Honey was half out of her gown—she was used to undressing before other women and girls, and Joe, the Negro boy, had gone off as soon as he set down the tub--before she realized that they'd nothing but boys' leggings and shirts to put on afterward. She stopped, stricken, and Sarah did too, of course.

Molly looked at them with a frown. "What's the matter? Isn't the water hot enough for you? But I told you, it's prodigiously warm. And you've got to make yourselves neat and clean. What if Papa comes home? He's expected presently, and he fancies ladies to be always neat and clean. Even me. Even the house servants. He's known to be peculiar that way. Mama might not care, seeing as she's just been delivered. Oh, but you want your clean garments laid out. And they haven't been aired." She knelt by the saddlebags lying in the corner, and pulled out everything, inspecting leggings, shirts and jackets, two of each.

"But these are <u>boys'</u> clothes. And mighty ragged, too. Here, May. Take them. Give them to Joe to take to one of the quarters. Don't you worry, Honey. Lucky you're so little. I'll wager you'll fit into one of my gowns. Sarah's bigger around, so I'll look in Mama's French press. She has heaps of gowns." And off she skipped.

Her leaving unloosed Sarah's tongue. "Can it be that folks live so fine as this?" she whispered. "Feel the water, Honey. I declare! It's truly warm." At home they never washed themselves in winter. In other seasons they washed in cold water, standing in half of an old barrel. Here, right up close to the fire was a shining copper tub, big enough to sit in with your knees folded up, and the Negroes had poured in several pitchers of hot water to mix with the cold. "They won't hardly let us stay here, will they, Honey? Fine people like this?"

"I don't know. I kind of wish they won't. We don't know how to act around gentlefolk. We'll surely shame Papa and Mama." If they got turned out, in spite of her trying her best, then Papa could not blame her, could he?

"But Honey, where would we...?"

Just then Molly returned, her wiry arms laden with clothes, and a pair of shoes, <u>leather</u> shoes, in each hand. "There! Try if these will do. Do you mind if I call you 'Honey'? If I must, I'll call you Cousin Caroline. But it's a deal of trouble. But you never did tell me why you're called Honey."

Honey felt the blood rush to her face. "I reckon it's because of my hair," she stammered. "And my freckles, that used to be brighter, like pollen."

"Well, jump in the tub then, Sarah. Shall I call May to wash your hair? Or no, I'll do it myself. How pretty and thick and long it is! Almost as pretty as Mama's. Mine's so thin and pale. Like corn silk on a dried-up ear. I truly despise it."

Soon they were washed and clothed in ill-fitting finery. The gowns were of cotton, cloth they'd never had on their backs before, wool and linen being all they'd ever known. Sarah put on shoes of Mrs. Waverley's that Molly swore were cast-offs, and seemed only a little too big. The shoes that Honey was given pinched her sorely, but of course she couldn't complain so she said they fitted just right. Then the bossy child demanded to show them the house.

"I can't show you <u>my</u> room," she explained, "because it's directly over Mama's and the boards squeak something awful." So down the back stairs they went, also "so as not to disturb Mama," and thence through a hall and into a huge room, lighted by three big glass-paned windows with heavy crimson cloth draped over their tops and sides. On the floor lay a splendid wide rug adorned with flowers in reds and blues floating on a creamy background. The walls and even the ceiling were perfectly smooth– no beams showing– and painted a deep, smoky blue like a fine sky in evening. The chairs were covered in cloth like the curtains and had carved legs. Most wonderful of all was a fireplace made of gleaming white stone with pretty gray threads running through it.

Molly was clearly delighted by the round eyes and open mouths of her cousins, and even more so when a sudden clang rang out from the hall, just when they were standing by the doorway. Honey and Sarah jumped and sprang to grab each other's hand, while Molly whooped with glee. "It's only the grandfather clock. I truly love to see it wake Grandmama when she's dozed off." Honey knew well that their fright convinced the child all the more of their ignorance, but there was no help for it. And their trials were not over yet. While they stood speechless in the middle of the parlor, Molly spied someone in the back hall and ran that way with a shriek, followed slowly by her cousins. When they reached the pantry Molly was tussling with a man, he holding her by her braid and she struggling to poke him in the stomach with her elbows. Mr. Waverley? No, for this was not much more than a boy, with the gangling long limbs of that in-between time. When he looked up at the newcomers Honey shrank back, bumping into Sarah who was trying to keep safe by hiding right in back of her. The boy's head was narrow, with dark hair cut short above a high forehead, and cheekbones jutting out under deep-set eyes. Like a skull, thought Honey.

He started too, at first, and let go of Molly. But he quickly seemed to figure out who they were, even though he looked everywhere but at them. Of course Molly jumped into the silence:

"This is Nathan, my cousin. And yours too, of course. He's seeing to the people shoveling paths for us, so we can get to the necessary!" She laughed, clearly hoping this would shock somebody.

Nathan gave her a little cuff on the head and hastened to say: "It's so people can get here from the home quarter, and the smoke house and dairy, and feed the animals in the stables and the barn. We have your horse safe inside, Miss," and he gave just a flick of a glance at Honey. "He's in bad shape. Lamed and wheezing hard. But he's drinking and eating a little. I doubt he'll be good for much."

Honey enjoyed for a moment the picture of old Dasher in a warm, dry stall, eating clean hay. He too had come into unknown splendor. "Thank you, sir," she managed to say, real low, without daring to look again into those sunken eyes. She'd never felt quite safe around men. And this kind, the ones too young to be wedded yet, was the most dangerous. Always on the watch to catch a girl in a lonesome spot and make trouble for her. Here she would have to keep a sharp eye on Sarah, too. At Granny Harriet's there wasn't no need. No one dared (even the strongest man) make trouble around Granny Harriet. And afore that, when they had first left home, Sarah was only a child.

Then the brown woman called Joan came bustling into the hall, yelling to Joe to bring more wood for their mistress's fire, and telling Honey that Mrs. Waverley wanted to see her.

Honey's heart set to thudding like thunder. She had not feared the night before when they fetched her to help with a difficult birth--that was the same anywhere, and she was used to it--but now she was surely being called to be peered at and questioned.

The room was the same one as the night before, but how different it looked! Yellow curtains now hung from a little roof over the bed, pulled back like a window on the sides. The walls were the color of a ripe peach, and a thick brown rug had been laid on the floor. Never had Honey seen such bright colors inside a house. The old lady who had let them in and shown them to their room the night before was sitting by a window and knitting, very slowly, with her work way off at arm's length. She raised her eyes, giving Honey a placid look, as though she had been there for a long time. On a table next to the bed sat a white-painted basket with the newborn sleeping inside. The lady leaning against cushions on the bed, under a rich, embroidered coverlet, seemed a different person entirely. The wild eyes, the grimacing mouth, the wet hair plastered against her head, had disappeared. Only a paleness of skin (perhaps natural) and a slight darkness around the eyes suggested her long hours in labor. She beckoned Honey up close to the bed, and Honey observed a woman not in her first youth, but the most beautiful lady she had ever laid eyes on. Her hair rolled in dark-red waves over her shoulders. Her nose was narrow and straight, her mouth thin but graceful and her forehead high over large, gray-green eyes.

She stretched out a large, shapely hand and made Honey sit on a chair right up close to the bed.

"So you are the angel who appeared out of nowhere to save me," she said with scarcely a smile. "But you're barely more than a child. Who are you? I think someone told me, but I was too tired to listen."

Honey started to explain and was instantly commanded to "Speak up!" which she forced herself to do.

"So you are Mr. Waverley's cousin, once removed, as they say," remarked the lady when Honey had finished her brief tale. "Out of the wilderness. I do recall hearing something of a black sheep who long ago disappeared out that way and never returned. Now you are left an orphan, with a younger sister. And where is she, pray? Oh, never mind. I'll see her another time. How on earth did you contrive to get here, all that long distance, two young girls all alone? And a stormy time of the year as well. No, it's not possible."

"On no, ma'am. We wasn't alone so much. We was with folks, kin of our neighbor, part of the way. They was coming this way, toting tar and pitch and such to market. And we was ketched in just one storm that wasn't too bad. Just at the end me and Sarah was real lucky we got here afore the snow got to coming down real thick last eve."

Mrs. Waverley suddenly winced and let an "Ai!" escape her lips. She then tried to pull herself higher up on the pillow.

"Don't you fret yourself, ma'am. Them afterpains will soon go away. They do get a little worse at each birth. But they leave off just as quick."

"Indeed! This is my sixth, and I hope the last. I suppose I'll have to suckle this one quite forever, or at any rate until I'm too old to conceive again. Tell me, how does the baby look to you?"

"Oh, he looks better already, ma'am. A little peaked still, for sure, after such a long birthing. It's a shame they tarried so long to call me." Right away she felt uppity for saying this, but another groan from Mrs. Waverley took her mind off that.

"You sure do look tuckered out, ma'am. You shouldn't ought to be setting up like that. Let me help you lay down. You need to rest a good long spell." And she carefully pulled the cushions away and laid the lady back on just one fat pillow.

"Yes, that's better." She drew a number of deep breaths in silence. Then: "What a nuisance this baby-making is! My dear child, we must see to it that you marry as late as can be, and then to an old man who will die as soon as you've two healthy boys." Her laugh rang out, full and rich like a song. "Oh, you mustn't mistake me. Your cousin is an excellent man, a true gentleman who will do his best for you and your sister. A trifle too generous, perhaps, but isn't that the mark of a gentleman?"

Mrs. Waverley's earlier words had shocked Honey. Perhaps they'd given her too much laudanum for her afterpains? She'd heard that rich ladies in the East took that for all their ills.

After a while Mrs. Waverley turned toward her and smiled for the first time. "Well, child, you came at an opportune time. This little hand of yours," and she took and held it up, turning it this way and that while Honey squirmed under the scrutiny, "so narrow even at the knuckles, so different from the fat, clumsy hand of our midwife who wouldn't touch me anyhow because of my overly solicitous husband and because she's a fool in any case. This hand kept my new baby from dying in the womb. So you are doubly welcome. We will fatten you up and marry you a little sooner than I said a moment ago." She laughed again that laugh that made Honey smile to hear it. "Joan tells me we have a rich lamb stew and succotash for our dinner. Do you and your sister drink tea, child? Good. Then take the biggest key from that drawer there, and give it to Joan when you leave. Tell her we will go on serving tea only until the master returns. My husband gave up tea to spite the British before the war, and has never gone back to it. Are you quite comfortable where they put you? Do you have all you need? His aunt tells me the water in her washbasin was frozen this morning. I must scold Joan for that."

Of course Honey assured her that everyone had been good to them, and even remembered to tell Mrs. Waverley about the apples, nuts, and ginseng they had brought. "Shall I give them to the dark lady, ma'am?"

"Dark lady? Oh, you mean Joan. Yes, by all means. And bring me that wool shawl on the chest by the window, to wrap round my neck. No matter how good the fire, one shivers five feet away from it. But why are you limping, child? Good Lord! Those are Molly's shoes. Where are your own?"

"I've only moccasins, ma'am, and it didn't hardly seem fitting to wear them here."

"So it's more fitting to limp about in pain? Get those things off, and wear your moccasins until we can have a pair of shoes made for you. If there's one thing I can't abide, it's a martyr. Now let me look at you better. How light your eyes are! Just barely tinged with blue. You've a pretty nose and mouth, but your face is raw from the wind. Tell Joan to find you some salve for it. Do I spy freckles under all that red? Didn't your mama tell you never to go out without a bonnet? I'll give you my old leghorn that has an enormous brim. And you're frightfully thin. We must fatten you up. Oh, and by the way, tell Joan to put the ginseng in the locked cupboard. Too much of a temptation for one of the servants to steal. When I'm up and about we'll see to your clothes. That old yellow muslin of Molly's looked frightful on her and looks even worse on you. Now leave me to rest."

Honey crept out of the room, confused in her heart.

This house and its lady was strange beyond belief, but the lady seemed to expect them to bide for a while, and her words about the gentleman, Honey's cousin, promised good rather than ill. She and Sarah would stay where they was, and try if they could be tolerated.

Chapter 4

"Thank God you are safely delivered, Mrs. Waverley," said a tall woman, plainly dressed but clearly a lady, who walked briskly into the master bedchamber. Her face, plain as her gown, showed permanent lines of care, though she looked in other respects no more than thirty. Heavy responsibilities rode on the square shoulders of Kate Nelson, shoulders quite capable of bearing them.

"Moses must be whipped. Oh yes, indeed he must." This last was in response to a shake of Charlotte's head. "I have only just learned that Aunt Abie sent him for me yesterday forenoon. And when did he appear in our back hall? Not until this morning. The rascal claimed to have lost himself in the snow, and then when he finally got to Farrington, 'couldn't find Miss Kate nowhere.' It's true I spent the whole afternoon either in the infirmary with sick servants and their crying babies, or else in the laundry where the women of the crop had been sent to wash wool, since nothing can be done in the fields with the snow so deep. But the lazy fellow had only to bestir himself and look about. Doubtless he spent all that time lolling with my woman, Sue, who assures me she knew nothing of his errand. I cannot conceive of such recklessness. Even in a Negro. If you or the child--well, it appears that all finally turned out well, but you had no lady to comfort you and assure that everything possible was done. Poor Aunt Abie could be of no use, of course." Miss Nelson appeared genuinely outraged.

Remarkable, thought Charlotte. Despite years of struggling to manage the neighboring estate of Farrington with only a sickly stepfather, a profligate stepbrother, and a pampered young stepsister, Kate was still shocked by what she perceived as gross dereliction of duty in anyone, she who never strayed a tiny stitch from her own.

"My dear Miss Nelson, calm yourself. Come, ring for someone to bring us tea and seat yourself in the armchair. All has ended well, as you see."

Charlotte did indeed feel surprisingly well. Her afterpains were already beginning to subside. She arched her back languorously over the plump pillows and rubbed her cheek against the yellow satin that covered them. She had finally produced a healthy son. He was already sucking greedily at her breast, though the milk had not yet come. Poor Kate. She was the orphaned daughter of Mr. Ludwell's first wife. Now that he too had died, she had no close relations except her young stepbrother and sister, wastrel Stuart and naive Lucinda. Her only help came from Matthew, who had served as her brother's guardian until his recent majority and still exercised this duty toward Lucinda. But Matthew was a man laden with numerous obligations of his own, so the daily round of plantation management fell to Kate.

"Joan tells me you walked all this long way, my dear. You should never have attempted such a thing in the snow. And quite alone, I'll wager. What if you had turned an ankle, and been unable to move? Think of the anguish of poor Lucy, of all of us, when they found you stone dead in a snowdrift. Wasn't it only a fortnight ago that Tom Pettigrew was discovered frozen solid on the riverbank?"

"Tom was far gone in his cups, and had soaked himself trying to ford the river. Who could I have taken with me, Mrs. Waverley? Sue, with her pleurisy? Or old Jed, with his bad leg? Our two sound house servants are off with Stuart in Richmond. If I'd sent to the quarters for someone, it would have taken twice as long."

Her sister Lucy was left unmentioned. Kate's habitual rationality stumbled here. She saw Lucy as a delicate creature requiring constant protection, whereas for all outward resemblance to a violet, Lucy seemed to have the vigor of a dandelion.

"And as for walking," Kate continued, "it is certainly the surest way. I'd not venture to take Red Lady out in deep snow. She is far from sure of foot. If she stumbled and injured herself, where would I have been then? We can ill afford to lose a horse. Me, yes. All I am is a fly in the ointment of pleasure, or so my brother opines."

This last was thrown out with a hearty laugh that dared her hearer to take it as self-pity. Such small dashes of humor saved Kate from being a dreadful bore. Still, it irritated Charlotte that Kate found so many occasions to remind everyone of the Ludwell family's straightened circumstances. It was purely imaginary poverty. Charlotte knew to the acre the extent of their holdings, rich ones that suffered only from Stuart's waste of the income. The Ludwells were cash poor, of course, like so many of their fellow Virginians. But most of them would have bitten off their tongues rather than confess to any decay of their fortunes. Ease and openhandedness were the marks of a gentleman. And so it should be, thought Charlotte.

High time, however, to save the hide of Moses. Feckless, and a shameless chaser of wenches, the big black man pleased Charlotte with his unfailing good humor--never surly like the others so often were--and his funny, gossipy prattle about everyone: servants, neighbors, even the family, even herself.

"Miss Nelson, in the name of Heaven do not say a word to my husband concerning Moses' fault. He would have the fellow sent out to the River Birch quarter. I want Moses here. He's a good worker, as long as you keep an eye on him. Aunt Abie should have known better than to send him on such an errand."

"If that is what you wish, Mrs. Waverley. I only thought that an example should be set. And I really must say that you'd best look closer to your women servants. Once you are on your feet again, of course. On my way to the house I took a half-dozen jars of quince preserves to your cook, and found a woman and two girls chatting and laughing there in the warmth of the kitchen. Not doing a speck of work."

"Ah well, they'll not dare when all is back to normal. But you know I don't care to eye the servants exceedingly. Joan does that for me. But now she is occupied with me and the baby."

"At any rate I charged the woman with starching and ironing the clothes piled up in the laundry, and the girls with hauling wood into the house. But do please tell me about this unknown cousin who they say appeared from nowhere and delivered you."

Charlotte told the tale as briefly as possible, for she was already tired of it. "So you see," she concluded with a smile, "between this new cousin who proves to be an excellent midwife, and Joan, who for all other affairs is invaluable, I want for nothing. Indeed, I am particularly pleased that Maudy has returned. You remember that favorite of mine, the light-skinned girl whom we apprenticed to a dressmaker in Richmond? She's come back with such nice manners and speech that if you didn't look at her, you'd think her white. She has a heavy cold, and can't be allowed in to see me, but I've sent word for her to make over mourning gowns for the new cousins--there's a young sister, you see."

"By the way, Mrs. Waverley, may I order a cord of wood taken to the Clancys?" (This was the impoverished family of a crippled farmer living a little farther up the river.) "I could also send them a barrel of meal and a large box of tea. They will surely have finished the sheets for Mrs. Levier by now. The girls have got so quick at their loom, poor things. Perhaps you might order another pair of sheets? They will want more flax, of course. What fine, soft fibers the girls produce. I believe they comb them three times."

Kate could indeed be useful just now by taking over those charitable duties usually carried out by Mrs. Levier, Charlotte's mother-in-law. These were obligations that Charlotte accepted but did not care to undertake in person. She spread her hands to signify agreement to whatever Kate thought best. Finally, Kate brought up her greatest current worry.

"Our house rings with the songs of Lucy these days. I've never seen her so happy. As you well know, I had hoped her affections would go in a different direction. Mr. Miles Waverley has long been devoted to her. But who can rule the heart? Your dear brother, Mr. Burnham, is charming indeed and has quite conquered her."

"Of course he has," laughed Charlotte. "He has been on the scene, and his rival far away in the wilderness."

"Still, I'm a little uneasy, Mrs. Waverley. Lucy has had only one letter from your brother since he left here. He is doubtless much occupied, but if you could see how the poor girl waits so eagerly for the post. And then how earnestly she tries to hide her disappointment."

How to reply? Charlotte was not easy in her own mind on the matter. Geoffrey had been the picture of an eager suitor during his summer stay at Laurel Hill, riding over to Farrington each day to spend long hours in Lucy's company, and so clearly captivated by the girl that no one could fail to remark it. Lucinda's portion was modest, perhaps twenty adult Negroes and five hundred acres settled on her through her mother, but that little would mean independence to Geoffrey, particularly if he should fail to salvage any part of their uncle's Virginia holdings. Equally important were the Ludwell family connections, distinguished people settled throughout the Tidewater. The luster of Charlotte's and Geoffrey's aristocratic English background was now tarnished. Their noble uncle, Lord Ashton, had died, leaving a much-diminished fortune and his place in the House of Lords to an imbecile child. Only the American holdings had been left to Geoffrey.

Lucy had good looks to recommend her as well, though she had not much height and was rather lacking in color. She was an amiable creature, but perhaps too clearly in love, too dazzled by her newfound happiness, for a girl not yet officially betrothed.

In short, marriage to Lucy would be a stroke of good fortune for a possibly landless gentleman whose good repute had suffered grievously from his leaving the country and spending the time of hostilities in England.

"Now Kate--you will permit me to call you so since we will soon be related--you know how essential it is for Geoffrey to look closely to his lawsuit. I'm sure Lucy herself understands this. It is difficult for a man engrossed in affairs and the rowdy company of men to find the moment to write."

"But an aunt of Lucy's wrote that she saw Geoffrey in Portsmouth. That is not where the property is, is it, nor the law court?"

"Heavens, Kate, it's a good thing you're not married. A woman does best tending to her own household, leaving men's business to them. How can a woman understand these things?"

What nonsense I'm speaking, she thought. Of course Kate must concern herself with men's business, because the so-called man of her family is only a foolish boy. Yet Charlotte could not admit to doubts concerning her brother and perhaps damage his hopes of allying himself with this well-connected family. He was genuinely fond of the girl--that she knew--and he was neither carouser, nor gamester, nor brawler. Not the paragon of honor and wisdom that she herself had married, but a good sight more jolly in company.

Kate said no more of Geoffrey, nor did she venture a comment on woman's sphere. But she did direct a sharp glance at the older woman. "You seem more eager than I to see Lucy married. I wish her happy. Most fervently I do. But will not you, as I, sorely miss her? Every time I hear her light step on the stair or look up to see her smile, I dread the day she will leave me."

To this Charlotte must nod assent, but some part of her, a part she preferred not to think on, would not regret Lucy's departure.

———◦◦◦———

Next day, toward the noon hour, Molly and her new cousin Sarah were cooperating in the construction of a snowman on the broad slope of land that descended to the Solway River from the front of Great House. At first Molly had protested mightily at being told to keep Sarah company because Joe, Molly's frequent companion on hunting expeditions, was off after turkey that morning with Old Tan, the finest hunting dog on the plantation. He knew what creature you were looking for directly upon your signal: in this case, a turkey call. There was nothing Molly so enjoyed as a hunt with Joe and Old Tan.

But once the snowman project was under way, Molly quite threw herself into it. Bright sunshine had turned the snow on the trees and on the lawn into the brilliance of diamonds and caused the girls to squint as they worked. The snow was melting fast. Already furrows of soggy green and brown were breaking through, and the bright mounds of white on the branches were dripping steadily, shrinking minute by minute. The girls' work was considerably hampered by the excitement of Silky, who kept barking and circling and leaping upon their snowman despite many sharp smacks at the hand of Molly. She, of course, was boss of the project and kept urging Sarah to make haste, not yet knowing that Sarah was never a girl for haste.

Still, the girls meshed well in their labors. Molly contributed by far the most to rolling three snowballs into three tightly packed rounds, small for the head, middling for the chest, and a great one for all below the waist. Then she ran into the house and returned with a battered three-cornered hat of green felt trimmed in black, a frayed yellow silk stock for the neck, and an old mustard-colored broadcloth coat with magnificent horn buttons. But Sarah exhibited her special talents in a trip to the kitchen where she somehow wheedled, despite her shyness, a mass of fine tow for hair, shiny ends of eggplant for eyes, a fat carrot for the nose, and a great crescent of pumpkin for the mouth. As they stepped back to admire their creation, Molly pointed to a clapboard house of modest size a little downriver and closer to it than the more imposing brick dwelling where most of the family lived.

"That's Grandmama's house that we call Old House. She's very strict. She doesn't approve of me and Mama. Or even Papa. She likes Nathan because his papa, who died long before I was born, was her favorite. Nathan can do near anything and Grandmama won't scold. Did your Grandmama like you?"

"I never knowed her. She was dead afore I was born."

"Lord Almighty, Sarah. You talk like a bumpkin. You'd best start right in learning to talk properly. My papa is most particular about that."

But now Molly was peering far into the distance downriver. Suddenly she deserted Sarah and tore off in that direction, leaping light as a hare over the snow. Against the white riverbank she had made out the figure of a man on horseback. As she ran, the man urged his horse into a trot. When they met, the rider jumped off, lifted Molly into his arms and then set her upon Dauntless, for it was indeed Papa and Dauntless. The two approached the house diagonally up the slope of the hill, talking eagerly, with questions from Papa and eager answers from Molly, much embellished with extra details about her own exploits until he broke in with another question. As they neared Sarah and the snowman Molly jumped down and tried to pull her father toward them. But he, with only a brief glance in that direction, handed the horse's reins to his daughter and set off at nearly a run toward the front steps of Great House. Poor Dauntless shied and stumbled as Molly threw the reins to the ground in front of his forelegs, and stamped her foot in disgust. After a moment she bent to pick up the reins, jerking them out from under a hoof, and trudged slowly, head down, toward the stables.

Molly's papa, who had left Uncle Miles and Stove behind in Petersburg to bring on the wagon and baggage, took his supper that evening with her mama in their bedchamber. Conversation around the family dining table was no more lively than it had been all through the previous fortnight, when Mama felt too ill to leave her chamber and cold and rain had kept visitors away. Miss Kate Nelson had been persuaded to stay the night, but seemed quite absorbed in her own thoughts. Aunt Abie counted for little. She hardly knew what day it was anymore, so she scarcely dared venture a remark on aught but the weather. Nathan, never a talkative fellow, appeared cowed by the presence of the two new girls, who themselves were silent as bullfrogs in January. Molly herself was wont to introduce at supper a number of topics she considered immensely interesting, and was indulged in this when only family was present. But tonight she had no wish to entertain anyone, even herself. She sat glumly in her chair and wouldn't even respond to Sarah's gentle smile across the table.

When her papa finally joined them for the dessert of apple tart and vanilla custard, he appeared unusually easy in mind. Molly stole half-angry, half-anxious glances at his calm, kindly face. Aside from a few polite inquiries of Miss Nelson, his attention was directed mainly to Honey and Sarah. He asked about their papa and mama and brothers, their home and country, and more than anything else, their journey hither. He seemed to think it quite astounding that they had reached this place at all. Nathan and Miss Nelson, too, looked at the girls with wide eyes as though they were two Little Red Riding Hoods who had triumphed over the wolf. Honey gave such short answers and in such a soft voice that Molly wondered her papa could hear half of them. Yet he didn't once tell her to speak up, nor act one bit impatient at her meager little replies. Papa was so kind and gentle. To everybody but her!

At the end of the meal her father arose, excused himself with a bow to the ladies, passed into the pantry for a few words of instruction to Joan, then returned with a slight frown upon his face and said to Molly: "Please go attend me in my cabinet, Margaret." He dropped a large brass key into her hand. He then ushered Aunt Abie, Miss Nelson, and the two newcomers across the hall into the master bedchamber to keep Mama company.

Molly's throat got so tight she could hardly swallow. What had she done wrong? He was the one who had wronged <u>her</u>. She passed through the bookroom, turned the key in the lock, and pushed hard against the heavy door of Papa's cabinet. The room was usually entered, even by him, from the outside, through a door in the side of the house. In that way clients, overseers, and agents could come and go without disturbing the family, and in turn, since the inner door was kept locked, family and guests were discouraged from invading this place of business. Not a large room, it was dominated by a massive secretary with cubbyholes bursting with papers. Books and papers covered the surface of a large mahogany table, and other books, on law and agriculture and medicine, filled a wall of shelves. Molly stood stiffly looking out the only window into darkness. She had not long to wait.

Papa came in with Nathan, saying "I'm sure I can lay my hand quickly on my record of how many bushels we planted last year." Seeing Molly, he asked her to wait for a moment in the bookroom. She slipped out, but did not close the door, and was not asked to do so. She could have amused herself with a book, for here they covered all four walls, and there were a few of interest. She was already quite proficient at her letters and she knew where <u>Pilgrim's Progress</u> and <u>Robinson Crusoe</u>

were to be found. But listening to the men's conversation would serve better to distract her from her fear.

At first it was only about farm work: how much winter wheat had been planted, how much barley and oats, for how many days they had burned hickory fires to cure the tobacco (given the dampness of the weather), how much of the tobacco was already struck. She could see Nathan standing stiff as a cedar tree beside the chair he had been offered, puffed up with pride, no doubt, because Papa was inquiring of him concerning the crops before talking to the overseer.

"You and Amos have done well, my boy. But I think we must burn some more hickory before we strike the rest. And now, tell me how your poor mother is getting along."

"Well enough, sir, I suppose." What a booby Nathan was. She could tell a deal more about Crazy Mary, as everyone except Papa and Nathan called her. How she'd nearly choked Juno to death one night when Cyrus was asleep. She was kept on the upper story of Grandmama's house, where Juno and Cyrus, Grandmama's freed Negroes, had to feed and dress her just like she was a baby. Most of the time she sat staring into her hands all day, but every few weeks she suddenly scared somebody half to death.

Her father asked no more, just touched Nathan lightly on the arm, and Nathan suddenly said in a rush of words that he'd visited his mother every day because his grandmother was from home. Molly was surely glad that Grandmama saw it as her Christian duty to keep Nathan's crazy mother in her own house, so that she, Molly, didn't have to hear the lady's screams and curses. Not close up, anyhow.

"And have you yet finished reading Gibbons' history?" Papa was asking. Papa supervised Nathan's education. Of course Nathan could hardly pretend he had read that big, long book. She herself had already read almost as many books as he. She was sure of it.

Her father gave his usual little lecture about the value of book learning. Then he fell silent, and began gnawing on his thumb, his habit when thinking hard. "I wonder did I do wrong in not sending you to an academy in Richmond, rather than leaving you entirely in the care of Mr. Higgens. I thought it best to preserve you from the infection of vicious examples found in towns. Also to avoid spending your small fortune before you were grown. But I fear Mr. Higgens does not inspire sufficient respect. He is well enough as our pastor, and to teach Latin and arithmetic, but for the larger ideas I have some doubt. Well, be off now. We'll speak more of this later."

He heaved a big sigh and called to Molly, who came in slow as a snail and took her place exactly where Nathan had stood. Her father looked at her, again with the slight frown. "Dauntless has been injured, Molly, and I fear it is by you."

"Papa, I didn't do anything to him." She swayed a little, so intense was her fear.

"Listen to me, child." He made her sit down, and drew up a chair for himself. "I left the horse in your hands and of course you took him to the stable and left him in Pram's keeping. But when I looked him over this afternoon, to see if he was breathing well, I found ugly wounds on his forelegs. I questioned Pram, who said he had marked it shortly after you handed him the reins. Now, I do not think Pram lied, and I'm sure this did not happen on my way hither. Despite my haste to arrive, I was very careful of Dauntless. I also know, only too well, that you have not yet learned to master your temper. This truly alarms me."

There was no use trying to lie to Papa. Not that he saw right through you, like Mama did, but Molly simply couldn't do it. Besides, she well knew that lying was in his eyes a worse offense than almost anything. "Papa, you wouldn't look at my snowman, not even for one minute!" Her voice sounded to her like someone scratching on a windowpane.

He regarded her for a long moment in silence. "Yes, I was so anxious to see your mama that I was brusque with you. I am sorry for that. But Molly," and here he leaned forward and took her two thin, long-fingered hands into his own bigger ones, cut from the same pattern, "it grieves my heart to find you subject to such spurts of passion you would harm an innocent creature. An animal, a servant, a smaller child. If you cannot erase anger from your heart, then you must make a good resolution to hide it, and spare others, especially those helpless to protect themselves from its fury."

He had sprung up now and was pacing the brown and yellow painted floor covering. "Don't think that I preach to you from some exalted perch, as one above such weakness. I have struck a Negro cruelly, more than once, in my youth. I still must have one whipped from time to time. I even sold one once to one of those despicable traders, in a fit of anger. That turned out to be a great...evil that I will never forget. Thank God I've never mistreated a woman or child. But if anger is bad in a man, how much worse in a woman, who is here on this earth to soften and bring mercy into human dealings."

He sat down again opposite Molly, peering into her face with those dark blue eyes of his. She noticed for the first time deep lines fanning out from their corners, and how his face sank in a little at the temples. "Someday you will be the mother of children, the mistress of house servants, perhaps mistress of vast holdings that you must manage on your own because you find yourself a widow, or wife to a man much occupied with public affairs. And who knows? You may still fall heir to this estate. Who can ever be sure that tomorrow will not rob us of our hopes? Being a girl, and such a fine, healthy one, thank God, your life is less subject to danger than those of your brothers. And in any event I count on you to be an example to them."

He had laid his hands on her shoulders. How small she felt, and how heavy, like leaden bells, were his hands! She stiffened her back, as stiff as stiff could be, to bear the weight. She didn't want to have to be an example to anyone. That wasn't fair. She couldn't look at him, nor say a word.

"All right, little Molly. Dauntless will heal. You needn't fear. But

I want you to go thrice a day and put liniment on his legs with your own hand. Pram will show you how. And remember, <u>noblesse oblige</u>. That means that privilege brings high duty. And one of the highest, and most difficult, is control of anger so that those less privileged never suffer unnecessarily or unjustly at your hand. Come to think of it, I believe that your newly arrived cousins will be a good influence. The older one, in particular, has such a modest, gentle air. Soft complacency can do so much to sweeten the cares of a father or husband. Now go along and bid goodnight to your mother."

Clenching her teeth, Molly slipped almost unnoticed into the back of her parents' large bedchamber, behind the ladies chatting with her mother, or rather the lady, because Miss Nelson and Mama were doing all the talking. Molly stared hard at Honey, who was seated on the edge of the least comfortable chair, head and eyes bent meekly toward the floor. Mealy-mouthed mouse! Did her papa truly want her to be like that? She couldn't and she wouldn't. She truly hated her newfound cousin.

Chapter 5

Matthew took his son Edward from the arms of Joan, and dismissed the servant with a distracted gesture. He seated himself in a straight-backed chair with his knees pressed against the bed where Charlotte sat propped against plump pillows with her baby at her breast.

"I do believe Edward's color is a bit improved," he said as he searched the boy's face, the furrow between his brows deepening. He had fed the child his breakfast every one of the four days since returning from Richmond, and this morning for the first time Edward accepted his father's touch without whimpering. Matthew reached for the small silver spoon with "E. W." engraved in gothic letters on the handle that curved backward until it almost touched its bowl. It was made to be easy for a child to grasp, but Edward waited passively to be fed. Matthew dipped the spoon into the bowl of hominy, and gently coaxed his son to open his mouth. When he repeated his observation about Edward's color, this time in a questioning tone, Charlotte merely shrugged her shoulders, further exposing their milky roundness, and looked down upon the infant sucking at her breast.

"Curious. My other babes curled up against me like snails clinging to a branch. This one stretches himself out full-length as if to draw the milk into every inch of him. A true sensualist. Beware, Matthew. This boy will become everything that you despise: tippler, gamester, petticoat-chaser."

"Pray don't even think it. I've seen too much of that, and too close to home. Miles has markedly improved, thank God. I have good hope for him. Stuart Ludwell, however, only goes from bad to worse. But dearest one, I wish to think only of the happiness I have in being here again with everything I love. You, above all else," and he contrived to hook the spoon onto Edward's small fingers and draw Charlotte's plump ones to his lips.

"Well, you see that I succeeded in expelling this lusty fellow, despite his having stubbornly set his backside in the place where his head belonged. No thanks to your high and mighty doctor from Petersburg, who never came. Your young cousin Honey managed to dislodge the babe, but you cannot be credited with that, since you did not send her, no, nor knew a jot of her existence." She was laughing at him. Matthew was well used to that. Indeed, he found it reassuring to hear her in top form and clearly enjoying his presence, if only as a butt for her raillery.

At that moment the infant flung back his head, and a stream of creamy liquid sprang from her nipple. "You see that," she exulted, "such a vigorous babe, and my milk has come in thicker than ever before!"

"But you must not continue suckling him yourself, dearest. It saps a woman's strength, and now you have more tasks than ever to attend to, with two new and probably illiterate girls to educate, and Molly of an age to need more of your attention. I'm sure we can find a healthy servant with child, to be wet nurse to ours. My mother will no doubt object, but I'll persuade her it must be done."

"Not on your life!" Charlotte cried, startling Edward who began to whimper and was rocked soothingly by his father, while Charlotte hastily stuck her nipple back into the baby's mouth, which had opened wide to let out a scream. "Not that I care a whit about your mother's objections to 'handing our babes over to black wenches,' as she would say, but I have no intention of conceiving another, and suckling seems to prevent it."

As Matthew remained silent, she continued. "Now as for my added duties, I have a notion that the elder of your young cousins will prove more help than burden. She will need to learn her letters, certainly, and something of speech and manner, but she has already won Edward's trust and been wonderfully attentive in the care of this babe. By the by, we must settle on a name and--but let us rid ourselves of both these young ones who in any case are dozing off. No, do not trouble yourself to rouse Edward to eat more. The water in the warming dish is surely cooled, and he will never take his hominy cold."

She pulled on the bell rope and instantly May appeared. The little black girl liked to listen at doors. "Put this babe in his cradle, <u>carefully</u>, child, and call Joan for Edward. Then run tell old Sukey to make us up a batch of waffles, light golden the way the master likes them, and brew us some of the West India coffee."

As soon as both children were gone she allowed Matthew to wipe the milk from her breast and cover it with kisses. Then she gave a small slap to his cheek and drew her shift up over her shoulders. "What would you say to Charles as a name for the babe, your father's, since we named Edward for mine?"

"The very thing I had in mind. And how about Patrick for the child's second name? We can thus honor my stepfather, and Mr. Patrick Henry by the same token, whom I know you much admire."

"Yes, why indeed not? <u>Our</u> Patrick will be highly flattered. He still feels himself such an outsider in the family and indeed, in the country. As for Mr. Henry, never shall I forget the time you took me to hear him defend a debtor in Williamsburg, back in our courting days. That voice! It sent shivers up and down my spine. Yet a moment after he ceased speaking, I could not have told you a single idea he expressed."

Saying this, she moved to get up from the bed, but Matthew laid a hand on her shoulder.

"No, dearest. You are but ill able to sit, much less stand. It is not a week yet since your lying-in."

But she threw off his arm. "I am not an invalid, my dear, except in that one place you would like to treat me as quite recovered." Seeing him crestfallen, she healed the sting with a sudden spattering of kisses over his face, during which procedure he could only close his eyes, part for protection and part in bliss. She then threw on her green silk shawl and took the few steps needed to seat herself at her secretary by the east window where sunshine turned her hair to fire licking over meadow grass, the very color of her shawl. "Now, sir, what orders has my lord to give?" She had a pen in hand and her daybook in front of her.

"Your servant relies on your judgment in all things," he smiled, still dazzled by the vision of fire and grass.

But Joan arrived with their breakfast at this point, cutting short such thoughts. He spread a little warmed honey on his waffle and allowed the seriousness so basic to his nature to return. "I was distressed by the spelling in our daughter's letters to me. The matter that she writes appears quite advanced for her years, yet from the look of the page, in penmanship as well as spelling, one would think her a child of six. I wonder Mr. Higgens tolerates it. Didn't I persuade him to give her lessons two days of the week?"

"Molly is impatient of trivial details. Her mind races on and her pen must keep up, no matter the cost."

"But if one cannot read her?"

"Those to whose benefit it will be to read her will take the trouble."

"And what of the piano-forte? Lucinda Ludwell most graciously consented to teach her the rudiments until we can procure a season of a music master's time. Yet when I asked Molly to play last evening, I was not at all pleased to hear her reply that she knew not a single note. And I have yet to see her, at any hour of the day, applying her needle. Do you know what she replied when I asked, in a brief moment I had, what she has learned during this last absence of mine?"

"How to distinguish between rabbit and raccoon tracks, perhaps, or set a trap for some other hapless creature?"

"Nearly as distressing as that. She has learned third-congregation Latin verbs, and is starting to read Caesar. I confess I am alarmed."

"What wonder in that, my dear? Is she not your daughter? As for being a roughneck, did I never tell you what a wild one I was at her age?"

"You are jesting, as always," he sighed, "but in truth, such pursuits and such learning can only be frivolous play for a girl. They will be worse than useless. They will be a detriment, for they will teach her to play at the work of others, rather than perform assiduously her own."

There was so much of importance that Charlotte refused to take seriously. Education was a matter that he himself took most seriously of all. He certainly delighted in learning, more than in any other activity. If he had not inherited land and its responsibilities, he would most certainly have joined the Church, where he could have freely indulged his taste for study and teaching. But that was out of the question for a man of substance. And a woman of any station, high or low, could ill afford to devote herself to book learning. Women's minds were not suited to abstract thought, any more than their bodies to hunting or war.

"Pray don't distress yourself about Molly, my dear. She learns quickly what she wants to know. She can set a hen and make a pudding, and she directed the planting of the whole of the winter vegetable garden. She does lean toward men's pursuits. I've even heard her question Miles about his surveying work. But can she know too much about managing an estate in all its aspects? Her chances of drawing a blockhead or a laggard for a husband I calculate at twenty to one."

"You show little indulgence for our sex, my dear."

She ignored his remark and continued. "Molly certainly likes better to give orders than to do the work herself, but what harm in that, provided her orders are sound? Needlework is too dull for her, and I think she has no ear for music. Best to give her her head. Lively colts make the best horses, you know."

"It turned out so for you at any rate, my dearest," he said, mightily tempted to slide a hand under that glorious hair and fondle her soft neck. But he forced his attention back to serious matters. "Will you have time to teach our two recent arrivals?"

"I'd sooner leave that to your mother. She will like their meek manners, and can readily turn her parlor into a schoolroom. These new duties will help me persuade her to curtail her good works among the farmers. It's a pity to behold her dragging her rheumatic legs in and out of their houses. And now, my dear, give me your arm back to my bed. My strength has not come back in force, after all, and I must rest."

Once ensconced against her pillows she went on. "One thing before you go to your duties. Honey and Sarah will need shoes. I thought of having Cato make some as soon as he returns from his year out to hire. But truly that would be niggardly. His shoes are only good enough for the servants. The question then is, since I know you will send Nathan to Petersburg with the tobacco, could he choose shoes for the girls? He has no experience of such things, but perhaps it is time for him to learn? Could he also purchase eight yards of dark gray muslin for gowns? I'm having Maudy make over two of your mother's old mourning gowns for them, but they must have another each, for spring. Send Nathan to me if you think he can be trusted."

He left her, her dark lashes already resting upon her cheek. How beautiful she was. Unreasonable, volatile, but wasn't this the universal character of woman? All that truly mattered was that she was safe, already almost back to health, and she was his.

Nathan had been counting hogsheads of corn in the shed by the old barn when summoned by Amos, the home quarter overseer, to the east tobacco barn where "Massa" wanted to see them. Thirty-four hogsheads. Nathan had counted them twice, knowing his uncle's exactitude.

Three days of rain had washed away much of the snow, leaving only a thick carpet of wet leaves on all open ground. The trunks of the trees, mottled gray and brown, were slowly drying under a cautious sun. A few large leaves still dangled from the branches of the oaks. Now and then a breeze swept through the branches and a leaf would let go its tenuous grip and flutter, twisting this way and that, to the earth.

Smoke from the hickory fires still hung lazily over the fields, softening the sunlight that filtered through it. Soon the smoke would lift for good, until next year, because the tobacco was being struck from the last of the barns, where Nathan found his uncle watching the people stemming the dried leaves from their stalks, tying them in 'hands', and pressing them into the open hogsheads.

"Good morning, Nathan, my boy." Matthew Waverley drew in a slow, deep breath. "No more savory aroma than that, is there? And no better sight than hickory smoke rising in the sunshine. How glad I am to be home." The older man had forgotten how smoke affected his nephew. Nathan always did his utmost to conceal his weakness, professing a cold whenever anyone remarked on his running nose and swollen eyes. "Amos tells me you've been improving your time these past six weeks. Up every morning and out at the quarter before the gang have even opened their eyes."

Nathan wasn't sure he liked this praise, coming as it did from the report of a Negro. Amos had certainly not seemed pleased to see him appear at the quarter every morning. Yet he always answered Nathan's questions with proper deference and even complied without comment to those few orders Nathan ventured to give. He had returned six weeks earlier from a summer's stay in Kentucky Territory with his uncle Miles, learning surveying. Miles had come back east with him, but had spent scarcely a day on the home plantation because of business of his own to attend to at the other end of the county. Then Miles had had to accompany his mother to her youngest daughter's estate for her lying-in, before going on to Richmond to work with Matthew on the filing of land warrants. Nathan had consequently been the only white man on the home plantation for several weeks, had taken pride in the fact that his uncle had explicitly placed him in charge not only of the home quarter, but of Black Oaks, Stony Creek and Sims quarters as well, even though two of those had white overseers. The trust was flattering indeed, but had he proved worthy of it? So far, no word of complaint.

"You were verifying the corn? Thirty-four hogsheads is a good return for the seed we planted. You will ask Old Sukey how much she needs ground, and have an additional hogshead ground for Mr. Clancy, who has asked for another advance of meal and salt. The poor fellow struggles mightily, yet goes deeper in debt every season. He'll bring his tobacco to go down river with ours. By three days hence ours will be ready. You see how high the river is running. It will go hard with the boats, I'll warrant. Let us hope we have no more snow, or rain, for a while. Though the snow has made the winter wheat sprout quite famously."

"Yes, sir, but I'll take good care with the canoes." Nathan could scarcely wait for the trip down the Solway, high water or no. He and two strong Negroes could manage well enough. He foresaw no trouble at the warehouse. The tobacco inspectors knew him and respected his uncle, whose leaf never had to be rejected.

"The barley has sprouted as well as the wheat," Uncle Matthew continued. "Both will come on fine, if only God sends us more sunshine. By next year we'll have one of those new seed drills. They say it puts down seeds in rows as straight as a sword. What do you think of that, Amos?"

"We tries to make 'em straight, Massa." Amos was standing a few feet beyond the other two, looking straight through them as though they weren't there. Short, thin, and very black, with hair the color of pewter, he was a man who never said three words if he could get by with two. Yet he was the best overseer ever seen at Laurel Hill, at least since Charles Waverley's death had obliged his eldest son Matthew to take over the plantation at the age of fifteen. God knew what Amos thought, but what he <u>did</u> was entirely satisfactory.

"Now we must get the livestock penned in the east fields. With a good dressing of manure they should give us one more year of tobacco. The west fields don't need it. And we must begin plowing for next year's crops. We need to get back the plows loaned to Mr. Swope at Black Oaks quarter. I sent for them three days since, but that man is not to be trusted."

"Shall you clear some of the woodland acres bought from Col. Meachem?" Nathan ventured to ask. "That's good virgin land and will yield a rich plenty of the best, sweet-scented leaf."

"No. I'll put no more land to tobacco. Prices soar and plunge too precipitously these days. One goes from lord to pauper from one year to the next. Besides, I want no more land gone sour in a few years. There's market enough for wheat in England, France, and the Indies. I asked Mr. Levier to order us a model of the new Meikle threshing machine. We'll build one as soon as it arrives. We must also improve the livestock. And increase it."

"Then what will you do with Swope's gang? They won't be needed for wheat or animals." Nathan had so carefully thought out his suggestion. Why must his uncle disagree with it in front of Amos? It was humiliating.

"We must think on that. Perhaps hire out the men this coming year and train the women to something else. I will ask Mrs. Waverley about that. By the by, she wishes you to shop for ladies' things whilst in Petersburg. For the new girls, you see. I said I would send you to her."

Nathan felt his face grow hot. He never knew what to say in the presence of his aunt. No matter what he said, she always seemed to be laughing at him. Hard to remember now that time so long ago of sinking and churning in his stomach--was he seven or eight?--when his silent, soft-handed mother began to frighten him. He couldn't recall just why. But his mother had gone to live in Old House, and for years he no longer saw her. Then his great object became that of grabbing a fold of his aunt Charlotte's gown in his fist and holding tight as long as she would allow it. Her voice was loud and her hand heavy, but her embraces were frequent and no one was permitted to scold him or drag him from her side. At that time his grandmother had seemed frighteningly stern and forbidding. Yet in time he had learned to please her and to rely on her. Whereas the closer he grew to manhood, the more his aunt Charlotte took him for an object of ridicule.

He knew she was still keeping to her bedchamber, her lying-in being so recent. Never would he enter there! Why was it that just as he was anticipating a successful trip doing man's business, he was told he must make trivial purchases for young girls? Aunt Charlotte would most certainly judge ill of what he bought, finding it the choice of a boor and a fool.

"Don't look so black, my boy. No telling when your uncle Miles or I can get back to town, so you must see to absolute necessities for these girls. Shoes, for certain. For that you must obtain an outline of their feet. And yard goods, she said. She'll surely order a few sundries, as well. Buttons, perhaps. Time you were broken in to shopping for the ladies."

Nathan had accompanied his uncle on one such visit to a milliner's shop two years ago, and endured the smiles and whispers of the ladies sitting there sipping their shrub while they fingered the cloth and ribbons and other trifles. If only he weren't so devilish cowed before ladies. If only he could, like his uncle, exchange pleasantries with them as easy as you please. Of course, one of the old biddies would be bound to cluck her tongue and remark, supposedly too low for him to hear, what a shame it was about his mother, poor boy. "Raving mad, they say." Well, no help for it. He must bear this life among the know-it-alls and the busybodies until he could be off to live in the wilderness forever. There, no one knew more of him than that he used his surveyor's level with accuracy, could fell a deer so as not to damage the skin, and had plenty of heart where squatters or Indians were concerned. There he would cut a flash due to his own merits, and no one would shame him because of his mother.

He started as he felt a hand on his arm. His uncle was guiding him toward the old barn, both their boots making sucking noises in the wet earth. Amos had disappeared, his head no doubt filled with five or six orders to obey before noon.

"I have a parcel of things to look at, my boy, and I want you to stay with me. I shall be glad to have your views."

This was sheer nonsense. His uncle was flattering him, attempting to put him at ease so as to draw out his opinions and then correct them. Nathan was weary to death of the role of pupil.

However, once they entered the darkness of the barn with its musky smell of damp hay and rooting pigs, Nathan's opinions were not asked for. The older man drew a thick book of small dimensions from his pocket and made notes in it as he talked.

"Twenty-one pigs from the three breeding sows, ten from this monster alone," he said, bending to pat a huge gray-and-white creature covered with squealing, squirming bodies all vying for too few teats. "You see the benefit of feeding and sheltering the beasts during bad weather. I used to bristle at the remarks of Englishmen about our slovenly ways--leaving our animals to root about in the forest most of the year--but I must admit they are right. Next we must reshingle the roof of this building, make it good and snug. Noah will soon be back, the man I hired out this year as apprentice to be trained in carpentry, you remember. We'll keep him on the home place this coming year. Plenty of work for him here. Making at least two thousand shingles for this roof, to begin with. And we'll need another loom, a wheelbarrow, and new cow stalls. These are rotting from the damp."

The voice droned on and on. They looked over the harnesses, the plow handles and blades, and the cows' feet and udders. Or rather, Uncle Matthew looked these over, made his comments, and wrote in his neat round hand in the little book. Nathan found himself succeeding less and less in even <u>appearing</u> attentive.

"Come, Nathan, you are not attending a tenth of what I say." The slightly nasal voice was more resigned than annoyed. "Let's go take a look at the river, inspect the rafts and canoes, and give some thought to your future." That sounded a bit ominous. On the walk down the slope toward the swollen river Uncle Matthew's eyes kept glancing upward to where dark clouds were moving in to mask the sun. "No more rain, please God. The wheat's so well sprouted and we'll have seventy bushels if only the sun deigns to shine steadily for us."

When they reached the river they inspected the bottoms of the overturned canoes pulled up on the muddy bank. Then from the dock they stepped carefully onto each of the rafts to test its soundness. Nathan had no need to feign attention to these things over which he would soon assume complete charge. Apart from one leaky canoe that might safely carry a man, but not barrels of tobacco leaf or wheat flour, all was in order.

"We must needs set a clear course for you, my boy," said the older man as he sat down upon the dock and leaned his shoulder against a mooring post.

You mean <u>you</u> must set a course for me, thought Nathan, who chafed at being called a boy. Was he not nearly eighteen?

"You could settle on your father's land. It was thoroughly soured by the time he died. As you well know. But in these sixteen years I've let the worst of it lie fallow, grown a little rye and barley in the better fields, and sold off a little at the eastern edge for the parish school. That paid for your Bascomb fields, you know. But it will still be years before the land will support you well. Years of attention and patience."

Nathan had spent many of his days, these last two months, on his own acres that were being passably managed by the next best overseer, after Amos, that his uncle had. It was the same struggle every year against bad weather, erosion, soil depletion, malingering Negroes, and drunken overseers. He had seen all this and heard men's complaints of it his entire life.

"I see that you scorn such a life," said his uncle with a great sigh. "Patience is not your strong point. Well, well, you are young. That is why I've sent you west these last two summers to learn surveying with your uncle Miles. He has done well at it. That course may suit you also. But the times have changed. Since Kentucky will become a state next year, you would no longer be able to get the legal work done through me in Richmond, as Miles has done. You would work with a lawyer in Lexington. If that is the work you determine on, you will do best to sell your land here and settle there with good virgin land."

"But that is exactly my wish, sir! If you will but allow me to sell my land here, and perhaps advance me a little cash of your own, I know where good land in the Ohio Valley is still to be had. But it's going fast." Was it possible that the moment of freedom was at hand? Uncle Matthew had been his own master at fifteen, with only distant guardians who interfered but little. At twenty he'd been off to distinguish himself in the Continental Army. Even been wounded! Then Uncle Miles, a big lad already at fourteen, had run off to join the Army in '79, been detached with his regiment to join General Benjamin Lincoln in South Carolina, and promptly been captured at the fall of Charleston. Nathan's misfortune was to be born too late, when military glory was nowhere to be had. Instead he was saddled with this all-too-closely-watching uncle who restricted his every movement.

"I've no objection to your going west, my boy, but you are too much in a hurry. For one thing, I do not trust this current scramble for western land. Men are falling over themselves to buy, borrowing on land they haven't yet paid for in order to buy more. Mark my words, many will rue the day, and find themselves in debtors' prison."

"But sir, Uncle Miles has made good profit in that manner."

"He did not go far out on that limb, you may be sure. He has a deal more experience than you, and has sold off most of that land by now. Besides, I would be remiss in my duty if I allowed you to go off permanently to the Kentucky wilderness with your education incomplete. Miles could leave all legal matters in my hands, but you, dealing with strangers, must know what you are about. You need grounding in the law, not only to prevent your being cheated in your surveying, but also in managing your property. Have you heard that that brave fellow you so much admire, Mr. Daniel Boone, has been careless--out of ignorance, I'll wager--has failed to file land warrants as required. Now he finds himself mired in legal difficulties, as well as gravely in debt. I would not have a like thing happen to you."

Mr. Waverley pulled himself to his feet, raised his arms and stretched his long, spare body. Nathan could see a strip of fair skin usually covered by his neck cloth. "Come, Nathan, do not stomp about so. This dock is much weakened by the recent freeze and thaw. You have always been too quick to throw aside your book. Miles was the same, but he regrets it now, and though he still loves to play the rough and hasty lover of good cheer, I've noted that his late-burning candle doesn't always light a deck of cards."

What could Nathan reply? It was a matter of course that he could not budge his uncle one inch. What if, instead of arguing that he could make his fortune without all that tedious book learning, he admitted the shameful truth. He simply could not learn from books. When he tried, he read so slow and painfully that it drove him wild. He learned far better when he could be told the matter by word of mouth. But if he confessed that, his uncle would only answer that he must apply himself more diligently. And he would look a fool. Nothing for it but to comply with as good a grace as he could summon.

"What do you require of me, sir?"

This brought a frown to his uncle's brow, as Nathan well knew it would. The man wanted agreement, wanted to persuade, not command. Any suggestion of submission, particularly unwilling submission, even from a servant, seemed to disturb him. But had he not been trained from babyhood to command? Then his father's death had made him master of Laurel Hill and at least forty souls, if you count family, overseers, and Negroes. And this when he was no more than a schoolboy. What arrogance to pretend to rule only by reason!

"I require nothing, Nathan. My dearest wish, as you well know, was for you to study at the College in Williamsburg. For two years, at the least. You could have lived in Mr. Levier's house, had all the advantages of daily contact with educated persons, made valuable connections, as I so wished to do and would have done, had it not been for my father's death and then the War."

"Yes, but Mr. Levier had not yet married your mother. There was no thought of your lodging with him and enduring the disgrace of living in the same house with his nigger mistress and their bastard brat!"

Instantly the brick-red skin of Mr. Waverley's face turned ashen. Nathan saw his hands tighten into fists and almost feared his uncle would strike him.

Instead, after a long moment of silence, he said, very low: "Sir, you forget yourself."

But Nathan could not hold back. "I've heard you tell me all this a thousand times. The fine opportunity I've missed. The excellent occasion to dwell in Williamsburg with Mr. Levier, distinguished printer. And I've kept silent. But everyone knows what goes on there, in Mr. Levier's house, and goes on <u>openly</u>. Yet you pretend ignorance, and keep telling me that that is where I should be."

Another silence. Then: "Excuse me, but everyone does not know this. Do you allow yourself to believe malicious rumors concerning the gentleman that your grandmother is married to? How dare you voice such rumors on the very land where she lives? What if a servant heard you, and spoke of this within her hearing?"

Nathan felt the sting of tears springing into his eyes. He turned his head away and blew desperately upward to dry them. He was a child! A woman! He knew he should apologize, but could not trust himself to make a sound.

Finally his uncle spoke again, this time in a kindly tone that almost brought back Nathan's tears. "Enough. I'm certain you regret your words and you will endeavor to mind your tongue better in future. I was wrong to bring up once more the matter of your studying at the College. Let's speak rather of what I have in mind for you. This winter you will read law with me. In spring I will stake you to a partnership with the surveyor that Miles and you became acquainted with in the Territory. He of whom you think highly, if I'm not mistaken? In a few years, when you are ready to make your way on your own, your land here will most probably bring a better price, and you can then repay me and still have enough to buy land out there. What do you say to that?"

Nathan knew he ought to be profuse in his thanks. Yet he could manage only a stiff "Thank you, sir." His earlier anger and his shame had left him befuddled. He kept his face as blank as he could and searched feebly for an excuse to get away. Fortunately his uncle saved him the trouble by hurrying away himself, reminding Nathan to see

Mrs. Waverley about the purchases she wished made. Nathan stumbled off, paying no heed to where he stepped, and thus sending spatters of mud even higher on his smallclothes than those already soiling them. It was a dirty day: mud, patches of snow, pools of water underfoot. From above, as added insult, drops of icy water from thawing branches struck him on the head. All nature seemed to remind him that freedom was still far off. Would it ever come? Even if he did finally escape to the West, what good would it do to cut a flash, however bright, way out in the Ohio Valley, among rough folk dressed in rawhide and dwelling in crude cabins? Who would ever hear of any fame of his? Unless he could somehow quell the red savages and stop the British from egging them on to attack settlers. Then indeed his name would be heard on the streets of Richmond, Charleston, and even Philadelphia.

But instead of leading a party of sharpshooters in pursuit of savages in the wilderness--he had plenty of heart for that--here he was faced with seeking the orders, and bearing the scorn of his aunt. And it would have to be in her bedchamber, after all. She would be with Miss Nelson, perhaps, or the new cousins. Or worse still, alone.

How about Miles? There was a happy thought. He would ask Miles to go with him. This younger uncle was an easy fellow. He took Mrs. Waverley's jests in stride and returned them back to her. Besides, Nathan had noticed that when Miles was present Mrs. Waverley fired all her teasing shots at <u>him</u>, ignoring anyone else who happened to be about. What a shame that Miles was bent on settling here in the home county. His companionship these last two summers in the West had been both agreeable and instructive. When he was doing something that was new to Nathan, he did it slowly, and commented slowly on what he did. Next time he would ask Nathan to do it, and walk away, not hover over him, as Uncle Matthew would have done. Miles seemed to take for granted that it would be done correctly. And if it were not, he would comment with an easy air on what must be changed. He was nothing like Uncle Matthew with his anxious watching, as if one mistake would mean the death of both of them. Yes, he would take Miles along when he went to take his orders from Mrs. Waverley.

But where was Miles to be found? He suddenly remembered hearing Molly complain over breakfast that her uncle had gone to Farrington, the Burnham's estate, to visit the ladies there and had refused to take her with him. This was strange, for Miles usually indulged Molly in everything. Well, nothing for it but to await his return.

———◦◦◦———

Late that forenoon Honey stood in the middle of the Waverley parlor twisting about uncomfortably in her new black gown. It was longer than she was used to and too tight in the waist. But Maudy, the young Negro woman who had taken such neat tucks in the bodice, insisted it had to be so. "<u>Ladies</u> wears 'em like that," she had said, letting Honey know she wasn't no lady in spite of her being kin to the Waverleys. Honey didn't need anyone to tell her that. Why, she was such an ignoramus she did not even know a person was supposed to wear black after a death in the family. Mrs. McNair, whom she'd always taken to be a learned woman, who could read her bible from one end to the other, had never said a word about wearing black clothes to mourn your kin. Honey dreaded the return of Mrs. Levier, Mr. Waverley's mother, who was to return any day now. This gown had been hers, and wouldn't she surely be mad as a treed bobcat when she saw what had been done to it? Luckily, it had just been taken in and hemmed, and no fabric cut off, so it could be changed back. Honey had begged, and been allowed, to do the hemming herself, but she had to do it under the eyes of the black woman, who remarked several times on the bigness of Honey's stitches. If truth be told, Maudy wasn't black at all. Her skin was a pretty golden color, and her eyes were light green. She wore quiet colors like the white people, not bright ones like the Negroes. But she was one of them, all right, for everybody treated her like one. She was Joan's daughter, they said, and Joan was the color of a chestnut. This was beyond Honey's power to figure out.

Honey had begged for other work to do, and Mrs. Waverley had set her to inspecting the dining room and parlor for dust and had told her to get after May, the little housemaid, if she found any. Of course she would not "get after" anyone, but found a bit of rag and was prepared to take care of any dust herself. Only her too-long and too-tight gown, and the splendor of the objects before her gave her pause. Everything seemed to be made of gold or glass or china: little clocks with china flowers all round them, looking glasses with gold eagles perched on top, large vases with blue and white scenes painted on them of strangely-dressed ladies with parasols walking toward bridges beneath trees she had never seen the likes of. She dared not touch any of this.

The looking glasses bothered her the worst, and it was not just the gold on their edges. The pictures they threw back at her were so clear, as clear as if she saw another Honey staring back at her. Especially upsetting was the enormous glass over the side table across from her seat at table. Each mealtime she tried her best not to look. But yesterday afternoon, sitting there for the first time in this black gown with the words of Mrs. Waverley saying how washed-out she looked worrying her ears, she couldn't help looking in the glass. Her picture there showed how true Mrs. Waverley spoke, especially when Honey looked at the reflection of Sarah, sitting next to her, with her hair that rich brown and her cheeks so pink. No wonder Sarah was quite taken with looking at herself in the glass.

The only things that seemed sturdy enough to dust here in the parlor were the smoothly carved chair backs and legs, and the wondrous brass dogs in the fireplace. She was crouched before one of these when a voice made her start up and tear loose with a sickening rip the waist of her new gown. How could she be so clumsy as to catch the hem under her moccasin?

"Massa say you come to the cabinet." It was little May, the housemaid.

"Yes, ma'am," said Honey without thinking, and bit her lips together because Mrs. Waverley had scolded her twice already for speaking so to servants.

She grabbed hold of her dragging skirt and scrambled to the back of the house where in a corner by the back stairs she had stowed the gun and the skins she had brought from home. Mr. Waverley had told her at breakfast that he would want to speak to her later in the forenoon. She had not yet seen him but at the family meals and that was no time to present their precious gifts. Not precious to <u>him</u>, she knew, but still the best she and Sarah had to offer. Would he think it mean-spirited of her to hold off until she could hand them to him direct? That thought took her aback but it was too late to think on it. She must go ahead and hope the gifts would win her and Sarah his good will.

She tucked the top of her skirt carefully into the tight bodice, draped the deerskins over one arm and took the gun in her other hand. She walked back up the hall to the door that May had pointed out to her, and knocked softly. No answer. She was summoning her courage to knock more loudly when the door opened and Mr. Waverley almost ran right into her.

"What? You're here? I was coming to look for you, child. Come in. Come in. But you are burdened down." He took the skins from her arm and led her to a chair.

"We brung these for you, sir," she said in the tiny voice of her shyness. She held out the gun to him as soon as he had laid the skins carefully over a table covered with books. "Papa shot these here bucks. Him and Dan and Josh surely done most all the scraping. I finished it myself. See how fine and big them two critters was. And you can't see no bullet holes at all." Something about Mr. Waverley, despite his fine clothes, eased her fear and allowed her pride in her papa to come right out.

"And this was Papa's best gun, that he had as long as I can recollect."

"Ah, a Pennsylvania rifle," he said as he turned it over, moving his long fingers slowly over stock and barrel. "The best there is. Light and prodigiously accurate. We can be proud it was developed here in our own country. Very well cared for, too. Your father was a careful man."

"Yes, sir." She couldn't help thinking, though, that his gun was about the only thing Papa took good care of. But that was hateful of her. She brushed the thought away.

"Well, well. You and Sarah are brave indeed to have made this long journey to Laurel Hill. And some of it quite alone. It shows quite singular resolution. Mrs. Waverley tells me that you brought a good lot of ginseng as well. Remarkable that you could find so much."

"It's right easy in October, on account of the leaves. They turn so fiery red they jump plumb out at you."

"They tell me it brings an exceedingly high price this year in the China trade. And the skins will sell well too. All that, together with what we can get for the rifle, will make a good beginning for dowries for you and Sarah. And I design to increase the sums as my circumstances permit."

"Oh no, sir! Indeed, it's all for you! So as not to burden you and Mrs. Waverley. Leastways no more than we can help. Me and Sarah are surely so beholden to you. But couldn't you yourself use the rifle?" Tears blurred her eyes at the thought of her papa's gun in the hands of a stranger.

She saw the line between his eyes go deep whilst he thought on it for a good space. "Very well, my child. Let us come to a little compromise. I will keep the gun, and be assured that never will I use it without I think in gratitude of your papa. Mrs. Waverley has told me of other things, edibles, I believe, that you brought, which we are happy to accept. But whatever are the proceeds from the ginseng and the skins must be for you and your sister. Agreed? May we shake hands on it?"

She dared not protest further, and allowed him to take her hand in his, which was firm enough, but felt smooth as though it had never done a lick of work.

"I asked to see you not just to attend to the gifts Mrs. Waverley told me you brought. I also wanted to assure myself that you and your sister feel perfectly welcome in my house. I had not the honor of knowing your father. The bad blood between him and my family, which I'll warrant you know something of, had its beginnings far in the past. I don't know the particulars, nor do I care to know them. Experience has taught me that there are always two sides to a quarrel. And both will have some merit. I detest feuding, whatever be the reason."

She could only stare at him. She had never been talked to like this.

He took hold of her hand again, and peered so deep into her eyes that she had to look away. "You are but a girl, yet you strike me as being a thoughtful one. I'll be bound that you and your sister are a little frightened at finding yourselves in such a strange place. And deeply grieved as well. I don't forget that your father died only a month ago. I lost my own father when I was still younger than you. But I was a boy, brought up to stand on my own feet, and I still had a mother, though God knows I saw little of her. She had her hands full with four younger children and all her woman's duties. My father was the very sun of my life, big and jovial and strong in mind, though quite uneducated. The world grew dark when he left it." He sat quiet for a while, with his eyes looking into that old darkness, she supposed. She couldn't imagine such a smooth-talking, finely dressed gentleman ever grieved like herself. Still, he was the first person in this new world who had spoken to her kindly of her papa.

Then he shook himself a bit and stood up. "You will be in the care of Mrs. Waverley, to be sure, and of my mother, Mrs. Levier, when she returns. But they are both much engaged in the care of all the family and all our people. Pray come to me if you should find yourself in want of anything. As a rule I keep to this cabinet in the late forenoon after my rounds." His mind seeming to wander off on some other matter, he gave her shoulder a distracted pat and guided her to the door.

———◦◦◦◦———

At that moment Kate and her half-sister Lucy were sitting in their large, comfortable parlor, Kate bent over an account book at the scarred oak secretary, and Lucy near the fire, working a piece of needlepoint destined to replace the worn upholstery of the chair on which she sat. The room had the faded elegance that marks a house once furnished by a proud and lavish hand, but long fallen into less ambitious and less affluent ones. The once-rich blue of the walls had grayed, the wine velvet draperies had frayed, and the Turkey carpet had suffered too much wear.

Hearing a masculine voice in the hall where their maid had just opened the front door, the two ladies put aside their work, smoothed their short gowns and petticoats, and poked stray strands of hair into their caps. Then both cried out "Miles!" at once, and sprang up to welcome the big man who strode into the room without ceremony. Miles, equal in age to Kate, had always been like a brother to both of them and to Lucy's brother, Stuart. Lucy was the first to give him both her hands, remarking on how fine and strong he looked, bigger than ever if that were possible. Kate welcomed him just as warmly, and the three were soon seated close to the fire, to which Kate ordered a log added.

Lucy was full of eager questions about Mrs. Waverley and the new babe, the newly arrived cousins from the backcountry, the public debate in Richmond, and most fascinating of all, Miles' adventures in Kentucky Territory. Lucy had been visiting an aunt when Miles and Nathan returned from the West, so had not seen them since the past spring. So much to learn! But she soon noticed that Miles' answers were short and his air quite distracted. Stranger still, Kate appeared ill at ease and would look at Miles with eyes almost apologetic. Was there something they were keeping from her? Both of them had always treated her like a child. That irritated her at times. Yet there was something pleasant in it too.

Of a certainty, Miles was not his usual jovial, blustery self, teasing her out of countenance one moment, and then bringing her a bright yellow finch to sing in the willow cage he had made for her, or a bunch of wildflowers for the bowl on her bedside table. This day he sat stiffly, regaled them with none of his humorous tales, and most surprising of all, once past the required question about her health that courtesy demanded, he did not inquire about her amusements, nor ask to see her latest drawings or hear her play on the forte-piano.

Instead he posed sundry questions to Kate about the crops and the livestock, even though she was only a woman. Of course he well knew that Stuart had not been home for months and that Kate must needs take some account of these things. He then asked news of Stuart.

Kate was proud, and would surely say nothing to Miles of their troubles. To Mr. Waverley, yes, she was obliged to confide because he had been Stuart's guardian for a year, until he turned twenty-one, and was still guardian to Lucy. Kate had to depend on him for advice concerning the farming. But no one else had to know of their affairs, especially those concerning Stuart. So Lucy was taken aback to hear Kate's next words.

"Stuart stays too long in Richmond." This was murmured low, with head bent, and was so unlike Kate, usually so firm and direct though always, somehow, perfectly ladylike. Miles leaned forward in his chair to hear her, something of his stiffness seeming to loosen. Kate glanced quickly at her half-sister, and then looked up at Miles. "I have no doubt that Mr. Waverley has acquainted you with something of our misfortune. Even if not, I fear it's the tittle-tattle of the whole county. Ever since his majority Stuart has been amassing debts. For a while we could pay them out of the tobacco crop. But now they are too great.

There are lawsuits threatened. If this continues, we will be forced to sell off land or have it confiscated. And now this provoking girl . . ."

Lucy felt the blood flood to her face as Miles turned those large, almost-black eyes of his full upon her. Never would she have believed that Kate would tell Miles about her intentions. But then, why not? He could be expected to take Kate's part against her. And she dreaded his disapproval worse than that of Kate or even Mr. Waverley.

"What is this, Lucy?" he asked with more mildness of tone than any he had used that day."

Perhaps he would understand her after all. "I only want to be of help to Stuart," she said. "He has been a little foolish. That's common with young men, is it not? I only wish to sell one part of the Winfield property left me by my mother. Stuart assures me that would settle all his debts. He would be so grateful. And he is contrite. He has promised to mend his ways." She looked anxiously at Miles, pleading with her eyes, her voice, even with a beseeching gesture of her hands. She knew she was pretty, and usually gave it little importance. But at this moment she was aware, and a little ashamed, of hoping this would help her win Miles over.

"Fiddlesticks!" cried Kate. "She says one part of her land? It's more like two thirds, and the best two thirds, to boot! The foolish girl would strip herself, and for what? The notion of Stuart's contrition and reform is a pipe dream. What, Stuart Ludwell? The darling of the tavern crowd? Perhaps ten years' time will put a check to his conduct. Mr. Waverley will have none of it, to be sure, and Lucy can do nothing without his consent. But she reaches her majority in ten months. Then what she does with her land will be in her own election. I fear an overindulgent heart will be her undoing."

Kate's voice had risen. Abruptly she pressed her lips together and walked over to the front window, where she stood clasping her strong hands to compose herself. Her square face, under the plain mobcap, seemed all cheekbone and jaw.

"I beg your pardon, Miles. I ought not burden you with our troubles. And on your first visit. Pray excuse me while I go see to tea for us. Perhaps you can talk some sense into this girl."

Lucy stifled the protest she would have made had Miles not been present. She had no thought of looking pretty now. No, nor any hope of winning him over to her side. She could see this in Miles' face, which gave clear assent to the words of Kate. She would bear his scolding in silence. Her best course lay in patience.

But Miles had come to sit in the chair that Kate had left vacant, nearer to Lucy, and his tone was not scolding. "What a loyal sister you are, Lucy. It must signify much to Stuart that you, at least, don't condemn him. But have a care before you come rushing to his rescue. It may well be that the best way to help a dog caught in a thorny thicket is to let him fight his own way out and take all the scratches that rake him. If you cut away the brambles, how will he ever learn to brave them on his own?"

He paused, and some part of her acknowledged the wisdom of his words. But this was wisdom that would require her to harden her heart to Stuart's pleas. And brook his anger. Such wisdom was beyond her strength.

"My brother and Kate," he continued, "feel strongly their duty to protect you. And so do I. Who knows when you may need every acre of your inheritance? We cannot suffer you to despoil yourself."

His friendly words brought back to her, in a rush, those happy days when he would ride ahead of her on narrow trails throughout the hilly countryside, warning her of every overhanging branch or rock-strewn slope. He was her big brother and her friend. It hurt even worse to displease him than to annoy Kate and Mr. Waverley. She must make him see that her future was now assured.

"Oh Miles, you are very good to advise me. But you see, I already know my future. Surely they've told you. Geoffrey is the dearest, kindest man alive. He loves Stuart as I do. He understands that a young man must sow his wild oats. He is so wise, Miles! And so accomplished. You have heard him sing. And he has such gentlemanly manners. He can converse on any subject. Isn't it a wonder that he, who has met so many fine ladies in England and even in France, has chosen a simple girl like me?"

She hadn't meant to go on so, but she was so full of this joy that now filled her life that the slightest sympathetic word made it burst out as though in song. Besides, Miles could not but be pleased with this match. It wasn't as though some strange gentleman, unknown to him, had sought her hand while he was away. Geoffrey was Mrs. Waverley's brother. He had passed many a month at Laurel Hill. His sweet nature and fine manners were well known to the whole family.

But Miles took a long time to respond. He rose abruptly and walked over to the hearth, where he stood with his back to her. When he finally spoke, his voice was harsh. "Has he declared himself?"

"Miles! How can you ask? Of course he has let me know his feelings." She was quite taken aback by his tone. Surely he could have nothing against Geoffrey. Neither Kate nor the Waverleys made any objection. They were not, perhaps, as enthusiastic as she had hoped. But it would have been natural for them to wish to see Geoffrey make a more advantageous match. Someone with more of a fortune than her modest one. Perhaps they feared that Geoffrey's claims to his English uncle's property would not be honored. But she knew for sure that they would. Hadn't he told her so, told her that he had never, at any moment, lifted a finger to help the British fight their war against us? And therefore there was no obstacle in the way of his claim to his property. But even if he were left with nothing, she had enough for both. They could live modestly, happy in their love for each other.

The look on Miles' face when he turned toward her was even worse than his tone had been. She had never seen such anger in him before. And at her! She bent her head to hide the tears that came, and somehow managed to say, as she swiftly left the room, "I must help Kate."

Instead of going toward the pantry, however, she fled up the stairs. They had all deserted her. She had not liked to admit it to herself, but she knew well enough that Kate and Mr. Waverley did not truly favor her love for Geoffrey. Mrs. Waverley did, it seemed, but Lucy had always been a little afraid of her, especially during this past year or so when Lucy sensed a growing coldness in that lady's manner toward her. And now Miles despised her. She had so eagerly awaited his return and counted on his friendship. Now she was alone. Judged wrong in wishing to help Stuart, and somehow judged wrong even in this new happiness that meant everything to her.

And Geoffrey did not come and did not write.

Miles stayed planted where he stood, his back to the waning flames of the fire. All he could think of, all he could see, was the glow in her dark eyes, the delight playing on her lips, as she spoke of the man he detested. How could such crushing pain come from the look in an eye, the bend of a head?

At that moment Kate bustled in with the tea tray. Setting it down, she glanced about for her sister, then turned to ask Miles what had become of her. But instead, seeing his face, she exclaimed: "Miles! What on earth? Are you ill?"

He could not stay to answer her.

Chapter Six

"My dear Mrs. Levier!" said Charlotte. "I am rejoiced to see you up and about so soon after your bone-crushing journey. And come down into this frigid cellar, to boot! Joan, help Mrs. Levier up to the dining room and have Joe build a fire for her."

Elizabeth Levier and her servant, Juno, had been the first to descend into the storage cellar of Great House on this morning three days before

Christmas. Joan, May, Old Sukey, and the cousin from somewhere out west, each with a basket on her arm, had joined them one by one in the narrow, dirt-floored aisle between well-stocked cubicles containing barrels and bins of flour, fruit, vegetables, wine, everything that cold was needed to preserve. It did not surprise Elizabeth that her daughter-in-law was the last to arrive, she who should rightly have been the first. Was it not the duty of the mistress of the house to set an example by being prompt to her daily task of distributing foodstuffs for the day? Particularly now, so close to Christmas, when timely preparation was vital and when servants were more than usually tempted to pilferage. Elizabeth suspected that Joan had been entrusted with a key to the cellar. Charlotte had blind faith in that woman.

Now, because of Charlotte's words, they were all gazing at her with pity, as though she were an invalid. Yes, she was past sixty, but an upright character and wholesome habits had kept her sound. The coach journey from Norfolk had been a mighty ordeal, and that ruffian Miles, come to accompany her, had been in too great a hurry to cover the miles. But three days in bed had quite restored her. She, who had spent the whole of her girlhood in the chill of Philadelphia's climate, could certainly bear the cold of her daughter-in-law's cellar.

Elizabeth twitched her elbow away from Joan's grasp and straightened her shoulders as much as she could, given the permanent stoop that age had given them.

"No need to waste firewood, Charlotte. I am quite well where I am. I will take back my charge of the infirmary today. I've already studied what is needed in supplies, grown sadly low, I must say, in my absence." Elizabeth liked seeing to the needs of sick field hands and servants. It somewhat relieved her Quaker discomfort at living in a slave-holding family. "And Charlotte, I must say that I've waited upon you here for well nigh a quarter hour."

Her daughter-in-law shrugged aside these well-deserved reflections on her tardiness and negligence. Years ago, when she had first come to Laurel Hill as Matthew's bride and had much to learn about estate management, she had paid some heed to her mother-in-law's observations. Now, puffed up with knowledge and her power over her overindulgent husband, she barely noticed them. Elizabeth sighed. She might as well talk to the wind.

"Madam," said Charlotte in her blandest tone, "be assured that nothing pleases me more than to see you back in that infirmary. Yesterday I had two injured men and three sick women, one with her incessantly crying baby at her breast. I swear I'd have gone out of my mind were it not for Honey's assistance in the afternoon."

Elizabeth regarded the thin little towhead with the foolish name. She looked a sly baggage, with her downcast eyes. And the younger sister, Sarah it was, who was not present to lend a hand, appeared the picture of sloth. A sly young woman and a slothful child. What woeful additions to this extravagant household.

Charlotte's voice changed now to that commanding tone she used with the servants. "We must open a new barrel of flour, Sukey. Have Joe--where is that boy?" She gave an impatient jerk on the cord that hung from a rafter. "Have Joe pry open the barrel for you and bring me five pounds for the apple tarts I'll make this morning. Get three hams from the smokehouse; also eight jowls and four shoulders for the servants' dinner." She detached the smokehouse key from the ring around her wrist and handed it to Old Sukey. "The cakes have been baked, and I've already had five, no, six bottles of Madeira brought up for the gentlemen."

"Ah yes, there you are, Joe." The gangling son of Big Moses had come down and stood quietly at the foot of the steps. "You did broach a pipe of the dinner wine, did you not? Have you filled all the bottles--there should be a good twenty dozen--and corked them well?" A mumbled "Yes'm" followed each of her questions. "As for today's and tomorrow's meals, just for the family, let's keep them as simple as possible. I entrust that to your judgment, Sukey. Why not have a basket of Indian corn and one of butter beans brought up and make your excellent succotash, for one dish?"

Elizabeth was losing some of Charlotte's words. Why did she mumble so? Then the walls seemed to lurch a little to the side and she felt something clutch her from behind. She stifled a gasp and turned her head, to find the boy Joe holding on to her. "Keep your hands to yourself, boy!"

"Joe was only trying to steady you, Mrs. Levier. You were about to fall," said Charlotte with her superior smile. Why had Matthew chosen an Englishwoman, all stuck-up creatures as they are? She did feel a little unsteady, but she must needs have her say about the supplies for this holy day.

"Pray have two more chickens stewed for the infirmary people. And let us have for the servants a particular treat for the Yuletide. You could make your custard, Sukey. Poor Mary could be taken some as well. She does so relish it. She would devour three great bowls of it if we would let her."

"By all means, my dear Mrs. Levier. Mrs. Mary Waverley will have her custard, and for the matter of that, I fail to see how three bowls of it can do her harm."

What impudence! To remind her elder of how Mary should be spoken of before the servants. According to her aristocratical lights, to be sure.

"But Sukey will have enough on her hands already," Charlotte continued. "And you, Joan, will have to spare May to the kitchen all this day and the next. You yourself will be occupied in polishing the silver and cleaning the fancy glassware. I can trust no one else for that."

"If you please, ma'am," suddenly piped up the girl called Honey. "My sister can make a right tolerable custard. That is, if you would try her."

"Splendid," said Charlotte. "And you, my dear, I am counting upon to supervise the care of Edward and Charles today. Joan will be too busy."

Then Elizabeth did allow herself to be taken upstairs, by Charlotte, whose hand could not in politeness be shaken off. But once out of earshot of the others, she could make the observation to her daughter-in-law that she had grave misgivings about allowing the cousins from the backcountry so much contact with the children, especially Molly.

"May one know what you object to, madam?" asked Charlotte.

"What do we know of these girls and their upbringing, Charlotte? We do know that the two of them, so young and unprotected, traveled the highroad for weeks, sometimes <u>alone</u>, so I'm told. You know as well as I that the roads and the forest are frequented by runaway slaves and roughnecks of every description. What decent young woman would even think of such a thing? And Molly told me they had both lived from home, with God knows whom, for a long spell before the father was murdered. Murdered! I shudder to think what goes on in that violent country. What tales this 'Honey' could tell our Molly, who is already all too prone to wildness and a fevered imagination."

"Oh well," said Charlotte, "I'd as leave let Molly learn as much as she can of the wider world, as long as it is through talk alone. Surely she is safe enough in the midst of all of us proper people." Elizabeth did not much like the tone in which Charlotte said "proper," and was suddenly reminded that there was much unknown in Charlotte's own background. Why would a young woman, niece of a lord, no less, have come alone across the sea to her brother's care in the Colonies? Indeed, that too was a daunting and dangerous journey. Matthew had never enlightened his mother on this question. Perhaps he knew as little as she of the matter. And would not have insisted on being told, since the foolish fellow had been so smitten with the redheaded Englishwoman.

"All the same, I do not like it. Who knows what iniquity those two girls may have fallen into, living far from home, and then wandering about the country on their own."

"Then indeed, madam, they deserve our pity. And as Christians, we owe them our protection. Are they not your blood, or to be exact, Matthew's?"

Lord, how provoking! How dare she take that pious tone? Charlotte was the most worldly of women. Why, it was she, Elizabeth, who did her utmost to maintain some semblance of respect for Almighty God and His laws in this household.

By this time Elizabeth was settled into a rocking chair near the hearth where Big Moses, whom they had found loitering there, was set to work building a good fire. It had just begun to crackle encouragingly when Molly burst in through the pantry door, tracking great globs of mud onto the floor. Charlotte made a quick lunge to stop her, pointed to the chest where rags were kept, and told her to clean her shoes and the spots on the floor before the others came up from the cellar and made the mess worse.

"No one can be spared to clean up after you today, young ragamuffin. Joan has driven the servants mercilessly to scrub the house spotless and I refuse to listen to laments from her this day."

Elizabeth was glad to see Molly, whom she considered shockingly spoiled, put to a bit of work. Yet since the task had been set by Charlotte, the grandmother could be sympathetic, at least to the extent of chatting with Molly while she mopped the mud.

"Are you glad St. Nicholas will be coming soon, child? I'm sure you wished for a fine doll when it was your turn to stir the plum pudding ten days ago."

"Oh Grandmama! St. Nicholas is for children, and I'm not a child anymore. I didn't wish for a doll, though I'm sure to get one, for Papa orders one from London every year. But Mama, may I give it to Sarah this year? I'm too big for dolls, even lady dolls. And Sarah looks at my old ones as though her eyes would pop clean out of her head. She'd never seen a doll before, not a real one. Just stupid things made of reeds and corn husks, like the niggers make."

"Mind your tongue, Molly! I swear I despair of ever making a lady of you."

"When will they bring in the Yule log, Mama?"

"Your uncle Miles had it cut and dragged into the smokehouse a week ago. A good thing, else with all this damp weather it would never burn a whit."

"And Colonel and Mrs. Meachem, will they bring their grandchild, Mama, even if her mama and papa don't come? Little Becky is excessively fond of Silky. Won't she jump for joy when she sees his new collar we ordered from London? Have you seen it, Grandmama?"

Molly scurried on hands and knees over to a cupboard, jerked open its door and drew out a tooled-leather collar with tiny brass studs all round it.

"That must have cost monstrous dear," remarked Elizabeth, "money far better spent on new eating utensils or cooking pots for your slaves." She saw the quick hand of Charlotte cover Molly's mouth, which would doubtless have made a saucy retort. Elizabeth knew perfectly well that referring to those they called "servants" as "slaves" was considered indelicate. Yet as she aged she found herself returning more and more to the Quaker principles of her girlhood. The good Lord did not intend any of his creatures to be enslaved. She lived among slaves, but she could refuse to mince her words in referring to them.

Thank God she no longer possessed any slaves of her own. Of those left her as part of her dower right, the two who had skills to maintain themselves decently had been freed, and the rest sold to Matthew. Only Juno and Cyrus, a couple middling in age, freed and given their keep and small wages, remained to help her with the care of Mary, Nathan's poor deranged mother, and the widow of Elizabeth's middle son. So Elizabeth's Quaker conscience was at rest on that score. Almost at rest. She could not prevent the troubling thought at times that her acres were worked and her food prepared by slaves belonging to her son, but that was beyond her control, was it not?

The noise of heavy feet coming up the stairs from the storeroom broke in upon her examination of conscience. Old Sukey pulled her bulky body into sight, her black face drawn from the strain. She was followed by Joan, self-contained and impassive as usual. After her came her own Juno and then the black children, Joe and May, with the thin little Waverley cousin in the rear. All but Old Sukey carried provisions of one sort or another in their baskets.

Elizabeth started to rise from her chair, saying she would be off to the infirmary. She could not abide sitting still, especially when others were at work. But Charlotte stayed her, signaling to Honey to tarry with them while the servants went off to their tasks.

"My dear Mrs. Levier, with your permission I hope to see Honey become an aid to you in your work, and you to her in her education. She has confessed that she and her sister barely know their letters, scarcely enough, indeed, to write their own names. Yet she is quite the wizard in the sickroom, are you not, my dear?"

"Just only tolerable, ma'am," Honey murmured, "account of because Granny Harriet taught me all she could."

"She knows her herbs, Mrs. Levier. She can direct the gathering of them, and I dare say can prepare them better than...that is, relieve you of the tedium of crushing and boiling and whatever else you do. Then, as you have the time and strength, perhaps you will be good enough to teach her and Sarah to read and write. I shall esteem myself much obliged to you, for otherwise I would have to undertake the task myself. Besides, they will be of use to you by reading prayers to the sick servants, and to all the others at your evening prayer service. You've remarked on the strain this has become for your eyes."

Elizabeth said nothing. Charlotte and Matthew never paid the least attention to her efforts to bring the word of the Lord to the slaves. Respectable people read prayers daily to all their household, masters and slaves, but her son and daughter-in-law were lax to the point of scarcely deserving to be called Christians. Perhaps she could do something with the two young cousins. If only she could look for a little assistance and encouragement from Mr. Levier. He too had had a good Quaker upbringing, had grown up only a few streets away from her home in Philadelphia, though a few years younger and barely known to her. That had given her the courage to accept him as her second husband, hoping that in matters of faith and principles he would be closer to her than Charles Waverley, who had swept her off her feet by his assurance and courtliness when she was too young to know better.

But Patrick Levier had not taken to plantation management and had soon used what money could be borrowed on her land to set up the print shop in Williamsburg. He had henceforth been required to spend most of his time there, but had insisted that his wife not risk removing to the ague-ridden climate of the lowlands. He now had a second shop in the new capital, but found Richmond still too rough and ramshackle for her comfort. Doubtless he was right.

Yet now that he was here for the winter season, she was never alone with him. He came to bed long after she was asleep. It was the fault of Charlotte. She bewitched him with her pretty face and flirtatious manner. A wonder that Matthew stood for it, but of course Matthew had never had the backbone to keep his wife in line as a true man should.

"No need to decide these matters just now," Charlotte was saying. "But let me beg you to remember the recent fatigue of your journey, madam, and allow Honey to assist you to your chamber."

Elizabeth Levier was shortly left quite alone, and sighed with a familiar sense of uselessness in her own home.

———◦•◦◦•◦———

It was past seven o'clock when Madam Charlotte arose from the remains of her sumptuous Christmas Eve repast and led the ladies to the drawing room, leaving the gentlemen to their port, Madeira and peach brandy. Their hostess was more than usually resplendent in emerald-green silk with a white lace fichu that emphasized her deep décolletage.

A handsome onyx pin set off the auburn curls above her temple, and saucy burgundy slippers peeped from the hem of her gown. What a lucky dog is that stepson of mine, thought Patrick Levier, and allowed himself to picture his daughter-in-law reclining on her bed quite bereft of silk and lace. Alas, he was never able to visit when Matthew was not at home, and in any case, though she clearly enjoyed his attentions, he suspected that he would receive no better than a playful rap on the knuckles if he attempted further liberties. Nothing ventured, nothing gained, however. Such had ever been his policy with the fair sex, and it had occasionally shaken unhoped-for fruit from the tree.

Patrick would just as soon have followed the ladies, whose company he much preferred during his leisure hours. But he must tolerate the gentlemen's company for half an hour, at least, for propriety's sake. In truth, he was not adverse to Matthew's peach brandy.

He loosened the tie at the waist of his small clothes to ease his overfilled stomach and watched contentedly as the servants carried off dirtied china and glassware, pulled the stained damask cloth from the table, and brought in sparkling wine glasses and a silver dish piled high with walnuts and pecans. Decanters of wine and brandy were placed on the table, where they beckoned to Patrick with the ruby and gold lights sprinkled over them by the candles in the chandelier. The Negroes also brought more wood for the fireplace and more coal for the stove. The latter was nicely placed behind him, so Patrick shoved his chair a half-foot back and unclasped his stock, the better to enjoy the fire's warmth on his neck.

Lastly, the outsized chamber pot was carried in and placed in a dark corner. The black lacquered screen, the one with clouds of apple blossoms inlaid in mother-of-pearl scattered over it, was moved forward to conceal whoever had to avail himself of the pot.

Yes, Patrick's stepson spared no pains in making his guests comfortable. Patrick was not unmindful of his good fortune in having this pleasant establishment to come to whenever he could absent himself from his affairs. In addition, he could leave his wife Elizabeth here in her old home where she was welcome and well looked after. He was free of her the greater part of the year.

If the men of the family had been the only ones present, he would have been entirely content to spend an hour sipping his brandy with them. Matthew was a gentleman of the first order, and Miles a jolly fellow, leastways when not love-smitten. As for young Nathan, he was over-conscious of himself, and skittish as a colt. A boy, in short. Time would improve him.

The Meachems, those pesky neighbors to the west, were another kettle of fish. The Colonel would most assuredly try to pick a quarrel with him. The argument would be about politics, but the real bone that stuck in Meachem's craw was Simon, a free Negro now in Patrick's employ, but once owned by Meachem.

Then there was Dick, the Colonel's son. Surly, morose, he had a disquieting reputation for violence. His wife Sophie had not accompanied her husband and their little daughter Rebecca to the Yuletide festivities. Her absence was a frequent occurrence that lent itself to conjecture in the countryside. Both male Meachems had freely imbibed during dinner and would doubtless finish the evening in a deplorable state of inebriation.

"A toast to our lovely hostess who has offered us a magnificent repast and graced it with all the charms of Venus," Patrick cried, seeing that by now Matthew had filled each man's glass. All raised their glasses, and then of course toasts must be drunk to each of the other ladies in turn, though none compared to Charlotte, not even the Ludwell girl, little Lucy, for whom that great oaf Miles was eating his heart out. Patrick saw through the fellow's attempt at nonchalance, like failing to seize the opportunity of sitting by the girl at table. Lucy was a mere sapling, too young, of too meager proportions and too little color for Patrick's taste. Miles, poor fellow, hadn't the whisker of a chance, with the polished Geoffrey Burnham in the race.

There was something about those Burnhams, Charlotte and Geoffrey. Their good looks clung to them through the years. The brother must be nigh forty, yet he was still the handsomest devil in any drawing room he entered. And where was he at present? Nowhere near the girl he had made so much show of courting. Patrick had heard an intriguing rumor about Geoffrey's whereabouts. But far be it from him to say a word of it here. Matthew disapproved of gossip, particularly about his relations. Perhaps a word later to Charlotte would be favorably received. She had none of her husband's scruples along that line.

Once all the toasts were drunk, Col. Meachem launched into his attack. "I suppose you are still defending this farcical 'Bill of Rights,' Mr. Levier? Milk and water amendments, and weak as they are, with no chance in Hell of being enforced, is what I say."

"I heartily approve of them, sir. Quite unnecessary, I'd say, but needed to reassure those still fearful of their liberties in spite of our excellent new Constitution." Patrick was feeling quite merry now, with that delightful brandy added to several glasses of wine at dinner.

"Those bloody amendments are nothing but a thin sop to blind us to the dangers of this Yankee government being thrust upon us," growled the Colonel. "And now, deuce take it, it's the law of the land, through the foolish acquiescence of the gentlemen of our House of Delegates. More fools they!" His voice rasped like teeth crunching into toast. "And now what hope do we have of getting passed the further amendments we need, those with real teeth in them?"

"None whatsoever, sir," said Patrick. "Those amendments 'with teeth,' as you put it, would have gutted our new national Constitution." Patrick beckoned to Joe to bring him the bowl of nuts. "Just imagine," he resumed, "there were some who wanted to deny Congress the power to tax. With no funds, where would be the power to protect us from our enemies?"

"What protection, sir?" interposed Miles, appearing to shake himself out of the lethargy in which he'd been sitting, slumped in his chair with arms dangling like great sausages at his sides. "Did they protect us on the Maunee River last month, where Federal forces were soundly beaten by the Cherokees? Egged on by those pestilent Spaniards in Louisiana Territory. And that despite General Washington's fawning attentions to that half-breed Creek, Chief McGillivray. Paid him £25,000, by God, to keep the Redskins at peace with us. Should have had him hanged and quartered, I say."

"Hell and furies, you hit it!" barked Dick Meachem, from the foot of the table. His eyelids drooped over glazed eyes. He probably hadn't followed anything that had been said, but was responding to the sound of anger, always welcome to him.

"Those Yankees," continued Miles, "bought up our certificates at four shillings to the pound, mind you, in '85. The scoundrels were re-selling them at fourteen last year. And now, with Congress backing them at par value, Mr. Hamilton's Yankee friends are enriched with bonds on the new Bank of the United States paying six percent interest, interest we are paying, sir, while our farmers scramble to mortgage their land to pay their taxes."

So Miles was lined up against him too, thought Patrick. Only to be expected. These planters could see no farther than the boundary of their most distant acre. Well and good. Patrick was cautious of being drawn into disputes in the tavern where they could so readily turn violent. But here in private company he could exercise his superior knowledge. The Colonel was no threat, and Dick Meachem, apart from that brief outburst, seemed determined to drink himself into a stupor. The sooner the better. The guzzling sot took no interest in public affairs.

"It is an unfortunate rule," said Patrick in that dry, offhand tone that he loved to use when other men were becoming heated, "that some people must lose in any financial arrangement. But our national credit must be made good, else what nation would trade with us, or give us respect?"

"The deuce with respect!" The abundance of red in Col. Meachem's skin deepened with his rising ire. "Is it respect the English show us when they still occupy western forts on our territory, when they incite the Redskins against us? When they cut off our most lucrative trade with the Islands?"

"Not to mention the infernally high tariffs they have slapped on our exports," put in Miles. The big fellow was up and ponderously pacing the floor in front of the fireplace. Remarkable to observe him so heated, as it had been to see him sunk in gloom up to a moment ago.

Patrick leaned over toward Matthew who was watching his brother with a worried eye. "Better he vent his spleen on the English than sulk over the filly, eh?" he whispered.

"The knaves lure us deeper and deeper into debt," Miles was saying. "And what to pay with? The price of tobacco rises and falls with no rhyme or reason. We never know what profit to expect. If any, indeed."

"By my soul, they bilk us coming and going!" cried the Colonel, slapping the table with such force that two glasses of Madeira overturned. He rose unsteadily and made his way over to the screen at the end of the room. Patrick hoped he'd hit the pot and not the nicely polished floorboards.

"Stability, gentlemen, stability. I do believe that order and stability are what these United States need. Do not you agree that Mr. Adams, Mr. Hamilton, and our own Mr. Madison are all devoted to this end?" This was the quiet voice of Matthew, smiling amiably all round.

"The devil they are! Madison, mayhap. Curse me if those Yankees haven't just voted to line their damned pockets." The Colonel stopped on his slow way back to his seat and fastened his somewhat shaky gaze on Patrick. "As some right here in this very company do most all the time."

The Colonel was accusing him of investing in those hated certificates and in United States bonds, and there was truth in both accusations. But Patrick chose not to be affronted. As a man of sense, he had learned to feign obliviousness to insults. He also reminded himself again that the true source of Col. Meachem's enmity toward him lay elsewhere. The planter had sent his slave Simon as substitute to serve in the Virginia militia during the war. After the surrender, Simon had come to Patrick complaining that Meachem would not free him as the law required. Patrick knew the man to be a good worker because he had leased him from Col. Meachem before the hostilities. So he paid for the successful lawsuit and now had an excellent assistant, at wages, in his Williamsburg print shop. Well worth the cost. Indeed, Simon was so reliable that Patrick could leave him in charge while he himself did business in Richmond. Small wonder that Meachem still held a bitter grudge against him.

"Damn Yankees! Damn British toads! Damn speculators! Crew of devils!" This exploded from the mouth of Dick Meachem, who had suddenly shot upright, and leaning with both arms on the table, stared into space with bloodshot eyes.

"I think, gentlemen, that the wisest policy in these trying times is to diminish our reliance on foreign goods. Particularly in view of the high tariffs imposed by the Congress." This came from Matthew, again attempting to head the conversation along a safer path.

"It's those bloody Yankees again, pox take 'em," muttered the Colonel.

"I've received quite satisfactory tools and furniture from Philadelphia," Matthew continued. "Also, because of such uncertain prices, I've cut back on tobacco acreage, as many in the tidewater lands have been doing from necessity, and we should do as a precaution."

"Ay, and what's more," said Miles with an angry laugh, "send what tobacco we do grow to a runner. Get a far better price when it's sold in those nice little hidden coves on the English coast."

"Unless the runner is caught and all is confiscated." This was the exact comment that one would expect from Matthew.

"God's life! It's worth the gamble," cried Miles. "Mayhap I'll give up my notion of settling down and living the humdrum life of a planter. Damned if I won't buy me a fast little schooner and make me a fortune on bootleg tobacco right under the noses of those English bastards."

Patrick observed his younger stepson with amusement. Miles had been a jolly drinker in the past, and more recently had moderated his elbow-raising. But tonight he was neither jolly nor moderate. Ah, the power of dark curls and demure eyes. Patrick glanced at Matthew, who was again regarding his brother with quite unamused surprise.

"God's ass, fellows, let's drink to the drowning of the whole British fleet," said Miles, raising his glass of brandy so unsteadily that half sloshed over the edge, "and while we're at it, let's send every damned Tory back to grovel at King George's feet. We don't want 'em."

"Particularly if they have the effrontery to pay court to our loveliest young ladies," laughed Patrick, raising his glass perfectly level.

Miles sprang to his feet quicker than one would have thought possible in his condition, as also did Matthew, the picture of alarm. But Miles only glared at his stepfather for a long moment, then sank back down on his chair, his shoulders sagging. "Right," he muttered. "Only too right."

Matthew moved quickly to Miles' side and urged him up again with a hand under his elbow. "Brother, be so good as to take Col. Meachem outside for a turn in the garden." By this time the Colonel was sitting still and silent, his eyes open but seeing nothing. "He is assuredly not fit to be seen by the ladies. Perhaps a half-hour in the cold air will do him good."

You had to give it to the man, thought Patrick. Always sober, always able to make the best of the worst occasions and usually able to keep at least his relations out of trouble. Miles obeyed him like a good hound, and the two of them managed to get Meachem up and out the door.

Then Matthew turned toward the end of the table, where the younger Meachem was sprawled forward, his head on the table and his hair soaking in a patch of spilled Madeira. "I think he'll be safe here for a goodly time. I'll send for Big Moses to watch him and warn us when he wakes." He came closer to where Patrick and Nathan were standing and placed a hand lightly on the arm of each. "Shall we join the ladies, gentlemen?"

———————◦◦◦————————

Charlotte stood on the drawing room hearth where she was overseeing Big Moses as he touched the flame of a candle to the kindling under the enormous Yule log that filled the fireplace from end to end and halfway up to the opening of the flue. It would take a while for the log to catch fire, and by that time, she hoped, the gentlemen would have finished their carousing in the dining room. But if they returned too late for the most splendid effect of leaping flames, so much the worse for them. Poor little Edward was drooping sleepily over his new wooden horse, sitting still and pulling it on its big red wheels a few inches to one side and then the other. His small fists kept tight hold of the string lest vigorous little Rebecca, the Meachems' grandchild, grab it away from him.

It irritated Charlotte to see the little girl, the same age as Edward but nearly half a head taller, eyes sparkling and cheeks round and ruddy, skip from one lady to the next, and back to Edward. She was the center of the ladies' attention as a healthy child will always be. Time for the Yule log to burn, the pudding to be served, and the two small children put to bed, gentlemen or no gentlemen.

She dismissed Big Moses and approached the circle of ladies and children. Honey, seated between Mrs. Meachem and Lucy, was repeating once again, at their behest, the story of her and her sister's journey from the North Carolina mountains, while Lucy listened round-eyed and the older woman gave little shrieks of shock and pats of sympathy at hearing of such extraordinary perils. Kate, surrounded by ladies and girls in their silk and lace, looked plainer than ever in her brown, unadorned flannel. She sat next to Mrs. Levier and was listening politely to what was surely some complaint from that lady. As for Aunt Abie, she was dozing, mouth open, in her rocking chair, and jerking dazedly awake from time to time, as was her wont at this hour of the evening.

Molly and Sarah shared one chair as they bent in deep concentration over a card table. As soon as she saw her mother approach, Molly jumped up and called out in a voice that hooted like a teakettle. "Mama! Can you imagine? My Tablets of English History is missing a piece!" She pointed with outrage at the jigsaw puzzle laid out almost completed on the table. Indeed, a piece that should have pictured Queen Elizabeth's nose and chin was missing. "It is really too bad of them. What good is a puzzle that isn't all there?" And Molly kicked a leg of the table, sending half the puzzle over the edge.

"Mary Margaret!" exclaimed Mrs. Levier, the arm of whose chair had been struck by the card table. "What a wicked, ungrateful girl! You know very well that anger is a sin, and so is ingratitude for the gifts God brings. You deserve to have all your Yuletide gifts taken from you and given to the poor."

"They are not from God! They're from Papa and Mama, and I'm sure they're angry too, at the English factor who never gets things right."

Charlotte quickly put a hand to her mouth to hide a smile. How she enjoyed hearing her daughter nail a truth on its head, and seeing Mrs. Levier quite beside herself with that dreadful sin of anger that she so righteously condemned. No doubt she felt disgraced before the company by her granddaughter's behavior. Charlotte, on the other hand, rejoiced in her daughter's mettle. Full of spirit, Molly was a true child of her own. Still, she must learn to control her temper.

"Enough, Molly," she said in a level tone. "You are too old for such a display of temper. Leave the room until you are calm enough to return and apologize to your grandmother and all the company."

Mrs. Meachem spoke up as soon as Molly had disappeared through the archway. "My dear Mrs. Waverley, the child is right. The Colonel ordered me such a beautiful bonnet, far too dear, of course. And what do you think? It is too small! I shall have to slit the band and straw. Goodness knows if it can be rewoven without quite spoiling it."

"Yes, Charlotte, you must speak to Matthew," said Mrs. Levier. "My new leather chest has two of the brass knobs missing. I vow the London factor bought it that way, thinking a mere Colonial would not notice."

Charlotte wanted to snap out: "Speak to your son yourself," but she restrained herself. "We are Colonials no longer, madam," she said instead, "whatever the English may call us. But indeed, I have complaints of my own. I tried last year to persuade Matthew to change factors."

At this moment the gentlemen entered, or at least Mr. Levier, Nathan, and Matthew did so. Nathan pulled up a chair next to his grandmother. The other two drew Charlotte aside.

"Miles was reluctant to join you ladies this evening, my dear," said Matthew. "He's still quite cast down by what he considers Lucinda's poor choice in encouraging Geoffrey's suit. As for the Colonel, he is deep in his cups, so I asked Miles to help him walk it off a bit."

"Miles is pretty far gone himself, poor fellow," laughed Mr. Levier. "Ah, the power of a pretty face! What think you of that, lovely lady?"

"The subject is beneath my notice," she replied, a little surprised at her own curtness. But Mr. Levier was sometimes insupportable with his frequent allusions to intrigues where none existed. Anyone could see that Miles looked upon Lucinda as a little sister in need of protection. No doubt Matthew thought his wife rude, for he darted a disapproving glance at her, but changed the subject.

"What have you ladies been chatting about, my dear?"

"We've been complaining about our gifts, as usual at Christmas, Matthew. Parts missing, clothes not fitting, you know how it always is. Why on earth don't you find a more capable factor? Would you not be likely to get better credits on your tobacco, as well as more satisfaction on your orders?"

"My dear, I have told you before. I am still too heavily in debt to this one. For the third year in a row, he has sent me a notice of debit rather than a letter of credit. I'm gratified to say that the amount of indebtedness has diminished each year and I intend to continue it so, by ordering less and less from London."

"Oh but only think, Matthew, of how it will look," she protested, lowering her voice so that only he and Mr. Levier could hear. "I'm sure that the Meachems and Kate and Lucy have already noted that our orders were niggardly this year. Soon the whole countryside will suspect a decay in our fortunes!"

"Indeed, Matthew, the lady speaks truth." She could rely on Mr. Levier to defend the reputation for easiness of the Leviers and Waverleys.

"Be that as it may, I will not be beholden to those rascally English merchants any longer than need be. Besides, you know quite well that we have been pleased with orders from Philadelphia. The Encyclopedia, the Windsor chair, the cutlery."

"Now that is the soul of wisdom!" chimed in Mr. Levier once more. "We must encourage our own American manufacturers. The expense is less, and with no excise taxes to pay. However, I fear the government in Philadelphia is bound to impose them as their need for money increases."

"Oh, when you gentlemen begin to speak of manufacturers, and taxes, I can say nothing."

"Of course, my dear, not fit subjects for ladies." Matthew smiled at her in gentle condescension. She enjoyed flattering him and other gentlemen by encouraging their assumption that ladies were incapable of understanding matters of public interest. In point of fact, she was quite certain she could grasp such subjects if she chose. But great heavens, how they bored her! When released momentarily from the multifarious demands of running her household that gobbled her time like a ravenous gosling, she sought the pleasures of reading novels and corresponding with her friends.

The two gentlemen now excused themselves and left her side. Matthew drew near the group of ladies and children, while Mr. Levier sauntered over toward the pianoforte. After bowing to each of the ladies, and making an especially graceful leg to Mrs. Meachem as the eldest of his guests, Matthew bent over Lucinda's chair and gestured toward the pianoforte where Mr. Levier was officiously arranging sheets of music on the rack.

"Pray do not be shy, my dear. Oblige us with some of your sweet songs. As we all know, you are the only accomplished musician among us this evening."

"Oh indeed, Lucy," chimed in Mrs. Meachem to second Matthew's urging, "however could we name this a true Christmas Eve without your delicious warbling. The Colonel quite delights in it. He would, I am sure, join you on his flute, but they tell me he is quite indisposed at the moment." She tittered knowingly, having decided long ago, it seemed, to find her husband's frequent drunkenness a subject of mirth, at least in company.

Lucinda was protesting that she was unused to playing and singing alone. "Would you not be good enough to join me with your violin, Mr. Waverley? I'd be so grateful."

"Dear me, child. I've not touched it these three months. And before that, I played all too seldom. But since you ask it as a favor, I'm sure our friends here will make allowances." He sent Joe for the instrument, and went to kneel by the pianoforte bench, shuffling through the many sheets of music, most of them woefully dog-eared by wear and mildew.

"Ah, here is the little Haydn rondo we were practicing at Michaelmas. As I recall it wasn't excessively difficult." He placed that piece upon the rack, and took the battered case that Joe now handed him, drawing out his violin with loving hands.

"Please, ladies, please, resume your conversation while I tune my fiddle." He was in high spirits now, Charlotte noted, as always when given the chance to play or hear music. "Music is the favorite passion of my soul," he liked to say, "after you, my dearest," and would kiss her hand. She loved him best as he was now: eased of his cares, a small smile flitting on and off his lips, the line etched between his eyes almost erased. If only he could be persuaded to give up standing for the Assembly, and would stay at home, with only the brief absences occasioned by pleading cases in other districts. The power she enjoyed while he was gone and she left mistress of the place was beginning to pall.

She had not been educated for such a life. On the very day of her and Matthew's wedding she had overheard Mrs. Levier confide to Aunt Abie: "Mark my words, Aunt, this girl will spend her days lolling in her silks in the parlor while I must needs go on as before seeing to everything." Those words had sparked her determination to prove herself fit for her new duties. Now those duties were old, and increasingly tiresome. She had shown the old woman that blue blood will tell, even in this wilderness, but what did that leave her but boredom and fatigue?

At that moment cries of "Oh" and "Ah" broke forth from all round her as the Yule log roared into a huge burst of flame, sending red-gold light onto every face, and in the same moment there rolled into the room a tall fellow in a long red robe that barely reached to his calves, scarcely stretched round his broad shoulders, and opened wide over a rotund belly that appeared somewhat askew. Shaggy white hair and a mangy beard hid his face. Behind him entered Molly, who ran quickly to drop a curtsey and say an apology to her grandmama and the other ladies. Molly was not one to miss out on any merrymaking out of pride.

Who on earth was this Father Christmas? Patrick Levier had played the role in the past, but Charlotte had dissuaded him this year because Molly was now too knowing to enter into the spirit, and the excitement might well be too much for Edward.

"I declare, madam, it must be Miles, and I fear the clumsy oaf is still quite merry from drink," whispered Mr. Levier into her ear. "Heaven knows what's become of Col. Meachem. I think your husband has gone to see to him."

Rebecca was jumping up and down and pulling on Father Christmas's bag, from which she received a spinning top, and a whistle to give to Edward who hung back clinging to Joan's skirts. Of course the commotion had drawn all the servants, who crowded along the wall, whispering and nudging each other. Molly was laughing uproariously and trying to pull off her uncle's fake beard.

Charlotte called for the trestle table to be brought in, and then the plum pudding. Nothing like rich food to calm people down and even sober them a bit. Tradition demanded that you serve this pudding on Twelfth Night, but since Matthew insisted on releasing the house servants for nearly a fortnight after Christmas, so they might visit even distant relatives, Charlotte found it convenient to do all her seasonal entertaining beforehand.

Mrs. Levier commanded Father Christmas to sit down in the wing chair, and little Rebecca scrambled instantly onto his lap. She was soon delightedly feeding him huge mouthfuls of the first piece cut from the pudding, while Edward, still holding tight to Joan's skirt, inched closer and closer.

Soon all were eagerly spooning pudding into their mouths, savoring the dense mixture of beef, veal, raisins, currents, dried plums, spiced with cochineal, cinnamon and cloves, and moistened with sherry, old hock, and lemon juice. Of course it was not long before the silver farthing was discovered, in Nathan's piece, and all congratulated him on this promise of worldly fortune. It was Kate who discovered the ring. It was a little hard to believe that marriage might still come for this old maid, but perhaps, thought Charlotte, belief in the charm would somehow bring it about. Why not Miles? A sober woman like Kate would steady him--for he still seemed in need of steadying--and the thought of them as a couple was somehow pleasing to her.

She looked over at him, having the crumbs wiped from his chin by a giggling Rebecca who had quite a struggle with the enormous linen handkerchief she had found in his pocket. Miles was still playing the role of oafish, disheveled Father Christmas; not so far from his true character, Charlotte thought with sudden disdain as she spied Lucinda also contemplating him. Lucy's eyes were filled with gentle indulgence. What a soft, spineless little creature. Just the sort sought by the vast majority of gentlemen. Well, she would have need of all her indulgence if she wed Geoffrey, and not only when he was tipsy.

This last thought recalled Col. Meachem to her mind. She made her way to her husband, and learned that Miles had delivered the Colonel into the hands of his man Caesar, who had found a bed for him. As for Dick, Moses had got him onto a pallet in the pantry where he would certainly stay the night.

It was time to send the younger children to bed. She so signaled to Joan, and ordered the other servants, all of whom had received a piece of cake and a glass of wine, to clear away the foodstuffs. This made way finally for the promised musical duet by Lucinda and Matthew.

The Rondo was not ill performed, considering Matthew's want of practice. There was then a chorus of requests for a ballad. "'Lord Randal,'" commanded Molly at the top of her voice. "'Sir Patrick Spence,'" begged Kate. Miles called for "Bonny Barbara Allen" in a dejected tone. (He had pulled off wig and beard and abruptly lost his jolly air the moment the smaller children left the parlor.)

All requests were agreed to, but from the first measures of "Lord Randal" all were sadly aware of the absence of Geoffrey's fine baritone. Matthew himself complained: "What a crying shame our Geoffrey is not here! The ballads call for two voices."

Then all felt themselves obliged to tell Charlotte how much they missed her brother.

"Don't look to me for an explanation," Charlotte protested. "I know nothing of his whereabouts. But Mr. Levier here delights in hinting that he knows more than he tells." That would serve the old gossip well! She was fond of him, but he could become tiresome with his none-too-subtle insinuations.

"But I know nothing! Or next to nothing." Mr. Levier's little eyes danced behind his spectacles. He so enjoyed being the focus of expectant attention. "Our paths crossed, most briefly, in Williamsburg, where his phaeton splashed an enormous wave of mud upon me as I stood in Queen Street. Turned my new coat from blue to brown in a trice, I assure you. He said he might soon be off to Portsmouth where he has a relation arriving from Santo Domingo. Fleeing the horrid violence there, you see. And to think that the poor lady had quite recently taken refuge in the Islands from the troubles in France."

"Lord have mercy!" exclaimed Kate. "They say the black monsters in that wretched place have murdered people in their beds. Cut the throats of women and children. It grieves one's heart."

"Not only murdered, but raped and mutilated as well," growled Miles, in a tone that suggested a certain satisfaction in the thought. Foolish first, then morose, then murderous, and for what? A mealy-mouthed little snippet who sat all this while quietly on her music bench, head turned demurely away and in all probability dreaming of Geoffrey who most certainly was not dreaming of *her*. Charlotte's thoughts were interrupted by the voice of her daughter, who along with Sarah had been permitted to remain with the grownups.

"Papa, Papa! What is 'raped and mutated'?"

Her father took a long look at her and Sarah's round eyes and half-scared, half-excited faces. "That is nothing you need trouble your head about, little one," he said, "and I think it is time Miss Lucy and I continue our performance in spite of the unfortunate lack of a second voice."

"My sister has a pretty voice, sir," spoke up Honey of a sudden, no one having heard more than a "yes, ma'am" or a "no, sir" from her once she had answered all the questions about her journey. "Granny Harriet used to make Sarah sing the old songs when Granny's rheumatism plagued her. She said it cut the pain better than liniment."

Matthew led Sarah, too flustered to resist, to the pianoforte and spoke to her gently with words (murmured so that no one else could hear) that soon caused her to stand, flushed but smiling, by his side. Barely had she joined Lucy in the first ballad when exclamations of surprise and delight arose all round. Sarah possessed a fine contralto voice, absolutely accurate in pitch and surprisingly full for one so young. The effect of her low voice, harmonizing instinctively with Lucy's soprano, supported by violin and pianoforte, was so perfectly pleasing that soon all the company grew quiet, calmed and enchanted by the music.

They were even more enchanted when the trio launched into "Bonny Barbara Allen."

The girls took it into their heads to sing only the narrative portions together, and to take solo parts for Sir John (Sarah) and Barbara Allen (Lucy). The older girl's cool soprano fitted well the cold resentment of Barbara Allen, while Sarah put surprisingly strong feeling into the anguished complaints of Sir John.

> O hooly, hooly rose she up,
> To the place where he was lying,
> And when she drew the curtain by,
> "Young man, I think you're dying."
>
> "O it's I'm sick, and very, very sick
> And 'tis a' for Barbara Allan;"
> "O the better for me ye's never be,
> Tho your heart's blood were a spilling."

The scrape of a chair caught Charlotte's ear--all the others seemed too engrossed to notice--and she caught a glimpse of Miles' back disappearing through the archway. Lovesickness! She had no tolerance for such weakness.

"Wherever did you learn all these songs, child," Mrs. Levier was asking, during a pause in the singing. She clearly could not understand how these niceties of civilization could have penetrated so far into the wilderness from which the young girl came.

"Honey learned me, ma'am, and she learned them from Mama. Mama's mama was 'dentured,' you see, in a fine house. I don't remember where. But her papa was a gentleman and he . . ."

"She means 'indentured,' ma'am," Honey broke in, coloring deeply, "but that was way long ago, when our grandmama first crossed the sea, way afore she got wed and our mama was born."

So the distaff side of the family was not quite mentionable, concluded Charlotte. The mother had most probably been a bastard, and Honey was either lying, or had been lied to. "Enough of songs of death and heartache," she exclaimed. "Christmas day comes on the morrow. Let's all join in carols. That will lift our spirits."

Soon all voices rose in the strains of "Good King Wenceslas," broken by laughter at their dissonance, while Charlotte had the great bowl of wassail brought in and set on the card table. Tumblers full of the steaming golden liquid were being passed to every hand by the servants, when right in the midst of "Adeste Fideles" Joe, who had been sent for more napkins, strutted in empty-handed and full of importance.

Charlotte stopped him in the archway. "Titus be here, ma'am. Be just come. He say he must speak to Missus Kate. He say quick." Titus was Stuart's manservant who was supposed to be with him in Richmond. Titus stuck to his master like a bur, on Kate's orders, to head off the scrapes the young man was always getting into, or pick him up afterward when prevention proved impossible.

Kate had already noticed the eyes of mistress and servant fixed upon her. Since she had to disturb the whole circle around the pianoforte in order to make her way across the room, the song ceased abruptly and all turned faces flushed with wine and excitement toward the hall, where Titus could now be seen. A few words from him sufficed to turn Kate's face the color of chalk and her hand grasping for support. Lucinda rushed to her side and was soon clasping her stepsister round the waist. Matthew helped the faltering sisters to a bench in the hall and ordered brandy for them.

It was Charlotte who had to announce to all the terrible news. Stuart was dead. On the field of honor, she said, for Kate and Lucinda's sake, though it was more than clear from Titus's words that the "field of honor" was outside the lowest class of tavern and the combat a mere drunken brawl.

Everyone crowded into the hall, clustering around the sisters with clucks of sympathy or around Titus to draw out further details. Only Mr. Levier remained in the drawing room, where Charlotte soon joined him.

The first words he said were the very ones that were running through her own head.

"What an alteration this makes, do not you think? Our lovely Lucinda becomes a notable heiress."

"Assuredly," she replied. "I marvel at the rapidity with which your mind seizes on the practical consequence. What a shame that your married state does not allow you to aspire..."

"Ah, madam, you do me wrong. I was thinking only of your fortunate brother."

"Geoffrey may not be fortunate at all. To all appearances, something else lures him to the seacoast at the very time his true duty is here. He may well have lost his chance. But I pray you, do not speak of that. I must say that your company is sometimes rather less than edifying, my dear Mr. Levier."

But she smiled at him as she left to do her duty as compassionate hostess and neighbor.

Chapter 7

January had set in with cold more bitter than any remembered by even the oldest Virginians. For three weeks the bare ground had been frozen solid. Any attack by plow or pickax was not to be thought of. Thus no preparation could be made as yet for this year's tobacco crop, preparation that must always await the January thaw. This was just as well, perhaps, for sickness was rampant in the slave cabins as well as in the houses of the masters. All hands that could still be mustered were needed to preserve as many farm animals as possible. Cows were dropping their calves, sheep their lambs. The tender creatures must be found and brought into the barns in haste before they froze to death. Chinks in walls and leaks in roofs must be plugged, and straw kept dry.

All this formed the subject of Matthew's conversation with his brother as they rode one afternoon toward the Ludwell plantation. On their left, the large pond that marked the eastern boundary of Laurel Hill was frozen solid almost to the middle, because the sun, low to the south, did not rise high enough to reach over the trees, leaving half the pond deep in shade all day long. The ice was a silvery blue with patches of white where snow from an earlier day still lingered. Dark blue ripples showed on the open water beyond.

The two men allowed their horses to choose their own slow pace, the ground being treacherously slick with ice. They posted from time to time to get the blood running in their legs, and gazed bemused at the hoarfrost clinging thick to the trees and at the clouds of steam rising over the horses' heads every time they exhaled. Miles' two spotted hunter bitches, Shot and Flint, ran in great circles from pond to road to woods, barking merrily as they went.

Once the brothers had exhausted the subject of the rigors of this winter, they came to the more immediate object of their visit. But before they had exchanged more than two sentences concerning the offer that Matthew intended to present to Kate Nelson and Lucinda Ludwell, they began to hear the crack of other hooves on the ice, and soon could make out, on the road ahead, two mounted gentlemen, and beyond them, a cart with four men aboard.

The gentlemen on horseback turned out to be Col. Meachem and Dick. The Colonel's florid face was more than half concealed by a black felt hat and a red plaid scarf wound round neck and chin. Dick was bareheaded and wore only a tan coat over his shirt and breeches. It would seem that the combination of black bile and strong spirits kept him constantly warm. On the cart's board sat Phillips, the Meachem's home overseer, next the drayman, both well bundled in cloak and blanket. On the floor of the cart, huddled close against each other so as to share one ragged cloak, sat two Negro men, their knees drawn up to their chests and their bare feet in chains.

After the gentlemen exchanged the usual greetings and inquiries after the health of each one's family, Miles, who was not so loathe as Matthew to ask about other men's affairs, sought to know the Meachems' destination.

"Petersburg, sir," said the Colonel. "I've been told that trader Scudley is still in town, not having purchased as many Negroes as he requires at the first of the month. So I'm going to rid myself of these two troublesome fellows. I doubt not I'll get near a hundred pounds each. Cuffee's lazy as an old sow, and a very great rogue as well. Insubordinate as they come. He's been beat 'til the blood ran, given as much as sixty lashes, but there's no mending him."

"I've told you to leave him to me and Phillips, Old Man. We'd soon break the cur-dog."

"Oh yes, you'd soon ruin me if I left the niggers up to you." He turned back to Matthew and Miles. "I'm certain you heard of how Phillips, probably at the behest of my know-it-all son here, tied an insolent rascal naked to a tree at the edge of Bryan's Swamp. Of course the fellow got bitten so bad he swelled up to twice his size. As soon as I heard of it I had him brought in and cared for, but nothing to be done. Died of inflammatory fever. Yes, you'd take care of my nigger problems, Dick. You'd kill 'em all off."

"As for Ginger here," he continued, "he keeps running off. Stays away for days at a time. I give them three days at Christmas, but this bastard was gone near a fortnight. Last July he got all fired up by the Independence Day celebration. 'Freedom Day,' he called it. That time he was gone a month before we caught him. He's humble enough. Promises to mend. But he's sly. Always in the woods. Have to have him do his work in chains. Got tired wasting our time tracking him down, didn't we, Dick?"

"Damned right. Beatings don't signify a thing to his tough hide. Time in the stocks neither. You can't cut 'em anymore. Folks are too squeamish nowadays, I say. This old man says it would damage his reputation. Anyhow, you know what this impudent dog Cuffee dared ask us this very morning? To stop at Ludwell's to say goodbye to his sister."

"Yes, and I might have done it, too, as a favor to Miss Kate," said the Colonel. "It's hard for a woman to manage her people without a man on the place. Seeing these fellows in chains might strike some fear into their black livers. But we haven't the time. The going is so slow on this cursed ice, and I don't know how long the slaver will stay around."

Matthew would have preferred to remain silent, knowing how greatly he and Meachem differed on the subject of the Negroes. But the longer he observed the condition of those men in the cart, the stronger his conscience goaded him to speak.

"It would be well to cover your men's feet, Colonel. They'll be frostbitten in no time, if they're not already." Though the men were struggling to make their cloak cover their feet, it was too short by a hand's breadth.

"Well, sir, I had them trotting along to keep warm up until a quarter of an hour ago, but the ice was cutting up their feet and I didn't care to bring them up before that slaver, with them unable to walk."

"I'll warrant you they'll soon be in worse shape with the frostbite," commented Miles.

"Well shit upon it! Phillips! Take that blanket off your delicate person and throw it on the men's feet. Your breeches are plenty thick enough."

The overseer, a thickset man of bilious complexion and greasy gray hair, cursed mightily as he threw the blanket at the two Negroes.

"Doesn't your man Cuffee have a wife and children, Colonel? Couldn't you sell them all, keep the family together?" Despite the little time Miles had spent in Solway County in recent years, he had made it his business to learn all he could about the land and all the people on it.

"What kind of fool do you take me for? The woman's a good stout field hand, and a fine breeder to boot. She's already produced four healthy offspring, and another child on the way."

"Mighty comely wench, too," chimed in Dick. "She'll be lonely now her man's gone."

"Mayhap things are different in the West, young man," said the Colonel to Miles, "but if you're going to settle in this county you'd best learn to take a stern hand with the niggers. Your brother here is too soft, as I've told him many a time. He seems to manage passably well, but it's by expecting precious little, and turning a blind eye to their tricks. Am I right, Mr. Waverley?"

Matthew bowed his head. "Yes, Colonel. I confess I do set my workloads low, and ignore small infractions." He said no more. No use arguing with a mind made up.

"Anyhow, this will serve the fellow right for his insolence. Besides, he'll soon find another woman in Georgia."

"Not likely to make him forget the one who's borne him five children," said Miles in his driest voice.

"Borne <u>him</u>?" laughed Dick. "Maybe one or two. The rest are yellow as cream. The oldest is a nice little morsel almost ready for the 'guest' cabin."

Enough! No effort on Matthew's part (and he had made some in his younger years) could persuade the Meachems to alter the way they treated their people. But he was not obliged to listen to things that sickened him. Indeed, the sight of those two wretched creatures in chains brought back an extremely painful memory. As a youth of eighteen, shortly after his guardians had handed over to him full command of his estate and while still feeling woefully unequal to the responsibility, he had sold an obstreperous young Negro named July, a man who at once frightened and enraged him. Not long afterward he learned that the man, who left Laurel Hill a strong, healthy young fellow, had died of fever in the swampy sugar fields of South Carolina. His woman promptly threw herself in the Solway, was pulled out, but was never right afterward. Not long after that, someone rode Matthew's favorite horse to death. Smitten with remorse about July, Matthew had made little effort to find the culprit.

"Excuse me, Colonel," he said, but Miles and I will go on ahead. Miss Nelson and Miss Lucinda are expecting us, and are doubtless fretting themselves over our tardiness." This was a lie, but a necessary one. They saluted the Colonel and his son, nodded to the overseer, and urged their horses forward despite the treacherous footing.

When he thought them safely out of hearing of the other party, Matthew slowed his horse, and heaved a great sigh.

"Ah, Miles, I do feel the weight of this wrong I've inherited. This infernal blight on our land and our lives. Now that Virginia law allows manumissions, I've freed a few of my people, as you know. Those who have served me well and who have learned a trade that will support them. Those I retire in age, and maintain, as I will soon do with Amos, are a drain on our resources."

"Well, Old Fellow, I agree it is a nefarious institution, but take heart from the '1808 clause' in the Constitution, for then, no doubt, importing slaves will be forbidden everywhere in the country, as it already is in Virginia. The Negroes are much less needed for other crops, now that tobacco is failing. The whole institution will decline and die here, as it already is doing in the North."

"I wish I could be as sanguine as you. But Negroes are as a drop in the bucket up north, compared to the ocean of them here. What would become of them, and us, if they were all freed?"

"Well, that is all conjecture. I must pay mind to the present. I'll buy most of Mr. Humbolt's people, and will deal with them humanely, I hope. But will doubtless require more from them than do you. I'll be the new planter in the county, and must make my way."

"It won't be as easy as it was out west, I assure you. As you'll soon see in managing my Stony Creek Quarter, and the Ludwell home quarter if they accept our proposition."

"Come, Matthew, Negroes are Negroes. It took some doing to manage them on the Kentucky farm."

"Yes, I am sure of it. But you had only a handful of Negroes to manage. And you and your partner worked right along with them in the fields. Did not you say so? Here you will have many more to deal with, particularly when you finally settle on the Humbolt plantation. You will have to rely on overseers, and they are a lazy, drunken lot, on the whole, if not worse. Which is why I've had to fire Mr. Coles, whose place you are taking for now. And if you wish to maintain a reputation as a gentleman, you will not work beside them in the fields. Indeed, you will have too many other duties: in the militia, as justice of the peace, as delegate in Richmond, I hope, one of these days. And of course all the poorer folk in the area will quite constantly apply to you for help."

"Ah well," said Miles, stretching hands up toward a pale winter sun, which had emerged from the clouds and shone on their hair and their horses' coats in the opening of the avenue leading to Farrington. "I can do no more than my best. I mean to set a reliable Negro or two over my people, as you have done with Amos."

"If you're fortunate enough to find one. Even then, prepare to contend with feigned sickness, broken tools, ruined horses, thieving, unallowed absences at the very times when they are most desperately needed in the fields. Over the years I've transferred the most unruly ones to River Birch Quarter, because it is distant and because Mr. Stokes, who oversees them, rules with a sterner hand than mine. But he cheats me, the scoundrel. You must prepare your mind for these annoyances."

"Well, I mean to offer divers rewards for good work, and the milder punishments for misdoing: demotion, extra work, withholding passes, solitary confinement. I know the gamut. But all else failing, I will whip, or sell, as need be."

"Indeed, you will surely have more stomach for punishment than I."

Matthew was aware of the bitterness in his tone, and hoped it was not apparent to his brother. As Miles had observed, he had yet his way to make in Virginia. Still, Matthew had nourished the hope that with Miles establishing himself in Solway County, he, Matthew, would find a sympathetic ear to his increasing discomfort, nay, even distress, at holding other men in bondage. It seemed quite beyond belief to him that most of his fellow Virginians did not perceive the incongruity between all their talk about freedom during the war and then about equality as they created a new country, and the glaring lack of freedom or equality for so many human creatures they lived among. Even Mr.

Higgens, professing to be a man of God, saw no difficulty here, or would admit to none, even though the Baptists and the Methodists, who were drawing away so many from his parish, spoke of it loudly.

Matthew reflected on these things as he balanced carefully on the frozen ridges in the path that led from the Ludwells' stable, where he had left Miles and their horses, around the side of the house to the front door. Mr. Lucas Ludwell, Lucinda's grandfather, had built his house at the foot of a steep hill, surrounded by a stand of oaks and hickories. It was less imposing than Great House at Laurel Hill, and caught little breeze in summer, but in the raw and windy cold of this January day its site gave protection. Miles had refused to go on to the house with him, giving as excuse that he could better occupy his time inspecting stables, barn, and other dependencies of the plantation. Matthew was sure that Miles wished to avoid meeting with Lucinda just at present, and would naturally feel some embarrassment about the proposition that Matthew intended to present to her and to Miss Nelson.

The Ludwell house, of dark-red brick like his own, and embellished by toothed cornices and a four-column porch of two stories, was graceful and well built, but the pillars were moldy and blistered from lack of regular applications of paint, as was the wood trim of the window sashes and door jambs. Matthew noted that several of the roof shingles hung drunkenly askew. He thought he glimpsed a movement of drapery at the parlor window and just as he raised his hand to the knocker, the door was opened by Miss Nelson herself. Her face wore the usual blend of anxiety and relief that it held whenever he appeared. Her manner, however, was always calm and dignified.

"Come in, Mr. Waverley. How kind of you to brave the cold to visit us. Come warm yourself by the fire. I've already asked Sue to prepare you a cup of coffee, good and strong as you like it." She led the way to the parlor where Lucinda was hastily stuffing what looked like stockings into the bag under the sewing table, and a servant with a blanket in her arms was going out the back door of the room. Lucy, looking even paler than usual, was recovering from a severe pleurisy, but she came forward with her usual light step to hold up a soft cheek for her guardian to kiss.

The ladies seated themselves again, but Matthew took a few minutes to stand before the fire, warming his numbed hands and exchanging inquiries and answers about everyone's health.

It was now a month since Stuart's death. The funeral, held here at Farrington with Reverend Higgens reading the service, had drawn only one Ludwell relation, a male cousin from somewhere on the Potomac, and one aunt of Lucinda's on her mother's side, in addition to a modest number of neighbors. One circumstance noticed by Matthew, and surely by everyone present, was the contrast in manner between Miss Nelson and Lucinda. The grief of Lucinda was painful to behold. She looked seriously ill at the funeral, and soon was so in fact. A scarce two weeks later, from her sickbed--she clearly thought she was dying and the doctor was not strong in a contrary opinion--she insisted on Matthew's drawing up legal papers bestowing on Kate Nelson all the property she had inherited from her mother. This was a large and valuable piece of land to the east, currently leased to a member of the Bixby family, and not far from the small holding, also under lease, left to Miss Nelson by her own mother, Mr. Ludwell's first wife, a widow with Kate her only surviving child. Matthew had of course argued against such a hasty action on the part of Lucinda, but the sick girl was so distraught that he submitted in the interest of restoring her calm and her health if only that could be achieved.

But as soon as this gift to Kate Nelson had been effected, Lucinda had begged Matthew to draw up a will for her, leaving the rest of her considerable property, all that came to her through her brother's death, to Geoffrey Burnham! Here Matthew had to draw the line. How could he accede to such a foolish and even unseemly request? Mr. Burnham was not even officially betrothed to Lucinda. He and Miss Nelson contrived by soothing words and delaying tactics to avoid taking this drastic action. Once Lucy's fever subsided, she seemed to forget the whole matter of the will, her grief for the loss of her brother consuming all her being.

Miss Nelson, on the other hand, though she wore mourning and did everything that propriety demanded, did not pretend to any regret over the death of Stuart. When tempted to disapprove of her indifference, Matthew reminded himself of all the trouble that wild young man had caused her. In any case, if a tall, strongly built woman with olive skin that never changed its color could be said to bloom, this might be said of Kate Nelson. There was now more sureness in her step, more command in her manner, more satisfaction in her smile.

"My dear Miss Nelson," said Matthew, getting to the purpose of his visit, "I sorely regret that neither Miles nor I has been able to attend to the state of your fences and barns as yet. Deep into winter as we are." He took a seat in the straight-backed chair facing Lucinda, and smiled at her. "You, my dear, will be glad to know that all but one of the newborn calves and sheep, so far, are safe and thriving. But the new barn needs half its roof repaired. Miles came with me today, and is at this moment looking into it."

"Yes," sighed Miss Nelson. "Jed grows more and more lax. He is more than sixty, you know, and can no longer control the gang. He was wont to keep the hands a middling much in line by the threat of Stuart's return. And indeed, our brother's sudden, unexpected appearances, and his wrath when he noted something amiss, would indeed set them quaking. He was not wanting in knowledge, or a strong hand. Only in steadiness and restraint." She glanced at Lucy, but the girl only closed her eyes, apparently to shut out what she did not care to hear.

"Indeed," Matthew agreed, "a man's hand is sorely needed here."

"Oh, but most happily for us, Mr. Waverley," spoke up Lucy with a grateful look, "your hand..."

"Is turned to too many plows," sighed Matthew. "Well, I have a proposition to make you, which I hope you will accept. Miles has been a brother to you both. As I'm sure you know, he is determined upon settling in the county, and so will not return to the West. He has already contracted to buy the Humbolt estate. But he is good-hearted and he will not settle there until Mr. Humbolt, sick and hard-pressed in the pocket as he is, quits this earth. That will doubtless not be long in coming, but who can tell? Meanwhile Miles has agreed to take the direction of my Stony Creek Quarter. I was obliged to dismiss Mr. Coles, who nearly killed two of my hands in a drunken rage. By far the worst overseer I've ever had. I could have sent Amos to Stony Creek, but the old man is such a boon to me at the Home Quarter that I cannot do without him."

Miss Nelson sighed. "I own I'm not proof against the sin of envy when I think of what a prize you have in Amos."

"Miles can be an even greater prize for you. Just for the present, until Lucinda--or you yourself, of course--decides to wed. Miles has already ordered his belongings carried to Coles' cabin. Since Stony Creek is closer to you than to us, from there he can easily oversee the work here on Farrington's fields as well."

"You are both much too good, Mr. Waverley," said Miss Nelson. "But why shouldn't Miles stay here with us where we can provide him with much greater comfort?"

"I took the liberty of sounding him on that, knowing you would offer, but the fellow absolutely refuses."

"Oh, but Mr. Waverley," Lucy broke in, startling them both. "Mr. Coles' cabin can scarcely be more than a shack. Mr. Miles cannot live there."

"He assures me it is decidedly more comfortable than the cabins he inhabited in the West. Or indeed, the bare ground he sometimes slept on. Coles was not bashful about demanding improvements. And I confess that I question the propriety of his residing with you. With two unmarried ladies alone in the house. You might persuade him to take dinner with you now and again."

Lucinda turned her head away, appearing somewhat distressed. "My dear," said Matthew, "I do not wish, and of course Miles does not wish, to impose his care upon your property. It is yours now, and with your majority fast approaching it will soon be yours to do with as you see fit."

"Oh Mr. Waverley," she replied, distress in her eye and in her voice, "how could I know what is fit? Kate is so very much more capable than I. Yet I do know that this burden is too great for her. I have always looked to you as a second father, and Miles as my big, kind brother. It distresses me to become a burden to him, too, as I already am to Kate and you. But it appears I have no choice. Please do, all of you, as you deem best."

She hurried out of the room, tears glistening on the tips of her lashes.

Matthew and Miss Nelson stood looking after her in silence for a long moment.

"She is still not herself, Mr. Waverley," said Kate at last. It's not only Stuart's death. That still pains her sorely. But whilst she never breathes his name, indeed <u>because</u> she never breathes his name these days, I am sure that the absence of news from Mr. Burnham wounds her nearly as much."

"That circumstance is exceedingly vexing. Even Mrs. Waverley, his sister and only relation in this country, receives not a line from him."

"Would that poor Miles had captured her heart instead," said Miss Nelson with a sigh of exasperation.

"Perhaps her heart will change."

Miss Nelson shook her head. "I fear Lucy's heart will never change. We must hope that Mr. Burnham returns, as affectionate as ever, and that all our fears are for naught."

***

The Waverley ladies and children spent all that morning huddled close to the fire in the parlor of Great House. Even Elizabeth Levier and poor Mary Waverley had been obliged to seek shelter there because both chimneys in Old House where they lived were not drawing properly, making the house uninhabitable in the severe cold. Mary had been found that morning with the covers thrown off her feet and these half-frozen. Now she sat in the Waverleys' most capacious wing chair, facing the center of the fireplace and close up to the blazing fire, with Big Moses standing close behind her lest she cast herself of a sudden into it. This appeared unlikely because the white-haired, emaciated creature sat curled with her knees drawn up to her chest and her head leaning against a chair-wing, staring glassily into the flames.

Elizabeth, too, held a privileged position, sitting on the right side of the fireplace. Opposite her sat Honey, not that she ranked such a spot for her own self, but because she was holding little Edward, miserably sick with a cold. All the others: Charlotte, Aunt Abie, Sarah, Molly, and Maudy (Joan's daughter and an expert seamstress), had pulled their chairs as close to the hearth as possible.

Elizabeth surveyed the group with satisfaction. All but poor Mary were engaged in useful occupations: Aunt Abie, Sarah, and even Molly in knitting stockings for the female servants, Charlotte and Maudy in cutting out shirts for the men, Honey in crooning softly to Edward and working, every now and then, a few drops of goldenrod syrup into his mouth. Baby Charles' cradle had been placed near her foot, with which she kept it gently rocking. Big Moses tended the fire as well as keeping an eye on Mary.

Elizabeth laid aside her mending for a few minutes to ease the pain in her rheumatic hands. Yes, it did her Quaker heart good to behold everyone busy with useful work, so different from the evenings when she reluctantly gave in to her daughter-in-law's urging to join the rest of the family, only to find them frittering away their time with cards, idle chatter, ungodly reading, or even singing. She preferred her simple old parlor in the house she had come to many years ago as a bride from Philadelphia, to this luxurious "drawing room," as they pleased to call it, adorned with velvet draperies, gilt-edged mirrors, and a Turkey carpet, in the house that Matthew had built for his English bride. She wondered if she should send Big Moses to learn what progress Nathan, Joe, and Cyrus, her manservant who together with his wife Juno looked after her and Mary, were making in repairing her chimneys. No, she decided, because no one else in the room had the strength to restrain Mary should she suddenly take it into her crazy head to lunge at the fire, or worse, at one of the children. Elizabeth murmured a short prayer to the good Lord for patience.

A series of tearing coughs suddenly exploded like firecrackers from Edward's small frame and waked the baby who began to wail. Honey must have sent some wordless message to her sister, for Sarah flew over to take up the infant and carry him to his mother's breast. Charlotte certainly took her time in offering it to him, heaving a great sigh of annoyance as she put down her scissors. Why she chose to nurse this babe, when she had left all her previous infants to be suckled by black wenches, was beyond Elizabeth's comprehension. She did have to admit, however, that both these newly arrived cousins were good with children.

Molly, who always seized any excuse for leaving her knitting, had run over to look at Edward, who lay coughing weakly as Honey rocked him and rubbed his chest with the contents of a small wooden bowl on the table beside her.

"Honey, don't cry. Don't cry! He'll get better, won't he Mama? Honey's dropping tears like rain. Phew! How he stinks, Mama! I swear I can't stand near him." Holding her nose, Molly retreated to stand next her mother's chair.

Molly's words broke the anxiety that had risen like steam from a boiling kettle at the sound of Edward's wretched coughs. All eyes had turned to him, then hastily withdrawn from his flushed, hollow-eyed face, smeared with mucus and tears.

"Molly, for Heaven's sake, hush! You know perfectly well that Honey is rubbing the poor little fellow with onion and butter, to open his nose and throat," said Elizabeth. "Of course it makes her cry." She turned to her daughter-in-law: "Are you certain the infirmary fire is burning well, Charlotte? Joan is there, I know, but could you not take a look, as soon as the baby finishes feeding? My rheumatism is so bad today I can't get out of my chair."

"Lord Almighty, madam, cannot you see that I have more than enough on my hands? You insisted that I release Joan from her other duties so as to tend to your infirmary, and now you doubt her competence!" Well and good. Once in a while the calm, patronizing tone that Charlotte was wont to use toward her mother-in-law gave way to reveal her true, snappish nature. This did not displease Elizabeth. It gave her occasion to exercise her Christian forbearance. And set the young girls an example of sweetness of temper.

"Forgive me, my dear. I did not intend to overburden you. I worry about my woman, Juno, hard taken with the quinsy. Jake and Hattie, too, from the Stony Creek quarter, though I think them on the mend. There's nothing but sickness in the home quarter as well. But mostly I fear Juno will just let herself die, with her baby dead yesterday of the quinsy as well. And little Edward here--it looks very like the same thing."

Charlotte suddenly sprang up, almost dropping the baby at her breast. She clutched him tighter, stood for a few seconds as though confused, then quickly left the room. Molly ran after her.

"Well! I never!" exclaimed Elizabeth. She looked for disapproval matching her own in the faces of the other women and girls, but every one of them had her head carefully bent over her work. As for Mary, she seemed to sense something in the air and began to bang her head against the back of the chair. "Lord have mercy!" Elizabeth got Moses to cup his hand behind Mary's head while she herself searched for the corn cake she had brought in her purse. "This all comes of our having to bring her here. The poor dear requires quiet. Peace and quiet." Of course she knew that Mary's spells could come upon her at any time, even in the middle of a quiet night.

This time they were fortunate in that Mary stuffed the whole corn cake into her mouth and gradually the banging of her head grew weaker. She finally fell asleep, letting her head rest against Moses' big black hand, which he gently extricated without waking her.

Little Edward, too, had now fallen into a quietly rasping sleep. Elizabeth was aware of all the female shoulders rising and falling with sighs of relief. In winter everyone had to accustom herself once again to huddling close together before the fire, but the presence of Mary, and Edward so grievously ill, was unnerving to all. Silence enfolded them all as each gave full attention to her work, or to thoughts she did not care to voice.

Charlotte found May in the pantry stacking plates in the cupboard. She sent her to fetch Joan from the infirmary. Then she delivered baby Charles into the arms of the young black girl, and found a dozen sharp observations to make to her, to Molly and even to Joan, who would no doubt repay her mistress with grim silence for two or three days.

Needing to escape the three sullen faces, two black and one white, Charlotte crossed the hall and entered her chamber, slamming the door shut behind her. Then, her anger suddenly spent, she sank heavily onto the chair by her bed. She was not a wretched, tearful sort of woman. She prided herself on that. And now she did not cry. But she felt a blast of withering blame, like an icy wind, from the whole pack of humans that clustered round her. Matthew, his mother, Kate, Molly, Joan, and all the Negroes, of course. Even Honey. Charlotte thought she knew all the reproaches one or another of these people made against her. She was overly lavish in her expenditures and niggardly in her religious obligations. She wounded sensitive souls with the keen edge of her tongue. She was overly severe with the servants. But it's of course that all servants complain of harshness in their masters. True, she did lose her temper at times and boxed an ear or slapped a face. Not that the careless or insolent creature didn't deserve it, but Charlotte did not like to be seen as out-of-control.

She always made a great show of ignoring all this disapproval, and did indeed ignore it the great part of the time. But once in a way, of a sudden, she could not. Particularly where her babies were concerned; when the word in someone's mouth, the look in someone's eye, implied that she neglected her babies.

She was worn to a ragged clout after the night she had spent. She had wakened to the sound of crying. She knew it was Edward. Quietly, so as not to wake Matthew, she had slid out of the covers, slipped into her mules, and clutched her shawl tight around her shoulders, for the cold was cruel, the fire having died hours ago.

She climbed the stairs to the floor above, hearing as she approached the sound of crooning under the cries (now more whimpers than cries) of Edward. Honey was on her knees before the stove, holding Edward close-wrapped in a blanket. The acrid smells of vomit and urine assaulted Charlotte's nostrils.

"Oh, Mrs. Charlotte, I'm sorry you got waked."

"All right, Honey. It's a good thing the stove was kept burning." (A coal stove had been purchased for the nursery, and coal brought all the way from Richmond.) "Where on earth is Joan when she's most wanted?"

"She's gone to the infirmary, ma'am. One of the hands is took real bad. I sent May for warm water from the kitchen, but there's a little here in the basin on the stove. I feared washing the poor little mite 'til I had somebody to dry him as soon, but now you're here..." She handed Charlotte a warm dry towel from the stove. At that moment May came in and added a good quantity of warm water to the basin.

Honey opened the towel and quickly stripped Charles of his wet nightshirt. As soon as she rinsed off a small arm or leg, Charlotte dried it. How light and gentle were the movements of this young girl!

Charlotte felt heavy-handed beside her. And how thin was her little boy! Yet even so, he was perfect as only a small child could be, with skin absolutely smooth and unblemished. Honey had a fresh nightshirt at the ready, and then Charlotte wrapped him in a warm blanket and hugged him to her breast. Tears did well up then, as images of the three babies she had lost rose up behind her eyelids.

Charlotte then sent May and Honey back to their beds, and stayed a long while with Edward, holding him in her arms. She'd not failed to notice how he reached out his arms to Honey as soon as he was dried, how he was restive in his own mother's embrace. What else should she expect, since Honey and Joan attended the little boy far more than she herself? She was too busy to be much with him. That was true. But it was also true that seeing his hollow eyes hurt her so much that she welcomed the duties that took her away from him. But that one night she held him close in the darkness and felt against her lips the fine dark curls on his brow.

Remembering those hours alone with her son brought at last a return of calm and strength to Charlotte. She returned to the drawing room where the women were gathered and was able to apologize to Mrs. Levier for the rude response she had made her. Much as the older woman irritated her, Charlotte's pride forbad her from permitting an open rift. Gentlemen might settle their differences on the field of honor, but quarreling ladies only descended to the level of fishwives. Wishing to make further amends, she asked how Honey and Sarah were progressing with their education under Mrs. Levier's tutelage.

To be sure, Charlotte had not waited all this time to check on both girls' progress. She knew that Honey was learning quickly. She had committed the alphabet to memory and learned to recognize the letters in a matter of days. She could form only a few of them, and most crudely, with her quill, but she was beginning to sound out the words in the primer. Mrs. Levier had reported this, a bit unwillingly, for she still had grave misgivings about taking in these wild creatures from the backcountry. But she took apparent satisfaction in making the following observations:

"Sarah appears most tractable indeed. She looks at me with her eyes big and wide, and says 'yes, ma'am' when I ask if she understands, but the next day you would think she'd never seen a single letter. I declare I don't know what to make of it. I fear what we have in Sarah is a pretty face on a leaden head."

"Oh she does try, she truly does," said Honey, wiping her eyes still teary from the onion-butter salve as Maudy, at a sign from Charlotte, took the sleeping Edward carefully from her lap. She would try to get the limp form into his bed without waking him. "It takes Sarah longer, but she'll learn," Honey insisted.

"I should think so," said Charlotte. "Does she not know to read music already? Such a repertoire of songs and their melodies as well!"

"Oh, she don't <u>read</u> music, ma'am. She just hears a song oncet, and she knows it."

"<u>Oncet</u>!" Molly shrieked with laughter. "Is that your hillbilly talk again?"

"Keep a civil tongue in your head, Molly. Both your cousins are far more educated in common politeness than you," scolded her mother. "Honey is learning fast, and as for the music, Sarah will learn to read it properly, by book, according to the gamut."

"The gamut, ma'am?" asked Sarah.

"Yes, the notes of music and how they follow one another and how they are written down on paper."

Molly could no longer contain herself. "You must hear me read my Caesar, Mama. I can read as far as book three of the <u>Gallic Wars</u>. Nathan can barely read three sentences of it."

"Latin!" humphed Mrs. Levier. "And wars, as well. What business has a young girl with either?"

"Papa says it's a crying shame I'm not a boy. I'm so smart I'd make a brilliant figure in the House of Delegates. I'm reading the "Spectator" with Papa, and Mama's going to teach me French, aren't you Mama?"

"That's enough, Miss. Have you never heard that children should be seen and not heard?" In asking this, Mrs. Levier was looking straight at Charlotte, as though to ask her why she did nothing to enforce this excellent maxim.

Of course Molly paid not the slightest heed to the interruption and proceeded to tell them all, with increasing excitement, about the dancing master who was to be lodged at Laurel Hill in the spring and who would teach them all, even Nathan (and what a lark it would be to watch him!) contra-dances and minuets, perhaps even cotillions and allemandes that are ever so difficult.

"Child, you already know quite enough of dancing." That really meant "too much." For of course Mrs. Levier disapproved of dancing.

"Oh I know reels, jigs, and scampers," answered the child with scorn. "Dances for country bumpkins."

Molly could not tell them more about her educational ambitions because at that moment the gentlemen trooped in from out-of-doors, and attention must be turned to them.

What a bustle there was then! Miles announced to the company that Mrs. Levier's chimneys were now drawing as well as ever, and both her parlor and Mrs. Mary's chamber would soon be warmed to a tolerable degree. Mrs. Levier insisted upon returning to her own house immediately. Big Moses would carry poor Mary and Miles would assist his mother.

Charlotte protested, of course, but feebly. She'd be glad to be rid of them. She did think to tell Maudy to go along to serve them their dinner, which brought an ugly look to the wench's face. Because of her light skin and skill at needle and shears, Maudy considered herself too good to wait at table. Well, Mrs. Levier would have to put up with her surly manner.

Charlotte then urged Aunt Abie, Honey, and Sarah to draw closer to the fire and take their dinner there in the warmth of it, along with

Molly. Less than half the dining room was tolerable in this piercing cold, and there she would cluster the gentlemen. May would serve Aunt Abie and the girls, and she would have Joe attend to the gentlemen's wants. What a nuisance that Joan was needed in the infirmary! Another female servant was sorely needed. But Matthew was adamant against any further purchase, and training one from the fields, providing one could be spared, was such a burdensome task.

Miles strode back and forth on the cold side of the dining room while the platters of pork shoulder, Irish stew, and sweet potatoes were carried in; not to keep warm--the activity and excitement of the morning still had his blood racing--but merely to calm his thoughts and, above all, dismiss his wild hopes. Yes, installed as he was at the Stony Creek Quarter, and charged with the oversight of the Ludwell's Home Quarter, less than a three-hour ride away, he would surely see Lucinda with some frequency. But that meant nothing, he told himself. She would be incessantly mooning over her Tory suitor and yearning for his return.

Would to God he would never return! Miles thought of the Lambert ferry crossing near Portsmouth, the most dangerous in the entire Tidewater region, where Geoffrey was thought to be at present. He pictured to himself the steep bank, the frozen water along it where men would be overly confident and leap onto the ice to guide their horses over the plank to the ferry and prevent them from stumbling and breaking a leg, which happened not seldom. But the man could suddenly break through the ice, plunge down into black water, and die in an instant in its freezing embrace. Miles was half shocked, half delighted by his murderous imaginings. If this company could read his thoughts, what would they think of "jovial, good-hearted Miles"?

"Come, come, Miles. Take a seat next to Nathan. You tire my eyes pacing about like a caged bear." Mrs. Waverley's hand was at his elbow.

Her words, her touch, so imperious, brooking no possible resistance, irritated him. But he did as he was bid, sitting on the side of the table next the fire with Mr. Levier and Nathan, with Matthew at the head and Mrs. Waverley at the foot. Molly, the only one who seemingly had no fear of Mrs. Waverley, was pulling at the rich blue wool of her sleeve and begging to dine with the gentlemen, insisting she would be quite warm enough on the cold side of the table and jumping with delight when the bare, rounded forearm pointed her carelessly to a seat.

For a spell everyone was occupied with adding the warmth of the hot stew and potatoes to his belly, to supplement the heat from the fire. Faces grew ruddy and bodies began to relax from the strain of bracing against the cold.

Mr. Levier had his plate filled three times, but he it was who finished first, for he had never bothered to learn the gentleman's leisurely manner in taking his meals. Leaning back comfortably in his chair and unbuttoning his waistcoat on which a few drops of gravy shone in the candlelight, he pulled from his pocket the latest copy of the National Gazette, waving it before the eyes of Miles so that it brushed against his lifted fork and got stained by the morsel of succulent pork that had almost reached his lips. This Mr. Levier did not notice.

"You see, Miles, and you too, Nathan, my boy. This rabble-rousing rag which you were so certain would be 'mislaid' in droves by order of Mr. Pickering, our new 'high Federalist' postmaster general, as you name him, has arrived in remarkable time. Less than four days from its printing. What do you say to that, unjust young men that you are?"

"That Mr. Freneau's admirable little semi-weekly reached us," laughed Miles, "signifies only that our postmaster's watchdogs have not been diligent enough to waylay them. A good thing, too." Miles, who had been making his remarks between mouthfuls of pork and fricassee, now wiped his lips and pushed back his chair, signaling Joe to fill his glass with port. "You must admit that Mr. Jefferson chose his man well. Mr. Freneau is a fine poet, in addition to possessing all the correct views. I beg you to recall the inspiring lines from the first issue of the <u>Gazette</u>, which reached us only a month ago. Suspiciously late, don't you think? I came across it while moving my few necessities to the overseer's house at Stony Creek today."

He stood up to his full six feet and two, drew a crumpled sheet from his pocket, and making the most of his resonant baritone, read:

"From the spark that we kindled a flame has gone forth
To expand thro' the world and enlighten mankind.
With a code of new doctrines the Universe rings,
And <u>Thomas</u> is preaching strange sermons to kings."

"Papa, Papa!" cried Molly, who had remained attentive and unnaturally quiet until now, but was perhaps emboldened by having seen her mother leave the room to attend to the ladies in the parlor. "Has Mr. Jefferson become a preacher?"

All the gentlemen laughed. "No, child," said her father. "It is Mr. Thomas Paine, who penned <u>Common Sense</u>. And he has not turned preacher. It is merely a way of speaking."

"Ah yes, Tom Paine," said Mr. Levier, "that angry corset maker, that vagabond with a golden pen."

"But sir!" cried out Nathan, forgetting his usual reticence, even though Mrs. Waverley had reentered the room and was seating herself with a piece of embroidery by the window. "How can you speak so of Mr. Paine who wrote so truly of the folly of our subservience to England?"

"Yes, yes, my boy. I grant you that that winged eloquence of his united us (as far as we ever became united) in the cause of independence. But do you know where he finds himself at this moment? In Paris, of all places, doing what he can to pour oil on the flames of revolution, and I would give my oath he knows not a word of French. He has only narrowly escaped imprisonment in England for his efforts to incite an uprising there. His is a soul born to destroy, but entirely wanting in capacity, nay, even in desire, to build."

"Zounds, sir, you do him wrong." Miles leapt at the chance to defend one of the two men he most admired, now that Patrick Henry had settled into the conservatism of advanced age. These two were Tom Jefferson and Tom Paine. "Have you read his <u>Rights of Man</u>?"

"That's of course, Miles. The wonder is that <u>you</u> have done so. What? Have you exchanged the dice box and the petticoat for dull volumes under the evening candle?"

Miles ignored the question. "Then you know that Mr. Paine has utterly destroyed the arguments of Mr. Edmund Burke against the wondrous events in France. He has shown that Mr. Burke's horror at a little bloodshed in Paris, his aristocratic scorn of the patriotic members of the French Assembly, his condemnation of the salutary changes brought by the new French constitution, are the timorous ranting of a worshipper of old ways." As if to punctuate his words, Miles took a chestnut from the bowl and crushed it without mercy in his strong hands.

Mr. Levier, for his part, laid his hand on a plump pickle on the tray that Joe was lifting to remove it from the table. He was immensely fond of Mrs. Waverley's pickles, though biting into one with his usual enthusiasm sometimes caused his removable teeth to slip from their moorings. This time he was lucky, and was able to make a response to his firebrand of a stepson.

"Has not the world seen enough bloodshed these latter years? We against England, England against France. You do not conceive, you young men, how dreadful would be war within England herself, or within France."

"If that is the only path to liberty, then so be it," cried Miles. Indeed, visions of musket fire, of volleys laying low whole companies of men, quite suited his mood these days. "As Mr. Paine says, when Burke recoils in horror from the scene of the people carrying the head of the Mayor of Paris through the streets on a spike, he forgets where the mob learned this practice. From the methods of the Old Regime, of course. Look what this small bit of bloodshed has brought. An end to the superstitious belief that the King is there by divine right. In its stead, complete sovereignty in the people through their elected Assembly, freedom from arbitrary imprisonment, freedom of opinion, even religious freedom. I call all this worth the lives of a handful of men who were plotting against the people."

"All that is admirable, of a certainty," said Matthew. "We can find no objection to those principles. But this change has come about so precipitously. This Assembly has such uncontested power--the King now a virtual prisoner and much of the nobility fled into exile. I think Mr. Burke has reason to distrust such radical change. To write that liberty, when men act in bodies, is <u>power</u>, and to ask what use will be made of this power, particularly <u>new</u> power in the hands of new men."

"How could it be otherwise? One would not expect men <u>old</u> in power and in years, to give up their power and embrace the new." Miles felt a surge of pride in his ability to hold his own in this debate. He had not as many years of study and experience behind him as did his brother and stepfather, yet he felt altogether their equal. After all, his ears had been wide open during those games of chance at the tavern and he was always as hungry as the next man for every word of news that reached the frontier, be it on printed sheet or by word of mouth.

"What did I tell you, Matthew?" said Mr. Levier. "Our young man is ready for the House of Delegates. His retorts are quick and to the point. You can retire to this country seat where men of learning, long experience, and moderate views are still admired, and where you can escape the rising dust of partisan clashes." Mr. Levier laced chubby fingers over the blue bulge of his waistcoat and beamed all around, as though he were indeed father to both brothers, and should be credited with their merits.

"Nonsense!" exclaimed Mrs. Waverley, rising abruptly and looking at Miles with her lovely brow scrunched into a formidable frown. "Miles does not even own property yet in the county. And my husband is still at the crest of his powers. How dare you suggest he retire from public life?"

"But madam," replied Mr. Levier, not in the least intimidated, "you yourself have often complained of your husband's absences, and the drain on his health caused by being burdened with so many duties."

"Ah well. If you must listen to ladies' complaints and their quite natural concern for their husbands' health."

Why is she so vehement, wondered Miles. Does she think ill of my abilities? Up until now she had often teased him, as she did everyone, but seemed to entertain a certain respect for him all the same. Perhaps because he had made his way in the West, of which she knew little except that it was wild and dangerous. Did she think him incapable of success in civilized climes? This thought irritated him. It reminded him of the over-civilized, foppish Geoffrey with his auburn hair so delicately curled and his waistcoat and stock looking always as though his man had just dressed him. If only he could be called out and killed in an affair of honor. No, he was too great a poltroon. Besides, what could be more ridiculous than to think that Lucy would turn to him, Miles, in such a case? She would detest him forever. He began to scratch furiously at his hands, already red and rough from chilblains.

"Ah, I see that you and Matthew both are itching cruelly. I will have Joan prepare some of my sulphur and lard ointment for you," said Mrs. Waverley, her sudden anger as suddenly disappeared. "But must you continue so much out of doors in this excessive cold? I declare, it's the worst winter in my remembrance. Stay close to the fire, and if you must keep occupied, use the time to catch up with your accounts." This last was addressed to her husband.

"If that could only be, my dear," said Matthew, "but the ink refuses to flow freely in this cold. Besides, we must keep the men busy. Nothing can be done in the frozen ground, but in the barns harness can be mended, stalls repaired."

"Yes, and there are still oats to thresh on the Burnham place," said Miles. "I purpose to set some fellows to making shingles, as well."

"The cattle must be fed, too," Nathan chimed in. "This is the first winter we've had to bring them in to the barns."

"The first in your short life, my boy," Matthew remarked. "Is it not strange that after the more-than-ordinary heat of the past summer, the drought, the hurricanes, our land should be frozen solid in January for day after day?"

"Perhaps the deity is punishing us for our impertinence in throwing off the authority of our dear mother country," smiled Mr. Levier.

Miles opened his mouth with a scowl, but Matthew raised a hand to stop him. "He is jesting, Miles. But I see your knees are troubling you sorely again, Mr. Levier. Take my arm and allow me to lead you to the ladies' fire in the parlor. It burns more heartily than this one."

In truth the old man moved as though on legs of ice as he was led slowly from the room, with Matthew giving him advice all had heard before. "If you would only allow the doctor from Petersburg to look at your legs when next he calls in upon my mother."

"No, I pray you! These doctors view rheumatism as an open invitation to take out the lancet. An opportunity to satisfy their ardent craving for blood. I won't be bled to death if I can help it."

"You are severe, sir," said Mrs. Waverley, who with Molly, Nathan, and Miles, was following behind the pair. "It's only that it distresses us all to see you limp along so painfully."

"I'll tell you what aids me more than being punctured by any doctor, for all his diplomas. The gentle administrations of this young lady here." He pointed to where Honey sat bent over a stocking she was knitting. "She has sweated me and poulticed me and rubbed my aching joints. Red Indian remedies are far superior to your learned medicine. She gives me hours of relief. Do you not, my dear?" Honey sprang up, coloring deeply. Her chair scraped across the floor boards as she pulled it into a corner far from the fire, making way for Mr. Levier and Mrs. Waverley to take seats near it. The other gentlemen called for their cloaks and went out to face the piercing wind.

Honey was grateful for the dimness of the corner she had chosen, even though she must strain to see the coarse gray wool on her needles. She reckoned Mr. Levier meant well to say fair words about her. But it made everybody stare at her and that was right much to bear. More and more she felt herself all alone in this place, in spite of how there was a sight more folks about her than she had known in her whole life before.

A year ago, at Christmas time, only Granny Harriet and Sarah and she were living in a two-room cabin at the far edge of a settlement of nine families. Granny didn't take to social calls, so folks just came for liniment or syrup or suchlike. Or Granny and her went to them, ofttimes as far as fifteen miles away, to birth a baby or set a bone. Granny was a tall, skinny woman with a raspy voice and a face like a ripe persimmon. She had rescued Honey and Sarah from the house of her own daughter, where at age fifteen Honey had found work as a hired girl after she and Sarah had run away from home. Granny's daughter was a pale woman with too little strength and too many children. She had worked Honey hard but wasn't too mean until she caught her husband with his pants down and Honey's skirt up. He was a man who couldn't be content with just one woman. A little chunk of a man he was, but strong as a wild boar and there wasn't any way he'd listen to "no." That woman, his wife, made him hold Honey down while she beat her so bad she couldn't stand up. So Honey and Sarah went to live with Granny Harriet, who somehow made the little creature growing in Honey's belly disappear. Or mayhap it was the beating that did it.

The three of them were cheery as crickets that Christmas, with Granny telling the story of Jesus' birth and them all saying the few prayers they knew. Granny kept Honey busy learning where to find healing plants, and when to pick them at their prime, and how to crush and boil and mix them. And she taught her bone-setting and birthing, of course.

Here in this place Honey had nobody to turn to. Even Sarah barely paid her any mind now. Why right this minute you could tell just by looking at her where Sarah's heart had gone to. She was sitting on the hearth next to Molly who was reading to her from a big brown book. But Sarah's back was wedged up against a leg of Mrs. Waverley's chair, and her pretty head was tilted to catch that lady's words to Mr. Levier. Truly, Sarah was in a spell cast by Mrs. Waverley. As much as she was allowed, Sarah followed on Mrs. Waverley's heels just like Silky, the spaniel, did on Molly's. When shooed away, Sarah became Molly's playmate, or servant, more like, for she jumped to do the least thing the younger child commanded.

To these gentlefolks Honey was still a bumbling backcountry girl. Mrs. Waverley was all the time vexed with her. She fussed at her over and over again to speak up, look folks in the eye, and when asked to give an order to a servant, do it like a lady, instead of begging humbly, or worse, doing the chore herself. She tried ever so hard to do right, to speak right. But it was no use. No matter how hard she tried, Mrs. Waverley faulted her for being a "meek little mouse," and Molly laughed at her for "talking funny."

With old Mrs. Levier it was worse. She talked a great heap about sin. Some sins she laid on Molly's head, like sloth and gluttony and pride. But when the worst ones came up in the book called Pilgrim's Progress that Molly was reading aloud to them, Mrs. Levier didn't say a word, but her eyes like slate buttons stared at Honey as though she could actually see her stealing the family plate or lifting her petticoat for every man's pleasure. At those moments all the sins of Honey's past swarmed over her like angry fire ants: the bible and rifle and horse she had taken from home that ought rightly been left for James, the times she had been nasty and lewd. But not from wicked lust. No. From fear.

Truly, truly from fear.

Honey had been pure for nigh on two years now, as much as a girl once stained could be thought pure. She'd been kept safe from sin as long as Granny was close by. But what now? Like a hare caught in a trap in a clearing, she was exposed in this vast open place with no trees close by to shield her, no mountain to cast its shadow over her hiding place. Men of every sort came and went, black and white, some living right in this house or nearby. Even Mr. Levier, old man that he was, would pat her on her backside in a way she did not like, when she was bent over to rub liniment into his sore legs. But who could she complain to? Who wouldn't laugh at her if she did? She would surely fall prey to some man's need. And be turned out again, with no Granny to take her in.

Mr. Waverley was the only one who was perfectly kind to Honey. Twice he had sat down next to her after supper and questioned her about her life back home, the animals and the plants and the weather mostly. But he also wanted to know what Papa and Mama and Honey's brothers and neighbors were like. Honey had never known anyone as curious as Mr. Waverley. She'd found herself telling him about how every summer Mama coaxed along a little corn patch and a few beans and carrots so they could have vegetables and pone most every day. There wasn't much space for growing these things because Papa had cleared so little land. She'd told Mr. Waverley how when Mama was alive Papa distilled spirits of turpentine from pine sap and carried some in his saddlebags when he drove his hogs to market in Fayetteville in the valley. But after Mama died he didn't bother to do any of that anymore, and of course they didn't grow hardly anything because Honey couldn't do it like Mama. Folks used to say their land was so poor it wouldn't raise a cuss-fight. The only victuals they had then were rabbit and squirrel and sometimes deer meat. And fish, of course.

She told how Papa said to her, just before he died, that he'd gone as far as Petersburg once, and spied a Mr. Waverley. She wondered if it was this very Mr. Waverley she was talking to. He bit on his thumb and thought hard. He said it might have been him, but he was sure her father hadn't spoken to him.

Both those times Mr. Waverley had made her speak about her life before; she had somehow managed to hold in her tears while he was by her side. But they sprang right out as soon as he moved away, just like he'd opened a sluice gate as he left. It was just rightly because he was so kind that he made her cry. She felt all shook up when he was near. She didn't know why, because she did trust him, didn't she?

She had to get out-of-doors. She got up with a start, jerking several stitches off her needle. They'd think she had to visit the necessary, and if she didn't come back right away nobody would mark it.

Outside the dark had already fallen. It was the time she liked best. Night dropped a dark curtain all round her, hiding the too-open land. To add to the comfort of darkness, snow had begun to fall. Great wet flakes drifted down slowly, slowly, glistening in the light of the rising moon that hung round and white, quite low on the horizon. The shadows of the snowflakes glided over the white ground like troops of gray spiders. Clumps of snow were slowly swelling on the branches of the proud red cedars that marched along both sides of the path leading up to the road, and tiny crystals gleamed on the smallest twigs of the fruit trees. A layer of white lay all along the top of the boxwood hedge that guarded the flower garden.

Honey pulled her shawl close around her shoulders, tied on her feet a pair of pattens that lay by the pantry door, and walked down the path that wound through the orchard on the east side of the house, the side away from kitchen, dairy, and all the other workplaces. Consoled by the silence and the snow and the dark, she right quickly saw how wicked it was for her to complain, even in her own head, of the people in this place. Hadn't these folks taken her and Sarah in and fed them and clothed them and were even learning them their letters? It seemed like God Himself was looking sadly down at her from that big white moon--for it did have a face, didn't it? She looked timidly up at Him and said she was sorry. And she said a little prayer of thanks for the dark and the snow.

Chapter 8

"Why can't we ride Dauntless, Papa? Pram says his leg is quite mended. You can't even see where the wound was." Molly's folly of three months earlier still stung her. She longed to ride into town behind her father, as in former years, mounted on the fine bay thoroughbred, and bask in the admiring glances given her handsome papa and his handsome horse.

"Yes, Molly, he is healed. Do not fret yourself. But Dauntless is old, as old for a horse as is your grandmother for a lady."

"Oh, Papa!" giggled Molly. "You'll catch it presently, when I tell Grandmama you think she's like a horse."

"What a little hellion you are, Molly. You know very well that... but you'll tell your grandmother no such thing. As for Dauntless, I would not have him carry two riders, even though you're a mere sprig of a girl and I have too little meat on my bones, as old Sukey persists in reminding me by sending in my plate piled high with fatback and potatoes dripping with butter."

Molly sat alone upon the broad rump of Boston, an ordinary roan quarter horse who would impress nobody. Still, she would ride behind Papa, just the two of them, all the way to church. That was a great deal.

Boston shifted a step or two from side to side, echoing her own impatience. She leaned forward over the saddle to lay her hands on the animal's shifting muscles and smell the rich, horsy odor. Papa was standing at Boston's head, holding his bridle and giving last-minute instructions to Pram, though why, she could not imagine, for the servants were at leisure on Sundays. They were encouraged to attend Grandmama's prayer service or go to meetings of their own.

Papa at last placed his foot in Pram's laced hands, swung his right leg carefully over her bent body, and landed in the saddle. Molly smiled. Papa was just as limber as Nathan, and much more graceful. Then her father accepted the crop that Pram handed him and nudged the horse forward. Boston whinnied happily and set off at a brisk trot.

The day was bright and clear, the first clear morning in a fortnight. The January thaw had finally come, but not until February this excessively severe winter, and with the thaw had come day after day of rain, making the fields leak their precious riches in rivulets that flowed toward the Solway, changing the frozen road into a river of mud. No one could travel under such conditions, even to the nearest neighbor. Fields could not be worked. Tempers of masters, servants, and field hands had corroded in the tedium of petty, indoor tasks.

Now, finally, on this second Sunday of February, the sun shone warm and it had not rained in four days. Papa had judged it possible to attend services, if they rose very early and moved cautiously over the partially dried-out road. He had helped Mama, Mr. Levier, Honey, and Sarah into the wagon, which had set out in a crunch of gravel more than half an hour ago. Grandmama Levier never attended the church in the village. She would hold services as usual for the servants and for Aunt Abie who was too addled to be taken out in public. Aunt Mary was usually kept in her room lest she have one of her fits, and disrupt the prayers.

Papa gave Boston his head the whole length of the avenue from the back portico to the road. There at the gate he reined in the horse and turned him about so as to observe the effect of the long drive bordered by red cedars that sloped gently down to the north entrance of the house.

"I own I'm not displeased that I chose cedars for the avenue," he said. "Your mother urged catalpa, like those before the Governor's Palace, but I fancy they don't flourish so well here in the Piedmont. Besides, it lifts the spirit to see branches still green amid the brown and gray of winter. And look, Molly," he added, tightening the reins to restrain the restless animal under them and extending an arm to the east, "when have you seen such a glow all along the horizon? The rising mist from our deluge of rains is still making magic of the morning sun. I only regret our land does not rise higher, so as to have a more lofty view of river and valley."

People called her father "poetical," and though it was usually said with a deprecating smile, Molly was certain that being poetical was a virtue if it belonged to her papa, but for the life of her she could not stare at trees or sun or river with any pleasure at all. To interest her, things must move at a much faster pace than these. Or they must, like books and songs, excite her with thoughts of action and adventure.

"It's very fine, Papa," she humored him. "But pray let us move on."

They started along the gradually rising road toward the west, a dirt trail that soon dwindled until it was scarcely as wide as the wagon the others had taken. The farther they went, the more frequently they encountered patches where the mud was still soft and Boston lurched to right or left as a foreleg sank in it up to the hock. Molly struggled to keep an old servant's cloak pulled close around her because Mama would scold if she allowed her gown to be spattered with mud. Meanwhile her father was craning his neck to observe the look of the earth in his western fields that had been left fallow last year.

Molly had known well enough that she would have little of his attention riding along a road bordered by so much of vital interest to the planter that he was, but it was of course that she would choose his company at its worst over that of anyone else. Even when they had passed beyond the boundaries of his own land, his attention to every field, fence, and building was acute.

"Aha! I see that Meachem has added to his dependencies," he exclaimed, as they came in sight of the main buildings of Col. Meachem's plantation, built closer to the road and farther up from the river than those at Waverley. "How is it I didn't remark that sooner. But of course it was hidden by the young oaks and elders still in leaf." He was staring at a low rectangle of brick, covered with wooden shingles. "Brick, no less. Must be a new stable. I recall hearing him say at Christmas that he had given two hundred pounds for the finest stallion offered in Richmond. He hopes to have all his mares in foal by him next year. He offered the creature's services for my stock. But what price did he mention? I can't recall it. Monstrous dear, even for such fine blood. Perhaps he'll abate the sum a little."

"What's his color, Papa? How many hands is he?" Her mama and the other ladies complained of how the gentlemen talked eternally of horseflesh. The ladies would open their mouths in small, ladylike yawns covered by plump white hands as they said it. But Molly was not bored one bit. How lucky she was that her papa and mama still allowed her to ride astride. Mama did so herself, on their own land or to visit Miss Kate and Miss Lucy. Once in a while Papa even allowed Molly to tag along behind a fox hunt, though he made her stay back from the kill the one time they made one when she was along.

"He's a chestnut, I believe, and a fair height but I don't recall exactly how many hands. His sire has won innumerable purses, and fine saddles and bridles, and appears to breed remarkably true."

All of a sudden Boston pitched forward, plunging his forelegs, up to the cannon, into a huge puddle, splattering horse and riders with great blobs of mud. Molly did not fall off--she thanked her luck again for having a leg on both flanks of the animal--but in throwing her arms around her papa's waist she did lose hold of her cloak which floated gracefully downward until it lay slowly sinking into the ooze.

"Confound it!" exclaimed her papa, the worst language she and the ladies ever heard from him. He himself had been thrown onto the pummel and was clutching Boston's mane with one hand and his private parts with the other, screwing his face up in pain. But he soon broke into a laugh as he surveyed himself, turned to look at Molly, and saw that even Boston was standing stock still, head down, as if ashamed of his own coat that had turned from gray to brown. As though to console them for their spattered garb, a sleek brown thrasher, his white breast richly speckled with nutmeg spots of which he seemed proud, sang to them from his perch on the curled up shingle of a hickory trunk.

"Well, Molly," said her father after pausing a long moment to admire the bird and his song, "our clothes look like a parcel of dish-clouts that have just wiped a stew pot. What a fine appearance we'll make in the village. We'll leave your cloak to be picked up on the way back. Our only consolation is that everyone at church will be in a more or less sorry state, unless it be the Meachems who will come in their closed carriage. Providing it makes it all the way to the village without capsizing."

They were now proceeding on their way, their mud bath having occurred at the lowest point of the road, so that they were mounting back toward higher and somewhat drier ground. Oaks and chestnuts formed a vast canopy over the open floor of the forest, stretching as far as one could see in all directions. Sunlight poured freely through the denuded branches, spreading a mottled gold carpet over the ground. A great singing of frogs drowned the thud of Boston's hooves.

"Be still, will you!" commanded Molly, who could not abide their guttural cries.

"It's the warm rains that have waked them, child," said her father. "Soon a frost will put them to sleep again. I wonder that the wagon made it through that enormous puddle at all. No doubt we'll catch up to them soon. But wait! Who is that fellow up ahead?"

Walking along the side of the road, going in the same direction as they, was a young, husky Negro dressed in split work shoes, tattered shirt, and pants that allowed a gaping view of his thigh. At the sound of

Boston's hooves he turned and seemed about to leap into the darkness of the woods, but thought better of it. He snatched from his head a hat that consisted of scarcely more than a blackened straw crown, and waited while they came up to him.

"Who are you, boy? I don't know you."

"I is Jim, Massa. Missus Hanna's new boy. Missus say I can go see Keeny and the new baby I ain't never seen, at Massa Clancy's place."

"Very good of her, and on a Sunday, her busiest day." (Mrs. Hanna was keeper of the village tavern.) "Where's your pass, boy?"

The fellow made a show of looking in pockets that clearly didn't exist, and then clutched the little round of straw tighter and kept bowing and raising his head, saying "Musta fall, Massa, musta fall."

Molly could tell that her papa couldn't make up his mind. This could be just a Negro taking a day off without asking. He could be a runaway. Or he could even be telling the truth. Planters were expected to look out for possible losses to their neighbors' property.

Papa must have decided the fellow was at least not a runaway because he let him pass, which brought several more bows, and then a sudden fast walk past them, almost a run.

"I may regret this. I must address Mrs. Hanna on the subject first thing. Perhaps the fellow really is a new father, and she a kinder mistress than has appeared up to now. That's why I don't like my people to marry any farther than the next farm."

"Oh Papa, I'm certain he's a runaway. Didn't you see how he was about to dash into the woods as soon as he spied us?"

"That signifies nothing, Molly. All the Negroes try to keep away from the road when they go from one place to the next, whether they have permission or not, to avoid being stopped and questioned. Like as not they've pilfered some little thing, so best not meet white men at all. It's a sorry system we live under, Molly, we and they."

Molly waited, not unwillingly, for him to say more. She had heard him complain of the problems of managing the Negroes before, as all the grown-ups did at times, and she had heard him deplore the injustice of "owning human beings," as he put it. This last didn't seem to bother the others, except for Grandma and Mr. Levier, and they didn't count because they were Yankees. And Quakers, to boot.

But her father remained silent, and before long they overtook the party in the wagon. That is to say that they came up to the edge of a huge puddle and spied the wagon just barely out of the muddy water on the far side of it. Two of its occupants were a still sorrier sight than she and Papa! Mr. Levier and Honey were closely wrapped, he in a blanket and she in Mama's old cloak, but these had soaked up mud from their bodies, and their faces and hands were covered with slime. Molly shrieked with laughter, and even Papa had to chuckle. Mama joined in, but Mr. Levier appeared not to see the humor of it, and Honey and Sarah, well, those little ninnies dared not laugh at anything when grown-ups were about.

"I hope you don't think your appearance improves on ours!" exclaimed Mama, whose aspect was speckled, but not soaked. "We came within a thread's width of capsizing when our right wheels dipped into a monstrous hole over there. (You'd best keep hard to your left.) Poor Mr. Levier pitched in head first--I thought for sure his neck would be broken. But Honey here is a regular Joan of Arc! Jumped right in after him to the rescue. Helped him up and beat the horses into pulling us out before supporting the dear man back into the wagon. All this while the rest of us sat like stone pillars, unable to move." Mama recounted all this with verve. No one liked an adventure better than Mama, unless it was Molly herself. Their country life was all too humdrum, especially recently when no visitors had come and they'd been cooped up so long they'd grown jumpy as fleas.

Papa got Boston to pick his way very slowly through the water. He dismounted and approached the wagon on Mr. Levier's side, asking him questions to which the gentleman barely responded.

"He is hurt, my dear, and hurting more by the minute. Perhaps no more than bruises, but we must examine him betimes. We're not far from Mr. Crawford's house but I don't think his condition is so grave that we should stop there. Crawford would have no place of any comfort to put him. Molly and I will go on ahead and warn Mrs. Hanna that we'll need tubs of warm water for Mr. Levier and Honey, and fresh clothes as well. The rest of us will look no worse than most."

He turned to Mr. Levier. "Try to compose your spirits, dear sir. We will soon have you warm and dry at the tavern. You too, my dear." And he reached over to pat Honey on the shoulder. She looked none the worse for her dunking, but Molly could see that the old man's face was drawn together like the top of a purse. Papa told Boston to walk on.

"I should have known the road was still too infernally uncertain for travel. I should not have succumbed to their pleas. If Mr. Levier has broken a bone I shall never forgive myself." Her father's shoulders squirmed this way and that as he thus muttered to himself so that Molly, who was tired now and tried to rest her head against his back, had it bumped off over and over again.

"Oh, Papa," she complained, "Mr. Levier is much, much older than you and may do as he pleases." (How she envied him this!) "Besides, he it was that most insisted we go to town. He was so cross at being cooped up and seeing no one."

"He could not have come, had I not allowed the wagon out. You know he does not ride. Now, not a word more about it." His back did stop pitching about, and they rode on in silence as the road turned away from the river and thus grew muddier still in the deep shadow of trees on both sides.

Then they were passing the small farm of Mr. Crawford, one of the Waverley tenants. It was to the north of them, with no frontage on the river. No Great House here. Only a four-room cottage of clapboard, its moldering sides cruelly exposed in the sunshine. Farther up the hill was a burned-out barn, one end already collapsed and the blackened roof of the rest sagging pathetically like the back of an ancient nag left out in the pasture to end her days. A makeshift shed had been built to house the animals.

"Well I'll be bound!" he exclaimed. "Crawford hasn't felled a single tree on that land he aims, so he says, to clear for tobacco. And that barn burned way back in October. I offered him two of my people to help rebuild it, not a difficult task with his two Negroes to help. Not to mention his sons who doubtless did not lift a finger. And all they managed was this miserable shed? And take a look at his wheat. A sorry year for it, but he could have salvaged <u>some</u>. But it's clearly been left to rot."

Even Molly, talkative as she loved to be, knew when to keep silent. Papa wasn't talking to her, anyway.

"It's of course that Crawford will ask for another loan betimes. I'll wager he'll be at my cabinet door within days, asking for a bigger loan than ever. He managed poorly enough last year, but this year still more ill than before. His land is good, more level than the greater part of my own. I give him the use of my dock without fee. But he manages his Negroes poorly, and his sons worst of all, letting them saunter about the country associating with bad company. It will go hard for them, and it's the fault of the father. But he'll come begging for his loan, and despise me more if I grant it than if I don't."

After a long sigh he shook himself and took up a different subject. "By the by, while I was inquiring in Richmond for a dancing master I heard of one who may be available come spring and who can teach French as well. Your mother could teach you, of course, but she hasn't the time. So if I find that your spelling has improved by then, you may begin studying French, a language suitable for a young lady. Meanwhile, mind your book. I particularly like the idea of your reading the Almanac regularly. Become familiar with coach and ship schedules, and nature's schedules as well: times of the rising and setting of the sun, the ebb and flow of the tides--in short, nature's laws by which we all live."

But Molly cared not a whit for nature. However, the prospect of learning French, and how exclusive her claim of doing so might be, interested her a good deal. "Will Honey and Sarah also study French, Papa?"

"Ah, you wish for companions in your study," he commented. It always surprised her to see how dimwitted her learned papa could be at times. But she was glad of it. "No, I'd as leave they put all their efforts into learning to read and write their own language. Time enough for niceties later. Like as not Miss Lucy will care to chat with you and the tutor in French."

"Oh, Honey won't ever go far with her letters, Papa. She still talks like a bumpkin. And she takes no interest in history, not the kings and queens of England or even General Washington's famous battles. Only some paltry skirmish her father took part in way out in the backcountry. Nobody civilized ever heard of that!"

"Why Molly, this is distressingly mean-spirited of you." Her stomach shriveled as he turned in the saddle to give her a piercing look. "You must allow for her not having all your advantages. She is bright, and certainly most willing. She has experience well beyond yours, and even mine as far as the wilderness is concerned. She knows how to scrape and tan hides, spin flax and cotton, shear a sheep, and set a bone. She could teach you a great number of things. I have learned from her of animals different in size or markings from those hereabout."

So that was what Papa and Honey had conferred about several times at such exasperating length. He had drawn her cousin aside after supper and shown by the way he turned their chairs away from the rest of the room that he did not care to be disturbed. Honey had sat there in her sheepish way, looking uneasy, but inside she must have been proud as a rooster that the master of the house paid her such attention. Well, Molly had one consolation. Of a certainty, Mama was not so taken with Honey. She found her excessively meek and mousy. Molly had heard a remark or two to that effect. Also, Grandmama was beginning to warm to the girl. And Mama never cared for anyone or anything that the old lady was fond of.

Molly grudgingly acknowledged that her cousin had vast stores of knowledge, and promised to help her as she could with the book learning. Anything to bring herself back into Papa's good graces. Then she was able to doze for most of the remainder of the journey with her head against his quietly swaying back.

Those ladies whose menfolk had no further business to transact in the county seat had departed promptly after church service, leaving a handful of others to while away the time in conversation at Mrs. Hanna's tavern. Since the day was mild, they chose to gather on the east porch where the morning sun had left a pleasant warmth, rather than the upstairs ballroom where they sat on Sundays when the weather was inclement.

Honey had washed herself quickly in the tavern scullery, where she put on a gray linen gown, shiny from wear, that Mrs. Hanna lent her, and a threadbare woolen shawl and cotton cap quite yellowed with age that belonged to the tavern cook. Dressed thus, she had slid quietly into the very back of the church, where she was later joined by Mr. Levier, also clad in dry clothes. However, that gentleman slipped out again before the benediction, no doubt not wishing to be seen by the entire congregation.

Here on the tavern porch Honey marveled at Mrs. Waverley's commanding air as she directed potboy and barmaid to place rocking chairs for Mrs. Meachem and for old Mrs. Humbolt from the western end of the county, and straight chairs for the rest of the ladies. She insisted that each chair be placed so that its occupant could admire the stand of sycamores and oaks that graced the gentle slope toward the river, and beyond their calm dignity, the youthful rush of earth-stained water. Each lady could also keep an eye on the knot of men, horses, cattle, and swine in the corner of the tavern's paddock.

Mrs. Waverley placed Honey and Sarah on either side of her, something she always did when they accompanied her abroad, so that they could observe and imitate her manner and hear any observations she chose to make to them without being overheard. Since they had not had the benefit of early training in manners, she'd told them on more than one occasion, they must look sharp to make up for lost time.

"That sorry cap is too loose," she'd remarked as soon as she spied Honey. "Your hair is escaping all round and I must say, it's too stringy to be fetching. Take the cap off at once and let me pin your hair up tighter. Now mind you don't forget to collect your own clothes, dried or not, before we leave."

Honey was sure she could never take such a commanding air with the servants, as did Mrs. Waverley. "Neither surly nor excessively amiable," was her command, and she did as she advised. Honey remembered now not to sit until all her elders were seated, but Sarah needed a stern reminder. Besides Mrs. Waverley, Sarah, and Honey--Molly could be seen down in the paddock close to her papa--there was Mrs. Meachem, smiling and chattering merrily, and then there were several ladies that Honey had never seen before. Mrs. Humbolt, whose husband was said to be at death's door, was a tiny old woman whose large rocker seemed to swallow her up, but whose little black eyes, staring fiercely out of a crumpled rag of a face, seemed to stab into you and twist about with glee. Young Mrs. Sophie Meachem, married to Mrs. Meachem's son Dick, could not be called a more comfortable person. She was pretty to look at, with fair skin and tight black curls. But she had thus far said not a word. She just stared into the distance, yet would abruptly dart a glance at someone who was speaking, and buckshot of scorn seemed to spray from her eyes. Honey tried not to look her way at all. Finally there were the Cracklethorpes, Mrs. and Miss, the mother pale and plump, the daughter pale and thin, both with hair the color of a shammy cloth. These two spoke so fast that Honey could scarce follow what they said. Their talk treated mainly of bonnets, sashes, buckles, sleeves, and gloves, which fabrics and shapes of these were "the thing" and which were not. Honey and Sarah were quite in ignorance of these matters, as Mrs. Waverley had not yet seen fit to instruct them.

The company had barely settled themselves when a figure emerged from within the tavern, oddly clothed in nankeen small clothes that hung so long they had to be tied below the bulge of his calf, and a yellow lindsey-woolsey waistcoat so small that not a button of it could be fastened over his ample belly. Around his shoulders was draped a faded puce shawl and atop his head sat a nightcap of blue flannel.

"Lord bless me, I believe it is Mr. Levier," exclaimed Mrs. Waverley, laughing heartily as she helped him to her own chair and called out loudly for another. "I'm relieved to find you still in the land of the living. Not only that, but vying with the finest of the dandies in your attire." The other ladies tittered gently.

"Yes, madam," he replied, not forgetting to bow to each of the ladies present, "I am the grateful recipient of charity from Mrs. Hanna, her potboy, and even her grandsire. I am honored that you find my ensemble fashionable, but I confess that what makes me truly rejoice is that every piece of it is dry, and was even warmed at the hearth before being so kindly put on my humble person."

"Oh, Mr. Levier," spoke up Mrs. Meachem, "when I did not see you at worship, I promptly inquired and found to my horror you had been thrown from that wagon--not quite a steady one, I believe--right smack in the middle of a large puddle. 'Gracious Heavens!' I exclaimed to the Colonel, 'would to God the poor gentleman is not killed!' But how do you find yourself now, dear sir?"

"A trifle the worse for my adventure, madam, but your kind sympathy spreads like a balm upon me." He patted his right hip and knee with his left hand, the right one being immobilized by a splint. "Only a sprain of the wrist, says the barber."

"What a shame, sir, that you had to miss Mr. Higgens' edifying words this morning," cooed Miss Cracklethorpe. This surprised Honey, who had noticed that young lady's head lolling upon her mother's shoulder through the greater part of the sermon.

"Bless you for your kind thought, dear young lady," responded Mr. Levier, "but I must confess that I sneaked my old self in at the back, and fully availed myself of all that edification." The old gentleman winked his eye at Honey. Heat rose from her neck to her cheeks, and she turned her own eyes downward.

"'We'll take him up in our carriage for the ride home,' said the Colonel," Mrs. Meachem continued. "Oh yes, indeed! It is not at all out of our way. Our carriage is <u>enclosed</u>, as you know, and the Colonel has only this fall put in new springs and marvelous plump new cushions."

"The silly woman is excessively proud of her carriage," murmured Mrs. Waverley to Honey and Sarah. "She clings to it despite the declining fortunes of the family." But aloud she said: "Most gracious of you, madam. I'm sure my father-in-law will be grateful." Mr. Levier nodded, giving Mrs. Meachem a broad smile.

"But mercy me," cried that lady. "We will refuse to carry you all the way to Laurel Hill. No, no question of that. Instead, we'll take you in at Fairhaven, prepare a treat for you, and indeed we beg the honor of giving dinner to all of your dear family."

"Ah, I wish we could accept your kind offer," said Mrs. Waverley, much to Honey's relief, for spending all the remainder of the day in the company of strangers appeared to her quite fearsome, "but Mr. Waverley designs to break the custom of entertaining company on Sunday, so that all our people can go to church, including the kitchen Negroes. He forbids us to go abroad as well, else we put the burden on others' servants."

"Ah, but my dear, not one of them, save our coachman, comes to <u>our</u> church. Nor do many attend services at all, but drink and dance and otherwise cavort. Working them on Sunday keeps them out of trouble, I say."

"Oh, that husband of yours," suddenly screeched Mrs. Humbolt, her voice surprisingly penetrating for such a tiny creature. "He'd have us free half our niggers and let the rest loll about guzzling corn liquor and sticking pins in those little dollies they make to look like us."

No one made a sound for a long moment. Sarah's eyes opened round as teacups and Honey was afraid her own looked the same. Mrs. Waverley glanced at the two of them and laughed. "When you get to be as old as Mrs. Humbolt," she said in a low voice, "you too may say whatever you like and in the most vulgar language. Honey, you and Sarah go find Miss Lucy and ask her to come to us. I fear she's gone apart somewhere to mope."

When the young girls had left Charlotte spoke in a louder tone, for Mrs. Humbolt was hard of hearing. "That's of course, madam, but fortunately for all, there are few gentlemen in Virginia of my husband's turn of mind."

"I thank you for your offer of dinner, Mrs. Meachem," put in Patrick Levier, clearly wishing to turn the conversation, "but I invariably accede to my stepson's wishes. Besides, my poor body is already on the mend. However," he cried suddenly at the top of his voice, "there is one of our acquaintance whose health gives true cause for alarm. I hope your attendance at worship signifies that your husband improves, Mrs. Humbolt?"

"You know as well as I, sir, that a dying man does not improve. He only lingers. Out of spite, in his case, if you require to know."

In her younger days Mrs. Humbolt was known as the quiet little shadow behind the hearty sun of her big, handsome husband who charmed the ladies with his fulsome compliments. Charlotte remembered that Charles Humbolt had always left <u>her</u>, at any rate, after church service or a visit on his part to Laurel Hill, feeling herself the most beautiful and most delightfully witty woman in the Commonwealth. Well, it was clear that the little shadow had not been charmed.

Only slightly nonplussed, Patrick responded: "Dear lady, I am sure we all wish him a peaceful end. But where are our young friends, Miss Kate and Miss Lucinda? Ah! I recall. Miss Kate has turned a Baptist. She has joined the company of the New Lights." He clicked his tongue loudly against the roof of his mouth. "So be it. But what of little Miss Lucy? Surely she has not deserted the sacred fold?"

"She is still in the chapel with Reverend and Mrs. Higgens, trying out the forte piano she so graciously has given to the church. Trying to see if moving it has put it too dreadfully out of tune. She herself, being the only musical lady hereabouts, will play at services now that Mrs. Higgens' rheumatism is grown so bad." This information was supplied by the elder Cracklethorpe lady. "Poor dear, it will give her some occupation to divert her mind from her brother's death and being cruelly deserted by that fickle Mr. Geoffrey Burnham. My, how these young gentlemen play fast and loose with a girl's affections."

"Mama!" cried young Miss Cracklethorpe.

"Oh Lord, Lord! Do please pardon me, Mrs. Waverley. I plumb forgot he is your brother. Such a fine gentleman he is. I'm sure Miss Lucy mistook his genteel manners for attachment."

"Oh, don't concern yourself about me, madam," said Charlotte with a shrug. "I quite agree that Geoffrey is something lacking in steadiness. What a wise girl was your daughter here, in not misconstruing Geoffrey's genteel attentions to <u>her</u>."

That would serve the silly goose and her mother right. For despite the girl's simpering efforts, Geoffrey had of course barely noticed Miss Cracklethorpe's existence. She had neither the looks nor the property to merit his attention. Nor the wit, thought Charlotte with an inner smile, for the girl did not even perceive the barb. Her mother stiffened, however.

"Perhaps dear Lucinda will enjoy a revival of interest from Mr. Burnham. Since the death of her brother leaves her such an heiress, you know."

"Quite considerate of Stuart Ludwell to get himself killed," cried

Mrs. Humbolt, who doubtless had not yet shocked the company to her entire satisfaction. How the old biddy enjoys her new freedom, thought Charlotte, not without a touch of envy. It was known that Mrs. Humbolt would go live with her son in Baltimore once her husband died and the estate was sold to Miles, as was already contracted. Therefore her reputation in these backwaters of Virginia no longer concerned her.

"The young rapscallion took up swords with some ruffian outside the tavern, according to report," continued the old lady, "and got himself cut so bad he bled to death before anything could be done. Quite the profligate, so they say, and would have reduced the estate to penury had he lived. But Lucinda had best take care, and not take some whimsical puppy for a husband. They wouldn't be the first to start out fond as doves, but once shackled in matrimony, turn into cocks thrown into the pit."

Charlotte was thoroughly enjoying the old woman's brash remarks, but she had to shush her brusquely because she saw Lucinda picking her way across the soft earth between church and tavern porch. That young lady was carefully holding her plain brown linen skirt up out of the mud with one hand and her brown wool shawl around her shoulders with the other. Really, the girl looked more the docile hare than ever. Hard to say who looked worse, she or Honey, who followed in her wretched borrowed get-up. Sarah formed a pleasant contrast as she brought up the rear in her well-fitting puce cotton gown laced closely under her already-growing breasts.

"Miss Lucy! My dear girl!" exclaimed Mrs. Cracklethorpe, who had not seen her since Stuart's funeral. "You're thin as a starved rabbit. You must make yourself eat, child." Both Cracklethorpes clucked loudly, joined by Mrs. Meachem. Lucinda had always been too thin, but now she looked downright gaunt, with violet shadows around her eyes. Whether this came from grief over the loss of Stuart, or Geoffrey, or both, no man was worth this. Charlotte was sure that this thought was behind the look of mingled disdain and resentment on Sophie

Meachem's face as she gazed upon Lucinda. Sophie, a woman yoked to a worthless husband if ever there was one, might well be asking herself how this skinny little filly could have attracted to herself the affections of <u>two</u> respectable gentlemen, and that even before her fortune rose as suddenly as the water in a mill race when the sluice gate is opened.

Come to think of it, Sophie had probably felt the force of Dick Meachem's fist again recently because she had tied the ribbon of her bonnet so that the brim shadowed half her face, and she had pulled forward a bunch of curls to cover her cheek.

Mrs. Hanna herself brought a chair for Lucinda, and after doing her share of clucking over the girl's appearance, addressed the Cracklethorpes: "So clever of you, dear ladies, to give the gowns you brought to my maid to iron before the service. She did well, don't you think?" It was true that except for the Meachems, the Cracklethorpes were the only ladies who had attended worship in crisp and spotless attire, much to the envious murmurs of the others. "I asked the girl to try if she could wash out the stains in your travel gowns, which she succeeded in quite perfectly and now has them near dry by the kitchen hearth."

Mrs. and Miss Cracklethorpe visibly preened themselves on their cleverness and the fine appearance it produced. The fabrics clothing their persons might well be clean and smooth, but though the daughter was modestly attired, the mother was ridiculously festooned with little red bows all round the lace trim of her cap, and giant ones all down the front of her gown. Charlotte had to concede that Mrs. Meachem, on the other hand, was quite elegant in a blue sack-backed gown and embroidered silk stomacher. The fullness in back concealed her too-ample derriere. <u>She</u> had no need to pack her gown and yield it to the ministrations of Mrs. Hanna's maid. She could wear it in the safety of her closed carriage. A few wrinkles were the worst she risked. Charlotte sighed. Matthew was far too close-fisted. Why must he be so determined to reduce their debts? Everyone had debts. How could you live decently without incurring them? She must somehow persuade him to buy a carriage. Then she wouldn't be disgraced by riding abroad in that miserable wagon, and could wear fine gowns to church and balls and neighbors' houses, without fear of dirtying them.

"I do beseech all you ladies to follow the example of Mrs. Cracklethorpe on days so filthy under foot," Mrs. Hanna was saying, "and bring your church finery packed safe in your boxes. Then you can change in our ladies' chamber. Everything, combs, brushes, looking glass, water basins, is there for your convenience. Ah, and I hope you were all comfortable at church service this morning. I had such a charge of duties I could not attend. Was the fire high enough to keep you warm?"

"No need of that on a mild day like this," laughed Charlotte. "We would have done better without a fire. I might then have succeeded in staying awake through the usual tedious homily."

"Awake?" cried Mrs. Humbolt. "How can a body stay awake through such a lame discourse? I had myself a good nap from start to finish of the sermon."

It was scarcely to be hoped that the good Reverend had not heard her words, for there he was, approaching to join them on the now-crowded veranda.

"Welcome, Reverend," said Patrick, not a man to be easily disconcerted. "Mrs. Humbolt was regretting that weariness from her journey caused her to miss some of your fine sermon."

Mr. Higgens remained standing while he looked down sorrowfully upon his parishioners. Despite his humble Scottish origin and monotonous sermons, he was respected in the county as a schoolmaster completely in command of Latin and Greek. Tall, with a narrow face and a mouth constantly pursed, he prepared to continue his sermon. "We were pitifully few this Sabbath," said he. "As I already observed to Miss Lucinda here, we particularly miss her sister, Miss Nelson. Such a serious and rational member of our congregation. Yet she has deserted us for those of the Baptist persuasion. It is inconceivable that she has been led astray by the ranting and raving of those unprincipled charlatans. What can have led her to such a step, Miss Lucinda?"

"Sir?" Lucy looked her dismay. What could such a meek little mouse find to say? A lame "I cannot tell, sir" was all she could manage.

Charlotte, on the other hand, was more than ready to take Kate's part. "There is something of morality, a most strict morality, in the beliefs of these New Lights, don't you think, Reverend? Miss Nelson would certainly have an affinity for that." How delightful it was to provoke people, especially the pompous. Mrs. Humbolt was far too crude. Charlotte preferred a certain degree of subtlety.

"Good Lord, Madam!" exclaimed the good Rector. "But of course you are jesting. So our Mother Church is not moral enough for Miss Nelson? And all that riffraff that follow those Anabaptists, are they more moral than we?"

"Certainly not, Reverend," put in Mrs. Meachem, "but it is perfectly true that some of our servants, even the field hands, are filling the meeting houses of the dissenters. As for the vulgar classes, farmers, overseers, mechanics, and suchlike, they have deserted us in droves. It grieves my heart to see it, dear Reverend." The lady dabbed at her eyes with a fine silk and lace handkerchief that matched the blue of her gown.

Sophie Meachem slunk away to wander somewhere or other, as was her custom in any gathering. Mr. Higgens now made his way to the chair she had left, and dropped into it, looking quite overcome with despondency. But Charlotte felt no pity. "That was only to be expected. All those of mean and vile condition love the Anabaptists and the Methodists. They preach that all men are brothers, all equal in God's eyes. And I hear they let all sit mingled together, even the Negroes."

"Heavens!" cried Mrs. Cracklethorpe, quite overcome.

"That must be why your respected husband, Mrs. Waverley, whom I esteem for all other things, actually aided our storekeeper in establishing a Baptist chapel here." Mr. Higgens' pursed lips were pinched even tighter and the skin around his mouth had gone white.

"But Mrs. Waverley," said Mrs. Cracklethorpe, "your mention of the Methodists reminds me. Do not your tenants, the Clancys, hold meetings of that persuasion? And didn't I hear that this young lady here, your cousin from North Carolina, attended there?"

All eyes turned toward Honey, who shrank back in her chair and flushed quite as red as the chapped hands she held clenched in her lap.

"Yes, yes, the child walked all the way there this past Wednesday for some sort of class. Egged on by Mrs. Levier, it seems. Is that not true, my dear?"

Surprisingly, the girl found her voice, though she kept her head down. Perhaps Charlotte's commands to speak up, repeated daily over recent weeks, were beginning to take some effect. "Mother Levier--she begs me call her so--asked me had I got religion, so I told her about our preacher back home. He was Methodist, so Mother Levier said as how I should go to the meeting that's so near by. She said the Quaker faith was best of all, noblest she said, but seeing as there ain't, isn't, a meeting of them in these parts, it was best I go to the Clancys."

"I disapproved, of course, when I heard of it," said Charlotte. "I am sure that Mr. Levier will agree that his respected wife means well, but she is over-serious, as seem to be all these New Lights. They would squeeze all pleasure from life. Throw out the juice crushed from the grape, and eat the bitter skin. I expected the concurrence of Mr. Waverley. But he with his excessive notions of freedom objected only to Honey's walking to the meeting. He insists she drive the dogcart in future and that it be held available for her on the Wednesday. However, I insist she attend worship with us on Sunday, so as to be among the better sort of people. And be subject to your enlightened teaching, Reverend. So you see, I did not allow another complete desertion."

Charlotte thought she'd been kind to the girl and put an end to the questions, but of course everyone's curiosity was aroused.

"What on earth do you do at those meetings, my dear? I've heard they are quite raucous, with people behaving quite without decorum." This came from Mrs. Meachem.

"We sing hymns, ma'am. We pray to God to direct us aright. We read from the scriptures and the older people, they try to dig out what they mean."

"Lord have mercy! Don't you need a preacher for that?"

"He comes every two Sundays, ma'am. But just the elders is there on the Wednesday. Back home, our preacher couldn't come, even on Sunday, but every six weeks, or seven. He had lots of meetings to visit. But when he did come, oh how fine it was! He made the Scriptures like they was happening right there in front of us. Oh, he had a fine booming voice, and when he laid his hand on Lazarus (my brother Josh would lie down dead like Lazarus) it was so fine I cried and cried. Oh, if only Jesus could have come and done for Josh when he got kilt just what He done for Lazarus."

Charlotte was quite amazed to see meek little Honey standing up in excitement, and tears welling in her eyes. Sarah, who had sat frozen like a startled rabbit until now, jumped up and put an arm around her sister while silence reigned for a few moments.

"Yes, yes, do calm the poor agitated child. You see what harm those unprincipled mountebanks can do. Quite turn a young or ignorant person's head with their wild playacting." Mr. Higgens shook his learned head dolefully.

Charlotte pulled Honey down beside her and bade Sarah fetch her a glass of toddy.

"And now has come the crowning insult!" bemoaned Mr. Higgens. "We are to be shorn of our charitable duties. Mother Church has looked after the orphaned and the destitute for untold ages. But now our county turns its back on our vestries and will elect 'Overseers of the Poor.' Overseers! The very word suggests negligence or worse. And what of our churches? They are falling down around our ears. Did you note the cruel sag in the roof over the altar itself?"

Unfortunately, Mrs. Humbolt had caught the last of this, and cried out in a voice as loud as a sea captain's: "That's as nothing, Parson. I'd as leave have the roof sag all it pleases, if only I need not watch my step going down the aisle, and even sitting down in my pew, for fear of landing slap dab in a spatter of chicken shit! Or rat shit, for all I know. For Mercy's sake, could you not have the holes plugged?"

"Madam, I..." But his words were swallowed by a scraping of chairs. Someone had noticed a movement of horses and vehicles signifying that the gentlemen were finally ready to set out homeward. Never was a group of ladies more relieved, since this rescued them from the complaints of their pastor and the offensive language of this old woman (scarcely to be called a lady) whom age had robbed of all decent restraint.

Chapter 9

Patrick had been given the place of honor in the Meachems' carriage, on the right side facing forward so he might have a clear view of the river and a little splash of sunshine on his lap, but not in his eyes. A pillow had been placed on his right side to support his splinted arm, and the softly padded body of Mrs. Meachem provided even better cushioning on his left. Still, with each bump or lurch of the vehicle he felt more keenly the growing soreness in his right shoulder and the ache in the lower part of his back. Strange that he'd barely noticed his injuries while in the company of all those ladies on the porch of the tavern.

Mrs. Meachem was already dozing, emitting a soft buzz with every exhalation. The Colonel, seated on her other side, stared glumly ahead and answered no more than a gruff "Indeed, sir" to Patrick's attempts at conversation. Had he been bested at a horse sale that day, or did other worries absorb him? The fascinating Sophie Meachem, who sat opposite Patrick, always reminded him of a serpent because of her gliding movements and habitual silence. So he must now endure both pain and tedium.

Every winter he told himself he would not go through the monotony of another stay in the country, relieved only by a rare visitor or by the hazards of a journey to church in a village offering only a modicum of additional faces, and these of little interest. This time the hazards may have brought him a broken bone. Who knew but what something was broken, despite what that ignorant barber had said, perhaps merely to soothe him. How wrong he'd been to allow himself to be prevailed upon by his stepson, and some foolish notion of duty to his wife, to spend three months in this dreary backwater. How much better to go home to Williamsburg, the only civilized spot in the Commonwealth, and pass the winter at the window of his print shop, directly on busy Gloucester Street. From there he could watch all the comings and goings of people in the street, and converse with residents and travelers who gathered there for news brought by the post. His assistant Simon still asked him most deferentially for advice on how best to lay out the broadsides brought him to print, though he carried out these commissions quite ably on his own during the long months that his employer was away in Richmond or at Laurel Hill.

In Williamsburg Patrick was a man of importance. There his lack of land signified little. Here in the country he was merely the stepfather of a respected estate owner. Last, but far from least, he had in Williamsburg his young and very grateful Jenny, the very opposite of the reproachful old woman who was his wife.

Now that he was reminded of women, he could no longer fail to pay some attention to Sophie Meachem, seated, nay, sprawled carelessly on the seat facing him. Now <u>there</u> was a young woman whose every move, every glance, seemed to invite a man to take liberties with her. He'd observed her impudent, challenging looks directed most particularly at his younger stepson. Miles appeared not to notice, but surely he could not be insensible to her charms. A man could have fine sport with her, if it weren't for her devil of a husband.

Oh yes, the vixen had marked him looking at her and now leaned forward as if to adjust her skirt, giving him full view of a bosom that threatened, nay promised, to spill out of her bodice. When he forced himself to return his eyes to her face, he found her watching him with a look of contempt. But Patrick was not one to be shamed by such a little baggage. He gave her back the look he used on men who sought to bluff or cheat him, one of shrewd calculation. For a few instants two pairs of eyes stared into each other like pistols about to fire on the dueling ground. Patrick's spirits rose. Country life could offer its diversions after all.

Sophie was first to look away. She shrugged, closed her eyes, and let her head fall against the seat back. A kerchief of crimson wool was looped over the top of her bonnet and tied under her chin so as to hide most of the left side of her face. The color crimson, which she often wore, itself gave rise to gossip, for only servants and field hands decked themselves in vivid colors. Ladies wore gray or buff or puce.

It wasn't long before Sophie dozed off, her body sliding forward and her head flopping about on the seat back. The sway of the carriage, its gentle creaking, and the regular splats of horses' hooves on mud might have lulled Patrick to sleep as well. But Sophie's bonnet and scarf became dislodged by the bobbing of her head, revealing a blue and yellow bruise beneath her left eye and on her temple. The injury must be a couple of weeks old--there was no swelling and the coloring on the skin was pale--but the blow must have been a brutal one. Of that Patrick was sure. His stomach turned over. He abhorred violence of any kind, even among men, yet was surrounded by it. Every day he heard mention of a duel or a brawl or the whipping of Negroes. Some men beat their wives, he knew, though they didn't speak of it. But surely only farmers, and the lower sort of mechanics, and the rabble. Not gentlemen. Yet the minx was provoking, willful, a harlot at heart and perhaps in deed. Was she to be pitied? No, she brought it on herself. Besides, Dick Meachem was no gentleman, despite his family and his wealth. Ah well, sighed Patrick, not every man could evade the troubles of matrimony as cleverly as did he himself.

"Well, what say you, gentlemen? Is he not the finest creature in all the Commonwealth? Son of Straightway out of a daughter of Lanzero, who you know was the swiftest little quarter nag ever seen in these parts."

Miles listened idly as Col. Meachem bragged about his costly new horse. He and Nathan had ridden into town too late for church service, but in time for the usual business transactions and man-talk afterward. They had accepted the Colonel's invitation to dinner, with Matthew's approval. The approval surprised Miles, since his brother avoided giving or accepting Sunday dinner invitations.

It was mid-afternoon and a cold wind was blowing in from the southwest. While Nathan saw to the needs of the Waverley horses, Matthew, Miles and Col. Meachem leaned on the rails of the latter's paddock, their eyes following the restless movements of Prideful, the Colonel's new yearling, as he trotted to and fro in the mud. A magnificent bay stallion he was, with a narrow, even blaze.

"Straightway is brother to your Dauntless, Mr. Waverley. Only I think his son will breed truer."

Miles glanced at his brother, sure that these words would prick the pride he still took in his aging stallion. The slightest aspersion cast upon his beloved animal still wounded him.

But Matthew's face betrayed nothing as he mildly replied: "Do you think so, sir?" Come to think on it, Matthew's face wore an unwonted pallor this day.

"He's fully fifteen hands and a half, fiery as a comet, and I have his bloodline all marked out in Weatherby's stud book. Have you seen that marvel of a volume, gentlemen? At last we have a complete record, and none too soon in coming. I'll show it you when we go in to dine. Now we can trace with an absolute certainty the bloodlines of our nags. Our two, this fellow and your Dauntless, Mr. Waverley, stem from Godolphin Arabian--which we well knew, but now we have it clear and firm in the book."

"Indeed, sir. A great service Weatherby has done you. Even though he is an Englishman," Miles remarked.

Not used to the younger Waverley's sense of humor, Meachem showed him a raised eyebrow, but Matthew filled in the silence.

"He is indeed a well-made animal, Colonel. Broad chest, good scoop of the nose, high crest, eyes as large as ever I've seen. In short, all the points of the best thoroughbred. Pray have your boy bring him closer....But he appears to balk?" (Miles was delighted to detect a tone of satisfaction in this last observation made by his holier-than-thou brother.)

"He's something skittish yet. Oh, he's perfectly broken. But nervous. Part of the high blood, you know," Meachem hastened to explain.

"Is it indeed? Dauntless was so steady from the first. Eager, spirited, but quick to respond to the merest word."

Miles almost laughed aloud at the scarcely veiled rivalry between the two. He himself, as a boy, had fully shared most men's fascination with horseflesh. But ever since he had set out to fend for himself, at fourteen, first in arms and then in the West, the equine race had become for him a mere means of locomotion. He could not afford anything beyond the ordinary nag, dependable above all, and few men in the West had anything better.

Nevertheless, he knew in his heart that one day he would own a blooded mare, chestnut, with all the points of her Arabian ancestors. Suddenly the image of Lucy came to his mind, dressed in the white gown she had worn for the Christmas celebration, her lustrous chestnut hair pinned up in a sleek ball in back, and in front letting fall loose ringlets about her face. His chest tightened, whether from shame or anger, he knew not.

The appearance of Nathan, who emerged from the stable and came to stand beside him at the fence, chased away that disturbing image.

"What do you think of my new stable, young man? I aim to show it to your uncles here directly," said the Colonel.

"Oh it's a fine one, sir. Dry and airy, with ceilings a good two feet higher than ours. Big stalls, too, that invite an animal to lie down. And this solid brick wall to protect from the western winds. Any horse would be happy here. Really, Uncle, you should build one like it." He stopped short and flushed. Miles could see that the boy suddenly thought himself presumptuous.

But Matthew had taken four or five of his long strides toward the east side of the stable where he could see the head of a sorrel roan stretched out the window of her stall to nibble the bark of a young river birch. Several other newly planted trees stood within a few feet of the building. It was indeed an impressive stable, the bricks of motley colors and age, but tightly mortared, the shingles of the roof spanking new.

Miles, who had followed his brother, took a few steps inside the wide doors and noted that hardwood was used throughout. "Truly a splendid building, Colonel," he called back to the smiling owner.

"Indeed," Matthew added to the praise, "these trees will soon give welcome shade to your animals in summer. But I fear one is too close. Your sorrel roan will nibble it to death." To Miles he murmured: "The Colonel's horses are far more snugly housed than his Negroes."

"If you'll permit me to make a suggestion, sir," said Miles to the Colonel, "it is that you allow our nephew Nathan here to work with your new yearling a little. I'll warrant you he can calm him. He has a prodigious way with horses, and your boy strikes me as afraid of the animal."

The young Negro, scarcely more than a child, had succeeded in catching hold of the halter, and was pulling on it ineffectually while the horse strained away from him, his ears flat back and his tail swishing menacingly.

"Don't pull him toward you, you fool!" yelled the Colonel. He started toward the paddock gate, but evidently thought better of it. He was still dressed in his Sunday clothes. "This oaf will get himself knocked down and kicked to kingdom come for a certainty. Not a great loss, except that I've no one better for the stables at present."

While he talked Nathan had swung his long legs over the fence and walked slowly toward horse and boy, speaking as he went, but so softly that Miles could hear only a murmur. "He's a damned sight more at his ease with horses and dogs and the rougher sort of men, than with gentlemen," Miles remarked. "Plenty of heart though. I wish you could have seen him out west when we had to deal with squatters. I can tell you some of those fellows, standing in a knot with their rifles at the ready made the chills go down my spine. But Nathan was full of assurance, ready to brazen it out. He would stride right up to them by my side, looking just as mean and a hell of a lot more sober than them. I always played the reasonable, calm fellow, real sorry to have to displace them, but it didn't hurt to have Nathan there looking like he was spoiling for a fight. He's a dead shot, you know, and wasn't shy about showing that off."

A lucky thing that Nathan couldn't hear his words, thought Miles. He flushed as readily as a girl and purely hated to be talked of.

"What became of the trained groom you hired from the breeder of Prideful?" asked Matthew. "I heard he arrived a fortnight ago. With the horse, I supposed."

"Yes, came and was gone in a week. Half-killed by my whelp of a son. You recall that Dick ruined my bay mare Angel, best horse in the stable. Winded her, whipped her 'til she was good for naught but breeding. And she so gentle and swift. Almost as good blood as this animal. God's breeches, Waverley! How came it I was cursed with only one son, and him a deuced rascal. <u>Your</u> father was blessed with three good sons."

"But our father did not live to see even one of us grow to manhood," sighed Matthew, "and then our brother died so very young."

"Well, well, but your father was spared having to bear that. Besides, your brother left behind a fine son of his own." This was said as he watched Nathan, who had succeeded in quieting Prideful and was stroking his neck. The horse stood almost still, his flanks heaving, but his ears half erect and his tail barely moving.

"And your new groom, what happened there?" asked Miles, his curiosity getting the better of what little discretion he possessed.

"Well, it's of course that I gave him orders not to allow Dick to touch Prideful, much less ride him. You can well imagine what occurred when only three days after the animal arrived Dick came out to the stables and ordered that groom--only a little wisp of a mulatto--to saddle Prideful for him. The nigger had the courage to repeat my orders--I'll say that for him--orders that of course I'd repeated several times to Dick myself. Thank God I was at home. Randel, my home overseer, was nearby but the lily-livered fellow, white as he is and rough enough on the niggers, is scared out of his wits by Dick and could only come running to find me. I got out here in time to save the horse but not the groom. A fractured skull and a broken arm. His doctoring cost me monstrous dear, I can tell you, not to mention the heavy cost of placating that breeder so as to keep the affair away from the magistrates. And what if the fellow had been killed? He's worth three hundred pounds. Or so his owner tells me."

"Imagine that! A nigger worth three hundred pounds. That ain't right, when a white man can't put his hand on two shillings for a few swigs of rum at the Silver Stallion." This came from the deep shadow inside the wide-open doors of Meachem's stables. Dick emerged slowly, hands in the pockets of a buff coat of good broadcloth, much rumpled. His smallclothes were stained, but his large dark eyes were clear, peering from under black locks that mingled with thick brows. He appeared sober.

"So you're back, are you," muttered the Colonel, not looking at him. Matthew and Miles nodded to the man, who didn't bother to acknowledge their greeting.

"You freed any of your niggers yet, Waverley? I hear tell old Robbie Carter's let loose five hundred of them on us. As if we don't have enough of the critters running wild."

"Mr. Carter's Negroes will hardly run wild, Dick," corrected Matthew. "They're still on his land, working for wages. And not the whole five hundred. It's a gradual manumission."

"Well more fool he. However he's doing it, it's an insult to the rest of us. What's more, it's a threat. All the bastards prick up their ears when they hear of such a fool mass freeing as that."

"Well, something must be done with those on tidewater land, isn't that right?" remarked Miles. "Too many for wheat and the other grains, now that tobacco's petered out there."

At this moment two figures descended the back steps of Col. Meachem's house and started slowly toward the paddock. It was Mr. Levier, steadying himself on the arm of a young manservant. When they arrived at the paddock he laid hold of a fence rail and waved the servant back to the house.

"So you tired of the ladies' company, did you?" said the Colonel. "Wanted to see my new stallion?"

"No indeed, sir. The ladies deserted me. Gone off to fuss over the granddaughter somewhere on the upper story. So I thought I'd take some air."

"Well, sir," said Miles, "we were talking of Mr. Carter's big manumission of last August. You, with your Quaker views, must rejoice in it."

"By all means. Yes. Yes. I would that all would follow his example. You see, apart from the fact that slavery is one of the most abominable institutions ever invented by man, from the point of view of morality, and all decent men agree that it is..."

At this Dick Meachem gave a great snort, and his father kicked irritably against a fence post.

Mr. Levier paused as if to collect his thoughts, without seeming to notice these reactions. "In addition, the entire system violates the most fundamental laws of economy, gentlemen. If you've read Mr. Adam Smith, you know that when a man isn't free to sell his labor, when you remove from him all possibilities of self-improvement, you take away all incentive to productive labor."

"I say the whip's incentive enough," growled Dick.

"I swear I'd ten times rather hire free men," said Miles, "but where in hell do you find them here? White men won't touch field labor, and free Negroes can find plenty of work in mills or shops or taverns."

"Too God damn many of 'em are swarming about in Richmond and Williamsburg. Must be at least ten thousand," opined Col. Meachem. "Just figure what it'd be like if all the others were freed. There are more of them than us, you know. God Almighty! What a chaos that would be. Or worse."

"Hell and the devil!" cried Dick. "Our gentlemen in Richmond free all our niggers? Pox take them! We'll tar and feather 'em first. And I don't mean the niggers."

"For God's sake," said the Colonel, "freeing's not what's needed. We need sterner laws to control the ones we've got. Only think of the people on Santo Domingo, getting their throats slit as they lay asleep in their beds."

Matthew had remained silent. Miles knew that this subject, a not uncommon topic of conversation these days, troubled his brother deeply. Miles had known him to go into a brown study for hours after hearing it debated. Sometimes he spoke up, but only to ask a disturbing question or just to state a fact. Now he did the latter.

"There is talk of sending some of them back to Africa. Helping them establish a colony there. But I don't know. I don't know." He heaved a sigh.

Brotherly affection inspired Miles to change the course of the conversation, but an evil spirit chose the tack he took. Unmindful of the company they were in, he fell to teasing his stepfather. Perhaps it was the old man's pontifical tone and his highhanded way of condemning a system on which all here except him depended. He, with his successful printing business and outside investments, had other means of support.

"By the by, Mr. Levier," said that devil in Miles, "I read in the Richmond rag that there's a fine little house offered for sale on a pleasant street right next the house of Mr. John Marshall. Establish yourself there, so convenient to your Richmond shop, and have all the talk you could wish about the theories of Adam Smith and of our abolitionists. What's better still, it would be a comfortable abode for our mother. How content she would be to live all the year with you, and close to our sister Mildred as well."

Despite his long absences from Laurel Hill, Miles was well aware that Mr. Levier had no desire to have his wife live with him. Miles was not so tolerant of this situation as was Matthew. Perhaps because he was more fond of their mother. As the youngest son and only a small child when their father died, he had been held close and coddled in those years, whereas Matthew, at fourteen, had been forced into instant manhood with all its responsibilities. Besides, as his mother often repeated to Miles, with no warmth of approval, Matthew was the picture of his father and strove always to emulate him.

Mr. Levier was saying something about the climate of Richmond being only a little less pestilent than that of Williamsburg, where he already owned a house. "And you know, dear boy, that I am in

Richmond only for the sessions of the Assembly, and then am kept so busy I can scarce find time to eat and sleep, much less attend to the comfort of your dear mother."

At these unlucky words Dick Meachem jumped in: "It's of course that the gentleman would not care to stay long in Richmond when he could be cozy in his house in Williamsburg and pampered by his free nigger friends. Or are they servants? I couldn't rightly tell, Mr. Levier, when I paid a call at your house, or rather your shop in the front of it, last May. They acted mighty uppity. You'd think they were the masters."

"If you are referring to Simon, young man, he is not a servant, but my able assistant in the shop."

"Is that so, sir? Well I was just a tike fifteen years ago, before the War, but I seem to remember that selfsame nigger shuffling around the house here at Fairhaven, humble as you please. Damn if he didn't keep his proper place in those days. My old man here can vouch for that."

Col. Meachem, whose face had turned the color of a crabapple, began to sputter something but checked himself. Miles felt a mighty urge to knock the sneer off Dick's lips, but when he glanced at Matthew and saw the consternation in his eyes he felt more like kicking himself for bringing his stepfather's personal arrangements into the conversation.

As usual it was Matthew who first found words to attempt to retrieve the situation. "I'm sure that Col. Meachem will agree that that is an old story, long settled by the courts, whether rightly or wrongly. But you will tire yourself standing out here, Mr. Levier. Let me assist you back inside. We'll play a game of backgammon until dinner is served."

"No. No. The air and the movement is doing me good." And to prove it Mr. Levier walked a few steps this way and that, but stiffly and with a wave or two of pain washing over his face. He was enjoying the situation, thought Miles, not without admiration.

"Simon has become an excellent typesetter. Not that alone, but he edits copy as well as any white man I know."

"And what of that comely wench that served us tea in your cabinet? Is she a freed one too?"

"She is Simon's sister. He bought her freedom several years ago."

"Well, she gave herself plenty of airs, that one. And I remarked a mighty pale little brat tugging at her skirts. We don't allow nigger brats in the Big House here. But I suppose that one is a very particular one?"

Mr. Levier stopped in his tracks, his face as stiff as his walk had been. Only his lips moved. "What are you implying, sir?"

"I ain't implying nothing. Only that boy's pappy wasn't no nigger."

"That's enough, Dick Meachem! You think you can insult my stepfather because he's old, and injured to boot, you wretched poltroon! You'll answer to me!" The words were out in a rush of heat that burned Miles' neck and face, and seemed to singe the roots of his hair.

Dick laughed, the nervous, high-pitched laugh of a girl. Something in the sound brought Miles to his senses even as Matthew, clamping a hand hard as a rabbit trap on his arm, pulled him aside.

"Don't play the fool, Miles." He had Mr. Levier in tow with his other hand and drew them both several paces away. "The fellow's not worth an hour of your time. Been called out many times. Always arrives on the field besotted. Then what can a gentleman do but fire in the air, if the rogue can be made to pace off at all. Or call it off. Believe me, it would make you look a fool, given his reputation. It's you who gave the insult. Pray make no more words about it. He won't call you out, so just walk away. Remember, we are Col. Meachem's guests."

Mr. Levier appeared to have regained his composure and merely shrugged, wincing at the pain that evidently caused him. But Miles was not one to slink away like a scolded dog. He used his own greater strength to release his arm from Matthew's grip and turned back to see the Colonel gesticulating angrily as he spoke to his son. Nathan, who had mounted the new stallion, was walking him slowly at the far end of the paddock, as far from the angry voices as possible, but both horse and rider kept turning their faces toward the group of men outside the fence.

As Miles started back toward the two Meachems, not sure what he would say or do, but considerably calmer, Dick Meachem suddenly stalked off, rounded the end of the stable, and disappeared. This made Miles' task clear.

"Col. Meachem. Sir." He grasped for the right words, ones that a man of honor could say to ease the situation, yet not appear a coward. "I regret violating your hospitality with angry words. I mistook your son's remarks about my stepfather's servants." (Fortunately Mr. Levier was out of earshot and could not object to the term.) "His remarks were uncalled for, but of course they could not in any way have anything to do with Mr. Levier personally."

The Colonel merely bowed his acquiescence, turned and walked toward his house, motioning the others to follow.

There! Matthew would be proud of him. Indeed, Miles was surprised at his own restraint. He heartily congratulated himself.

———⟊∘⟊———

Matthew sat at an elaborately carved cherry writing table in the Meachem's second parlor, the one with draperies and upholstery of yellow satin set against wallpaper depicting a leering Pan and nymphs pretending fright amid the lush greens and browns of a forest. This elegant apartment, reserved for special occasions and elite guests, did not suit Matthew's mood, but it was the only one in which he could find solitude, giving as excuse that the post, picked up in the village, had brought reports from Richmond to which he must give immediate attention. Indeed, two long letters lay open on the table before him but he had barely perused two sentences before he raised his head and gazed at the pale afternoon sunlight on the trunks of a stand of beeches that rose above the deep green of the boxwoods bordering what the

Meachems called their pleasure garden.

Small chance that the Meachems found much pleasure there, or elsewhere. Matthew knew that the Colonel had been obliged just before Twelfth Night to sell the last remaining parcels of land that his father had amassed in the Ohio valley. All had gone to support the extravagance of a way of life that emulated the wealthiest of the tidewater plantations and was quite out of keeping with the simpler style of the Piedmont. But pursuing the road to financial ruin was not the worst of the Colonel's worries. Dick Meachem grew more quarrelsome with each passing month. The attack on the groom was only the latest and worst of the incidents that had reached Matthew's ears. Dick's father seemed unable to put a check to his conduct, could not even threaten to disown this only son, whose mother defended and protected him against her husband's frustrated rage.

He sighed, rose, and stretched in an effort to get that picture out of his mind, then crossed to stand looking out the leaded window with one of its small squares showing in colored glass the Meachem coat of arms. Matthew knew it had been purchased by the Colonel only fifteen years ago when he made a long stay in England seeking, without success, to find a genuine one. Matthew blew out his breath in exasperation. Here he was enumerating the woes of the Meachems; worse, passing judgment upon them. "Let he who is without sin cast the first stone."

He snorted wryly at the quotation. He considered himself enlightened, had risen above the harsh condemnations and intellectual narrowness of old-fashioned Christianity. But the words of the Bible, falling incessantly from his mother's lips when he was very small, still came back to him unsought. Particularly when the black fog was descending upon him. Well, that particular quotation merited respect.

He could feel the fog in the weighted lids of his eyes, in the taut wires that stretched from his eyes to his temples to his jaws. He recognized it in these judgments of others that began earlier on the ride to church with his damning of Mr. Crawford, even spoken aloud in front of Molly. Such judgments, he had learned by now, were a useless effort to stave off judgment of himself.

For was he not more to blame than anyone? Was he not here at Fairhaven, partaking of an abundant dinner prepared and served by seven or eight servants, and then requiring a fire and candles brought into this parlor against the dampness and waning light of a winter afternoon? He was the man who had adopted the lofty principle, known to all and doubtless laughed at by all, of not dining with company on Sundays so as to leave the servants a day of leisure. But he had let himself be persuaded: Mr. Levier needed a rest before continuing the journey to Laurel Hill. Oh, a very good reason, but were there not always good reasons for not following the principles so earnestly laid down for oneself?

That thought recalled a more painful matter that had been sticking him like a thorn lodged in his foot. Little Edward had been bled while Matthew was away in Richmond. The image of that frail little arm held over a basin with the thin blood spurting out brought pain all along his own arm and up into his heart. When Edward was smaller the doctor had not attempted such treatment. It was too difficult to find and penetrate such tiny veins. Matthew had long doubted the efficacy of bleeding, purging, and blistering, ever since he had witnessed the wretched death of his father, rendered so much more painful by the doctors' harsh treatments. When he had realized in the first months of Edward's life that the sickly little boy was probably not destined to live long, he had vowed that he would never let any doctor torment him. Yet the bleeding had been done. Charlotte had allowed it, though knowing full well his determination on the subject. Or rather, Joan had allowed it, for Charlotte had given over all care of the child to the servant. Charlotte, so jealous of her authority in all other affairs, had put this child into other hands, black hands. She had already lost two children. Perhaps she did not trust in the care of her own hands?

Whatever might be the cause, when Matthew had attempted one time to remonstrate with her about it, she had given him such a look, such a look...that he had not opened the subject again.

Yet after Charlotte had nearly died with the delivery of Edward, had he not shriveled up in panic, first vowing never to touch her in lust again, and when he proved too miserable a weakling to hold to his resolve, then commanding that one of those same doctors he so distrusted be summoned to attend her next confinement.

Great God! Not just the black thoughts, but the headache was coming. He might have known from those wires in his head. Now the yellow lights were flashing before his eyes. And the wires were tightening, tightening. He swayed as a wave of nausea washed over him, and sank abruptly into the armchair nearest the window, keeping his swimming head erect because the slightest bend would bring on vertigo. What a disgrace if he should spill his dinner upon the Meachems' fine Turkey carpet!

Finally the nausea subsided. But the black thoughts returned. A family, an estate, to a great extent a county, to a much lesser one, the Commonwealth itself, were entrusted to his hands. What a misfortune for all concerned. Even the estate, the precious heritage passed on to him by his father; he had not enlarged it, as his father had done. No. He had now gone a long way toward reducing the large debt owed to the British factor with whom his father had dealt. But was he not building up other ones, owed to Baltimore and Philadelphia merchants? All because he couldn't refuse his wife anything she wished and, to be quite honest, could not refuse himself his fine wines and blooded horses.

He should be guiding his ward Lucinda, and Kate too, toward good marriages. Yet Lucy would certainly accept Geoffrey, a most questionable suitor, if he offered. And there again, Charlotte wished the match, for her brother's sake, so how could he oppose it? And now there were his young cousins, for whom he must provide proper dowries. And there was Molly. And his new son.

A wiser and more energetic man than he would have the power

to fulfill this multitude of duties, as well as those of magistrate and deputy. Far better that he withdraw from public life. Miles had so much more of vigor, was so much more decided in opinion. Already he was of great help at Stony Creek. Where would he be without Miles to help there? He should not have turned off Hopkins, who, though brutal, at least got the work done and revenue in. It was all very well to play the humane master and not allow floggings. That was possible on the home quarter, particularly with Amos in charge. But on more distant quarters where he could visit only infrequently? Better to give the overseer his head and close one's eyes. Yet that course was out of the question for him. He was resisted, ridiculed. Even Charlotte, whom he made such efforts to please, was often irritated with him. She now accepted his embraces with only wifely duty, not with the enthusiasm she once had shown. She was disappointed in him. At this point he felt a sudden stinging in his eyes, and moisture filled them.

"Ah yes, it lacked only this!" he cried aloud and rose to knock his head against the window frame. Unmanned. Completely unmanned.

He started at hearing a knock on the door. He barely had time to blot his lashes with a finger when the door opened and a vigorous step, accompanied by a swish of skirt, told him before he turned that the intruder was Charlotte.

"Matthew! Why on earth have you closeted yourself away like this? It's downright discourteous to our hosts." But when she moved closer, took him by the arm and turned him so that the light from the window fell upon his face: "Ah, my dear. You are unwell. Surely you have not allowed a disagreeable hour at the Colonel's stables to make you ill. Mr. Levier told me of it."

"It was something worse than disagreeable. An affront that almost occasioned a calling out. But Miles' behavior, once he remembered himself, was exemplary, and all was mended. No, if I look ill, it's because I feel my migraine coming on."

He bent to pick up two sheets of paper that she had let fall, but swayed so that she had to steady him. Still, he caught a look at them.

"That appears to be Geoffrey's hand. You've news of him at last?"

Charlotte hesitated. She wondered if this was the right moment to give him Geoffrey's letter to read. It would of a certainty do nothing to soothe his spirit. He looked truly distressed, and his headaches were quite terrible. Yet he would be more disturbed if she held it back.

"Yes, it is from Geoffrey. He is well, but his case is still not placed on the docket. No news there. You can read it later. For now, my dear, do sit down...no, not at the writing table. No business for you today." (She snatched up the correspondence on it.) "Sit in the easy chair, and I'll be off to order the horses brought round for our departure. You will ride in the wagon with Mr. Levier and I will have Boston hitched to the Meachem's dogcart to convey Molly and me."

"No, no, my dear. The migraine has not truly begun as yet. Pray read Geoffrey's letter to me whilst I rest my eyes." He smiled and allowed his eyelids to droop.

Nothing for it but to comply. She sank upon a chair opposite him and read as follows:

Richmond
21st February
My Dearest Sister,
You will pardon this long lapse in news from me when you learn how taxed I have been in recent weeks. On the fourteenth day of September I received an urgent message from Portsmouth, from the captain of the brigantine Fulham, saying he had on that very day deposited Mme. de Coulanges, more dead than alive, in an inn of that town. You will doubtless recall that our relation, the Marquis de Coulanges, gave me all the honors of his estate during my youthful wanderings in France, and again took me in after I was obliged to leave Virginia during the hostilities here. Both he and Madame were infinitely kind

and gracious, so what could I do but depart instantly to Portsmouth to her aid?

The poor lady was indeed an object of pity. The voyage from Santo Domingo had been plagued throughout by incessant storms and the ship packed with miserable refugees of all conditions, some wounded or ill. I discovered Mme. de Coulanges racked by fever and unable to eat. The doctor gave little assurance, but I soon perceived that while her body had been ill-used, it was her spirit that suffered the most. She had fled to the Islands from the shocking upheaval in France, and had been settled with the family of her brother a scarce six months when the slaves there rose in their bloody revolt, inspired no doubt by the radical ideas promulgated by those lunatics in France. Mme. de Coulanges' brother, his wife, and their children were brutally slaughtered on their own land. She herself would have suffered the same fate had she not been visiting friends in the port town at the time. She took ship for Portsmouth within the month. You can well imagine the deplorable state in which I found her.

My arrival brought her more attentive care from the innkeeper, and the solace of finding herself in the charge of a relation and friend. She was soon out of danger, and even formed the brave resolution of traveling on to Philadelphia where she has connections. When I told her how severely the yellow fever was still raging there, that the city was virtually emptied, she abandoned that idea for the present, at least until her health should be completely restored.

I have now forsaken all hope of getting my suit placed on the docket before May, when your esteemed husband returns for the next Assembly sessions, and with his influence will readily accomplish what I alone have failed to do. Meanwhile my purse has shrunk quite flat, what with the expense of Mme. de

Coulanges' maintenance added to my own. (To be sure, she will repay me when M. de Coulanges, who has established himself in London, sends her the means.) Her health is improved, and as you may ascertain from the postmark, I have brought her to Richmond. There is nothing for it but to throw her upon your mercy, though she much protests. As I tell her, however, it is but a trifle you can do for a countrywoman of M. de Lafayette in exchange for signal services which, indeed, allowed your country to be born. <u>Our</u> country, I should say, for I am schooling myself to regard it as such.

I purpose to set out within the week for Petersburg, where I will leave Mme. de Coulanges. She will need to rest from the journey, and besides, she insists that I make sure of her welcome at Laurel Hill, which I do not truly doubt, having benefited myself from the hospitable nature of Mr. Waverley on so many occasions.

I delight in the prospect of embracing you, dear sister, and your dear children, including the newest (on whom I congratulate you), in a matter of days.

Your affectionate brother,

"Remark that he says nothing of <u>my</u> hospitable nature," laughed Charlotte, while Matthew sat staring at a spot beyond her head, his lips stretched back in pain. "My dear, you are very unwell. I shall ask the Colonel if he will have a bed prepared for you." She moved to the back of his chair and laid her hand across his forehead, gently tracing with her finger the furrows that she knew so well.

"No, dearest. By no means am I so bad off as that. I was thinking of that unfortunate French lady. Imagine fleeing one danger, only to fall into the midst of one far worse! In France all is upheaval, yet there has been little bloodshed, thank God. But in the Indies! Brutal slaughter by their own servants. Desperate fellows who have nothing to lose."

"Only their lives," said Charlotte, grimly.

"They may well have thought their lives scarce worth living. I confess that I am stricken with fear when I think of it. For it could happen here. It has happened here."

"Come now, Matthew. The migraine is affecting your nerves. A few small incidents, quickly punished. Besides, our Negroes, especially those here at Laurel Hill, live far better than those in the Indies. I am sure of that."

"Perhaps," he sighed. "But yet, think of the poor lady. Turmoil, horror, a sea voyage even worse than most, and then grave illness. We must send Miles, or perhaps Nathan, to Petersburg with the wagon at once. At a time like this I wish we had a closed carriage."

"I always wish it. But let us await Geoffrey's arrival. Time enough then to make any necessary arrangements. We must get you home, and then you must leave everything to me. Banish all cares and drink my potions. You'll take the Jesuits' bark of course, and I'll make you hop tea. Have they not always done you good? Then, when the headache subsides a little, cold baths and rides in the fresh air on Boston, whose gait is so gentle. You need only submit yourself to my care."

He admitted as much with a rueful smile, which quickly turned to a wince of pain. She gave orders, saw them obeyed, and felt within her bosom that elation that always came to her when she took command.

Chapter 10

One evening as Matthew came in muddied and weary from supervising the preparation of the year's tobacco fields, he was met at the door by his manservant Stove, eager-faced with a message.

"Mistress beg you come to the parlor as soon as you're refreshed, sir."

Trouble, he supposed, and more than Charlotte chose to handle alone. He would rather face it at once. "I'll go directly, Stove. But bring me clean shoes first. Then have water heated for my bath and lay out the old gray banyan for me to wear."

In the parlor a fire was roaring on the grate, and pulled close to it was the green brocaded armchair with Geoffrey in it, his legs propped on a stool and the whole of him swaddled in a jumble of coverlets. Charlotte, who was just taking an emptied cup from Geoffrey's hand, smiled wryly at Matthew, her eyes rolling toward the ceiling.

"Welcome, my dear fellow," said Matthew, relieved to see his brother-in-law finally come. "We'd begun to fear some mishap had befallen you. But it appears you are unwell? What ails you?"

"Ah, what does not! Flux, vomit, an infernal pain in the head, and chills that are shaking my bones apart." He did then give a convulsive shudder to illustrate the latter. "My coldhearted sister, and my only blood relative in this godforsaken land, refuses to send for the doctor. I vow she's had enough of me and is waiting calmly to witness my death."

"Come, Geoffrey," snapped Charlotte, "I merely suggested we wait to see how you do in the morning. And you insisted on appealing to the master of the house. As he is here, I withdraw." And so she did.

Charlotte was wont to be more patient with her brother, though he habitually showed his least endearing side to her, while saving his considerable charm for everyone else. But she had been increasingly out of sorts of late, for reasons Matthew could not as yet discover.

"I am sure these irritating delays with your lawsuit have undermined your health, old fellow, not to mention your trials in being obliged to take on the charge of your unfortunate French relation." Matthew spoke soothingly as he eased himself into the comfort of the red morocco armchair. He felt certain that a sympathetic ear to Geoffrey's distress would prove an acceptable substitute for the doctor.

"You couldn't speak more truly," moaned Geoffrey. "Attempting to move those gentlemen of the Court is more exasperating than whipping six winded carriage horses up an icy hill. Those pompous windbags must needs consult records, and then more records, some of which they are still trying to find, or waiting to receive from England. I assure you I hung about town paying visits to anyone I thought might speak in my favor, but in the end the Court adjourned without addressing my case at all."

"Ah well, we will hope for better things come spring. I will use my interest with Mr. Pendleton who has become quite a power on the Court. But tell me, how did you leave Mme. de...? I beg your pardon, but her name escapes me."

"A damned sight better off than I, I assure you. I couldn't raise my head from the pillow for a fortnight after we reached Petersburg. Marie--Mme. de Coulanges, that is--was up and about in no time. But when I was finally able to resume our journey, she refused to ride on here to Laurel Hill without being certain of a welcome."

"But surely you told her..."

"Yes, yes, old chap, but it isn't just a matter of courtesy. She didn't wish to leave behind her portmanteau, which we had no means of carrying. Doesn't trust the innkeeper to keep it. And she is in want of a maid. She has a stubborn notion of procuring one in Petersburg, though I told her a thousand times that we don't have white servants. Of course she hasn't the means to buy a Negro. Ah, such a parcel of difficulties! My head is quite pounding with them. And my poor stomach is churning. The uncouth victuals in that dreadful inn are what did me in. Can you imagine that they expected me to breakfast on porridge? And porridge stinking with grease, at that!"

With his thick auburn hair overly long and undressed, and his reddened eyes rimmed by puffs of pale skin, Geoffrey looked far from his usual comely self. Indeed, he looked all his forty years. Matthew suspected that an excess of food and drink, and of cares that he could not on this occasion shuffle off onto others, was the worst of Geoffrey's ills.

"For the love of God, my dear fellow, send for that Petersburg physician, Dr. What's-His-Name. I had him to see me twice, while at the inn, and he did me not a scrap of good, but perhaps three is the magic number. You have still no medical man in Solway County, I suppose?"

"My dear Geoffrey, let us see first what wholesome nourishment and rest can do for you. I trust to the gentle efforts of nature to help the body recover from its distempers. Far more than to physicians. My poor father lost his life to the ministrations of one of their breed, who talked and talked of humors and animalcules while he bled and purged the man's life away. Barely forty he was, and strong of constitution. The poor soul was suffering only an abscess of the throat when the physician arrived. In ten days he was dead. Perhaps death would have taken him in any case, but it might have done so peaceably. Instead he was tormented with the lancet and the blistering cup. He was vomiting one moment and pouring out his life's blood the next."

This speech had its desired effect. Geoffrey groaned and closed his eyes. With his vivid imagination, he was in all probability picturing himself a similar victim of the medical arts. It was not the first time Matthew had used this painful memory of his father's death to dissuade someone from a too-early recourse to the medical profession. He was aware of his inconsistency in insisting upon a physician for Charlotte's last lying-in. But the terrible time she'd had with the birth of Edward had destroyed his trust in the Negro midwife.

"Of course we will send for the physician if you truly wish it, Geoffrey," he continued, as Charlotte entered the room holding a tray with a cup, spoon, and small bottle from which she carefully poured three drops of a pleasantly green liquid into the water in the cup, "but I beg you to consider that some distemper is to be expected in a delicate constitution like yours when it is subjected to strange food and perhaps more drink and less sleep than usual. Then exposure on those foul roads to winds unusually chill for March. Old Doctor Thorpe, now dead, who seemed to do my mother good for her stomach ailments, prescribed these drops, which she swears by."

When Geoffrey had drunk eagerly from the cup and allowed Charlotte to smooth the covers around him, they left him to rest. Charlotte followed Matthew into the dining room where supper was already laid and where they were alone for a moment. She gave him a warm embrace, a rarity these days, alas.

"You don't really mind that I drew you into that. Geoffrey gives so much more weight to your opinions than to mine."

"Ah, my dearest, aren't you ashamed of your deviousness? Fooling the trusting sick with your colored water?"

"Not at all," she laughed. "Remember it was Dr. Thorpe himself who suggested the trick, which he used many times to good avail. 'One must give them something to hearten them, yet nothing to harm.' His very words."

"Of course you're right, my dear. Would that old Dr. Thorpe, who knew when to leave Nature free to heal, were still with us. They say the new physician is a furious bleeder and purger. But enough of that. Let's have Stove sound the gong for supper."

<hr>

A noon sun broke through the clouds a few days later as two horses skirted the large pond on the western boundary of Farrington, the Ludwell plantation. The surface of the pond trembled under the last drops of rain. Underfoot the pine straw glowed red as the sun shone upon it, echoed by the red of the few remaining berries on the holly bushes. The tiny pink buds of leaves just beginning to awaken to spring shone pink on every branch of the trees. The two riders paid no heed to this beauty and promise, so intent were they on reaching their destination.

The horses, breathing heavily, for they had been urged on too eagerly, soon trotted out of the woods and came up to the stable door at Farrington. Molly slid off her horse's back before the stable boy could reach her, but Sarah, who was learning to act like a lady, allowed herself to be assisted. She had to run to catch up to Molly who was already banging on the carved walnut door of the house. It took a long wait before Sue appeared, rubbing her eyes with one hand and pulling her yellow head cloth straight with the other.

"Taking a nap, I'll wager, weren't you, Sue?" said Molly. "I suppose Miss Nelson and Miss Lucy are from home, then."

The big black woman grinned. "I is tired, Miss Molly. I was up doing all night, helping Miss Kate make plaster and liniments for her sick folks she gone to see today."

"Where's Miss Lucy, then?" demanded Molly, sparing no sympathy for the maid.

"She be out of doors somewheres. You come on in and sit yourselfs down in the parlor. She sure to come back soon."

"You go find her, Sue. We've come on business." Molly strode importantly down the hall and into the dark parlor where she promptly pulled open the shutters and seated herself in the biggest chair, motioning Sarah to the sofa.

"Oh Molly, you shouldn't ought to do that," protested Sarah. "They don't likely want sun falling on the furniture. Your mama says it ruins it."

"Oh rot. Mama always lets the sun in when <u>she</u> is in a room, unless it's summertime, of course. What do you think Lucy will say when she finds out Uncle Geoffrey is back? I can't wait to see the look on her face. She's so sweet on him it's a pain to see. Maybe she'll faint dead away. You can be ready to catch her. What a lark that would be!"

"I can't say as I blame her. Mr. Geoffrey is so handsome. So pale and wan. Just like in the poem you read me. 'Why so pale and wan, fond lover, prithee why so pale?' You remember? Or like Barbra Allen's beau on his deathbed. And Mr. Geoffrey has such beautiful hair. So thick and curly and such a pretty dark red color. I ain't never seen nothing like it."

"Don't you go falling in love with him, silly. He'd never in this world look at you. Especially not talking the hillbilly way you do. Besides, he's old, and he's not nearly as handsome as Papa, even if Papa's hair is thin. Papa's strong and has a nice ruddy face and brown hands the way a man should."

"I ain't, I mean I'm not saying Mr. Waverley isn't a fine-looking gentleman, Molly."

"Well, you better not. I suppose Lucy and Geoffrey will get betrothed now and we'll have to put up with them holding hands and blushing and all that rot. But what I'm truly on tenterhooks waiting to see is the French lady. I saw a French <u>man</u> once. Not a gentleman. Just a dancing master on his way through to see who might want lessons, but I was too young and Nathan was away visiting his mama's folks. The funny fellow couldn't barely speak English, and he pranced about on high heels and wore the fanciest wig you ever saw."

"Will she wear fashion gowns--the French lady, I mean--and have her hair piled up high and have tiny hands and feet, and be just so beautiful you can't hardly believe it?"

"She'll be an old hag--she's much older than Uncle Geoffrey, Mama said. And she'll wear powder and rouge and gowns that leave her naked to the waist. I've seen pictures in Mama's fashion books. Oh, I do hope she comes soon!"

Molly couldn't wait another minute for Lucy to come. Who knew if Sue had even gone to look for her? With Miss Nelson away from home, and only Molly giving the order, Sue would take her own sweet time in going, if she would go at all.

"Oh let's find Lucy ourselves," she said, jumping up and dashing out of the room. By the time Sarah made it out of doors after her Molly had already run round to the back of the house where she commanded a view of the end of the pleasure garden on her right, the slope of new spring grass down to the river, and on her left the tall, thick mulberry hedge which enclosed the kitchen garden. That was where Lucy was most likely to be found, but before she set off in that direction Molly heard Sarah's voice plaintively calling her name from the front of the house. That girl never moved faster than a turtle, even the time Molly put a cricket in her chamber pot, just to see. "I'm here in the kitchen garden!" yelled Molly.

"Is that you, Molly?" came another voice, and Lucy appeared at a gate in the opening of the hedge. Molly ran in and received a gentle kiss, as did Sarah when she arrived. "My goodness, girls, you came by yourselves? To keep me company, I hope. I'm all by myself today." She led them to a wooden bench in the middle of a large area crossed by paths of scraggly grass surrounded by dirt beds, for the most part still bare. In some, however, young leaves peeped diffidently out of the earth. Molly's practiced eye recognized English peas, celery and green peppers. Elsewhere a few tired remnants of winter vegetables remained.

Lucy was wearing a mobcap that completely covered her hair, a huge apron that engulfed her whole figure, and pattens on her feet, but she looked something better than a month ago when they had seen her at church. A little less of a hollow and a little more color in her cheek? Molly couldn't be sure. She hoped Lucy hadn't already heard that Uncle Geoffrey was coming. Perhaps she felt better because Uncle Miles was taking such good care of Farrington and of Miss Nelson and Lucy too. That was what Mama said, without sounding very happy about it. With the two younger girls seated at each end of the bench, Lucy settled herself between them, and opened the daybook she had closed when she heard Molly's shout.

"Just let me finish writing the beans and spinach and peppers in their proper places. I do hope we didn't have the short dung dug in too late. Such a dreadful frosty winter. The ground couldn't be broken until nearly March. A wonder the sea kale survived and produced famously. I have the size of each bed marked, but which seeds must go in each is here only in my head. I'll forget if I don't write it down this instant."

She wrote slowly in her small, even script while Sarah watched with close attention and evident admiration. Molly sat silent, trembling slightly from the tension of holding in her exciting news. The page of the daybook was marked out in squares and oblongs, and into each, taking an unconscionable length of time, Lucy wrote the name of a vegetable. Just at the point where Molly felt ready to burst, the job was done, the book closed, and Lucy turned first toward Sarah and then to Molly.

"How is everyone at Laurel Hill? How are your Mama and Papa, Molly?"

"Oh, everyone's as fine as can be," said Molly, jumping up and grabbing Lucy's gloved hands in her bare ones, "but we've a visitor. Guess who it is. Don't you tell, Sarah!" as she saw the other girl open her mouth. But she couldn't leave time for a guess. "It's someone so very, very handsome, that you don't care for at all. Someone with wavy red hair."

At that the daybook slid off Lucy's skirt onto the moist earth. She looked more alarmed than pleased. "It can't be! You're playing me a trick, you wicked girl."

"Oh no, it's true, Miss Lucy," said softhearted Sarah, who couldn't bear to see anyone upset. "Mr. Geoffrey is your faithful suitor. How could he not come back, with such a pretty sweetheart as you? I told Molly . . ."

"Oh pish! Her head is stuffed as full as sausage skins with silly love stories. I say you must cut him dead if he dares come near you. Pay him back for a sorry lover."

Lucy had risen and was clumsily wiping the earth off her daybook. "Oh Heavens! It's dirtied," she wailed. "I'll never get it clean." Then suddenly she straightened and turned indignant eyes on the other two.

"Mr. Geoffrey is not my suitor. He never was. I forbid you to talk that way about him. Now we won't speak of it anymore."

Even Molly was struck by this unwonted firmness. But having made the most of her surprise announcement, she was willing to pass on to the important message with which she had been charged.

"All right. Don't fret. We see how it is," she said, nodding archly to Sarah who was sniffling a bit at the reproof. "Papa has sent us with a message for Miss Kate. You see, Uncle Geoffrey brought a lady with him. As far as Petersburg, that is. Some French relation of his. Since Uncle Geoffrey isn't well--no, don't worry, Papa says it's just fatigue--Nathan is going tomorrow in the wagon to fetch her, and Papa wonders if Miss Nelson would go too, since she said she had purchases to make. The French lady might not like journeying alone with a strange man, though goodness knows Nathan isn't a man," she laughed, "just an awkward boy. I wish I could go."

"You're sure Mr. Geoffrey isn't really ill?" asked Lucy, a little crease appearing in her forehead. Molly nodded. "Well, I'm sure Kate will be delighted. She's been complaining of having no one to send to town. Poor Stuart," she sighed, "used to shop for us thrice a year at the least. And of course Mr. Miles cannot be spared. His hands are full. He is so good to us."

"Uncle Miles is a brick," affirmed Molly. "He may be plain, but he's a Waverley. Ours is good stock. The best. He's worth ten of Geo . . ."

"Hush, Molly, don't you talk so. Besides, you're a Burnham too, you know." Lucy smiled. She seemed to have recovered her composure.

"No I'm not. I'm mostly Waverley. Don't I look like my papa?"

"That I own, but you've the temperament of your mama. Does she not, Sarah?"

That little mouse nodded, to be sure. She always agreed with anything a grown-up said. Besides, now that Lucy had given her a few music lessons, Sarah had become utterly devoted to their neighbor.

"Well, well, come along indoors and have some tea, girls. Sarah and I will practice some new songs that arrived with the post last week. You won't mind, will you, Molly? Then you must start home before the light begins to fade." Lucy's eyes gave a last sweep over the packed earth of the garden. "I must get Mr. Miles to send me a strong girl from the fields to dig up these beds, and then a couple of children can help me rake and sow."

<hr />

A wagon with two ladies in it sat in the shade of an oak tree near the ferry landing at New Kent. On the landing itself stood Nathan, watching as the boatman poled the barge toward him and waiting to catch a line and help the fellow secure his craft. John was a stocky but nimble young man who did his job tolerably well when he was sober.

On their way down to Petersburg Miss Nelson and Nathan had found the man snoring boozily on the dirt floor of his shack, an object thoroughly disgusting to Miss Nelson's eyes. But she had taken a vigorous hand in pummeling the oaf awake and throwing water into his face.

Today, on their return journey with the French lady, John appeared steady as a trout. Nathan was relieved: one less thing for the lady to complain about.

"Hallo, Master Nathan. Back so soon? I reckoned you'd stay a spell in town."

Nathan returned his greeting with no comment. He had too much on his mind to make conversation. He had a skittish horse and an impatient lady to worry about.

"Will you cross us directly, John? There's tuppence extra if you step lively."

Nathan approached the wagon to assure the ladies they would soon be on their way across the Solway.

"Parbleu!" exclaimed the French lady in that startling voice of hers, throaty and almost low enough to be a man's. "We are waiting here a full hour, no?"

"Oh, that is no time, madam," said Miss Nelson, eyeing the lady severely. "We are fortunate there is nothing to unload from the other side, and the current is not swift today."

Nathan now led the horses, already unhitched, toward the landing, praying that the young one, Jasper, would not balk this time. On the trip down, he had had to take Jasper across the Solway at a shallower spot upstream. But the river ran more smoothly today, so perhaps Jasper would follow the lead of his older mate and step docilely onto the barge. They would cross the horses first, then come back for the ladies and wagon, since the barge was not large enough to hold people, horses, and wagon all at one time.

Both men led Juniper, the older horse, slowly and with soothing pats and words, onto the barge that rose and fell at a fairly steady pace. No trouble with good old Juniper.

They took far greater pains to reassure Jasper, but as soon as he placed his front hooves on the planks and felt them move beneath him, he reared, plunged sideways, and knocked John flat upon the landing.

John swore a mighty oath regardless of the ladies' presence. Nathan stroked the trembling horse's neck and spoke to him gently. When the animal, with all four hooves once more on solid ground, seemed calmed, they tried again, with the same result except that John was quick enough to avoid the blow from Jasper's shoulder. They then tried tying a cloth around the animal's head to cover his eyes, but it was not the sight of barge and water, but the feel of motion that alarmed him. Then Nathan, thinking that the voice and touch of a stranger might be adding to the animal's fright, tried walking Jasper for a bit to steady him, and then leading him by himself onto the barge. But it was too late. The creature was thoroughly upset. Nathan cursed himself for not trying this first off.

He himself had been unnerved by the impatience of that damned Frenchwoman who had been complaining of the condition of the road, the pace of the horses, the stop he made to rest them, ever since they left Petersburg. He ran a hand along Jasper's damp nose. It wasn't the animal's fault. Horses were creatures of instinct. Nathan had no trouble accepting their fears, regardless of the trouble it caused. But people! Particularly ladies. They should know better than interfere in men's business. He looked at John, who merely shrugged and spit out a stream of tobacco juice. Despite his cursing, John was used to problems with getting horses onto and off his barge. These were always dangerous moments. A frightened creature could break a leg. This time, despite John's experience and Nathan's patient way with horses, there was nothing for it but to give up.

Miss Nelson was a sensible woman. When he told her he would once again, as on the journey down, take the young horse upstream to a place where he could lead or ride him across, with water probably no more than up to his flanks, she instantly agreed. He would go back to meet them at the ferry landing on the other side.

"Get back to us as soon as you can," she whispered. "I shall have to put up with a deal of squawking in the meantime."

Nathan smiled. He would enjoy at least two hours of silence.

His two hours passed as well as he hoped. The river at the fording place was less deep than he had expected and he was able to join a small hunting party going across, so that Jasper was put at ease by the presence of equine comrades.

But Nathan had to rejoin the ladies. He could see the peevish set of the foreigner's mouth from fifty paces off, and when he drew nearer, the skin the color of porridge that hung on her face. To him she looked sixty years old, but Uncle Matthew had told him she had not reached fifty.

"I do not comprehend why Mr. Waverley sent such a wretched animal," she complained as soon as Nathan came within earshot. "We already make poor progress with an ill-matched team. And now this ridiculous delay!"

Miss Nelson explained (not for the first time, Nathan was sure) that horses were much needed on the plantation at this season, and begged Madam to let Nathan help her into the wagon.

With the reins in his hands and his back to the ladies, Nathan would be spared the angry looks, but not the stream of complaints. Fortunately, these were sometimes muffled. He had noticed that the lady kept pressing a pink lace handkerchief to her upper lip. An affectation of those haughty Europeans, no doubt.

Nathan gave a flick of the reins and a click of the tongue to get the horses moving. The road would soon take them into deep, quiet woods. It was too early yet for snakes, so the only thing likely to spook the horses was a wild pig. The road was firm enough but not overly dry, so the lady would have no call to complain of the dust.

He could scarce credit his ears when her first words were ones of relief. "Thanks to God we travel alone. It is mercifully quiet here." But shortly the complaints began again. "Imagine yourselves! The stage from Richmond to Petersburg was full of drunkards. They were spitting and vomiting out the coach windows all the long of the way. I was the only lady, and Geoffrey protected me from gross insult, but it was a frightful journey. The road was so bad that everyone, even I, was forced to descend and walk up the most bad hills. I assure you I was certain I could not survive. Then, when we are finally arrived, long after midnight, those ruffians waked the whole town with their cries and laughter. And do you think we could finally take our rest once in our beds at the inn? No. Insufferable noise day and night. And when I tried to take the air at midday, my life was at risk from madmen racing their horses down the principal street."

"But surely, madam, you've traveled bad roads and encountered drunkenness in France." Miss Nelson's voice sounded dry as a snapping twig after the gurgling tones of the French lady.

"Ah, mademoiselle, even the canaille in France knows better to contain the alcohol. As for the roads, humph! They may be bad in the provinces, but rarely I subjected myself to them. We resided in

201

Versailles, and from there I traveled only now and then to Paris, when the Court was there. Ah, our poor king! His poor children. Prisoners in their own kingdom. The good Lord knows what they will become."

Mercifully, the voice was stilled for a time. Only the dull thud of hooves and the creaking of springs broke the silence.

"Mon Dieu! How dark it is in this forest! Tell me, are there no farms in this part of the country?"

"Yes, to be sure. We will pass some soon," said Miss Nelson. Soon, indeed, they emerged from the forest and passed a small farm of perhaps twenty acres, with a stand of winter wheat, a field of newly planted rye, a windowless cabin, and only an old man and a child out pulling weeds. Then a larger farm appeared on their left. Here three Negroes, two women and a man, were transplanting young tobacco plants into small hills. On both sides of the road cattle and hogs wandered quite free.

"My faith! How dreary it all is. How irregular the planting. And the cattle, how small. This is most slovenly. Yes, it is as my brother-- God preserve him--read in an English book. 'Americans are the greatest slovens in Christendom.'"

This was too much. Nathan could not be expected to remain silent at such an insult. But Miss Nelson's tongue was quicker.

"Our farmers live well enough, madam. They eat well, and so do our servants. I've heard Mr. Geoffrey say that your peasants starve, and have no freedom. Our animals may indeed be small, but we eat plenty of meat. And plenty of fish and game as well."

"But why are your cattle not fenced in? Where are your pastures?"

Nathan interposed here. "There's plenty of land for them to find food. We fence in our crops, to keep the animals out." Who did this lady think she was, and how could she know anything of farming if she had spent her days mincing about at a king's court? Oh, but better not let her think they didn't take proper care of their animals. "We fence in the sheep, of course. Else they would soon die of disease, or predators, or their sheer stupidity. And the horses we fence in as well. There are wild horses about, who would spoil our bloodlines."

"So you breed your horses. Why not your cattle? I wish you could see, young man, our fine, fat cows. And come! Our neat, rich fields, all planted in straight rows. Do you even fertilize your fields?"

"Of course, madam. We use stable dung and field dung. But not for our tobacco. It makes the taste bitter. And our sweet Virginia tobacco is the best there is!"

The lady continued her rude observations and questions, to which Nathan, his throat tightening more and more with anger, could give no more than a yes or no answer. He had thought that the raillery of Mrs. Waverley and the smirks of the town ladies were the worst a fellow had to bear, but this foreigner made them appear almost gentle. He urged the horses faster. Once he got this lady to Laurel Hill he would keep a good furlong's distance between her and himself.

Then she suddenly changed course, going off in a far more alarming direction. "This young man is clever, mademoiselle," she said, "so young, yet knowing all. He will possess much land one day, be a great planter, no? He is well-favored, as well, do not you think? Are all Americans so tall, so vigorous? I will have this young man show me over the estate, and explain to me everything."

This froze the very blood in his veins. Why did she speak so loudly? He would rather not hear a word.

"He is the son of the great Mr. Waverley, no?"

"No, madam. The nephew. Son of Mr. Waverley's brother, long dead."

"Now tell me, mademoiselle, about Mr. and Mrs. Waverley. She in particular. She is of a distinguished family, I know, and has married a man of moderate property and distinction. For this country, that is. She is the one to please. I must step cautiously with her. The husband? Geoffrey says he is kindness itself. Is that so? But with a gentleman, I do not think I have a difficulty."

What must Miss Nelson think of this? Particularly the careless use of Mr. Geoffrey's given name. They were not such close relations as that, surely?

"But come, mademoiselle," the lady continued. "I want to know about this Lucinda. Your sister, if I make no mistake. Much more young than you, surely. And pretty. Geoffrey will not say so, but I am sure of it. And an heiress? By cause of something, I do not recall, she and not you is an heiress of considerable property. Excuse me, I ask many questions, but my poor Geoffrey is so reticent on this matter. The English, they are like that. And you Americans also, perhaps?"

Nathan had listened to all this with disbelief, but he was relieved that the lady had left the subjects of poor American farming, and even worse, himself. Miss Nelson remained silent.

"Come, come, my dear lady! These are not secrets, surely."

Finally Miss Nelson spoke, almost too low this time for Nathan to hear. "I think...pardon me, madam, but I think you must learn what you wish about my sister, and the Waverleys, from your own observations."

"Ah, then perhaps this handsome boy will not be so reserved. He is old enough to have a little weakness for your sister himself, eh? He is her suitor also perhaps? And she, she cannot be indifferent to these black eyes, these long graceful hands." The woman actually leaned forward and tapped him on the shoulder with her sunshade. He started, and jerked on the reins, which stopped the horses and covered him with embarrassment.

"Ah, the poor boy, he is red as the flesh of those insipid melons of yours."

"Madam, please! Let the boy be."

"Oh well, what do you expect? I must amuse myself somehow in this wilderness. First the horrors of Santo Domingo. I will not think of them! Then the terrible sea voyage. The sickness. My maid died of it, did you know? Poor, poor Berthe. Then more frightful travel on your miserable roads. I wish I had never left home!"

Nathan silently and fervently echoed that wish.

There followed a long silence during which Madam opened her sunshade with a snap (though the day was cloudy) and held it tilted forward so that only flattened tulle roses and foliage could be seen.

"Could you not, madam," ventured Miss Nelson, "go back to your relations in France? Or better still, to your husband who you told me has settled in London?"

"Nom de Dieu! You expect me to return to a country gone mad? The hotheads control everything now, and soon it will be the canaille, the rabble, as you say. And Monsieur de Coulanges? Join his household, where his mistress flaunts herself openly and they live in rags with only two servants? Oh, I have been informed. Besides, London is a filthy, evil-smelling place. Dark, and the rain, it never stops. Still worse, those arrogant English regard us with their noses in the air. They think us so fortunate to be permitted to find refuge among them. It is not to be borne!"

Miss Nelson murmured something that Nathan could not make out.

"Yes, you are right, mademoiselle. One must make the best of things. But no! I will not be contented in any place. I refuse to be so. The world, it is become mad. Why would I be content? Excuse me, but you do not know the world. You cannot comprehend."

Madame de Coulanges lapsed into a silence that, this time, lasted for the remainder of the journey. Miss Nelson spoke a time or two to ask Nathan about a farmer or his crops. Nathan's shoulders and back began to ache as he relaxed them in the peace of the familiar road, the smooth-flowing river, and the gentle slopes of home.

Chapter 11

"I am rejoiced to find you up, madam," declared Charlotte as she discovered Mme. de Coulanges seated before the small glass above the dressing table in Molly's chamber. The lady started, and rose to turn and make a curtsy worthy of an assembly at the Governor's palace.

Charlotte smiled to herself, seeing such elaborate grace in a lady whose rumpled dressing gown revealed too much of her sagging bosom, and whose hair, though a pleasant light brown, hung limp and straight down her back. Charlotte had awaited the arrival of this French aristocrat in the expectation of impossible demands and unendurable arrogance. She had prepared herself by stiffening her resolve not to be imposed upon by anyone, no matter the rank. Was she herself not the niece of a lord? But it appeared that she had got her back up for nothing. For five days now the lady had kept to her chamber, making no requests that came to Charlotte's attention, accepting whatever was sent her to eat, and submitting her body to the ointments and poultices prepared for her by Honey. Most times when Charlotte took the trouble to mount the stairs her guest appeared to sleep; when discovered awake, she merely smiled feebly from beneath mounds of coverlets and managed to look exceedingly grateful.

According to Joan, who kept her distance from the "foreign lady," May and Sarah vied for the honor of serving her, and Honey had taken charge of mending her travel-bruised body and queasy stomach. It was Honey who mixed browned flour with water to form a thin gruel that she carried several times a day to Mme. de Coulanges' chamber to relieve her dyspepsia. Even Maudy had willingly undertaken the cure of torn lace and frayed hems. Doubtless she was eager to learn the secrets of high French fashion.

"Pray don't stand on ceremony with me, madam. Regain your seat, or better, your bed, for here is May with your dinner. I trust you slept well?"

"Ah yes, I am sleeping better, thank you. But I still do not accustom myself to your country noises."

"Set the tray down, child, and plump up Madam's pillows," said Charlotte to May who stood gaping by the bed. She herself settled into an armchair as Mme. de Coulanges eased herself onto the bed, leaning back with a sigh against the piled cushions and pillows. With Madam's portmanteau and trunk both standing open to reveal glimpses of blue, gray, and violet silks and muslins, and two screens over which were draped more gowns and petticoats, Molly's little room that had always stood empty except at night, had been transformed into a crowded jumble of exotic shapes and colors where young girls, slave and free, trotted in and out incessantly.

"I hear that May and our young cousins are quite mad to serve you," said Charlotte. "I don't vouch for the quality of the service, but their zeal, yes, that is apparent. Do be off, May. And see if Old Sukey needs you in the kitchen."

"Yes," smiled Mme. de Coulanges, "just at this moment I am popular. But would you allow May to return with a curling iron presently and do something with my miserable hair? I'm shamed to be seen by you like this."

Charlotte nodded to May who still lingered on the threshold, then waved her away.

"But madam, I hope you do not delay your own dinner to keep me company."

"Be assured that we have already dined. But truly, I am astonished to find you suddenly so sprightly."

"Indeed. Up until waking an hour ago I was feeling each day fatigued to the death. My limbs, they were so sore and my poor stomach, so weak. That little black girl you call lazy came each morning at break of dawn to bring me water for my basin, build a fire to lift the morning chill, and empty my chamber pot. This last she returned to do often, for my bowels have betrayed me. And the pretty young white girl called Sarah was also bustling about me. But best of all, the older girl with the strange name, Honey, has brought teas to calm my stomach, liniment for my aching joints, and rubbed me down like a horse. With all this care, could I be impertinent enough not to mend? You are silent, madam. My care, it disturbs the smooth running of your household. I confess I was surprised at the entire tastefulness of your appointments, which I glimpsed upon my arrival. You will forgive me if I say that in France we think of this country as a rude wilderness. Not Philadelphia or New York, perhaps, but everywhere else.

"We strive for some degree of gentility," laughed Charlotte, remembering her own fears of wolves and savages when she left England twenty years earlier. She could scarcely credit her own eyes and ears in finding this lady so charming, so light-hearted, after the disapproving report of her given by Kate, and Nathan's downright refusal to speak of her at all.

"But tell me, madam. Monsieur your husband is perhaps displeased with my presence here? He has not been once to visit me. Nor have any of the other gentlemen."

"Oh think nothing of that! My husband was attacked with his periodical headache a month ago, and since he was not able to lay aside his cares then and take care of it, it has lingered on. He must be up and about before dawn in this busy season, so by afternoon the pain quite subdues him and he is not fit to be seen by anyone. Just at the hour when you, madam, are perhaps in the habit of beginning your day. Besides, it is not the custom here for gentlemen to visit ladies in their chamber."

"Mon Dieu! You Americans are so energetic! At home it was my greatest pleasure to converse with friends and acquaintances, and give orders to the servants, from the comfort of my bed."

"Speaking of conversation, madam, I wonder at your proficiency with our tongue. But you had an English governess, of course."

"Oh certainly. And before that an English nanny and even an English wet nurse. You English have long been all the rage in France, you know. And pardon me, but this has been to our ruin. The English have a parliament that rules over their king? Then so must we, said our philosophes. Even I was in my youth seduced by such notions. But then what happened? <u>Nom de Dieu</u>! The American Colonials must rebel, helped by fools like M. de Lafayette, and establish a republic! So again, we must mimic you. But enough! Pray excuse my warmth."

"Did you never meet our American envoys?" asked Charlotte, hoping to turn the subject to something less distressing.

"Ah yes! That funny little man. Dr. Franklin. And the brilliant Mr. Jefferson as well. By this time I knew better than to take their ideas at the serious. And they were too astute to press them on us. How could we conceive of a land without a king at all? But Dr. Franklin, he is so charmingly rustic, with his beaver hat and outlandish manner. Quite a sensation. Can you credit that I kissed him once, oh, only for a greeting, as we do, and he, clever rascal, since we were standing a bit apart from the others, gave quite a squeeze to my <u>derriere</u>. The naughty man!"

At this moment Honey came into the room, followed by Sarah. Both started upon seeing Charlotte, but they dropped their curtsies quite correctly. These had become second nature to them by now, as Charlotte was gratified to observe.

"Good day, Mrs. Waverley and Madam Marie. May said you would have your hair fixed and be dressed this day, ma'am. But May is needed in the kitchen. Sarah will do for your hair, I hope? And I thought I'd best come and give you a little rub whilst she heats the curling iron."

"I am much obliged, my dear, that is, if Mrs. Waverley is agreeable." Upon a smile from Charlotte the lady stripped off her dressing gown and a gauzy shift made of fine cotton, not the sturdy linen most American women wore. Quite naked, she eased herself flat on her stomach across the bed whilst Honey climbed up to kneel beside her.

Meanwhile Sarah squatted by the embers of the morning fire and laid the tin holder with curling iron inside carefully in the smoking ashes. Charlotte watched with some surprise. Only Maudy had any skill in dressing hair. Had May and Sarah learned from her, or from Mme. de Coulanges herself?

Honey was spreading a yellow oil the length of the lady's back, plump and the color of walnut shells. No sign of bone or muscle, just soft flesh that Honey kneaded firmly with the heels of her hands.

"Ah," sighed Mme. de Coulanges when she could catch enough breath to speak, "how fortunate you are to have this young girl to soothe your aches."

"Good Gracious, madam! How can you think I have time for such things? I must be up at dawn to distribute supplies for the whole plantation and then there are the meals to plan with the cook, orders to be given for replenishing our stocks, then the spinning, weaving, laundering, ironing, butter churning and candle- making to supervise. Not to mention soap-making and house- cleaning. Then there are shirts and pants to be cut for the men servants, shortgowns and skirts for the women. Worst of all is the constant sewing, mending, and knitting of stockings. Every one of us must help with that, even Molly, whose baulking vexes me mightily. Yet we are never caught up. Oh, and I forgot about tending the kitchen garden and putting up preserves." How provoking to hear herself babbling on like this. Whining like a child. She must appear despicable in the eyes of this lady.

"I am quite exhausted just to hear you speak of all these burdens, madam. Yet you appear to have many slaves."

Charlotte winced at the word, but let it pass. "Lazy. Lazy. And surly, to boot. One or two can be relied upon. Joan, my head maid and nursemaid to the babies is quite trustworthy, though I must put up with her bad temper. And her daughter Maudy, who has attended to a few of your gowns, is excellent for fancy work like weaving and embroidery, but when told to help with ordinary mending and knitting, she becomes as sour as a green persimmon. A fruit of ours, madam. She gives herself airs since I sent her to be trained in fine needlework in Petersburg."

"Indeed, madam, you have much to annoy you."

"Oh, not as much as all that. I am a trifle out of sorts this morning.

We are most fortunate in our home quarter overseer, Amos. That I must concede. He is honest, and even more remarkable, has reasonable control over the others. But he gets sick! As do they all. And then we must nurse them. Amos is in a bad way at present with his rheumatism, which is why my husband cannot pamper his migraine, but must spend most of the day in the fields and barns. Oh, and right now all the Negro children must be wormed. Every spring and fall."

"Thank you, my dear," said the lady to Honey. "That has eased me exceedingly." She sat up and stretched nicely rounded arms above her head. "Oh! But my poor neck! Do but run your fingers along the back of it, here, before you help me dress. Pray continue, madam. Speak of your children. I have only one son left. My two girls were taken by the pox when still so small. You have, someone told me, a small boy who is not well, who must quite drain you with anxiety."

The old familiar hand, cold as spring water, clutched at Charlotte's stomach. She shivered and looked up to see, beyond the watchful eyes of Mme. de Coulanges, the sad ones of Honey, whose fingers had stopped their rhythmic pressing into the lady's neck. Charlotte was being pitied!

She stood up abruptly, squared her shoulders and shook out her skirts. "My son Edward is frail, yes. But so was his father as a boy. So they tell me. And now, apart from the headache, a paltry thing, never sick a day in his life! Not even the ague that everyone else suffers. Edward's is the same constitution. He will outgrow this weakness."

Mme. de Coulanges smiled politely. Not Honey. Though her fingers had resumed their movements up and down the Frenchwoman's neck, her expression still fairly dripped with sympathy for Charlotte. Damn the girl!

"Enough, Honey! You will leave bruises on Madam's neck. Leave off, and help her to dress."

With perfect humility Honey helped the lady into her shift, her stays—covered with satin, no less!--which Honey laced only loosely, and then into a simple but well-cut morning gown of muslin. Then the lady placed herself on the low chair in front of the dressing table, beckoning to Sarah. "Do it in a simple chignon in back, child, but leave this much hair free about my face." She held forefinger and thumb two inches apart.

"I mean to walk just a little this afternoon, to build my strength, you see. I am so hoping that I can join all your company for dinner one day soon."

The chignon completed, quite deftly, thought Charlotte, the lady took up her own silver hand glass, turned her back to the mirror on the dressing table, and surveyed Sarah's work with satisfaction. "Very nice, child. And now take the iron to make curls about my face. No, no, they must be more plump. And you must oil them first. Employ those little rats there on the table to puff them up. You are surprised, madam. You do not need such things, with that thick hair of yours. Yes, I can tell it is abundant even under your pretty little cap. With your fine figure and complexion like milk, what a sensation you would make at court! I confess that I am on thorns at the prospect of appearing in company by your side. Like a wretched little gray donkey next a blooded bay mare."

Ah, these French ladies of the Court were so skilled at flattery. It dripped from their lips as naturally as sap from a pine tree. Yet how could Charlotte help enjoying it? It was so much more pleasant than the everlasting disapproval of Mrs. Levier, the solemn earnestness of Kate, or the tiresome humility of Honey. But she must not neglect her own manners. "Nonsense, madam. You have suffered much injury in mind and body. But already you are gaining color. And these curls about the face become you exceedingly." In reality, Charlotte thought the stiff, oiled curls quite lacking in appeal.

"You are excessively kind, my dear." And before Charlotte knew it she was engulfed in an embrace in which were mingled the faint scent of lavender and a stronger odor of perspiration. Startled, she jumped up, knocking her head against that of the older woman who was bending over her. Each let out a yelp of pain and then fell into bellows of laughter as they came together in another embrace. When they finally recovered and settled themselves again on their chairs, the sight of Sarah holding the curling iron with a few thin strands of fawn-colored hair caught in it and her mouth agape in astonishment sent them both again into merry peals.

"<u>Ma foi</u>! I have done myself yet another injury," exclaimed Mme. de Coulanges, as she laid fingers gingerly on her forehead.

Truly, these French had a freedom, a warmth, unknown among the English and Americans.

"My dear Mrs. Waverley, I feel so deeply your kindness. Be assured that I shall not take advantage of it any longer than need be. I sent already a month ago to my husband in London and also to my son who serves under our minister to Vienna to apprise them of my circumstances here. M. le Marquis will without doubt find some way to send me money, on the condition that I remain in this country. The last thing he wishes is to see me appear in England to annoy him and his mistress. Or my son will send me something. I mean to set up a little school for young ladies of good family. I had thought to do so in Philadelphia with a French lady in similar condition. But they tell me that the epidemics of yellow fever are quite dreadful there, and the streets full of foul air from piles of filth along them. Is it not so? I think now of a smaller town. Charleston, perhaps."

"Be assured you are welcome to stay with us as long as you wish, madam. One who has been so kind to my brother when he was in your country . . ."

"Ah no, it is I who am in <u>his</u> debt at the present. When I was carried off the ship at Portsmouth and taken to an abominable inn where no lady would consent to descend, I was in despair. But what could I do? My fever was so high and my bile so black that the landlord threatened to send me to the pesthouse. He shouted and swore it was the yellow fever. But Captain Dupont, a fellow passenger, had sent immediately to Geoffrey, who fairly galloped to my rescue. It was only a pleurisy. So I was bled, and given vapor inhalations, and then in time brought here to throw myself upon your kind mercy."

Charlotte begged her to say no more. She and her brother were only too glad, et cetera, et cetera.

"I do hope to see Geoffrey's affairs put on a better footing soon," continued the lady. "His lawsuit. His marriage. Of course I would not be a welcome guest in his bride's establishment. A young American girl would not take kindly to the presence of a strange woman just as she learns to be a wife and mistress of a household."

She was speaking truth there. Charlotte did not think it worth mentioning that Kate looked to be a permanent member of Lucinda's household, the one truly in command, and she would certainly not welcome this lady's presence or approve of her at all.

"Pray tell me about this young lady Geoffrey pays court to. He says she is sweet-tempered and musical. And comes recently into a considerable property, no?"

"Indeed, all that is true. Perhaps I would have chosen someone more...forceful...if one is allowed to wish for that in a lady. Someone able to influence him to greater efforts."

"Yet perhaps through love? Do you think he truly loves her? Is she very, very pretty?"

Something in the lady's tone made Charlotte eye her closely, holding the other's gaze with the power of her own. "Tell me, madam. Do you think it well that Geoffrey be wedded?"

In the long moment of silence that followed, the other woman turned to face the glass on the dressing table, patting down one curl, fluffing up another, seemingly absorbed in surveying the effect of Sarah's efforts with the curling iron.

"But of course he must marry," said Mme. de Coulanges finally, with a not-quite-easy laugh. "It is high time, no? And this is a splendid match. But tell me, is there not a rival? Geoffrey spoke of a young man, brother to your husband, I believe, who is devoted to the lady, and has the advantage of youth and long years of proximity."

"Nonsense! Mere puppy love. Or rather, my husband's brother grew up with Kate, the older half-sister, as playmate and Lucinda as the little tag-along. His is brotherly affection, no more."

Charlotte could feel the penetrating look that the other turned upon her. Of course the lady would seize any chance for revenge. But what of that? Was it not clear that she held dear the interests of her brother and did not admit any obstacle to this advantageous marriage? If there were an obstacle, it was Geoffrey's own indolence. Could it be true that this Frenchwoman, who had surely been more to Geoffrey than a friend, was sincere in wishing his marriage? Thank God the woman's husband was still living. No real danger there.

"This younger brother of Mr. Waverley. He is not living here at present?"

"No, my brother-in-law is living in the overseer's cottage on a section of our estate, and serving in that capacity. Only momentarily, until he can establish himself on land he is soon to purchase."

"And this Mr. Miles Waverley, he is a strong, vigorous man. So Geoffrey says. Rather like the Irish. And quite unlike your husband who is more delicate. And perhaps rather phlegmatic, like the English." This was said softly, as though the woman were musing to herself.

But Charlotte heard it all quite distinctly. She clenched her teeth, grateful that she was not inclined to blush, and aware that she was closely observed. She searched for a reply that she would not regret.

"My husband is the finest man, in character and in appearance, that I've been privileged to know." She drew herself up to her most queenly posture, staring at the presumptuous Frenchwoman as she would at an impudent Negro or upstart farmer.

But Mme. de Coulanges was not easily cowed, and knew well how to recover from her error. "Ah, madam, you are magnificent!" She rose from her seat and turned to make a deep curtsy with a grace utterly unknown in these parts or probably anywhere but at the French court. "Forgive me, I pray. I am the naughty child of a corrupt old world. I have not yet learned the innocent ways of the new one."

"We are not so innocent as all that, madam. In Philadelphia, which my esteemed mother-in-law names a sink of vice, there is surely license aplenty, though nothing to rival the refinements you were privileged to witness at Versailles. Never to indulge in, of course," she laughed.

"But of course!" The lady's laugh was like the purr of a cat.

"But here in the country we are far too busy." She sighed and raised her hands to puff up the round crown of her cap, leaning sideways to catch sight of her head in the glass, now that Mme. de Coulanges had moved over to her wardrobe and was fastening a violet ribbon she had drawn from it into her fichu. "Our husbands are away half the year, at the least, leaving us alone to manage everything, or let everything go unmanaged. And when they are here, they are busy, preoccupied, weighed down still with public duties even here in the county, in addition to the cares of the estate. Of course many of them enjoy riding about, drinking their small beer, bragging about their horses, and exercising their power over their inferiors."

"You speak of gentlemen, men of property."

"Yes, I speak of them. My husband does not enjoy all that, but he is obliged to be gracious to all. When he has a moment free, he asks nothing better than to closet himself with a book. As for me, I have no moments free. Unless it be to submit to the appetite of this voracious babe."

Joan had entered the room with Charles in her thick, black arms. The baby was bawling angrily and stretched out tight fists toward his mother as soon as he caught sight of her.

"I swear, ma'am, I done looked for you all over the house, with this poor babe screaming so's I couldn't hardly think where you might be." Joan's tone was severe, her thick gray brows furrowed under her orange bandana. She continued to mumble under her breath even after Charlotte bared a breast and pressed the child's face into it.

"Ouch! For God's sake! This child's gums are as hard as teeth. He <u>bit</u> me in his rage. All right, Joan. Do be gone. I'll have Sarah take the babe back to you when he's milked me dry."

"You have a fine healthy boy there, madam," said Mme. de Coulanges.

"He's a monster. Soon big enough to be weaned. I'd planned to suckle him for the usual year, but I am sick to death of this. Look at that! The milk's leaked out of my other breast and stained my gown. I can't go visiting anywhere without dragging him along. Of course there is the risk of conceiving again and I am determined I am through with childbearing. I shall wait until Mr. Waverley leaves for the spring sessions before I wean the child, and in summer when he returns, well, our cousin Honey here, who is exceedingly knowing in folkways, assures me she knows an herb that will do the trick."

"Oh, it is not sure and certain, ma'am!" Honey's voice, coming out of the perfect silence she had maintained in her corner, startled both women. "Back home, when a woman starts to get poorly from too much birthing, she chews seeds of Queen Anne's Lace. I knowed two or three that never birthed again, but it don't always work."

"Doesn't, child. Doesn't."

"Yes, ma'am. Doesn't. So best keep right on suckling the babe as long as...as you don't mind it too much."

"I already mind it too much." How tiresome to explain things to those who had no comprehension. "I'll just have to take my chances. Picture me chewing on seeds the livelong day. May as well take up smoking a pipe, too. Become a true mountain woman."

The baby suddenly raised his head from his mother's breast, giving her a sharp knock on the jaw. "Wretch! You'll kill me yet. Here, Honey, take this fellow away. You go too, Sarah, and try if you can make Molly quiet down. I can hear her yelling for me somewhere in the house.

Get Charles away before she starts him crying again. Why am I cursed with such noisy progeny?" Even as she spoke, the image of quiet little Edward came to her mind. If only she could complain so of him.

Only a moment after Honey and Sarah descended the stairs with the baby, Molly burst into the room.

"Mama! I've been looking all over for you. Please, Mama, I can't abide sleeping with Aunt Abie one night longer! She's going to craze me for sure. She keeps waking me up in the middle of the night, and asking me who people are. Even Uncle Geoffrey and Honey and Sarah. You'd think the muddlehead would know by now. I've told her a thousand times. And she asks me when dinner is coming, when she's had it hours ago!"

"Do you know where you are, Margaret?" Charlotte had waited for her daughter to cease her chatter, and had now clothed her own words in ice, knowing this the best way to get the child's attention. After a long pause she continued. "Make your curtsy to Mme. de Coulanges and beg her pardon for your insufferable rudeness."

Molly did make her curtsy then, though not with the best of grace, and she did mutter something that passed for "Excuse me, ma'am."

Before Mme. de Coulanges could acknowledge the apology Charlotte spoke again. "Who gave you leave to trouble us here, in the chamber of our guest?"

"But Mama, it's <u>my</u> chamber!"

This was insupportable! Humiliating. In one swift move Charlotte sprang up and slapped her daughter across the cheek. Molly's eyes widened. A smudge of crimson suffused her cheek. No sound came from her lips, and she quickly blotted her brimming eyes with the ruffle on her sleeve.

Charlotte's anger, always quick to come and quick to go, turned to regret, especially when she noticed the lifted eyebrows of Mme. de Coulanges. She laid a hand gently on the child's slender neck, but Molly shrank from it. She withdrew it. "I asked you who gave you permission to intrude upon us here."

"Joan said you wanted me, Mama. I waited in your chamber but you never came. I called and called."

"Then you had only to sit and wait in patience. A trait you would do well to cultivate. But since you are here, I'll tell you what I wanted. By Mme. de Coulanges' leave, if she will give it."

That lady bowed, and then had the grace to turn her back and busy herself with a large powder-blue rosette of crepe bordered with cream-colored lace, which she had pulled from the top drawer of her wardrobe, and now pinned to the top of her coiffure.

"I've had disturbing reports of your conduct, Molly. You have hidden Honey's weaving cards, her primer, and other articles."

"Did she say so? What a tattletale. It's only joking, Mama."

"No, she is too sweet-natured to tell on you. But other eyes have remarked it. Why on earth do you plague her so, Molly? I've not known you to be malicious before this."

Molly's eyes were turned away, seeming to watch Mme. de Coulanges at her frippery. She remained silent.

"These are not simple childish pranks. I do not understand what has come over you, why you pick on this defenseless girl. And I have no time for it!" She was striving to remain calm, but the child's obstinate silence felt like slaps to her own face. "You've tried my patience too far this time!" She could hear her own voice rising in pitch. She clenched her hand to her thigh to keep from striking the child again. What must Mme. de Coulanges think of her, a mother unable to control her daughter, or her own temper?

"You will take your meals for the next fortnight with the babies in the nursery. And when your beloved father asks why he does not see you at table I will send for you to explain it to him yourself." (She felt the knife she wielded probing for the most sensitive spot to penetrate.) "As for your complaints about Aunt Abie's addled wits, it's only fitting you sleep with her since your own wits are not serving you well at present."

Molly kept her mouth shut and her eyes dry. But her steps, usually so light, were leaden as she left the room.

"Pardon me, Mrs. Waverley," said Mme. de Coulanges as she turned back toward her hostess. "Of course I would not presume to interfere. I see that your daughter is a girl of much spirit, and you are most wise to curb her. But somehow I find myself quite smitten with the child. Whenever it should meet with your approval, won't you give her leave to return to sleep here in her own chamber? I noticed the little bed under this one, which would fit readily over there by the window behind my trunk. She would cheer me, I assure you. As I have said, I do not care for solitude, especially in dark of night. I always had my maid sleep near me. Your daughter's presence, even asleep, would soothe me when I wake to the owl's hoot or the fox's bark."

"I'll be happy to oblige you, madam, when the fortnight of her punishment is over. Provided that Molly has not made me more trouble in the meantime. Now I'll leave you. Please feel free to walk out whenever you please and wherever you please. If you should wish for a drive, I'll have Nathan take you out in the dogcart."

This French lady promised to be rather more amusing than troublesome. She did not appear to be any threat to Geoffrey's chances of marriage with Lucinda. Age was against her. And clearly, she had never been a beauty, even in youth. But one couldn't be sure. These French courtiers had experience and secrets undreamed of by simple girls like Lucinda, or even by her own self who had never known the intrigues of court circles. It was best to be wary.

Chapter 12

The sun was already high in the sky and shimmering in the moist air after a night of rain when Geoffrey roused himself enough to recall that Miss Nelson had urged him to come early to dine with her and Lucinda that afternoon.

He stretched out at full length on the sun-warmed bed, then propped himself up against the pillows and surveyed the scene from the chamber window: beds of daffodils in bloom, laid out in patchwork squares, some golden-rich, others the color of cream, both set off by the vibrant green of their stalks. Beyond them an orchard bloomed in delicate pinks and whites. Yes, it was good to be alive in April, even in this wild country. Of course, one must be in a position to tame one's small part of it, as were his sister and her husband. It would be pleasant to possess such a plantation, where he could retreat from the debilitating heat of the Coast in summertime.

On this fine morning Geoffrey's heightened spirits promised him success in both his current endeavors. He would win his lawsuit to regain the tidewater lands his uncle had bequeathed him, and he would win the hand of Lucinda, which held within its gift not only Farrington Plantation and fifty Negroes to work it, but connection to the most powerful families of Virginia.

With the help of his man Pompey he dressed even more carefully than usual, choosing the fawn waistcoat and blue smallclothes that complemented the red of his hair. As Pompey smoothed over his shoulders the long blue cloak that would protect his garments from the splatters of the road, he lifted one stocking-clad leg after the other before the glass. Were his calves beginning to shrink ever so slightly? He'd always had such a good leg. He must make a point of riding out every day, now that his health was regained.

Suddenly he bethought himself that it would look well for him to arrive with a gift, perhaps a ham and a couple of bottles of port, which Pompey could carry in his saddlebags. He would go ask Charlotte himself; it was not a request to entrust to a servant, and there was no use seeking Matthew, who would be somewhere out in the fields at this hour. Once master of a plantation himself, he would most certainly hire a competent overseer, so as not to be riding about at all hours attending to wearisome affairs.

Finding his sister was not easy. He wandered from the house, where no one knew her whereabouts, to the kitchen garden, the root cellar, the icehouse, and the smokehouse, muddying his freshly shined boots and feeling an unpleasant sensation of moisture in his armpits. Finally he found Charlotte outside the dairy talking to a young servant who was standing with bent head, shaking shoulders, and hands dug in to her face. From the light color of the girl's skin and the grace of her neck and hands, he recognized the young quadroon whom he had noticed several times doing sewing in the drawing room. He remembered a pretty face, with pale green eyes and a delicate nose. On the other side of Charlotte stood another servant, a child who was lackadaisically moving the stick in a butter churn and listening in on the conversation of the other two. All three had their backs turned toward Geoffrey, so that he was able to come quite close before they noticed him.

"He'll find out, Missus. Sure as sure. Jed, he is my man since way long back when he come to prayer meeting here. Master says he'll get Col. Meachem to let us get married. But now he won't marry me when he find out. I know it for sure!" Here the shoulders that had stopped their shaking during this speech, began again more violently than before.

"Great God in Heaven!" exclaimed Charlotte. "How much more trouble must we bear from that whelp of the Colonel's?" She looked up to the sky as though truly asking Heaven for guidance, and in so doing caught sight of Geoffrey. She put up a hand to prevent him from approaching any closer, and spoke to the young Negro.

"There's no cause for all this fuss, Maudy. I'll fix things somehow, and if I can't, Mr. Waverley will. You were foolish to go see your man so near the boundary with the Meachem's land. Now go, and stay close to Great House. And you, Jillie," (this with a little slap across the child's head), "put your mind to that churn and keep it out of affairs that don't concern you."

As she walked toward him Geoffrey was shocked at his sister's appearance. She wore what looked like a homespun gown, had clumsy pattens under plain mules on her feet, and a simple mobcap on her head. From the latter sprang several limp strands of hair.

From the scowl on her face it was plain that she was not glad to see him. "So, Geoffrey, you are early abroad this forenoon. And you find me at work. Don't you know that in the country a discreet gentleman does not approach the lady of the house before the dinner hour? Particularly not out of doors. Well, what is it?"

She listened to his request, then strode so rapidly toward the house that he barely kept up with her. "No, don't you come in with those muddy boots," she cried as she removed her pattens at the back steps. She returned directly with the wine, which she thrust into the hands of Pompey, who was hovering close to his master, then made for the smokehouse at the same pace, her keys jingling in the basket hanging on her arm. As soon as Pompey, clutching a bottle in each hand, had a huge, redolent ham thrust under his arm, he was sent off to saddle the horses.

"You are truly a brick, sister dear," and he gave her his most charming smile and even a gingerly kiss, fearing to rub dirt from her gown onto his impeccable waistcoat. "But come, do tell me what that fetching little seamstress of yours was crying about."

She blew an exasperated puff of air from her lips. "It's not the first trouble we've had with that confounded Dick Meachem. He won't keep his hands off the Negro wenches. As long as they belong to the Meachems, I can have nothing to say. He and his father keep a regular harem of light-skinned ones for their use and that of their overseers and friends. It disgusts me of course. Once I overheard a fellow from Petersburg, come to do some carpentry for us, make the mistake of asking Matthew about that harem. Hopefully, you understand. Matthew turned quite livid and swore as I had never heard him do before."

Geoffrey couldn't help laughing. "Indeed, Matthew is the last person to ask for directions to such a place. He assuredly turned the fellow out."

"At any rate, you would think that Dick Meachem wouldn't bother our people. But it's not the first time. And now Maudy. That's the last straw. I raised that girl almost like a daughter. Why, I taught her to read and write, and to cut out and sew. And last year I sent her to a seamstress in Petersburg to learn fancy embroidery and weaving patterns. But the silly girl let herself be seduced by one of the Colonel's people, a mere field hand. A few of them sneak over here for prayer meetings (or such is their excuse) because the Colonel won't allow such things on his own place. Dick found her alone in the woods waiting for her man, and you can imagine the rest. What gall! He knows full well that she is a favorite of mine. Probably did it to spite me because I detest him and I don't try to conceal it."

"Ah, my dear," Geoffrey felt bound to tell her, "I'm sure he didn't need such a motive as that. The little wench is quite delectable."

She threw him a look like a sword thrust. "High time for you to be off, Geoffrey, and for me to see to the preparations for dinner. Our French lady has signified to me that she will join our company today. I'm determined she not think us ridiculously rustic. Pay my respects to Miss Nelson and Miss Lucinda, and advance your suit as best you can." Charlotte turned and left him abruptly.

Yes, of a certainty, he must marry Lucinda and play as best he could the role of American gentleman. Having bet on the prodigious might of England to put down the revolt of her colonies, and lost, he was left exposed to the resentment and even hatred of the victorious Americans. Could he hope for greater fortune than to marry into the Ludwell family? Besides, Lucinda was a sweet girl, and a pretty one to boot.

These thoughts meandered through Geoffrey's mind as he guided his horse at a slow walk toward Farrington. The image of Lucinda led him to that of Marie, whom he had seen only once, and briefly, since her arrival at Laurel Hill. At that one interview she had discouraged him from visiting her in her chamber, alleging that Mrs. Waverley had told her it was not proper. This was most unkind of Marie, after all he had done to care for her in her illness, and to bring her here to this comfortable refuge. Had her affection for him quite withered away?

———◦◦◦◦———

Mme. de Coulanges was at that moment preparing to descend into the dining room and take her dinner with the Waverley family at last. She had been much relieved by her recent conversation with the mistress of the estate, and had become familiar with the two young female cousins, but had been given only the time to curtsy to the master of all this property, had not been presented to the dowager his mother, nor met any other gentleman of the family. Ah, but she was forgetting the very silent and very awkward young man who had come with the wagon to fetch her from Petersburg. Nathan by name. Younger brother, or nephew, she could not recall.

A good thing it was that poor health had allowed her, without discourtesy, to keep to her chamber. Never had she so much looked the hag. But today she felt herself quite recovered. Indeed, her glass confirmed it. Now, with the help of the curling iron, the rouge pot, and her mauve lawn gown, she could assure herself that the figure she made would not disgrace her. A pity her first appearance was so early in the day. She could show very little shoulder and bosom. And these were her best features.

On first being led into the drawing room by Mrs. Waverley her attention was taken by the room itself, small compared to those she had frequented in France, and rather lacking in decoration. However, the furniture, vases, clock, and looking glass appeared of good quality, and the rug and draperies were fresh and bright.

She was guided to the chair of a broad-faced lady dressed all in black except for a capacious gray cap under which Marie perceived hard black eyes and a tightly set mouth. She was named Mrs. Levier, for although she was Mr. Waverley's mother, apparently she had married again. Marie curtsied deeply despite the pain this inflicted on her poor knees, and expressed herself honored. She paid no further compliment, for what use to waste effort on this lady who was clearly determined not to be pleased?

Next Mrs. Waverley turned around and indicated her husband who had evidently entered the room soon after them. Marie curtsied less deeply, but gave the gentleman her most beguiling smile, a smile that revealed only the tips of her best teeth. On his part he made an excellent leg for a colonial and said how glad he was to find her recovered and able to join the company at last. The man was tall and thin, with fine features set in a narrow face. His skin, burned brick red by the sun, stood out against his sand-colored hair. Except for the ruddy skin, he looked the finest type of English gentleman.

He indicated a richly brocaded Queen Anne chair for her, and drew up a matching one for himself. "I have closely followed events in your country, madam, and can well understand that you elected to seek refuge in the Islands. I am distressed that after the sea voyage, always uncomfortable and indeed dangerous, instead of a safe haven, you found yourself in the midst of a terrifying revolt. I believe you lost members of your family?"

Marie found herself quite taken with this American gentleman. She sensed in him a sympathy which both attracted and disturbed her. It was as though he might draw from a well within her water she did not care to have drawn. She shook herself back to his words, to which she must make some reply.

"It is true, sir. My poor brother and his wife were murdered in their beds! What is your English expression? I leaped from the fry pot into the flames. But then, sir, the loss of my brother was not the end of my woes. My serving woman, who was with me since childhood, took sick and died on the frightful passage from Santo Domingo to your shores." She was babbling on about private miseries when she had intended to impress these colonials with her lightheartedness and wit. And conquer them with flattery. An abysmal beginning, ma vieille, she told herself. She liked to address herself as old because she was convinced that she looked and behaved like a much younger woman.

"That is indeed distressing," he murmured, and looked as though he felt real distress. "Be assured that we will do whatever is within our power to give you comfort after all these losses. But allow me to present to you my stepfather, Mr. Patrick Levier, and my brother, Miles Waverley. I believe you are already acquainted with my nephew Nathan."

Two gentlemen had approached her chair and were bowing, while the young man who had driven her here stood in the background, clearly eager to escape. The older gentleman, rotund and balding, was peering at her with open curiosity, eyes sparkling and mouth spread in a wide smile. He kissed the hand she offered with too much enthusiasm. Aha! she thought, this one will be amusing to flirt with. The other gentleman, much younger, gave an impression of mass and physical strength. He said a courteous word or two and moved off, while the other, Mr. Levier, pulled up a chair and immediately launched into inquiries, not about her personal experience but about her country and its colony which she had left in such haste.

"Pray, madam, how long since you left France?"

"I embarked from Le Havre in September, sir. Why do you ask?"

"Why then, you were still there, though not in Paris, I trust, when the King and Queen were arrested at Vincennes?"

She nodded.

"What a shame! What a terrible shame they did not escape. I fear worse things for your country. Such drastic changes in the laws. Tradition thrown to the winds..."

"Excuse me, sir," Mr. Waverley broke in, "I am sure that Mme. de Coulanges does not care to speak of those public affairs. Such a subject is of no interest to ladies."

"Ah but no," cried Marie. "<u>Au contraire</u>, these affairs interest me very much. And Mr. Levier, I agree with you that all these changes are sheer madness. Indeed, our good king was quite amenable to reform, and some was being made. Although I scarcely saw the need. Once you open the gates of influence to those of low birth, who knows what evils will follow?"

Her words stirred the big man who had been introduced as Miles Waverley to step forward. "Pardon me, madam, but I follow the events in your country with great enthusiasm. They go to show that the common man cannot be crushed underfoot forever. Progress and enlightenment are inevitable even in the stultified societies of Europe and…"

Marie allowed the young man's stream of words to flow on while she surveyed his person with amusement. His clear indifference to her at the moment he was presented had been transformed into interest when she became part of this talk of her country's affairs.

"…and I do not perceive," Mr. Levier was saying as Marie's attention returned to the conversation, "how progress can come about without order, without maintaining the good in the old while gradually introducing the new, without wise and experienced men at the head of the state."

"Exactly," said Mr. Matthew Waverley. "You are exactly right about experienced men, sir. I beg you all to note well that the members of the Constituent Assembly, those who made all these fine new laws (and forgive me, madam, but I do believe these laws are excellent) have not only dissolved their Assembly, but decreed that in the forthcoming elections for a legislative body, none among themselves may stand for office. So new, untried heads will henceforth govern France."

Marie had noticed, not without satisfaction, that all the gentlemen, even the shy young nephew, were now gathered round her, while the ladies were left to themselves at the other end of the room. Mrs. Waverley and the old lady were casting glances of surprise and disapproval at her person. Ah well, so be it. She so enjoyed the attention of gentlemen and the excitement of controversy.

"I fear that you overlook, sir," she said, "the perfidy of the new constitution itself. For who is it who will elect these men without experience? Every man, no matter how lowly, has been given the vote. Journeymen, servants, peasants with no education, no breeding, only so long as they can pay three days' wages. I do not think that you have gone so far in this country."

"Indeed," confirmed Mr. Levier, "we do require that a man have property before he may vote. Landed property, that is."

"Ah," Marie laughed, for she had the good breeding never to become heated in a dispute, "so you see, you hotheaded Americans have exported these dangerous republican ideas to us, yet you are more cautious here in your own land."

At this moment Mrs. Waverley approached to announce that the meal was served. Portly little Mr. Levier jumped up to offer Marie his arm, and she was conducted into an ample dining room festooned with green silk draperies. The walls in this room were papered with hunting scenes in natural greens and browns, and the carpet underfoot was woven in brown and gold rosettes. The chairs were of the modern type inspired by Mr. Chippendale.

Except for size, and the lack of impressive picture frames, the room did not compare unfavorably with her dining room at home. She was seated next her hostess, at the head of the table, with Mr. Levier on her right. To her surprise, the table was already heavily laden with dishes of food of every sort. A soup tureen sat in front of Mrs. Waverley, a joint of what was probably mutton was found at the foot of the table before Mr. Waverley, and there were serving dishes of fish, fowl, vegetables, sauces, jellies, and pickles laid out to cover every available space. Mrs. Waverley ladled the soup into bowls that she passed to each person. Marie found it to be a delicately flavored mulligatawny. Then two Negro servants who looked to be no more than children took away the soup bowls and Mr. Waverley proceeded to carve the joint and pass plates of meat to everyone.

From then onward there was a busy movement of serving dishes up and down and across the table as each gentleman served himself and the lady next to him of whatever was desired. Such busyness at table Marie had never seen. She did recall having heard that the English dined in some quite uncouth fashion, and now she witnessed it. How much more elegantly it was done at home, having the meat carved on the sideboard by servants and then having them bring round the dishes and offer them to each person in turn. She had heard this present procedure described as dining a la russe. Had those barbarian Russians actually invented it? Quite impossible!

As soon as the scramble of dishes around the table had subsided, Mr. Levier began to recount his adventures in France.

"I determined to visit Europe for the first time soon after the end of the hostilities, or rather, after the Treaty of Paris was signed. For you will remember, dear madam, that the fighting ceased in our country two years before the Treaty brought formal peace. I thought it best to hasten abroad while I was still young enough to brave the horrors of the passage. I say 'young' although in truth I was already an old man of more than forty years. But could I live my whole life without seeing the wonders of Europe? I spent a few months in London, and a few weeks in Vienna, but they were nothing compared to Paris! Ah, the theaters, the cafes, the boulevards, the shops, the concerts, the galleries. I went quite mad with excitement. How I envy you, madam. You breathed this heady air all your life."

So the old fellow was a man of some cultivation and experience. And not so old, after all. Only a few years her senior. The lady to whom he was married, who sat opposite Marie on their hostess's left, was surely older than he. What had induced him to marry her? Had he been a nobody, who felt himself honored to ally himself with this family which appeared well-enough off, but was surely not of the first influence or fortune? She glanced sideways at his round face, which was becoming pink and moist in the warm room as he partook generously of food and ale.

"Do tell us about Paris, madam," Mrs. Waverley was saying. "Mr. Levier cannot resist raving about its distractions, especially when he becomes quite bored during his wintertime stay with us. He can scarcely wait to leave us in the spring, as he is now about to do, but of course he finds nothing in Richmond or Williamsburg to compare with Paris."

"Indeed, madam, one never risks boredom in Paris, but rather, exhaustion. You cannot imagine how people bustle about there, always in a hurry to get from a visit to a dinner party to a performance at the Opera."

"The Opera!" exclaimed Mr. Waverley from the end of the table. Other conversations stopped and all eyes turned toward Marie. "How I would like to hear a performance of 'Orfeo,' or perhaps Mr. Mozart's 'Marriage of Figaro.' Or at least attend a concert where his works and those of Mr. Haydn are played. I dreamed of continuing my studies in London in my younger years, but the war dashed all such hopes."

"Mr. Levier, please pass Madame's plate down to my husband for more mutton, and then help her to peas and some of cook's excellent mustard sauce."

But Marie did not allow him to take her plate or add anything to it. She knew she should force herself to eat more, and indeed, the victuals were surprisingly well prepared. The meat and poultry and fish, in particular, were well dressed. The vegetables were overcooked, but that was the only fault she could find.

"Thank you, madam," she said, "and you, sir, but I will attempt to do better justice to the next course. I'm afraid that my appetite is still impaired."

The serving dishes were removed and replaced by a different array for the second course, this time with a haunch of venison at the foot of the table and a fine-looking pheasant at the head.

Marie was now given time to begin on the meats, and a delightful blancmange and syllabub which were heaped in little hills and pyramids upon her plate, while Mr. Levier, at the behest of his daughter-in-law, described Paris to the two young girls at the foot of the table.

"There are thousands upon thousands of people, my dears, who live in stone houses of three and four stories, all attached to each other with no space in between. Offices and shops are found on the street level, then people of means live on the next two floors, with servants and poor people at the top. The streets are full of people and carriages, and are even lighted at night. You cannot imagine how convenient it is to go wherever you wish and see whomever you like."

"But my papa says cities are full of a terrible din day and night, and the smell is unbearable from the refuse in the streets," piped up Molly. "My papa has been to Philadelphia, and Grandmama comes from there. It's dark, too, because the tall buildings block out the sun."

Marie had been surprised to see Molly and Sarah sit down to table with the grown persons. She was used to seeing children appear before dinner, to be kissed and admired by the guests, and then reappear at dessert time to be given a few sweetmeats. But Americans seemed to dote excessively on their children.

"Oh, but ours is an age of progress, my dear child," said Mr. Levier, "and Frenchmen have gone farther along that road than we. For one thing, they have cut broad avenues through the dark districts, letting in the sunlight. For another, they pump water from the Seine up to the top of a great hill and send it through canals all through the city. Thus, water is readily at hand to clean the streets and put out fires when need be. It is all quite, quite remarkable, I assure you."

The mouths of the two young girls were agape upon hearing such wonders, and the rest of the company appeared to be duly impressed.

"But madam," cried Mr. Levier, "I see you have put down your fork. If you will not accept more of this delectable syllabub, may I ask you to tell us something of the enthusiasm for learning in the great city of Paris?"

"Certainly, sir. As you know, our <u>philosophes</u> have gained the admiration of the world for their studies in natural philosophy. All our cultivated people, even those of the bourgeoisie, are quite passionate about the new discoveries. Indeed, there are ladies who go quite beyond the bounds of good taste. They fill their apartments with burners and test tubes and scales and models of the universe. When one visits them one is forced to follow at their heels admiring every object and gasping at the success of their experiments. Such excess never appealed to me, I assure you, but it pleased me to attend the lectures of M. Lavoisier and M. de Buffon, and so many others. For I believe I may say, without undue pride, that France surpasses all nations, even England, in the natural sciences. Is that not true? But even more, I delighted in visiting the botanical and animal and mineral collections of M. Calonne and those of the Duke de Montmorency. And of course none compares to the King's Garden. One is quite dazzled."

"And then, madam," said Mrs. Waverley with a wave of the hand which brought the servants to clear away dishes and cloth from the table, and with a laugh that held a hint of disdain, "after you had drunk deep of all that knowledge, how did you pass your evenings?"

"There is always a ball to attend, an elegant private one, which I preferred, but many enjoy the one, every Sunday, at the Opera. It commences at eleven hours with a concert and then such a mob of persons, from the princes to quite ordinary persons, dance until dawn. They tell me that the principal charm there is the mask. One is so free to flirt, and to gossip, when one is incognito, you know."

Mr. Levier laughed quite immoderately at this, and owned that he had attended the opera balls quite assiduously while in Paris. "A capital way to learn the ins and outs of Parisian society, don't you know." He aimed multiple winks at the gentlemen and at Marie herself, even extending a plump hand to pat her on the wrist. Marie could see that his many refills of wine were taking effect, and was amused by this. She had been told that Americans were exceedingly heavy drinkers.

But Mr. Waverley appeared the very opposite of amused. "My dear," (this to his wife) "do not you think the ladies would like to make themselves more at ease in the drawing room?"

Mrs. Waverley rose, as did all the ladies, and Marie perceived that she must, however reluctantly, quit the company of the gentlemen.

Back in the drawing room Mrs. Waverley offered Marie a comfortable chair by a low table on which were laid out several books and portfolios. She asked her guest if she cared to peruse a set of prints of ladies' fashions, or perhaps read a few pages of a book brought as a gift by Mr. Levier. It was called <u>Les Liaisons dangereuses</u> and was quite shocking, but delightfully entertaining. Marie forbore to mention that she had read the book twice over. Mrs. Waverley took no work to hand and did not appear disposed to converse. She soon excused herself, "to attend to a household trifle," and Marie was glad to be left to her own thoughts, which were swarming about in her head, just as the overabundance of victuals she had swallowed were swarming uncomfortably in her stomach. She who had suffered so recently from indigestion, why had she not shown more restraint?

The thought that rode on the crest of all the others, the one she could not submerge, was that of Geoffrey's absence. Mrs. Waverley had told her he had been invited to dine with Miss Nelson and Miss Ludwell on the adjoining estate. She imagined him seated in a drawing room or at a dining table, his handsome face alight with pleasure as his eyes reposed on beautiful Lucinda Ludwell. Every time Marie attempted to picture her, and this was often, that young lady became more resplendently beautiful. Mrs. Waverley had described her as "pretty, in a quiet, unremarkable way." Even Geoffrey had spoken of her as "pretty enough, I suppose," but then Geoffrey had good reason not to extol his hoped-for bride to Marie.

He had been so good to her when he came to find her sick and helpless in Portsmouth. Much of the affection she had felt for him years ago had returned, but the taste of it was bitter because she knew herself so faded in looks, and so dependent on his kindness. In France it had been she who was kind to him, an unseasoned youth venturing away from England for the first time and overawed by the wit and elegance of the best French society.

Resumption of their former relations was out of the question. She was too ill and too ugly. But they talked in great confidence and when she learned of Geoffrey's half-hearted courtship of this young lady of good family, and particularly of the sudden change in her fortunes which had made of her a true heiress, eh bien, what could Marie do but conjure him to do everything conducive to winning the lady's hand? Her own presence need not be an obstacle--they were related by marriage, after all. But it would be well that he show indifference to her, Marie, and keep his distance, for fear of bruising the sensibilities of the young Lucinda, though she would doubtless be too innocent to suspect anything.

But Geoffrey had obeyed her behest too well! He had come once only to her chamber, to pay his respects, and that while Honey and Sarah were present. Since then she had seen nothing of him.

Mrs. Waverley came back into the room, followed by a black servant called Joe. She beckoned him to help her close the shutters as a gust of wind sent them clattering and several loose prints were sent fluttering off the table in front of Marie.

"Ah, madam!" Marie could not help protesting, "The breeze was so refreshing. Must it be shut out?"

"Against the rain, which has already begun, madam. Joe, fetch a fan and give Mme. de Coulanges some air." Mrs. Waverley took up the French novel and settled herself comfortably with her feet resting on a blue velvet footstool.

The small current of air from the fan only irritated Marie, so she waved the servant away. How content they all looked, even the children who had brought their game nearer the lighted tables and argued and giggled near the chair where Honey sat mending a pair of gloves. Every so often Molly would bump hard against Honey's legs, most certainly disturbing the older girl's painstaking handiwork. Marie recalled the scolding Mrs. Waverley had given Molly about pestering her cousin. Honey, however, gave no sign of annoyance. All the ladies, their faces softened in the beam of the candles, looked perfectly serene. Why should they not be? They were safe in their place, their undisputed place in the world, while she, Marie, where was her place? Not here with these strangers, these colonials. Not with Geoffrey, either, for he would soon have his own wife and estate. Marie noticed that Honey, against whose leg Molly had given an extra hard nudge, was moving her chair farther from the table and the light. As she reseated herself she glanced up and caught Marie's eye. A look of understanding passed between them, and was gone.

Chapter 13

The annual Waverley barbecue was planned for April 12. A simple but abundant meal would be served on trestle tables on the lawn: beef, chicken, potatoes roasted in their skins, apples baked in brandy, syllabub for dessert, and plenty of red wine and shrub, with rum or without. Everyone who could make the journey to and from Laurel Hill in one day was invited since Charlotte had no wish to fill her already-crowded chambers with overnight guests.

Those coming would include Miss Nelson and Lucinda Ludwell, Colonel and Mrs. Meachem, Sophie Meachem, Bessie and Ruth Clancy, Mr. Crawford and his three sons, Mrs. and Miss Cracklethorpe, and the Reverend Mr. Higgens (without his wife, who had just been brought to bed with her eighth child). Much to Charlotte's chagrin, Dick Meachem was also invited. Matthew, not wishing to provoke a scandal, had summoned the fellow as soon as he heard of the attack on Maudy. He had ordered him, in Charlotte's presence, never again to approach any of the Laurel Hill servants for any reason, not even the field hands. The rascal had blustered, had sneered, had claimed that the girl asked for it. But this had only provoked Matthew to threaten to take up the affair with the Colonel, who respected his judgment in most matters and might indeed finally carry out his own oft-repeated threat to disown his son and will the estate to a favorite nephew. As the whole county knew, Dick Meachem hadn't the heart of a rabbit. He had ended by begging Charlotte's pardon, almost abjectly. Thus the affair was settled.

Charlotte would have been glad to omit the barbecue this year. With her new baby, her husband's two cousins, Geoffrey and his Mme. de Coulanges, Nathan, and Aunt Abie (who was growing more dotty by the day), she had quite enough people to attend to. But Matthew insisted that it was an obligation. Generous hospitality was expected of one who considered himself a gentleman, particularly of one who had the honor of being a member of the House of Delegates. What would their neighbors think if the Waverleys failed to receive them at least twice in the year? It would quickly be bruited about that the family was sadly diminished in means or in manners.

When reminded of this, Charlotte was obliged to agree with her husband. And in spite of the burdensome preparations required, she always found diversion in observing her guests, particularly the young people when it came time for dancing in the drawing room. Perhaps a match would be made, or at least a courtship begun. Mayhap between a Clancy girl and a Crawford boy? Indeed, there was now Honey to think of. It was time to try the effects of her education already well commenced. She was minding her speech and her manners with some earnestness. But now she must learn to act lively with the young men.

Charlotte could scarce imagine such a transformation in the timid little mouse, but an effort must be made.

The day had dawned propitious: mild sunshine gleaming through a light haze. From their benches (for the young) and their chairs (for those whose backs needed support) the guests had a view of yellow daffodils and white-blossomed apple trees on their right, and on their left, of Matthew's "wilderness," a gentle slope of laurel and rhododendron, rocks and wildflowers, carefully planted to look as though it hadn't been planted at all. At the bottom of the lawn flowed the Solway, swollen and swift due to recent rains.

Yes, Laurel Hill was at its best. Charlotte took a moment now and then to congratulate herself as she walked from lawn to kitchen to house and back again, giving orders to servants, smiles to guests, frowns to Molly and Sarah, as they displeased her by commission or omission. Dick Meachem was drinking too freely as usual and casting surly looks at anyone who failed, despite their efforts, to avoid his proximity. But Matthew could be counted upon to control him.

Thank the Lord that Nathan's mother, Crazy Mary (a name that Charlotte never allowed spoken in her presence), had been taken away to spend the summer with her sister's family in the healthier climate of the region surrounding Charlottesville. That burden was lifted from her shoulders every spring. She always remarked a change in Nathan when his mother was removed. He did not turn cheerful, but something of the melancholy stiffness of his winter demeanor diminished.

He was eighteen now. More than time for him, too, to gain a modicum of manner with young persons of the opposite sex. What a shame that he was too young for Susan Cracklethorpe, a girl with neither looks nor sense, but with a tidy dowry of thirty slaves and considerable livestock. She was the right age for Miles, on the other hand, but when she, Charlotte, had mentioned the young lady's name to him that morning as one of those to be of the party, he had appeared to have no notion of who she was. Only one lady's name signified anything to him. This thought so annoyed Charlotte that she turned her eyes spitefully upon that object of her brother-in-law's foolish devotion.

The group of three sat a little apart, near the edge of the orchard. Kate Nelson, in a gown of dull brown, and Geoffrey, fashionably turned out in navy coat and breeches, provided a dark frame for Lucinda, all in white like a larger, more resplendent apple blossom. The breeze off the river, which was gradually waxing stronger, had blown several strands of her dark hair loose from her cap, and she kept making futile attempts to secure them. Her eyes never left Geoffrey, whether he sat and spoke to her and Kate--he alone doing the talking--or went off to fetch some trifle of food or drink for them.

Miles and Nathan were stationed at the stables to oversee the reception of their guests' horses and vehicles. Meanwhile Matthew was strolling back and forth near the dock to welcome any further visitors who might arrive by water, and Mrs. Levier sat with Aunt Abie in the drawing room where they would entertain any lady who did not care to brave the uneven footing of the lawn. Little by little that lawn, with its pale green sprigs of spring grass, became a patchwork quilt of moving colors as ladies, gentlemen, children (Molly, Sarah, Edward, the Meachem's Rebecca, the youngest Crawford boy), dogs, and servants strode, strolled, darted, or ran this way and that.

To Charlotte's immense satisfaction, Geoffrey was playing exceedingly well the part of assiduous suitor; indeed, he had been doing so from the day he recovered (quickly) from the malady he had complained of at his arrival. He paid a daily visit to Farrington where he often stayed through dinner and even supper. And now there he was, his red-brown curls falling prettily over his forehead (as white as any woman's), his soft brown eyes gazing tenderly at his beloved. But he was not forgetting, because Geoffrey possessed impeccable manners, to pay respectful attention to her elder sister as well.

Why was Kate sticking so close to the courting couple, as close as a cup to its saucer? Her gaze, persistent, observant, fixed itself as constantly on Geoffrey as did Lucinda's. You'd think she would leave them alone, thus favoring a declaration on his part. Perhaps she hoped he would declare himself in her presence, thus creating a witness to his commitment.

"Here, my dearest, here is a plate for you with just those dishes you most enjoy." Matthew stood smiling before her, blocking her view of the threesome by the orchard. "Sit here and eat while you can," he urged. "Soon enough someone will call you to nurse the baby or mix the syllabub. You've run about enough."

"Sit with me a moment," she cried, as he turned to go see to others' comforts. He did sit down next to her on the otherwise empty bench. "Oh, I am perfectly well," she replied to his glance of solicitude.

On the other side of the table Mme. de Coulanges was seated next to Reverend Higgens. The lady's looks were much improved with the artful aid of powder and paint. Though her stature was low and her face round, her lively dark eyes, mobile mouth, and graceful gestures made one find her attractive. Mr. Higgens, always bent on improving himself, was pestering the lady with questions. He wished to know the "best French-English dictionary, the best edition of Montesquieu." Should he purchase all thirty-six volumes of l'Histoire naturelle?

Charlotte would have to find a way to rid the lady of the tiresome Rector. But first she had something to say to her husband. "I am thoroughly vexed with your brother and your nephew. We are entertaining half the county, and they are skulking in the stables, pretending to be needed to greet our guests, though all are surely arrived. Here we have the Clancy sisters, Susan Cracklethorpe, and Honey, too. Four unmarried girls. (I say nothing of Lucinda and Kate, the former altogether smitten with Geoffrey and the latter quite resigned to spinsterhood.) Now who will keep these girls company? I must confess I am miffed that Will Cracklethorpe has not deigned to honor us. But you say that Susan's brother is too busy garnering votes at the other end of the county. So all we have at the moment to entertain our young ladies are the two older Crawford boys: Lazy Ned and Pimply Jake."

"You are too harsh, my dear. I see signs of correction in Ned. Indeed, I am arranging an apprenticeship for him with the new blacksmith in Simmons Corners. As for Jake, do not you see that he will be almost as handsome a fellow as Geoffrey when he has a few more years on him."

"Very well. For the moment we'll assign Ned to Miss Cracklethorpe. Though he can talk of nothing but horseflesh and she of nothing but hair and gowns."

"They will suit each other to a T. Two single-minded persons."

She had to laugh at that, but would not be diverted from her object. "Well enough. I appoint you to pry Ned away from Col. Meachem who is doubtless bragging on his splendid stallion, and bring him, Ned I mean, over to Miss Cracklethorpe who is looking exceedingly peevish, caught as she is between her mother and Mr. Levier, the charm of whose conversation cannot possibly appeal to her."

"Very good, my dear. I'll propose to the two young people a little walk to admire the new wheel on the mill. But I hope you aren't playing matchmaker. Mrs. Cracklethorpe would never consent to her daughter marrying a Crawford. However improved in character, poor Ned inherits only a run-down farm. An excessively mortgaged one at that."

"Fear not, Matthew. My duties end with keeping our guests diverted. Marriage is their own affair. Besides, if I did choose to interest myself in someone's marriage, it would be on behalf of your brother. I beseech you, once you bring Ned and Susan Cracklethorpe together, go find Miles and Nathan and drag them here by their stocks if you must. I hope to prevail upon Miles to pay Miss Susan some attention too. She will be delighted at having <u>two</u> gentlemen next her skirts, and you know, she would be a fine catch for Miles."

He gave her a reproachful smile, and set off to do her bidding. Such a compliant creature, when he chose. When he did not, so irritating in his lofty disapproval. Well, now she must do something for the Clancy girls who were lingering languorously over what was probably their third helping of barbecued beef and chicken, grateful, surely, for this unwonted abundance of victuals. She must rescue them from the perils of dyspepsia. They were not ill-looking girls. Only silent and gauche in company. At present it would be awkward to disengage the later-to-be-handsome Jake from Sophie Meachem, who was practicing her charms on him despite the presence of her husband. As for the latter, he was fondly embracing a bottle of claret and appeared as content as ever the sullen fellow could be.

Once all were settled in the drawing room--and that should be soon for the wind was growing stronger and more chill--she would make Jake and Miles and Nathan dance with the Clancy girls. And with Honey, too. Lucinda had been giving her instruction, and this would be the first occasion to make her dance in company.

She surveyed once more her company, all of whom (now that Susan Cracklethorpe had been provided a swain) appeared content. Or was there an exception? Mr. Levier had seated himself at the side of Mme. de Coulanges and drawn her attention to himself, thus relieving her of the Reverend's incessant questions. Poor Mr. Higgens could not hear what the other two were saying, so low were their voices as they chatted together, eyeing one guest after another and clearly making each the subject of their raillery. This was no doubt uncivil on their part, but the pedantic Rector almost invited such treatment. However, what had caught Charlotte's attention was the way Madame Marie's face kept turning toward the spot where Lucinda glowed in the loving looks and soft words of her suitor. The misery in the older woman's eyes belied the smile on her lips.

Charlotte was pleased with the appearance of her drawing room.

The new French chandelier, all its fifteen candles alight, shone brilliantly upon the crimson curtains and gave to the whole room a rich, warm glow. The carpet had been removed and all the tables and chairs pulled back to line the walls on which the candles in the tin wall sconces had also been lit. The two chased-silver candelabras sat glowing on the mahogany pianoforte where Lucinda sat playing a stately allemande. The instrument was in fine tune and the guests had been well fed. They now sat sipping cordials or tea or coffee, gossiping, laughing, flirting, as their inclination led them. Some of the older guests, Colonel and Mrs. Meachem, Mrs. Levier, and the Reverend Higgens (he not old, but too dignified for dancing) could be seen in the dining room playing whist while Aunt Abie looked on with a face sadly empty of expression.

Matthew had succeeded in corralling Miles and Nathan. They stood at the end of the room farthest from the piano. This was to be expected of Miles because on the piano leaned Geoffrey in all his grace of limb and dress, beaming upon Lucinda and turning the pages of her music as needed. Was he truly attached to the girl? He did not confide in his sister. Did he in the Frenchwoman who had surely been his mistress and who now watched him with a regard that was unfathomable even to Charlotte's practiced eye? They were apparently never alone together. Indeed, this was made almost too apparent.

No one danced as yet. People were always shy at getting started. The allemande was, in any case, too complicated a dance for most of the company this afternoon. Well, Charlotte would have Lucinda play a country dance, and if necessary stand up herself with Mr. Levier, whose round figure was surprisingly graceful at the dance.

As soon as Lucinda finished the allemande and began to shuffle through the sheets of music, Charlotte moved swiftly to her side and picked out a reel for her. Then she looped her arm through Geoffrey's.

"My dear brother, you must not <u>completely</u> neglect all the other young ladies. I'm sure Lucinda will excuse you, won't you, dear?" Without waiting for an answer she led him into the center of the room.

"Now ask our little Honey to dance, while I put the prod to those two oafs, Miles and Nathan."

He went off as asked, and she approached the oafs. Nathan shot her a look of anger, but did as he was bid, bowing awkwardly before the older of the Clancy girls. Miles acquiesced to her request with a shrug and approached the other Miss Clancy with an affable smile. They would make six couples (all the drawing room could comfortably contain), for Ned Crawford had stood up with Miss Cracklethorpe, and Mr. Levier, before she could invite him to be her own partner, had bowed before Kate. So much the better. She was free to check on the comfort of those in the dining room. She gave Lucinda a signal to begin, and the couples lined up with smiles (whether felt or assumed) on their faces and were soon skipping up to each other and back.

Then she noticed that Geoffrey was still standing before Honey, who was also standing, but with a stricken look on her face. What on earth could be the matter?

Honey was still wearing the black gown, taken in and shortened, that had been part of Mrs. Levier's mourning clothes. The ignorant girl had not even heard of wearing mourning when she had arrived, so far back in the wilderness had she lived, but once she learned of it, and was encouraged in it by Mrs. Levier as the proper way to honor her father (though from all Charlotte knew of him the fellow was no better than a rascal), Honey had insisted on wearing this dress for the full six months. Charlotte had at least prevailed on her to soften the worn and tarnished black with a white fichu at her neck, but of course with her sallow coloring the girl should never wear either black or white.

However, Honey's complexion was much improved at the moment due to the flush spreading across her cheeks as Charlotte approached.

"Oh, I assure you, Miss Caroline," Geoffrey was saying, calling her by her true name, "no one will take it amiss if you consent to a dance or two. Why only just now Mrs. Waverley gave me leave to ask you. But I do understand the delicacy of your feelings. Shall we await the next dance? I will ask Miss Lucinda to play a slow and dignified one."

Ah, what a blessing was an English education! Still further polished by a sojourn at the court of Louis the Sixteenth.

"What is this about delicacy of feelings, Miss? You have done quite enough honor to your father. It is high time you quit your mourning and behave as becomes a young girl of eighteen years. The six months since your father's death are all but over, are they not, and there may not be occasion for you to dance again for many a week. You must put in practice the lessons Miss Lucinda has given you."

"Please, ma'am." What a foolish, pleading look the little mouse was giving her!

"Well, speak up. I can't hear you above the music."

"I've not been able to go but once to Miss Lucinda. There's been so much nursing to be done. And then the weaving and knitting and hemming. Mrs. Levier says..."

"Mrs. Levier means well, but she has been something unwise in encouraging you to all that work." And I, she thought to herself but would not say, have been too willing to allow it, for convenience's sake. Had she not been pleased with the fine coverlet the girl had woven for the baby, and with the silk and wool workbag made for Charlotte herself?

"This must stop," she said. "Maudy will henceforth be charged with any fancywork required. We will train a servant to aid with the nursing, so that you may be concerned with only cases of some gravity. Your principal affair from this moment, miss, must be the arts of a lady: writing, figuring, dancing, and drawing. At fancywork you are already more than adept, and besides, Maudy is jealous at your taking so much of it upon yourself. A dancing master is expected to arrive any day now, and I require that you attend his every lesson."

"Oh please, ma'am! I'm not allowed...it's not permitted...to dance, ma'am."

"What on earth! Who in God's name does not permit you?"

"The Lord, ma'am. It's a sin!" Tears were welling in the silly girl's eyes, but Charlotte ignored them. Her breath came out in a great puff of exasperation.

"This is too much!" she cried, very loudly, so of course the heads of those sitting nearby turned to their little group.

"My dear." Matthew was there in a trice, at her elbow, so she unleashed the force of her frustration at him.

"This is what comes of allowing those New Lights to preach their ridiculous doctrines to our ne'er-do-wells, our servants, and our young people! And you permit this impressionable child to attend their wild meetings! They've encouraged her to set herself against such an innocent pastime as...yes, miss," turning back to Honey, "perfectly innocent, and perfectly essential if we're ever to marry you!"

"My dear Charlotte, do please listen to me." Matthew had taken a hard grip on her elbow, almost hard enough to hurt her. "This is not the place to speak so. Not in front of our guests. Pray, pray, compose yourself. And here, Honey, take my arm. Yes," he said to the girl with great mildness, "all will be well. You and Mrs. Waverley and I will go out into the foyer where we may speak of this quietly."

While Matthew spoke, Sophie Meachem had come up to Geoffrey and slipped her shapely little hand around his wrist.

"Won't you join me in the dance, Mr. Burnham," Charlotte heard her say as she herself was being led toward the archway by the iron grip of her husband. Insolent baggage! One day she would take a step too far.

Once in the foyer, Matthew motioned the two of them onto the settee beneath the tall clock. He remained standing. Charlotte clamped her lips together in an effort to bring under control her raging indignation, against Honey, of course, against Sophie, but most of all against Matthew who had humiliated her by shushing her before everyone. How she hated him at these rare times when he asserted his authority over her.

"My dear child," Matthew was saying to Honey, "we respect the religious teachings you have received, but sometimes it is necessary to adjust one's behavior to the customs of those around us. You have heard the saying: 'When in Rome, do as the Romans do'? No, perhaps not. But you seize the sense of it."

"Oh, sir, I know you are good, so good to me, and Madam too. But I have vowed to follow the commandments of the Lord. I was sinful, before, but the Lord has shown me mercy. How can I fall back into the jaws of Satan?"

"Child, child," Matthew murmured, "you are making much of small, childish weaknesses from the past."

"Oh no, sir! I was truly bad. Headed straight for hellfire!"

"For goodness sake, what nonsense! Who told you so?" Charlotte couldn't help breaking in, feeling Matthew's frown even without looking at him.

"The preacher, ma'am. When Granny Harriet first took me to bide with her, she said I looked so low in spirits, she sent me to worship and to prayer meeting when next the preacher came to a place I could walk to (since she had to have her mule close by for any call). Anyways, the preacher told me what a sinner I was for running away from my papa and taking Sarah with me. And he didn't even know the worst of my sins." Here Honey's voice went so low that Charlotte barely caught her last words.

"It does seem as though this preacher did you little good, Honey," sighed Matthew as he pulled up a chair from the other side of the foyer and sat down, leaning close to her. "I am sure you have led a good, Christian life ever since. And I wonder if such a little thing as dancing, quite restrained dancing under the eyes of all of us, can interfere with that?"

The girl's silence gave Charlotte an opening. "Yes, and didn't you yourself propose that Sarah sing for us at Christmas, and haven't we heard her sing many evenings since then? From what I hear, singing and dancing both are condemned by your Methodists and other New Lights."

A frown creased Honey's brow. "Yes, ma'am. Sarah hasn't yet found the Lord. But she is such a good girl! Pure and white as Christ's robes."

"My dear girl," said Matthew, "perhaps we'll speak more about all this at a later time. Meanwhile you will not be obliged to do what you think wrong. Perhaps you will like to join Molly and Sarah at their games in the bookroom."

"Oh thank you, sir." Of course the foolish girl disappeared in a quick swish of her dismal black gown.

"Yes, yes, my dear," said Matthew, "you are quite right that these people are fanatical. But I fear that Honey has suffered more grief than we know, and she is thus an easy prey to such teaching. Still, I believe that with steady kindness from us, their influence over her mind will diminish."

He now sat on the settee next to her, taking her plump hand in his lean one and brushing the hair at her temple with his lips. She felt a little mollified, but there was more to this problem of the New Lights than the small matter of Honey.

"What of our Negroes, Matthew? You know that they mingle freely with farmers and their wives, even with some ladies, so I hear, at these meetings. You know what they teach. That all the Negroes should be freed! Why I've heard that in Caroline the Methodists are planning to not admit slave owners to their worship. Everyone but you forbids their people to attend these meetings. And they are right."

He removed his hand from hers and leaned back against the hard wood with a sigh. "In terms of their self-interest they are right. In terms of the true right, they are wrong."

After a long moment of silence he straightened. "But do not concern yourself with these things, dearest. It is I who must, like Honey, try to 'do as the Romans do.' Come, let us rejoin our guests."

She willingly took his arm. Much as she sometimes resented his power over her, she was used to relying on his strength and knowledge, yes, even wisdom, in all matters beyond the family and household, and even there sometimes.

———————◦◦◦◦———————

One late morning, almost a month after the barbecue, Nathan was walking back to the house after completing his round of fields, barns and stable. His uncle was in Richmond for the spring public times, leaving Nathan again in nominal charge, at least, of the home quarter. This time he had Uncle Miles to consult with, if necessary, but he found himself less and less in need of advice.

Now, as he approached the pantry door, he saw that it stood open and Honey leaned against it as though she could not otherwise stand. Coming closer, he saw that her face was drained of blood, the freckles standing out upon it like crumbs of tobacco spilled on a tablecloth.

Her pale face and those blue eyes of hers quite dark with fright brought back to him as clear as glass the day of the barbecue. How he had dreaded that day, with its necessity of being sociable with ladies he barely knew. His heart had sunk into his stomach when Mr. Waverley had found him in the stables and insisted on his joining the group in the parlor where he knew there would be dancing. But somehow he had avoided the dance until all the ladies were already engaged, and when Miles suggested he go seek Miss Honey for a partner, he felt a sense of relief. Perhaps he wouldn't be able to find her, and even if he did, she was too simple, too backward, to be feared.

When he had found her, with Molly and Sarah in the bookroom, she had hung back with just the same look on her face as now and declared she could not dance. He had bowed quite properly, he estimated, and requested the honor with unwonted smoothness. How well he had behaved, compared with her gawky refusal! He actually felt sorry for the backwoods cousin when her sister and Molly laughed freely at her

249

expense.

Then Sarah had begged to dance with him, assuring him she knew how, and that Mrs. Waverley had told her she might dance if she wanted. So he had found himself leading her back to the parlor, and there both were welcomed and complimented on their steps. Sarah, being the child that she was, and her first time at the dance, was the center of attention, and was eager to help him when he forgot a step. He had come away thinking that dances were not quite such dread things as he had always held them.

And now he had to do again with Honey, whose wretched manners made his own appear almost graceful.

"What's the matter, Miss Honey? Are you ill?" Even as he spoke he congratulated himself on how easily he could talk to this girl.

She opened her mouth to speak, but nothing came out of her trembling lips and her whole body could be seen to shake in little spaced spurts.

"Have you seen a bear in the house? Or a wildcat?" As she seemed almost to nod at this, "Where is it?" Her eyes raised up high. "Above stairs? Then I'll go take a look. And chase the creature out for you," he said with only half a laugh. The poor girl looked so frightened.

He glanced into every room on the second story, and found nothing amiss. Then he mounted the narrow stairs to the loft rooms, in one of which he knew that Honey and Sarah slept. And there, warming itself in the patch of sunshine that fell on the bed lay a snake. It was only a garter snake, no more than two feet long, with a clear stripe down its back. Nathan flung his head back in a full-throated laugh.

Put on the alert, the creature slithered under the thrown-back coverlet. But it was no doubt still groggy from its winter sleep, and Nathan was quick with his fingers. Flipping off the coverlet, he caught it behind the head and held it while it writhed, sluggishly, to free itself. How could this harmless little thing have caused Honey such terror?

A backwoods girl who must have seen snakes aplenty, rattlers and copperheads among them, in her growing-up years.

He went slowly down the two flights of stairs, holding fast his captive and taking care not to trip on the worn steps. When he got to the pantry door, thinking to appear at good advantage as Honey's rescuer, yes, and tease her a bit as well, there was no sign of the girl. Instead, Sarah stood looking up at him from the bottom of the porch steps, and Molly leaned against the nearest tree, smirking. Sarah was certainly not afraid of the snake. She took one look at it and two spots of crimson appeared in her cheeks.

"You mean, mean man! I always knew you was mean! You've scared Honey nigh to death. She just run off, looking real miserable. Didn't she, Molly?" (But Molly had disappeared.)

"Hey! Hold your horses, girl. I didn't do anything. Only went and found this measly little garter snake on your bed, and caught it for you. What the devil she had to be so scared about I don't know." He threw the offending reptile off into the bushes in disgust. That was the trouble with women. And girls. They never behaved in a rational manner. No use trying to please them.

"Well I don't know either," said Sarah, coloring even more and probably ashamed of herself, as well she should be. "Anyhow, if you didn't put it there," she suddenly flared up again, "however did it get in our bed? Honey's plumb scared stiff of snakes. Always has been. I don't rightly know why."

"Well don't go accusing people when you don't know what you're talking about." He stomped off fast, having had more than enough to do with whimsical females for a long time to come.

It was late on the following day that Miles was riding slowly through the woods, on his way to the Waverley Great House. His hands lay so loose on his thighs with the reins dangling in long loops on either side of his mare's neck, that she took him a full half-mile along the well-worn path toward the Ludwell house before he roused himself and turned her back to take the path that led to the main buildings of Laurel Hill.

Word had been sent that his mother was unwell and had been moved to Great House with her maid so that Mrs. Waverley could keep an eye on her. Miles got on well with his mother. A small child when his father died, he'd been held close and wept over. Later he hunted and fished with the Negro boys, and when he ran away to join in the fight against the English he was sorely missed, and mourned when captured. Upon his return he was treated as a hero by his mother, despite her Quaker views about war. Since then, in the little time he spent at home, he respected her pious ways, even attending her household prayers upon occasion. Of course she knew nothing of his wilder ways when away from Laurel Hill. When she complained of Matthew and Mrs. Waverley he listened with a grave air and sympathetic noises; then he dismissed it from his mind. Matthew appeared to have as little affection for his mother as she for him, but he was scrupulous in his duties toward her.

Arriving at the back entrance to Great House, he dismounted, tethered his horse to a porch post, and made his way through the pantry to the master bedroom which had been given over to his mother and her servant Juno whom he spied curled up on a pallet in a corner with a bony black arm covering her face. Nathan sat next to the bed, his head lolling forward in sleep and a newspaper spread over his knees. Miles could barely see his mother in the shadow made by the bed curtains that had been pulled halfway closed. A floorboard creaked as he moved forward and both his mother and Nathan started awake. The young man jumped up and pulled back the curtains while Miles leaned down to kiss his mother.

"Miles! Thank God you've come. Juno and this boy went off to sleep leaving me in darkness and cold."

"Now Mother, it looked very like you were sleeping as well, quite warm and snug. Add a log to the fire, Nathan. Though I must say it is quite comfortable in here."

"Of course I feel warm to you. It's the fever." In truth, she did not feel or look feverish, but her voice was a mere rasp, and she now broke out in a paroxysm of coughing. He said words of sympathy and hoped she was being well taken care of. Should he wake Juno, whose dull snore could be heard from across the room? She couldn't speak for coughing, but shook her head no.

"The woman was up all night tending to Grandmama, and I think she's just about as sick herself," said Nathan. "Now you're here, I'll go have some supper."

Miles listened to his mother's complaints, which were mercifully brief, since they had to be gasped out between fits of coughing. Mrs. Charlotte should not have moved her to Great House, where she was not truly welcome, where there was no place but this pallet for Juno, where they barely paid her any heed, where the room was drafty, and where the children made an intolerable noise.

He thought of observing to her that Charlotte had given up her chamber for her mother-in-law's comfort and that spring was an excessively busy season in the house and dependencies. But he refrained; such remarks would only irritate her further. As her chest heaved and her eyes watered, he reached for the water tumbler. He suddenly saw not the strong, pious, sternly disapproving mother he knew, but a lonely, embittered old woman, scorned by her husband and living in the backwater of her son and daughter-in-law's busy life. A familiar vision, nurtured during his years in the West, of himself and Lucy strolling through the handsome rooms of their own house, a robust, big-boned infant in her arms and a slender, dark-haired little girl clinging to his hand, came back to him now enriched by an image of his mother presiding contentedly over a teapot in their parlor. For certainly his mother would be happier in the home of the gentle, pliable Lucy, than here in close quarters with the imperious Mrs. Waverley. He sighed and expunged that pretty dream from his mind, just as he habitually wiped clean the ivory surface of his chapbook.

When Nathan returned from his supper, Miles promised his mother to look in on her in the morning, and took his leave.

He found Mrs. Waverley, Mr. Levier, and Mme. de Coulanges still lingering at the supper table with the children, Molly and Sarah, and chattering in some excitement.

"Miles!" cried his sister-in-law. "Can you imagine anything more ridiculous? Honey, our quiet little mouse whom one is wont hardly to notice at all, has suddenly made herself the center of attention. She has disappeared! She who never strays from the grounds but to attend prayer meetings and church, has not been seen since yesterday forenoon."

"Yes, my dear fellow," broke in Mr. Levier, "and you will never guess the reason. So allow me to astound you by saying that it is all about a harmless little reptile that that rascal Nathan slipped into her bed. He denies it of course. Now I confess that if such a creature suddenly appeared in <u>my</u> bed, you would hear such an uproar! But my excuse is my city breeding. And if the creature were a lovely lady, instead," this with a sidelong glance at the Frenchwoman, "I should respond with admirable aplomb."

"Let us hope so, sir," the lady laughed. "But even a country girl may be allowed her fears."

None of them, not even Honey's sister, appeared perturbed about her disappearance. Miles saw the situation in a more serious light. "Have you sent out to search for her, madam?" he asked Mrs. Waverley.

"No indeed. Sarah says she has done this before, back in Carolina. She always comes back in a day or two."

"A day or two! I'll wager that my brother, were he here, would take this to heart." As he glanced with increasing annoyance at the empty place near the foot of the table he saw Molly slide off her chair and glide like a lynx out the doorway to the hall. Her complete silence, so unlike her, awoke an instant's suspicion, but her mother's next remark made it vanish from his mind.

"Yes, of a certainty, Matthew would put himself on thorns over nothing. A good thing he is from home."

Miles looked at this sister-in-law of his for a few moments in silence. He wondered, as he had done many a time before, how it had come about that Matthew, so serious, so scrupulous, so weighed down with care for the welfare of all those he encountered, could have married this proud Englishwoman who ignored all charges she preferred not to assume, appeared to care for no one, and openly derided most. He found it hard to credit the most evident answer: her flamboyant beauty, a beauty that stayed faithful to her through the years and the four or five children she had borne. He, of course, was quite impervious to her charms, and found her constant raillery, directed more at him than at anyone else, thoroughly irritating.

"Well, Mr. Miles, you are appraising me and I see nothing but disapproval in your stern visage. I stand condemned for neglect of the heavy duties that fall upon me in your brother's absence. But what extraordinary good fortune that you are arrived to assume them! Shall we summon a search party?"

"Nathan and I will suffice, madam. If we don't find her this night--thank God it is not cold--we will have the Negroes aid us in the morning."

"Ah well, I leave everything in your capable hands." She stared at them so fixedly that he shoved them under his coat. She flounced off with an unpleasant laugh. Her character did not improve with the years. This winter, in particular, her levity was laced more thickly with acid.

"Pray tell Mrs. Waverley that I will sleep in Old House. That she need take no trouble over me. But Sarah, run fetch some article of your sister's clothing that my hunter bitches may sniff. I doubt not they'll pick up her scent."

Of course the dogs had no trouble at all in finding Honey, who had taken refuge in the icehouse. Miles came upon her sitting on the packed earth that covered the winter's supply of blocks of ice cut from the pond. Miles had to laugh when he saw her surrounded by jars of preserves and barrels of pickles and cider.

She jumped up, shaking the dirt from her skirt and looking thoroughly ashamed, as well she should. "So here you are, young lady. Whatever got into you? A country girl like you running from a harmless little garter snake. And skulking here so as to worry all the household." Here he lied. But no matter. They should have worried.

"Come, come. Back to Great House with you. I assure you that Nathan disposed of that terrifying creature forthwith." No sooner were those mocking words out of his mouth than he regretted them. The poor girl had begun to cry. He reached out awkwardly to pat her shoulder, but she shrank back from his touch.

"Forgive me. I've only distressed you more. But you really must come back to the house."

She wiped her eyes with the back of a grimy hand. "I'm feared to go back, sir. Mrs. Waverley must be so angry at me. Now she'll sure and certain send me away."

"That's out of the question. I doubt she can do without you these days. But I do advise you to go straight to your room. I'll tell them you are feeling sick. And I'll send Sarah to bring you water to wash with and food as well. I'll wager you've not eaten since yesterday. Wait 'til morning to make your apologies to Mrs. Waverley. She's somewhat put out this day—oh not with you. With me. She'll have calmed down by morning."

Still looking quite wretched, the girl let him accompany her to the pantry door. He gave her what he hoped was a reassuring smile and bid her farewell.

Chapter 14

Honey squatted at the far end of the vegetable garden, her gown engulfed in an apron, her skirt hitched up across her knees, a trowel in hand. She was weeding among the carrot and pea sprouts, something Mrs. Waverley would not approve of, for certain. But how could she calm her mind and quiet her fears unless she busy her hands with something useful?

Sooner or later she would be summoned to appear before Mrs. Waverley and be scolded for her foolishness in running from the house and staying a whole night and day without anyone knowing where she was. But for now she was safe from the eyes of all except a handful of Negro children at work weeding near the kitchen. Mrs. Waverley, who was busy commanding all the house servants in the spring cleaning, had no time right now to concern herself with Honey's behavior.

She took off her big work glove and dabbed at the blood on the inside of her right thumb. Too vigorous weeding had worn a blister. She gazed at the loose skin that had slipped sideways to reveal a patch of deep red, and smiled. Working in the damp, fragrant earth soothed her spirit, even in the midst of her troubles. Feeling the soft young shoots reminded her of the one luxury of her new life that caused her no guilt. The abundant vegetables, fruits, and breads offered on the Waverley table were a welcome change from the constant diet of meat and fish of the mountain people back home. This had been especially so at Papa's house, since he took no care to clear land for planting.

The quiet of this place was not entirely a blessing. Bits and pieces from her past life had been swirling about in her head like leaves caught in a whirlwind. The snake that those people called harmless was not harmless to her. To her it was as though Satan Himself had come to remind her of the worst of her sins, the one she refused to think on. That slithery creature <u>made</u> her think on it.

Had Satan led Papa into that first sin, or had he led <u>her</u>, and she in turn led Papa? Like Eve had done. It was too long ago to remember. She didn't remember and she <u>wouldn't remember</u> those bad nights. But she did recollect the mornings, when her eyelids would be red from Papa's beard scraping on them, and the boys would call her crybaby.

For sure, in coming to this place, she had come to Vanity Fair. All the evils were here: rich houses, rich clothing, dancing, singing, Sabbath-breaking, drinking. These last things had gone on back home, but once at Granny Harriet's she was never called on to witness them.

Had she been wrong to obey the promise Papa required of her, even though a deathbed promise was sacred?

If only the folks here would just let her work and be quiet. She did truly love to nurse the sick, and to spin and weave and knit. Besides the ordinary handwork, she had made a fine coverlet for baby Charles, and had woven a workbag for Mrs. Waverley, made of wool and silk thread that she had spun herself. She had dyed it a rich indigo and embroidered it in gray and white. Mrs. Levier would have been pleased to have her use all her time doing such work. But Mrs. Waverley wouldn't hear of it. Honey must learn to be a lady. Mrs. Waverley said that an old lady in Mrs. Levier's position could afford to do as she pleased, but "a little waif like Honey must not play the fool." She must learn the proper graces, catch a husband, and so make a place for herself in the world.

As if that wasn't enough to worry oneself with, there was the trouble with Maudy, the pretty Negro girl, daughter of Joan. Maudy had done all the fancywork before Honey came. She'd even been sent away for a whole year to be specially trained for it. At first Honey couldn't understand why Maudy wouldn't look at her and wouldn't hardly answer when she tried to be friendly. Then she'd asked Molly, who'd laughed real hard and explained that Maudy was jealous. Since Maudy worked almost always in Great House, Honey had to bear those mean looks from her every single day.

Oh! She had stabbed with her trowel smack into a young pea plant. Split it in two. Even here in the garden she did nothing but damage. Well, she would beg pardon for this trouble she'd caused by running away. She would not set herself up pridefully to be holier than the others. But whatever she had to do, even dance, she would try to do with a pure heart. These thoughts calmed her so that she was able to go on uprooting the sturdy weeds that were threatening the delicate vegetable shoots.

In the strength of this calm she forced herself to face the one thing that scared her more than anything in this new life of hers: the feelings that sometimes sprouted up in her toward Mr. Waverley. Most times she looked upon that fine gentleman as sent by the Lord to be a new father to her, to guide and advise her, to tell her when she did wrong. It was true that he did not appear to be a God-fearing man. Even though he lived a worldly life, he was so kind and good that you just knew God loved him. But there were times when sinful thoughts came to her, quick as lightning: of Mr. Waverley holding her in his arms and smoothing her hair, like Papa used to do after the bad thing was over. This thought sent such queer shivers through her neck, her back, and even her belly, that she knew it had to be wicked. She would drive it out of her mind, only to have it come back again later.

Little by little she began to notice a shrill voice saying her name over and over. She wearily got to her feet and turned to see Molly standing a few yards behind her at the edge of the garden.

"I thought you'd gone deaf," said the child, staring at her more like she'd gone not deaf, but daft. Which of course everybody now thought she was.

"I'm sorry. I reckon I was woolgathering." Then she just stood there with her eyes humbly on the ground, even though it was only Molly.

Molly too said nothing for a few moments. She didn't seem quite herself. Finally she spoke. "I've got something I have to tell you. But we'd best not stay here, don't you think? In the sun and you without a bonnet. Mama would have a fit if she saw you."

Honey led the way to a section of garden wall that was shaded by two river birches. She sat down, but Molly stayed standing, shifting from one leg to the other and pulling strips of loose bark off one of the trees.

"I've got to tell you it was me put the snake in your bed." The

259

words rushed out and the child looked like she expected Honey to fall over from surprise. But somehow, it didn't really matter to Honey how the snake got there.

"Well, I guess you knew all along," said Molly, who looked relieved. "You did tell me once how scared you were of snakes. Anyway, Mama guessed. You can't keep any secrets from her. She sees right through my face into my brain. She's so mad at me. She hasn't ever been this mad. I'm sorry I did it. I won't ever do anything else to you. I swear it! I'll give you my Queen Charlotte doll, the one with the china head. If you don't speak up for me Mama will make me sleep in Aunt Abie's room again--I can't tolerate that--and she'll tell Papa about it as soon as he comes home and say I did it out of sheer meanness and then he'll hate me. 'If there's one thing your papa won't stand for, it's meanness,' she said. Which I already knew. And I won't be allowed to ride the pretty new thoroughbred mare he's going to bring home from Richmond, not ever!"

Molly was crying now, and not hiding her face either. She was staring at Honey with eyes wide open, tears streaming down and her forehead all in knots.

"Please, Molly, stop your crying. You've got no call to cry because of me." She groped for the purse tied with a cord round her waist. It always kept sliding from one place to another, but finally she found it, pulled out her handkerchief and handed it to Molly.

While the child wiped and sniffed and blew her nose Honey began to feel better. She said she'd ask Molly's mother to forgive her. Didn't she herself have to ask forgiveness for being such a goose and running away?

This speech cured Molly's sniffles in a trice. With a smeared but happy face she cried: "Oh, then you'll get to take dancing lessons with Sarah and me from the French dancing master. Mama was furious because Mr. Carter of Nominy kept him way beyond his time. But now he's in Simmons Corners and he's coming to stay with us for a fortnight! So we'll start lessons directly. He's such a funny little man. He jumps about and flails his arms and is always so excited. You'll see."

These were not words to bring comfort to Honey's heart. Papa always said Frenchmen were worse devils than the English, even though they had come and helped us in the War. Well, she had determined to do like those Romans Mr. Waverley talked about. Surely he would not bring a truly evil man into his house.

———◦◦◦———

Charlotte was feeling uneasy. Was it because of this silly affair of Honey running away? No. The little goose was back and everyone would know that a foolish prank of Molly's was the cause of it. As for Molly, Charlotte was sure she was properly chastened this time. No, there was something else hovering like a pesky gnat around her ears. It was Maudy. Charlotte had not seen her since Saturday, and this was Wednesday. Joan had said her daughter was sick and was keeping to their cabin. Any other Negro would have been forced to go to the infirmary (to make sure he wasn't just malingering) but Joan and her daughter had special privileges. Joan had been acting very strange the last few days. She hardly spoke at all, avoided Charlotte, and was evasive when asked about Maudy's condition.

Charlotte was not one to fret herself about something without taking action. She rang the bell, and sent May to summon Joan.

What a nuisance these servants were! She wished to God she'd never see another Negro in her life. But she must try to contain herself and not fly off the handle at Joan whom, if truth be told, she depended on all too much. Joan had her eye on everything. She knew when the pilfering became too blatant and whom to blame, when supplies of sugar or coffee were thinning out, when an "accident" was an act of resistance or revenge. She would report these things and many others that Charlotte needed to know. No, it was not advisable to antagonize

Joan. But restraint was not Charlotte's strong point. When things went wrong she could not sit still. As she paced back and forth across the worn pile of the Turkey carpet she heard loud voices in the hall. No, one loud voice, a man's, and the lower voice of Joan. What in the world?

Then the door was flung open and Dick Meachem stomped into the room. Behind him Joan's face was framed in the doorway.

"Mr. Nathan be afar off in the fields, ma'am," she said. "I'll run fetch Mr. Geoffrey." She took off at a trot.

"Ha!" the man yelled after her. "You think that little coxcomb is going to protect your mistress, you stupid nigger?"

The first thing Charlotte noticed about the man was the mud that his boots were stamping into her carpet. Then her eyes rose to his leather hunting jacket and the dead rabbits slung around his neck. From the mouth of one of them a trail of blood had trickled down his jacket. Then she took in Dick's face, not slack from drink this time, but tight with anger. It was too early in the day for his serious tippling to begin. Although he clutched his rifle in his hand, she feared no real violence. A surge of strength flowed upward from her belly to the roots of her hair.

"Have you not been informed, Mr. Meachem, that you are not welcome in this house or on our land? I made an exception for our barbecue, but the note I wrote to Col. Meachem was, I assure myself, perfectly clear. And my orders to my people were quite explicit." This she had done after Matthew's departure for Richmond.

"Your orders be damned! I don't take orders from a female."

"In the absence of Mr. Waverley I am in charge here, sir." She was pleased to hear her own voice, calm and cold.

"Hell and the devil! You ain't in charge of <u>me</u>, and I won't..."

"Excuse me," she broke in, surprised at the power of her voice, "but I will not stand here talking to a man in such a passion as you are in. Particularly one with bloody animals on his shoulders and a gun in his hand. Pray put them down on the table in the pantry, and then I will listen to whatever complaint you wish to make." While she was sure he intended no violence, the way he was gesticulating with that gun, it could discharge by accident.

"Didn't I just tell you..." But he hesitated. No doubt he wasn't used to having anyone stand up to him, particularly a woman. Mrs. Meachem quite doted on her son, and even the Colonel had given up trying to control him.

At that moment Big Moses stuck his head cautiously around the doorframe. Joan had apparently decided that the big Negro would be of more use than Geoffrey. "Moses, please put Mr. Meachem's gun and his kill on a table in the pantry for him." After a little hesitation, Dick just about threw them at the servant.

"Close the door after you, Moses. Mr. Meachem and I wish to have a private conversation." She seated herself on the imposing wing chair and motioned Dick to the sofa.

"Now, sir, are you here to protest against being banned from Laurel Hill? I should think that you know the reason. I will not have my servants interfered with."

"If your damned yeller gal don't want to be 'interfered with,' let her stay off our land." His tone had changed from belligerent to surly.

"She was never on your land, sir. Of that I am certain."

"She was fooling with my man Quash, for sure. He was a damned fair worker 'til she came along and put ideas in his head. Not just her, but all your gang of uppity niggers with their so-called prayer meetings. They're conspiring, that's what they are."

"You're wrong, Mr. Meachem. My people don't conspire. Perhaps if you'd allow your people to hold their own prayer meetings they wouldn't come here. And if you'd rein in that monster overseer of yours who beats them half to death."

"That's not your business, madam. Anyhow, your gal conspired. She and Quash have taken off, pox take 'em! Left Saturday, far as I can make out. I've been chasing after them since Monday, but I'm told they're clean out of the county. Quash don't have the brains to pull off a thing like that, but they tell me that gal of yours got to know people all around Petersburg, even Richmond, while she was away last year. Niggerlovers who'll hide other people's property."

"Have you lost your senses? Maudy is a quiet little thing who knows nothing but needlework. Besides, she's devoted to me."

"Well, all I can say is, you've a damned good conceit of yourself. You let her learn reading and writing, didn't you? More fool you. Seems she wrote passes for him and her, the jade. Signed my name on one, and your husband's on the other. You don't know a thing, Mrs. High and Mighty. But I tell you, I've hired some crackerjack nigger hunters, and when I find them that little gal will be sore in more than the one place I made her the last time." He laughed in anticipation, and eyed Charlotte up and down, clearly hoping to have jarred her calm.

Somewhere inside Charlotte a fear was growing that there was something of truth in what he said. But overriding that was the contempt in which she had always held Dick Meachem, and which was now greatly nourished by his words.

"Don't you dare touch my servant again, no matter what you may imagine she has done."

"And what'll you do about it? As you may know, madam, a runaway is fair game, just as long as we don't cripple her so's she's unfit for work."

"And as you may know, sir, Mr. Waverley has a deal of influence in this county. Your father respects him, and appears near the end of his rope as far as you are concerned." Charlotte despised her own weakness in calling up Matthew's name, but facts were facts: she could do nothing on her own. Even her order, to her own servants, banning Dick from Laurel Hill, was good only until Matthew returned and confirmed it.

At any rate, her surge of excitement in thus sparring with Dick Meachem was beginning to wane. Weariness was taking over.

"Well then, madam, perhaps you'll be so good as to send for the wench, since you're so sure she hasn't flown the coop?"

The fellow had cooled down enough to address her with some minimal courtesy, but still in a tone of intolerable superiority. Of course she would not deign to admit the possibility of his being right, so she drew herself up with as much dignity as she could muster, pulled the bell rope, and was glad to see Big Moses open the door instantly.

"Mr. Meachem, I see no point in talking further. I will not summon Maudy. She is sick. Joe, bring Mr. Meachem his things. And you, sir, please leave me now. I have much to attend to."

"I'm sure you do, madam," he said with an insufferable smile of triumph. The fellow was smarter than she had ever given him credit for, seeing him always in his cups. He certainly perceived that she was not so sure of herself as she pretended, and would have to look to her Maudy immediately. He took his dead animals and his gun from Moses' hands, made her an exaggerated bow, and left the room.

Almost instantly, Joan appeared in the doorway.

"Moses is gonna follow that gentleman, mistress. So as we knows he's gone. Is you all right? I looked for Master Geoffrey, but he done gone to the Burnham place."

"All right, Joan. I'm quite safe. Mister Meachem was only blustering." Charlotte heaved a weary sigh. Now she would have to find out the truth, little as she wished at this moment to know it. Knowing it, she would have to berate Joan, for which she scarcely felt the courage. She sank down heavily into a chair and looked at Joan's face. Except for her hair, tightly kinked under her red kerchief, and her full lips, you would have said a redskin. Her nose was straight, and on either side of it rose broad hills of cheeks. Her expression was, as always, blank. Only her eyes, wider open than usual, showed that she was distressed.

"Maudy is not sick in your cabin, is she? Mr. Meachem claims she has run away. And with one of his field hands."

"She done run off in the night, Friday, mistress. I saw her bed empty Saturday morning." Her eyes looked straight into Charlotte's.

265

Had the woman no shame?

"You lied to me, Joan. All these days you've been lying to me." Joan said nothing.

"Lord almighty, Joan! I can't believe it. No one ever laid the lash to that girl. I never even slapped her--once she was grown."

"No call to, Mistress. She works good. She don't sass nobody."

"Then why? Did she go listen to those Anabaptist preachers on Sunday? Those troublemakers who say all you Negroes should be free? Irresponsible fools. What would you do with yourselves? Who would take care of you?"

"She ain't gone to no preachers, Mistress."

"After all I did for her! Teaching her to read and write. Sending her to town to learn fancy cutting and sewing and weaving. She even has time to do needlework on her own account and keep the money she makes."

"Ain't enough light, evenings, for them fine stitches."

"Well, I must say I thought her too smart to do a thing like this. I suppose that hand of Col. Meachem's turned her head. That Quash. They went off together, didn't they?"

"They's married. Just about. Master promised."

"They'll be caught, of course. Mr. Meachem has the slave hunters after them. With their hounds."

At this Joan twisted her apron in her broad, strong hands and turned her head away, the first sign of emotion on her part.

"She'll come back, mistress," she murmured.

But Charlotte felt too much chagrin on her own account to take pity on Joan.

"Oh yes. Half starved, and beaten. You remember when Seth came back, nearly dead. He never was good for much after that. Serve her right. I've a mind to sell her to the traders. She'd bring a handsome price."

"Master wouldn't never do that!"

"Where could they go, anyway?"

"She say up north. Everybody free up there."

"Don't you believe it. Not anywhere they could get to. If they're not caught by the hunters, sooner or later they'll be kidnapped and sold. Foolish, foolish girl."

Joan just looked at her, impassive again. Worse, Charlotte sensed hatred behind those dark, veiled eyes. She suddenly felt ashamed. This woman had served her faithfully ever since her marriage, had silently backed her up in all those early struggles with her mother-in-law, had taught her, if truth be told, how to run a plantation household. She reached out and clasped one of the big, black hands in her own.

"It will be all right, Joan. I warned Mr. Meachem not to let her be harmed. We'll get her back and we'll...forgive her. Now bring me some tea, in my chamber. Don't let anyone bother me there."

It was morning in the Waverley dining room. The windows, facing west, were opened wide to catch the mild morning breeze before the heat of the day would force their closing and shuttering against the afternoon sun. Though it was only May, summer heat was paying an early visit to piedmont Virginia.

Honey sat at her humble place near the foot of the table and was glad that across from her the larger form of Sarah blocked her view of herself in the glass. Molly sat between them, at the foot of the table. Both younger girls were chewing on great slabs of toast, dipping them into their chocolate, and nibbling on crisps of bacon. Both were chatting eagerly, interrupting each other, about the latest excitement at Waverley. It seemed that Maudy had run away, and their neighbor, Mr. Meachem, the young one who always scared Honey, had frightened everyone by storming into Great House. How glad Honey was that all this had taken everyone's mind away from her own foolishness.

Joan had gone to tell Mrs. Waverley that Honey was back the very

267

moment she spied her, but the lady was resting and would not see her until the next day. Today. She would be scolded, of course, but mayhap Mrs. Waverley would be too upset by these other troubles to pay much mind to Honey.

The greatest relief was that few folks were at Laurel Hill just now. Or leastways not at Great House. Mrs. Levier was well again and back in Old House. Mr. Levier and Mr. Waverley were in Richmond at the sessions. (Though she had to admit that Mr. Waverley was the one person she'd have been gratified to see in spite of her shame.) Mr. Geoffrey Burnham kept to his chamber 'til late morning, and spent the remainder of his day visiting Miss Nelson and Miss Lucinda. Honey had caught a glimpse once of the French lady lying on a long chair in the drawing room, reading and being fanned by May, but she too kept to her chamber in the morning. And Mr. Miles lived away somewhere just now.

Mr. Nathan had been here for his breakfast, and that had made her mighty uncomfortable. But he, always so silent, had spoken to her twice, just asking about her health, and those sooty black eyes of his looked almost kindly at her for the moment she dared look up at him. His narrow face, with the bones of his cheeks sticking out, didn't hardly look so much like a skull to her anymore.

With a start she realized that the girls had grown silent. She looked up to see them staring at her, then up further to see Joan standing over her, looking like she'd asked Honey something and expected her to answer. But she had heard nothing! She sprang up, setting the cup down with a bang.

"Ma'am? I'm sorry, I didn't hear what you said." Even before Molly laughed, Honey recalled that she shouldn't have said "ma'am" to a servant. But Joan was so imposing that it still slipped out once in a while.

"I done told you. Mistress say you go see her now." The black woman's brows were drawn together in a stern frown. She seemed to be talking to a bad child.

At the door to the master bedchamber she forced herself to straighten her back and raise her head. Mrs. Waverley kept telling her to stand tall (as tall as she could with her small stature) and look like she was proud to be a Waverley. She found the lady seated at her secretary with a quill in hand. This she laid down slowly and looked Honey over from head to foot. Honey suddenly remembered to curtsy, and this she did carefully, remembering not to bob jerkily down and up, another thing the lady judged unworthy of a Waverley.

"Sit down, Caroline." Being called by her real name boded no good, but Honey forced herself to hold her head up despite her fear.

"Now it is a truth that Molly is a mischievous child, worse than that, a mean one of late. Out of jealousy."

Honey was startled.

"You can't believe that, can you? Well, I got to the bottom of it. Mr. Waverley has paid you too much attention. Molly cannot brook sharing her papa with anyone. Even I incur her wrath at times. That is not an excuse for her behavior. She has been punished and has been, for the moment, crushed." A slight smile flickered at the corners of Mrs. Waverley's mouth as she said "for the moment."

"At any rate," she continued, "Molly's behavior is clear to me now. Yours is not."

She again surveyed Honey in silence, and this time Honey could not help herself. Her head dropped.

"You're a backcountry girl, used to living in the wilderness until now. Bears, wildcats, wolves--God knows what else--and most certainly snakes. So why did you behave like a little fool over a mere garter snake?"

"I don't know, ma'am," Honey whispered.

"Of course you know!" Mrs. Waverley slapped her hand down upon the surface of the secretary. "Were you bitten by a rattler or a copperhead and almost died? Did your brothers torment you by hanging a snake round your neck as you slept?"

"Oh no, ma'am. They wouldn't do that. Well, they never did think of it, I reckon."

"Well then?"

Tears of shame and fear sprang to Honey's eyes. Mrs. Waverley would really despise her now, for crying like a baby. But she'd despise her still more, and send her away, if she knew the truth.

Then something quite unexpected happened. Honey heard a chair scrape, heard footsteps approach, shrank back for fear she was about to have her ears boxed. But then an arm dropped onto her shoulders. Mrs. Waverley had drawn up a chair right next to hers.

This made Honey's tears change to sobs.

"Listen to me, child. I'm not quite the ogre you think me. But I cannot tolerate strange things happening around me and not knowing why. I won't eat you, for goodness' sake. Just tell me the truth."

Honey was trapped. She thought for just a moment of making up some likely tale. She should have gone along with Mrs. Waverley's idea that she'd been bitten. But it was too late for that. Anyway, she'd done enough wrong without adding lying to the list.

Mrs. Waverley had never treated her like this before, holding her with that beautiful round arm Honey so admired, and speaking to her gentle-voiced. Maybe it would comfort her to tell somebody about it. She'd never told a living soul. Mrs. McNair had surely guessed it, and the McNair menfolk too, with the nasty looks they'd give her. But Mrs. McNair hadn't ever asked a question or said a word. Granny Harriet knew about the other thing, true enough, but she wasn't one for words, either. Just did for Honey what needed to be done.

Maybe this fine lady who never spoke of sin and let dancing and gaming go on in her house without as much as a frown on her forehead, no, even urged Honey to dance, maybe she wouldn't think Honey so terribly bad.

"Come, Honey, tell me what is so frightful about a little garter snake," said the voice again, just as gentle, and the arm was still around Honey's shoulders.

"It's my papa, Ma'am. My papa put snakes in my bed." This burst out loud, but then dwindled to a whisper.

"Your papa? Why on earth would he do that?"

"To punish me. Because I didn't mind him."

"You were a disobedient child? I don't believe it."

"No ma'am, I tried to be good, and get in his bed when he looked a certain way at me. But sometimes I just couldn't and I'd go hide outside. So when I sneaked up to the loft to sleep there'd be a snake tied up in the cover on my mat. Papa always knew where to find one, when the weather was warm." That old feeling came back, like an icy hand grabbed hold of her insides. She began to shake. The arm clasped her harder and she tried to stop, but couldn't.

"When there wasn't no snake in my bed I'd be so heartened, but then there'd be something else. Like my fry pan filled with dirt and the wood for the fire soaked, so it took forever to get breakfast cooked and Papa and the boys yelling at me, and Sarah crying."

"Quite a trickster, your papa."

"I...mostly did like he wanted, ma'am," she whispered.

"And when you did get in his bed...but you don't have to tell me. I can well imagine."

"I knew it was wrong, ma'am, but I just couldn't ... "

"Of course you couldn't. What a scoundrel! And your own father! Bad enough for an uncle, but a father! If I believed in Hell, I'd wish him burning there."

Honey had hoped to be comforted, to be forgiven. Not hear such things said of Papa.

"Oh no, ma'am. Papa had a mean streak. Even Mama said so, and he played her tricks, too, before she got poorly. But he wasn't evil. After Mama died Papa was all alone, with all of us to feed. And no woman to do for him. There wasn't no woman anywhere near by he could of wedded. He couldn't go looking for one in a place with more people because he couldn't abide 'swarms of folks all on top of each other,' like he said. I should have gone looking, for him. I used to think on that, but I never did get up the gumption. I did the bad thing instead."

"You do take everything on yourself, don't you? Just like Mr. Waverley. Well, you must look upon him as your father now. And forget that other monster." The lady had taken her arm away from Honey's shoulders and moved her chair back so as to look straight at her. Not angrylike, though.

"Oh please, ma'am, Papa wasn't a monster! He could be so good if only I did what he said. Next morning he'd pat me and comfort me. And he'd be so sweet to the boys and Sarah. It was like sunshine and birds singing in every corner of the house. He'd take the boys out and shoot some fine quail or maybe a turkey for our dinner and even pick me some flowers on the way home. It was only when he got lonesome for Mama and took too much drink that things got bad. I do mightily admire Mr. Waverley, and I do look up to him as a father. But my papa was a good man."

Mrs. Waverley just sat there giving her a look she couldn't make out. Not exactly angry, but not kind either. "Caroline Waverley, you're a strange girl. Beyond my comprehension anyway. I suppose it's because of all that preaching you've been listening to by those New Light people. But I say this: If you let them put the blame on you for what that blackguard did, you're a fool!" She said this with so much force and such a stabbing look that Honey flinched.

"I'm not angry with you for that." Then she got up and began to walk to and fro, clasping and unclasping those large white hands. "I could tell you something...but enough of this. I cannot think more about it right now. I'm certain Molly won't dare to trouble you again, but if she should, in any way, come straight to me. Do you hear me? Now be off. I have too much else to think of. A sick child, an ungrateful slut of a servant, a detestable neighbor. No, wait. I must inform Mr. Waverley of these affairs." She crossed over to the secretary, seated herself, and rapidly covered a sheet of notepaper with big round writing. She folded the sheet and wrote a direction on the outside. Then she warmed a wax pad with a candle and sealed her letter. "Give this to Joe and tell him to get it in today's post without fail."

"I'm real sorry I made trouble for you, ma'am. I'll try hard not to ever do it again," said Honey as she took the letter. She left the room in a confusion of thoughts that she would need to mull over alone.

Chapter 15

It was almost a fortnight later that Maudy was brought back. The slave hunters came late at night, waking everyone with their loud voices. They demanded to be paid forthwith, so Charlotte had to rise from her bed and descend to the cellar with her keys. Fortunately the stores of sugar and rum were high at Waverley at that moment. Told that Honey and Joan were tending to Maudy in the infirmary and that the girl was not in danger, Charlotte returned to her bed.

As soon as she awoke and recalled the scene of the night before, her anger at Maudy surged high in her breast, particularly at the thought that the foolish creature had got herself injured. She must take time to restrain her feelings. It would not do to storm into the infirmary and vent her wrath on the girl.

She carried out her morning duties as usual, doling out supplies and giving orders for restoring the stocks of sugar and rum. She also checked to see how the repairs on the roof of the smokehouse were progressing. All this time she railed inwardly at the absence of Joan, whom she had permitted to stay with her daughter.

The infirmary was a large cabin, double the size of the others in the home quarter and the closest one to Great House. It had a floor of planks raised four inches above the ground, and tightly chinked walls that protected the interior against the winds of winter. Matthew prided himself on the construction of all the slave cabins, but no other had flooring, or walls as tight as these. When Charlotte stepped inside she found Honey and Joan squatting by the mat on which Maudy lay, her whole body covered by a sheet of coarse muslin. Joan held a pewter basin from which Honey was bathing an ugly wound that ran from Maudy's temple across her cheek and over her jaw. At each touch of the cloth the girl winced and moaned. The skin all round the cut was so puffed up as to render the girl unrecognizable. If Charlotte's heart still held any anger, it left her now. Maudy, once so pretty with her pale skin and gently waving hair, would never turn heads again.

As Charlotte approached the mat Honey glanced up at her, murmured "Good day, ma'am," and went on with her work, but Joan started, letting water slosh from the basin. She made as if to get up, but gave up the attempt and simply turned toward her mistress with bloodshot eyes and sagging jaw. Of course she had spent more than this one night without sleep.

Charlotte, whose knees did not lend themselves to squatting, cast an eye about and found a somewhat mashed but usable reed stool in a corner and drew it up next to Joan. She took the basin from her servant's hands.

"Maudy is going to recover, is she not, Honey?" Honey nodded. "So I want you to go to your cabin, Joan, and sleep. You're no good to her, or me, in this state. Now go!" She gave the woman's shoulder a shake and added: "for I shall need you this afternoon."

With a groan Joan slowly pulled her heavy body up from the floor and made her way to the door without a word. How old she had become in a matter of days! She had always held herself so erect, appearing overly proud for a servant. Now her whole being sagged. Her head, bare of the maroon kerchief she was wont to wear, bent forward over her big breasts, which had nearly come to rest on her belly. Charlotte wanted her out of the way so she could find out the truth about Maudy's condition.

Honey was now spreading a piece of netting over four sticks that were stuck into the mat around Maudy's head.

"Won't you dress that cut?"

"No, ma'am. It wants to heal, and air will help it. As long as we keep off the flies."

"Is that all you're doing? Just the bathing?" Charlotte had dealt with many a wound, of course, but now that Honey was here she recognized a superior skill, and left all medical decisions to her.

"Once it dries good, I'll put on my salve. Later on I'll make me an elm poultice and lay it on. You'll see. It'll heal tolerable fast." Honey threw off the cloth covering Maudy's body and revealed a splint on her left wrist and forearm. This she untied and gently felt the whole swollen area. That brought a cry from Maudy. "I'm sorry, deary. I just need to keep a watch on it." She replaced the splint, and then offered the girl a drink, which was spurned.

"Please, Maudy, take a little sip of barley water. You've touched nary a bite of victuals, and you've got to get your strength back. Directly when you've drunk a little, I'll give you something for the pain." Maudy sighed, but took a few sips of the brown liquid.

Clearly the forearm had been broken. "Is it you who set this?" Charlotte asked.

"Oh no, ma'am. They surely took her to somebody right smart directly after it happened. The bone's set good, and the face cut washed and dressed. I can't hardly feature anybody doing so cruelly to a gentle little thing like Maudy."

"They're ruffians, that's all. Any other injuries?" Charlotte had noticed a strip of raw meat on Maudy's neck, and assumed there was bruising there, but nothing worse.

"Just between the legs, ma'am. I did wash her good there, and the bleeding that started up is clotted good now." Honey spoke matter-offactly of this, and Charlotte knew full well it was only to be expected. But she would not admit to such an expectation.

"The brutes," she murmured.

"Ay!" Maudy cried. "My arm do hurt so! You done said you'd give me something." She moaned and closed her eyes.

Honey reached for the apothecary box that sat open on the floor near Maudy's head. From it she drew a small bottle and dribbled a bit into a cup with a little water. Charlotte's nose told her it was camphor and cayenne in alcohol.

Charlotte sat back on the stool, letting her neck and shoulders relax, only then feeling the soreness that lodged there when cares came heavy upon her. She watched Honey as she supported Maudy's head and shoulders. How strong this cousin from the backcountry was, despite her small stature and little flesh. More to be wondered at was the different person she became in the infirmary. She held herself erect, she looked one in the eye; her voice, while still quiet, became firm and steady. Everyone, the old Negro woman who served as midwife, Joan, even Mrs. Levier, obeyed her without a word. Even Charlotte herself.

"Does she have a fever?"

"Only a little now. But it's so fearful hot. And not a breath of breeze comes in that door." She took up a fan and began to wave it over Maudy's face.

"What brutes men are."

"Tell me, ma'am, will they that did this get their comeuppance?"

"Don't be foolish. They've done no permanent damage. She'll be able to work again. The man, too, Col. Meachem's man that she ran off with, from what I hear he'll be back in the fields before long, though he was lashed to a bleeding..." She glanced at Maudy and was glad to see that she had dozed off.

"And where is Mr. Waverley?" she continued, as she felt a trickle of perspiration roll down between her breasts. "Away, as usual, leaving me to deal with everything. Maudy's a fool, an ungrateful fool, but she fanned away the flies at our table almost as soon as she could walk. She tended Molly from the day she was born. And when Molly got too big to need tending, Maudy learned fine weaving and needlework--thank God they didn't cut her hands!"

"It's a sin and a shame. I cannot feature it."

"But Honey, you know well that some men won't contain their anger and their lust."

"Well, I reckon I learned something about bad men after me and Sarah had to go away from home. You see, one day I begun to bleed real bad between the legs and I just had to go to Mrs. McNair for help. It turned out to be a baby I was losing. Mrs. McNair didn't say a word and she took care of me. But after that she did ever look at me so fierce I knew I was bound for Hell. So I just couldn't let Papa do it to me anymore. Right soon after that it appeared to me like he was looking wrong at Sarah. So one night real late when nary a soul was stirring we lit out for a little place I heard tell of round the back of Brooks Mountain. We walked for two days and nights and Sarah's moccasins got worn clear through and her poor little feet cut up bad so as I had to carry her the last day. But I found work right off in a house where the mama was sick."

"That was fortunate for you. Great heavens! You could both have starved in that wilderness."

"Yes, I recollect it was good for a time. The lady's husband was from home, out yonder in the West. But then he came back, and right off he started sniffing after me every time he could ketch me alone. And I just couldn't leave again so soon, not knowing what we'd find next. I tried to say something to the lady, but she wouldn't believe me. She'd been good to me at first, but now she began to fault me all the time, and when I got big with child, well then she had to believe it and she screamed at me and told the neighbors what a...slut...I was. It was terrible, I can tell you."

All this was told with a certain degree of spirit, but now Honey seemed visibly to shrink into the meek creature that Charlotte was wont to see.

"I reckon you'll be wanting me to go away, now you know how bad I've been."

"Don't be a little goose, Honey. You will certainly not be going anywhere. Do you imagine all the ladies hereabouts to be so perfectly pure?"

Charlotte said no more, but just stared at this girl she had thought so simple, so without experience, despite her long, arduous journey to Laurel Hill, merely because she came from the backwoods. Charlotte had considered her own early life particularly harrowing, but she had been fortunate compared to Honey.

The girl must have taken Charlotte's silence for disapproval. "I'm sorry I talked of such nasty things, ma'am. I won't ever talk of wicked ways again. Sure and certain, a lady like you oughtn't to even hear of such things. I reckon seeing poor Maudy like this got me all wrought up."

Maudy was tossing about now, perspiration sliding off her cheeks, neck, and forehead. Her hair was matted from the moisture.

"This water isn't cold anymore," said Honey. I'll fetch another pail from the springhouse." She handed the fan to Charlotte.

"No. Call Jillie to do that." But Honey was gone. A fly was trying to work its way inside the netting over Maudy's face, so Charlotte quickly went to work with the fan. Why hadn't she already called Jillie to do this? Still, it wouldn't have done for the child to hear Honey's tale.

So a lady like herself shouldn't even hear of such things? To be sure, this young woman--for she was, indeed, a woman, and Charlotte could no longer think of her as a child--this young woman from the backwoods had even less a notion of what a lady's life, in England or here in the East, was truly like, than she herself could imagine of life in that Carolina wilderness.

She wiped her damp face on her sleeve. With this fanning she would soon be as soaked as Maudy. She thought back to her girlhood in Hampshire, a blessedly cool land of rolling chalk hills, grain fields and pastures grazed by cattle and sheep. All was neatly fenced and carefully tended. A far cry from the open meadows and forests of her present home. Children of a younger son who had disgraced himself by marrying the daughter of a common harness maker, she and Geoffrey had lived pleasantly enough as long as their father, a naval officer, was alive. But when she was eleven, there came the terrible tidings that their handsome, good-natured father had been lost with his ship in a ferocious storm off the coast of Spain. Everything changed. Geoffrey was sent to the estate of their distinguished uncle, Lord Ashton, Earl of Surleigh, to be educated as a gentleman. But the harness maker's daughter, regardless of her qualities--and Charlotte's mother was as much a lady as any of them, better than most!--had remained with her daughter in the modest cottage on a quiet Southampton lane and continued to teach Charlotte what she could of the manners and graces worthy of the lofty paternal line.

But her mother's health and spirits gradually declined, placing Charlotte in the role of nurse and comforter, her one hope lying in the return of Geoffrey whose image (since he was never allowed to visit them) she imbued with all the gallantry of her lost father.

When her mother died she was indeed summoned to Lord Ashton's estate, where his dull wife and their idiot son dwelled alone for the most part, where there were no visitors to break the monotony.

All too soon the beauty she had inherited from her mother came to bloom. At seventeen she had the same milky skin, the garnet-red hair, the tall and shapely form that had led her father astray twenty years earlier. In the same year that Geoffrey was sent to manage their uncle's lands in Virginia, that uncle began to find Charlotte worthy of his interest. He installed her in his London house, with an impoverished cousin as chaperone.

At this point in Charlotte's reminiscences Honey returned with

May, one carrying a pail of fresh water and the other a small bowl and spoon.

"We've got some good hearty broth for Maudy when she wakes," said Honey as she took the fan from Charlotte and handed it to May. "She's sleeping peaceful now so we mustn't wake her." She proceeded to pat the injured girl's body all over with the cool water, during which Maudy stirred but did not wake.

"May can tend to her for a bit, ma'am. I'd best take a look at little Edward. His poor chest is taken bad this time. With a start of guilt, Charlotte nodded, realizing that since the news of Maudy's return she had forgotten her ailing son. But then, he was always ailing in some way or other, and was always attended by either Joan or Honey or Mrs. Levier.

They found the child breathing laboriously, but asleep. Mrs. Levier answered Honey's inquiries, gazing with disapproving eyes at her daughter-in-law. Edward's face was flushed, and his eyes were sunk deeper than usual into the hollow between brow and cheekbone.

Honey's gentle fingers felt the child's temple, his neck, and his wrist. His grandmother was in constant motion with a water-soaked cloth and a fan. If she had had to care for her sick boy herself she would have done so gladly, Charlotte told herself. But to stand by, useless and helpless, while others nursed him with such devotion, but to no true avail, that she could not do. She turned her back and left the nursery.

Slowly she descended the stairs, her body weighed down more heavily with every step. Near the bottom she sat down and let her head sink forward upon her hands.

Very shortly she felt light fingers on her shoulder and heard Honey's voice.

"Shall I help you to your chamber, ma'am, so you can lie down for a spell? Little Edward will be better soon, truly he will. Once he's older, he'll grow strong."

It was a lie, of course, but this one person, at least, did not speak to her with blame in her voice whenever Edward was mentioned. Even Matthew sometimes looked at her, if not in reproach, at least with a certain hurt puzzlement. Honey was trying to help her up.

"No, the sun beats on my chamber window. I'll go to the parlor." She pulled away from Honey who was holding her arm. "Come in here with me and close the door after you."

She seated herself wearily and looked up at Honey who was staring at her in great dismay. "Please, ma'am, don't send me away. I've been good. I swear I haven't let anyone touch me since I went to Granny Harriet."

"Hush. Didn't I tell you I have no intention of sending you anywhere? We need you here. And even if you hadn't made yourself so useful to us, you are our relation. It would be dishonorable in us to fail to look after you. Now, sit down. You can be spared for a few moments. Indeed, as soon as Joan reappears, you must rest."

"Now I'm going to tell you something that no one but my brother and my husband knows. I know I can trust you to speak of it to no one, not even Sarah. Once I tell you, you'll see that you have no grounds to creep about laden with shame and pretend to be the world's worst sinner. Do you understand me, and do you give me your word that you will say nothing to anyone?"

Those eyes, the color of a robin's egg, were wide open and still apprehensive, but the girl nodded and gave her word.

Charlotte drew her handkerchief from her bodice and wiped her damp brow and temples, then unhooked her fan from her sash and began to fan herself in nervous spurts. Honey tried to take the fan and do this for her, but Charlotte waved her hand away.

She quickly related those events of her childhood that had just now passed like a stream of pictures before her gaze.

"Now that my uncle had brought me to London, you see," she continued, "I was presented at his evening parties and invited to others. I had quite a success, though not of the kind that was to result in

281

proposals of marriage, since the Earl's reputation was excessively bad, and more important, he had given no sign that he intended to provide this obscure niece with much of a portion. So I found myself flirted with and admired by young men in the evening, and importuned more and more pressingly by my uncle in the afternoon. At first he clearly hoped to achieve his object by persuasion, by gifts, by turning my head with all the glitter of London life. All might have succeeded, I confess, had I not been repelled by his pasty-faced, corpulent person and by his slimy, insinuating manner. Then he lost patience and threatened to send away my chaperone, who always hovered near me, at least on the other side of the door."

"Oh Mrs. Waverley!" cried Honey, her hands clasped to her still childish bosom, "I reckon you were scared nigh to death!"

Charlotte couldn't help but be touched by the breathless tone and the anxious eye.

"Yes, my dear, I was frightened. There was no relation to whom I could appeal for help, Geoffrey being all the way across the sea by then. And what could he have done, in any case? Call out his uncle, who was his only hope of getting on in the world? So I took the one path that presented itself. One of my admirers was young enough, foolish enough, and besotted enough with me to beg me to elope with him to Scotland where we could be married without his family's consent."

"Oh, so you were married, ma'am, and then lost your husband and came to this country." Honey looked immensely relieved.

"We never reached Scotland. My uncle caught up with us. The foolish boy was wounded in a bit of ridiculous swordplay to avenge Lord Ashton's 'honor,' and I...well, there we were in an isolated village inn, and I no longer merited the slightest consideration, having already ruined myself. So the Earl 'had his way with me,' as they say. Still, I bit him so badly on the chin that I'm sure he could not show himself in society for a good while!"

Charlotte paused, triumphing in her memory of the Earl's swollen face and letting that image efface all that went before. Then, finally noticing the anxious question in Honey's eyes, she went on.

"I was more fortunate than you, my dear. I was not with child. He had gained his object. I had become an embarrassment, for rumors of the event were circulating. So the 'trollop' was bundled off to Virginia to live with her brother.

Both of them started at a knock on the door. Joan opened it just enough to stick her head in, looking startled herself at the untoward event of people closeting themselves in the parlor.

"I done lay down, missus, but it just ain't no use to try to sleep. What does you want me to do now?"

"All right, Joan. You may as well tend to Maudy, since you won't have your mind on anything else in any case. Send May to help Old Sukey in the kitchen."

"Where was I? Ah well, I'd come to the end of all that is pertinent. But what you must pay heed to is this, my girl. <u>I hold my head high!</u> What happened in that inn was forced upon me. I dare anyone to shame me for it. Is not the same true for you? If you condemn yourself as a miserable sinner, you condemn me as well."

"Oh no, ma'am!" The poor girl sprang up, the picture of complete consternation.

"Well, give some thought to what I've told you. No, don't speak more now. I have much to do. But do not let me believe, henceforth, by your foolish shamefaced air, that I have told you my story in vain."

Chapter 16

Honey was dreaming of blueberries. She and Sarah and Josh were picking them on Fox Bald. The sun was warm on their backs and a breeze blew the girls' hair up over their bonnets. Josh was eating more than he picked and when she called to scold him he turned a laughing face to her and stuck out a blue tongue. Suddenly a shadow fell across her and a hand took hold of her shoulder. Papa? What had she done wrong? But it wasn't Papa. She opened her eyes into darkness.

She was lying in her bed with Sarah curled up tight against her back. By pale moonlight she made out a shape at the side of the bed. She saw that it was May, and May had brought no candle.

"Auntie Joan say you come quick," said a breath more than a voice. "Don't you wait to dress yourself, she say."

Honey knew at once that the crisis had come. Edward had a violent fever, worse than any he'd had before. A few hours earlier the fever had let up a little, leaving the child sleeping almost peacefully when Honey left the nursery that took up more than half of Aunt Abie's large chamber, and sought a few hours' sleep. But sleep had been long in coming. Somewhere far off a dog had been ceaselessly howling. Back home everyone knew that was a warning of death soon to come.

Now she slid smoothly out of bed, so as not to wake Sarah, and groped her way into the hall and down the stairs. Bright light shone from the nursery where Edward, Joan, and the baby usually slept. Baby Charles had been taken to sleep in his parents' chamber as soon as the fever had seized his older brother.

A candelabra with five candles, all burning, stood at each end of the trundle bed where a tent of sheets had been erected leaving only one side open. On the floor close to the bed sat a pan of hot coals supporting a kettle of water from which steam rose, creating a warm mist to help the child breathe. One look at the small form lying there brought a chill to Honey's heart, as though an icy hand had closed around it. Despite cold baths, saltpeter, and camphor, the fever had risen again. Edward's face was flushed, his eyes deeply sunk in their sockets, and the pulse in the thin wrist that Honey could almost encircle with one finger raced like the feet of a frightened mouse. Worst of all was the roar of Edward's breathing that filled the room like the bellows in the blacksmith's shop, hardly to be believed as coming from a child so small. The end, so long dreaded, had finally come.

On the open side of the little tent Joan and Mr. Waverley were kneeling, he fanning the coals and she bathing the naked little body from a basin in which floated chunks of ice.

"There you are," said Mr. Waverley without turning his head from his task. "Joan must tend to my mother who is also ill. Please relieve her, and for God's sake do whatever you think best." His voice was thin and dry, as though it, too, was being drained of life. Honey knew he had been sent for from Richmond. He must have ridden straight through the night.

She hastened to take the icy cloth and kneel next to him. She was clutched by a desperate longing to do more, anything, to save his son. Edward's body was so thin you could count each bone. The network of veins under the transparent skin made his chest, his arms, and his legs look almost blue. She had known from the start that it would come to this. Everyone had known. Mr. Waverley, who had always shown himself so tender and so attentive to the boy, seemed almost serene as he steadily fanned the coals.

So it startled Honey when he suddenly stood up and turned toward the door, hand upraised. Honey had heard nothing, but Mrs. Waverley was there.

"No, not a step nearer!" he cried in that same thin voice. Mrs. Waverley stepped back, and also spoke in a voice new to Honey. It was pitched high.

"The doctor is here. I will stay away from Edward, for the baby's sake, but do let the doctor do what he can. He swears that just a little bleeding, from the throat..."

"No!" He himself seemed startled by the loudness of his cry. He was silent for a few moments, then said in a much lower tone: "My dear, not the lancet and no blistering. My child will not die with his tiny veins cut open and his tender skin burned. If I see that gentleman take out his cups and his knife, I will seize the knife and you will see where I plunge it."

The voice was quiet, entirely out of keeping with the words he was saying. He had knelt back down and resumed his fanning. Out of the corner of her eye, without stopping for a moment in her bathing of Edward's burning body, Honey could see Mrs. Waverley gripping the frame of the door as though she might shake it loose like Samson the pillars of the Temple. Honey sensed a tremor pass through the shoulders of the man next to her. He and his wife had become two different people from the all-knowing, all-seeing gods she so much admired and feared. She remembered being told that the other two children they had lost had died early, in the first few months of life. This one frail boy had lingered for nigh on four years, reminding everyone, more constantly than the family cemetery hidden behind the walnut grove, that death lay patiently in wait.

Now the gods were struck down. They suffered like ordinary mortals. Only the other day Mrs. Waverley had confided secrets that had begun to change Honey's view of her. While learning her letters from Mrs. Levier, Honey had heard much grumbling about Mrs. Waverley's extravagance and pride and yes, even about neglect of little Edward. But Honey had closed her ears to this. Whatever neglect there might be, she didn't believe it came from lack of love.

At that moment the doctor entered, a young man whose sharp step snapped against the rumble of Edward's breathing. Honey quickly retreated to a dark corner while Mr. Waverley and the doctor bent over the bed speaking in low tones. Mrs. Waverley, after letting the doctor pass, leaned her whole body against the side of the doorframe, her large hands open and slack against her skirt. Her face was turned toward the bed, but her heavy-lidded eyes looked sightless.

The whispers at Edward's bedside did not continue for long. The young doctor straightened up, raised his eyes to the ceiling and gave a great shrug to his shoulders. He stood for a moment as though considering what to do next, then reached to grasp the hand that hung limp at Mr. Waverley's side, lifted and shook it. Then he hastily left the room.

At a glance from Mr. Waverley Honey slipped back into her place at the bedside.

"Dr. Marsh wished to bleed him, of course. And he said we should keep him covered, to sweat the fever out of him. But good God! He's burning up. Still, perhaps just that thin sheet laid over him..." This was muttered in a voice so jagged, so out of keeping with his stiff, calm demeanor, that without thinking Honey laid her hand on his that now rested on Edward's forehead. She felt a surge of warmth at her own audacity, but he did not seem to notice her hand at all. He soon resumed his fanning of the coals, and she, after adding more water to the kettle, dipped her cloth once more into the icy water of the basin and slowly and gently cooled as best she could the feverish body.

They continued like this, in silence, for how long she hardly knew. From time to time Edward, in delirium, let out a little wail. It was almost past all bearing. Mrs. Waverley disappeared. Once Joan, once Maudy (who was much improved though she still wore the splint on her arm), and once Sarah too, came to relieve them, but each was waved away. Honey knew she had to stay, would stay even if Mr. Waverley ordered her to go.

Once only, Edward waked into a rational state, recognized his papa and gave him a wan little smile. At this the man's shoulders began to shake. Again Honey could not help laying her hand on his, which made him shake the more, without a sound.

The end finally came. As darkness fell at the end of the day, just two days short of Edward's fourth birthday, the roaring breath finally grew shallow and stopped. As the red slowly drained from the child's face, the whispers and rustling of people coming in and out of the nursery also came to an end. It was Honey who bathed the small body just as gently as if he could still feel her touch. She insisted on so doing, just as she had insisted on staying constantly by his bedside. Indeed, she had no need to insist, for Mr. Waverley made no protest. He again waved everyone else away. He held the basin and the towel while she worked. From the fine cedar chest under the window he had taken a coat and breeches of yellow linen for Edward to wear. Someone had brought a plain nightshirt and hood, as was commonly used as burial clothes, but he would have none of it. He also chose the position of the arms, crossed upon the breast. He at first balked at the cloths soaked in vinegar that Honey asked to be brought and wished to lay upon the face and hands. But when she gently spoke of the great heat, he sighed and nodded. He agreed to burial the very next evening, for the same reason.

Although Mrs. Waverley was brought word directly her son died, she did not come back to the nursery at all.

Edward looked so at peace, with the delicate lids closed over those hollow, haunted eyes, that Honey almost envied him. Such a thought was surely contrary to God's law. But it could not be wrong to be glad for Edward, who was with God in heaven and would never again wheeze and cough and cry until his throat hurt so bad he could barely swallow.

She dared to say a little of that to Mr. Waverley as the two of them sat by the side of the bed after the work was done. He said nothing for a long while. Then suddenly he asked her if she knew any prayers she would say now for Edward. This surprised her mightily because she knew he was not a God-fearing man and she expected, too, that Mr. Higgens, their preacher, had been called for such a purpose.

She scratched around like a chicken in the dust of her brain, but nothing more than the "Our Father" and the "Lord is my Shepherd" were stirred up and for sure and certain Mr. Waverley knew those prayers just as well as she did. But when she said so, he asked her in that strange, jagged voice to say them for him anyway because he couldn't get out the words himself.

She knelt then on the floor and folded her hands, feeling the heavy presence of his body bent forward on his knees. She managed to say the prayers steadily enough. He made her repeat them over and over for a long time. After a while she forgot him being there.

Then Mr. Waverley got up, so she did the same. He looked at her with his usual kind eyes and said in his usual quiet voice: "Thank you, my dear. Your prayers brought me back to a better time, a time long ago when I was a child and believed in the same kind of God you believe in. You're a good girl. I truly don't know how we did without you in earlier days." He gave a long sigh and then shook himself a little. "I must tell them to come take my son down to the drawing room. We'll have prayers said there by Mr. Higgens. And that will be all. No further ceremony."

"Please, sir, won't you let me tell them for you? I see Molly sitting out in the hall. I expect she's wanting her papa real bad right now." Honey had spied the child two or three times sitting on the floor just outside the door, hugging her knees and scowling when Honey met her eyes. She knew well enough that Molly hated her, and try as she would she hadn't been able to budge that stubborn hatred. The part she had played in this last illness of little Edward would only make it worse.

Mr. Waverley gave her a quick, surprised look, and then nodded and went to the door where he took hold of Molly's hands and drew her to her feet. They walked off down the dark hallway, hand in hand.

<hr/>

A week after Edward had been buried, in a simple wooden casket, the design for the flat stone to be placed over it had still not been decided. This was a decision that the grieving parents should make together, yet Matthew put off, and put off again, speaking to Charlotte about it. This was not because he feared causing her pain. No, he feared the coldness with which she responded to anything he said to her these days. Therefore little was said between them. Someone seemed to have erected an invisible fence down the middle of the bed they shared. They got in and out of it, each on his or her own side, without a word or a look, much less a touch. A gentle touch would have so consoled him in these forlorn days. Yet he dared not reach out to receive it.

Now the time for his return to Richmond and the Assembly session was at hand. He must speak to her.

He found her sewing in the drawing room, with Honey, Sarah, and that unfortunate girl Maudy, who did not raise her scarred face to look at him. "Young ladies," he said, "and Maudy, I wish a few words with Mrs. Waverley alone." All three hastily gathered up their work and left the room. He had addressed them, rather than Charlotte, for fear that she would refuse to dismiss them. What a coward he felt himself. He commanded, albeit politely, nearly sixty people, Negro and white, on his lands, but he could not command his wife.

She sat there, stiff and tight-lipped in her black gown unrelieved by any ornament, but as beautiful as ever. What had he done, that she should cut herself off from him so entirely?

"My dear, I leave for Richmond tomorrow, as you know." Silence. "I must tell Noah what to carve upon the stone. No word, I think, beyond his name and the dates. But would you like a winged cherub head, or a willow and urn?"

"Whatever you think best."

"Then the willow, I think. It is my favorite tree, despite the meaning we give it. It evokes sadness, yes, but also resignation and peace."

"I paid the doctor. He preferred rum to tobacco."

"I thought you must have done so."

Surely something more than this must be said before he left. It had almost always been she who brought words of more than everyday matters to their conversations. She might then voice opinions and emotions of which he did not approve. But at least there was warmth, though it be sometimes the warmth of anger.

"Dearest, you are angry with me. I beg you to tell me the reason. I don't believe it's because I am returning to Richmond. You well know that at one word from you I will delay my departure, much as my duty...but it cannot be that because your coldness toward me began even as our Edward lay dying."

He paused, but got no word from her.

"Is it that you blame me for his death? For not letting the doctor bleed him? I cannot believe you wanted him to be so tormented. We all knew he was going to leave us. I do blame myself, though, for his death and those of the others. You know I have never believed in a god who interferes in human affairs, not since childhood. But now, seeing our poor child born only to suffer countless illnesses and then... leave us, it almost makes me believe in the God of the Hebrews: cruel, jealous, wrathful. Cruel. But was I not cruel when I sold Joan's brother, those many years ago, merely because he was disobedient, rebellious, and I feared him? You know what became of him. You know he died in the sugar swamps of Carolina. I'll never forgive myself for that, and perhaps there is a wrathful God who does not forgive, either."

"For the love of God, Matthew! But in truth there can be no love of God in my heart after this. But you are inventing all this guilt because you want to hide the blame you have for me. No! Don't deny it. You all blame me. All of you. Ever since Edward was born. Because I did not devote myself to him as you have, and Joan has, and Honey since she came. Even your sanctimonious mother, as much as she is capable of devoting herself to anyone. She did it to show me up as a hard, cold, unloving mother. Not a true woman at all. For I have not that sweetness of temper, that softness, that submission, which is taken to be the mark of our sex."

He could only stare at her, so great was his surprise. And she stared back, as though defying him to contradict her. No thoughts, no words, came to his mind; only the urge to comfort her in his arms. He moved toward her, but she backed away.

"You think, you all think, that I cared nothing for him, but I cared more for him than for anyone. Only I could not be much with him. So if there is this God of Wrath, He has punished me, not you. I hate Him, for how could He allow a child to be born only to suffer for nearly four years, and then die?"

"Dearest," he was finally able to say, "I haven't the words to say to you. Only that in my heart there is no blame for you. None. Not ever. You are all the woman I have ever wanted, for me and for our children." He knew his words were not reaching her. He felt his helplessness. So he offered her the one comfort he himself had found.

"Perhaps you might ask Honey to be with you? Her simple prayers meant more to me than all the long ones of Reverend Higgens. Her faith and innocence, even for one like me who has so little of either, bring solace. Her God is a forgiving one."

This last made Charlotte bite her lips and raise her eyebrows.

"Indeed! With all her talk of shame in her past? Of being so laden with sin I must cast her out of Laurel Hill? But to you she speaks of forgiveness. Capital! Then let the sweet little creature comfort you. She, at least, is all a woman should be!"

Before he could raise a hand to stop her she gathered those black skirts together and swept from the room.

Nathan and Miles were walking slowly back from the west meadow where mowing had finally commenced, later than ever this year because spring had been so wet. Nathan breathed deep of the sun-dried air, enjoying the ease with which it filled his lungs and the sweet scent of fresh-cut hay. The earth felt firm under his feet. No mud oozed around his soles.

When they reached the feed barn and saw no sign of Uncle Matthew, whom they had been requested to meet here, they climbed onto the fence of the sheep pasture to await him.

"I suppose you'll have the oats mowed as soon as the gang has finished the meadow," said Miles. Nathan liked the way Uncle Miles always seemed to assume that Nathan knew what he was about. Not like Uncle Matthew who still treated him like a boy who needed constant reminding.

"Yes, sir. The crop will be but indifferent, because of the damp."

"Indeed," sighed Miles. "A farmer is nothing without weather, as the saying goes. And without tolerable prices as well. Those for tobacco are abysmal at present. But it's a good life, all the same."

After a winter of unnatural gloom, Uncle Miles' spirits seemed to have regained their usual buoyancy. Nathan could not quite understand why. Mr. Humbolt, who was expected to die months ago and thus enable Miles to take over his house and plantation, lingered on. Mr. Geoffrey Burnham also lingered on at Laurel Hill, paying regular visits to Miss Lucinda, a situation that could bring nothing but irritation to Uncle Miles. Nathan dared not ask him about this. It was not the sort of thing you asked a man. But then, just as he was wondering, his uncle brought the subject up of his own accord. His spotted hunter bitches, Shot and Flint, had come bounding up to his perch on the fence, the remains of a rabbit in both their mouths, and he patted them and scratched each behind the ears.

"Good girls! You might have saved that one for me, but you deserve your treat. You know, Nathan, patience can pay off. These girls were sniffing about, worrying themselves, for a good two hours before they finally caught the creature. As for me, I've been worrying myself for months watching that good-for-nothing Tory put on all his mincing airs and succeed in impressing a young girl who is as yet no judge of men. How could she be? I was champing at the bit to be away on my new land at the other end of the county so as to see no more of her."

He jumped down and picked up a large stick, which he threw for the dogs to fetch, each tearing away like quarter horses at the gun. "But now what I see is that the foolish fop is dragging his feet, apparently not about to set a date, probably because of the fascinating French lady so conveniently in the same house with him. It won't be long before the dear girl will see it all, will cast off her undeserving suitor, and I will be there."

Nathan did not see so much cause for optimism. He doubted he would ever understand girls; not ladies, at any rate. But it appeared to him that if this one was so intent on making a fool of herself over the Tory dandy, she would never appreciate the value of such a fine straight arrow as Uncle Miles. Plain looking and plainspoken as he was. Even if the other one threw her over. But best not say a word of his doubts.

"It's a right good thing you're here just at present, Uncle Miles. Because of the work. I've not had a word of direction from Uncle Matthew since poor Edward took ill this time. Of course I know well enough what needs doing, but he's so damned particular."

"He's taken Edward's death exceedingly hard. He knew it would come as well as any of us, but it's as though a wagonload of earth has fallen upon him. Just like that shoveled onto the child's coffin. He has the infant boy now, healthy as a mongrel pup, to pin his hopes on, but he was truly devoted to Edward. Mayhap because Mrs. Waverley was not. She's a queer one, that lady. One could never be easy with her for a wife. Small wonder since she comes from the same stock as Mr. Geoffrey Burnham."

"Sometimes I can scarce credit that Mrs. Waverley was so good to me when I was small. But now I've grown to manhood" and he cast a sharp glance at his uncle to see if he would smile at this, which, in fact, he did, "I keep as great a distance from her as I can."

"Indeed, she has a sharp tongue. She merely jests, you know, but her jests can sting. Best give her back as good as she gives, or if you can't find the words, merely laugh. A laugh pricks the tormentor's bubble."

"That's more than I can do, either one. I live for the day Uncle will let me go back out west. I'd give my ears to go this very moment."

At this very moment the "tormentor's" husband was finally approaching them, and caught the last words of his nephew.

"All in good time, my boy. All in good time." Matthew did not look directly at either brother or nephew, but gazed across the new-mown meadow and breathed in deeply as though seeking some illusive solace through his narrow nostrils. "I know you are burdened with supervision of the home quarter, Nathan, but as soon as I return from Richmond, which must surely be within a fortnight, you will be free to mind your books."

"Indeed, Nathan," said Uncle Miles, "I wish I had stuck my nose into the law books at your age. Now it's excessively hard to learn by heart all that tiresome stuff. Memory goes with age. Besides, why be in such a hurry to make yourself a target for the Creeks. Those redskins are raiding right and left in Kentucky territory. Goaded and bribed by the damned English, of a certainty."

"But how I'd like a good fight!"

"Nonsense," said Uncle Matthew, "there's no fight. They strike a lone cabin, kill a whole family, and are gone. Now I must be off. I leave directly after dinner. As you know, half the tobacco is drowned, but the remaining fields are not too weedy, and I commend your efforts for that, Nathan. Pray don't tarry in having it topped and succored. And the dung must at last be turned, seeing it's been too miry to do so up to now."

Nathan knew enough to attend to all that without being told. But he could at least take the initiative in another matter, before his uncle brought it up. "Two wheelbarrows are broke and rusted beyond use, sir. Shall I tell Noah to make new frames, and order wheels from Mr. Jameson in the village?"

"Yes, and have five or six new tilling hoes made as well. But come with me back to the verandah where we can seat ourselves more at ease." (Mr. Waverley was not one to perch on fences.) "And perhaps May will bring us a fruit drink, or whatever you gentlemen might wish."

All three men stopped abruptly in their tracks when they saw that the verandah was not unoccupied. Mme. de Coulanges was sitting there holding a cup in one hand and using the other to fan herself with what looked to be a newspaper. She beckoned them to take the seats near her.

"Come, we must join her," said Matthew in a whisper. "It would be discourteous to refuse. She will excuse our work clothes."

Miles laughed and whispered back: "You may have noticed, Matthew, that Madame is not over nice about her own attire in the morning."

"Sh! Good morning, madam. What a pleasure to see you about so early." And as she gestured to the other chairs, he asked if she were sure she wished the company of three work-stained fellows.

"But of course. I avow I was excessively bored. I awoke to this delightful sunshine and fresh breeze, and could not keep to my bed. I dared not hope for company. Everyone in your country seems to bustle about so busily in the forenoon. Yet here you gentlemen are. An answer to a prayer."

Nathan, who had never been in the lady's company in the morning, did note that the white cloth draped around her shoulders looked not quite clean, and that she showed much bosom for this time of day. Indeed, her bosom was the one attractive thing about her person, and he must endeavor not to let his eyes stray there too often. Of course, she ignored him and had looks and words only for his uncles.

She put down her cup and gestured with the newspaper. "I read of such shocking things that pass in the world that I almost determine not to look at another newspaper."

"May I ask what rag is that you've been reading, madam?" Uncle Miles inquired.

"It calls itself the 'Gazette,' sir."

"Ah, but which gazette?"

At this, she raised the sheets of broadside for him to see.

"Madam, I wonder that you would waste your time upon this rag. The 'Gazette of the United States' is a Tory organ, quite unworthy of your gaze. For you are not, surely, a lover of the British and their aristocratical ways."

"Come, Miles," said Uncle Matthew, frowning most pointedly at his brother. "That is no way to talk to Mme. de Coulanges."

"Oh do not rebuke him, Mr. Waverley, I beg you. I am so enjoying my disputes with Mr. Miles. When he comes here for a spot of tea, which is all too rare--only when my dear cousin Geoffrey is gone to visit your neighbors. I do not think he cares much for my cousin. Is it not so, Mr. Miles?"

Uncle Miles said nothing to this. Once again Nathan wondered at the audacity of this Frenchwoman. This was the first lady from that country he had met. Could they all be so brazen?

"So, Mr. Miles," the lady continued, with not so much as a blush for her rudeness, though she must have remarked the rebuke in his silence, "which 'rag,' as you put it--I do adore to learn your English slang--which rag should I read to know what passes in the world? For I must know, so that I may dispute about it with you or any gentleman I can find. It does so relieve the tedium of the day."

"Well, madam, you must read the 'National Gazette.' It's Mr. Jefferson's paper, though he does not acknowledge it. There you will discover the grave danger our new country is in at present. Mr. Washington's term of office is close to its end, and he is bent on retiring to his beloved Mount Vernon."

"And what danger in that, sir? You have other worthy gentlemen in your new country, do you not?"

"Yes, madam, but also some that are exceedingly <u>unworthy</u>. When Mr. Washington leaves office, the walls of our so hard-won republic may well cave in. Mr. Washington is our only bulwark against those who wish our country to become a monarchy."

"Ah, that would indeed be a strange reversal. Are your people about to recognize the value of kingship, whilst mine appear determined to throw off their king? And the fault of this last horror will be yours!

Oh not yours personally, dear sir. I mean the fault of your country's nefarious example."

"Dear madam," quickly interposed Uncle Matthew, even bending his tall body over her so as to put himself between her and Uncle Miles. "I am sure you would like another cup of tea. Do you find one of the servants, Miles, and have refreshment brought for all of us."

Uncle Miles sprang up quicker than you would think possible for a big man, and thrust his torso into the house doorway, clapping his hands and calling out with his voice roaring like a bellows: "Hey there, anyone! Come!" Then he was back in his chair in a trice, a wide smile on his broad face.

All laughed, even Uncle Matthew. "Ah well," said he, reseating himself, "if you are determined to carry on an argument, and Madame does not object, let me assure her that we, the instigators of this new form of government, are not likely to abandon it."

"There you are wrong, Matthew. You ignore the danger. Mr. Hamilton and his monocrats want nothing less than to give unlimited power to the Federal City, with him as its king, and his fellows from New York and Boston are as attached to him as the rattles to a rattlesnake. God's blood! They conspire shamelessly against us. Begging your pardon, madam."

At this moment May came in answer to the summons, and asked what they would have. All four simply asked for something cold.

"Look at the way the scoundrels are encouraging unnecessary debt," Uncle Miles continued. "And speculation, which of course favors those few northerners with ready cash to invest."

"That will not last," said Uncle Matthew. "There will be a reckoning for those risky practices."

"And consider the exorbitantly high tariffs they've imposed on the foreign goods that we need. All to benefit their manufactories. The farmer, even the middling sort of planter such as I will be, can only be hurt as long as they are at the helm."

"Well, I must say to you, gentlemen, with no disrespect for the importance to you of the price of your tea and your sugar and whatever else you must import, that the present danger to my country is much graver. The hotheads there have declared war on Austria, and of course with the best of our officers, our natural leaders, fled abroad, in every skirmish so far our despicable rabble have run from the field. Such a disgrace. My hopes attach themselves to the rising up of all our right-minded forces still within France, and all the powers of Europe coming to their aid. What comfort that would bring. What joy. But you would not approve of that, would you, Mr. Miles Waverley?"

The lady's bantering tone had changed. She gazed at her opponent with eyes wide in defiance.

"No indeed, madam. I hold no respect for kings and dukes who run roughshod over the common people, who dine on caviar while poor wretches scramble for a crust of bread."

"Our King is good, sir."

"Your King may be good, madam, but he appears to be led by his queen and the nobility, who, with the exception of a few like M. de Lafayette, are nothing but parasites."

"Miles! You forget yourself," broke in Uncle Matthew. "You forget to whom you are speaking."

"Yes, sir, you are speaking to one of that class which you scorn with such impunity. But wait. You will see what will happen when all the men of position and the habit of command are chased away, and the rabble rule! How would it be if your slaves revolted? If you had a bloody uprising like that I narrowly escaped in the Indies? You talk of our peasants. What of your slaves?"

Had the woman no sense of decency? For in truth, one could hardly call her a lady, so ungoverned was her tongue. This thrust had certainly attained its mark, for Uncle Miles only stared at her, opening his mouth a time or two, and then shutting it without a word. Uncle Matthew, who had been standing, sank like a shot hare into his chair.

Finally Uncle Miles spoke, and not at all as Nathan expected of that lover of argument. "Your words are perfectly just, madam. I could point out that according to the reports of travelers our slaves are better housed and fed than your peasants, but that does not justify us. We are saddled with a means of existence for which the only excuse we can give is that we ourselves did not institute it. You will say we should abandon it. Some among us say the same. But most of us have not the courage to face the chaos and near poverty that would bring."

"Exactly," chimed in Uncle Matthew. "So our circumstance is not so different from that of Madame and her people, those of her class, that is. Do they not fear poverty and chaos?"

Then something occurred that thoroughly nonplussed all three men.

"What I know, in my heart, is that I shall never see my son, my sisters, my friends, my country, again!" And the lady burst into tears.

Then there was such a commotion! Nathan could only sit frozen in his chair, but both uncles vied with each other in uttering all manner of apologies. Then Uncle Miles ran off to fetch smelling salts, he said, though the lady showed no sign of fainting. Uncle Matthew remained by her side, fanning her and murmuring reassuring words.

"Go call Mrs. Waverley, if she can be found," he said to Nathan.

"No!" the lady cried. "No, I beg of you. How stupid I am. It is the heat. Let me depart to my chamber to rest awhile." Uncle Matthew assisted her into the house.

When both men returned to the verandah Uncle Miles received a severe reprimand from his elder brother.

"Your behavior was quite unconscionable, Miles. How could you forget that you were talking to a lady?"

"But that is just the point! I confess I acted the boor, but this lady talks to one like a man. She has the mind of a man, sharper, indeed, in intellect than some we know. And then suddenly, this."

"And she bats her eyes at one, and wears her dress down low in front, even though she's old enough to be a grandmother!" Nathan could not contain his indignation any longer.

"That will do, Nathan. What we must remember at all times is that despite her intellect and education she is a woman, and subject to all their weaknesses. Their emotions are so volatile and their tears so ready. Above all, we must bear in mind that Mme. de Coulanges is our guest and has sought refuge in our country. You must apologize, Miles, when next you see her."

"As you wish. But if you'll permit me, just now I'm off to do man's work. Would that I never had to do with the fair sex." Nathan glanced at his Uncle Matthew and saw a smile play over his lips. They were both thinking of Miss Lucinda.

"Just one moment, Miles, if you please. There is still one matter I must take up with you both before I set off for Richmond. Just yesterday I heard a tale from Joan that has alarmed me. Indeed, I wonder that neither of you said a word of this to me. I'm speaking of Dick Meachem forcing himself into Mrs. Waverley's presence a month ago, despite his being forbidden by her to set foot onto our land. Indeed, I wonder that neither of you wrote a word of this to me nor have spoken of it since I came home."

Nathan felt the blood course into his face and any possible words drain right out of his throat. Thank God his Uncle Miles was there, for he spoke right up without a moment's delay.

"Yes I did hear something of the sort, from Joe. It seems that Nathan was off at Speckled Ridge Quarter when it happened and I of course was at Farrington. Nathan and I talked it over, and then I asked Mrs. Waverley about it. But she insisted there was nothing in it. The rascal did appear, but she chased him off without the least difficulty. Indeed, she rather preened herself on doing so. Didn't want me to say a word to Dick or the Colonel because this would 'demean her authority,' as I recall she put it."

"No doubt the blackguard got her dander up. She can be devilish imperious and did, I dare say, get the upper hand with him. She wrote me of his abominable conduct in regard to our Maudy. The fellow deserves to be throttled."

"He hasn't been seen hereabout since," said Nathan. "I told all the servants to send for me the moment he was seen again. Truly I did, and I would come at a gallop."

"Certainly, my boy. You are staunch as a hound. I count upon you. Still, I'm not easy in my mind. Dick has a fierce and wild temper, particularly when in his cups. And Mrs. Waverley can be heedless when in a violent passion. Do you both pay close attention to anything you hear of him, and take measures accordingly."

The older man gazed searchingly at both the others. While Uncle Miles reassured his brother with an easy nod, Nathan hastened to assent with considerable gravity. Then each went off to attend to his own particular duties.

Chapter 17

Late on a warm July morning Charlotte sat at her dressing table languidly brushing her hair. In the moist air of summer it needed no application of the curling iron. The long auburn locks fell in waves and could be readily twisted into the simple chignon that was good enough for everyday wear. Many ladies covered their heads with a mobcap on such days, but Charlotte considered that acceptable only for her rounds of the dependencies. Maudy could dress her hair better, and more quickly, but she no longer cared to call upon the girl for any personal service. She preferred to keep Maudy busy at her weaving, and out of sight. With her scarred face and her eyes so full of misery, she was not an agreeable thing to behold.

Charlotte's own appearance, to be sure, was nothing to be proud of. She bent forward to scrutinize her face: thinned, with the cheekbones standing out starkly against temple and jaw. And her eyes, hadn't they lost some of that famed violet hue? She glanced with disgust at the black gown she was wearing. Every time she caught a glimpse of it in the glass she was reminded of Edward. And him she must forget, else she would truly go into a decline. Why could she not accept this death, since she had known from the beginning that it would come? She had lost two other babies, with grief not near as deep as this.

Suckling the baby had become an ordeal. The monster had teeth now and a raging appetite, and did not scruple to bite the nipple that nourished him. Joan, Honey, Mrs. Levier, everyone indeed, beamed and chortled over the lusty creature, commenting on every sign of his prodigious health. Whereas she, Charlotte, who alone among them all could not banish the image of Edward from her mind, saw him as the devourer of his fragile brother, and now of her.

Was she quite entirely losing her mind? With two or three impatient movements she twisted her hair into a careless knot, stuck into it a few pins, and rising abruptly from her chair, went to seat herself in front of the secretary on which lay a half-finished letter to Matthew. Although the spring sessions of the Assembly were long since over, he had lingered in Richmond to fulfill the duties of executor for his brother-in-law's estate. He purposed also to catch up on legislative work he had fallen behind on because of Edward's death. Or so he said. She could well imagine that he was not eager to return to Laurel Hill after the way she had treated him before he left.

She drew Matthew's latest letter from the cubbyhole where it lay rolled, and smoothing it out with a heavy hand, ran her eyes over the two sheets--he used to write five or six--to see to what queries she must reply. Her eye fell on the following passage:

As to that scoundrel, Dick Meachem, I beg you be more on your guard. Of course you must take in his wife when she seeks refuge from his violence, but you must send instantly for Nathan and Miles and make sure of having one of the Negro males close by.

I do beseech you to continue suckling little Charles a few more months. I recall I did not approve of it in the beginning, but he does so thrive on his mother's milk. And now all our hopes are pinned on him.

She laughed. It was a bitter laugh. Her own welfare had once come first with Matthew. Now he too worshipped at the altar of the young heir.

She dipped her quill angrily into the inkpot and was rewarded by two drops splattering upon her letter. No matter. Since her husband's regard for her had already sunk so low, what further harm could a slatternly letter do? She added but two coldly compliant sentences to the blotched sheet, folded and sealed it.

When she went into the hall looking about her for a servant, she heard a rustle of skirts coming from the drawing room and was embraced, coolly of course, by Kate, whom she had not seen since the barbecue of the preceding spring.

"Why Kate! What a delightful surprise. Why did no one tell me you were here?"

"Oh, I asked them not to disturb you, Mrs. Waverley. Indeed, I feared you were ill."

"Because I still kept my chamber? It was from sloth, I assure you. So many tiresome duties and so few distractions. I'm heartily glad you've come. It makes a welcome change. But May will bring us a pitcher of shrub." (She had spied the girl's face peeking at them from the hallway.) "You must have had a hot ride to us." She led the way to the verandah, where they seated themselves and hoped to enjoy a breeze.

"Ah no. I drove over in comfort. Mr. Miles quite spoils us. He always keeps the dogcart handy. You remember that our last overseer usually claimed that he needed it himself. But Mrs. Waverley, I can scarce credit you are dull here. Have you not still Mr. Burnham and Mr. Levier and that French lady whose name I can never recall, all here to keep Laurel Hill lively?"

"Yes, indeed, they are here, but I scarce see any of them. Geoffrey dines constantly with you and Lucinda, as you well know. Madame finds our summer quite intolerable, and so keeps to her chamber throughout the day. In the evenings she and Geoffrey reminisce about Paris and Rome and God knows what else. As for Mr. Patrick, he came to escape the heat and the ague, but was barely here a fortnight before he was laid low with that malady. So now Mrs. Levier has her husband to herself, laying on the warming pan for his chills and clouts dipped in spring water for his fevers. And Mme. de Coulanges merely pouts and sighs when obliged to spend a few moments at table with only me and the young girls."

"I'm sorry to hear that, Mrs. Waverley."

"Oh but I forgot! We did have one quite stimulating diversion. Sophie Meachem suddenly appeared at Laurel Hill with a bruise upon her jaw the size of a duck's egg. What a flurry of bolting doors, alerting Big Moses and Nathan, stowing Sophie in Honey and Sarah's room! I swear I felt like the heroine of an old romance. Of course we expected Dick Meachem to come raging after his wife, but it turned out that he had galloped off to Simmons Corners to celebrate his brave attack on a helpless female. Only the Colonel, shamefaced and apologetic, appeared next day to collect his daughter-in-law. I confess that for me it was a pitiable anticlimax."

"Mrs. Waverley, may I speak of something that worries me?"

"By all means. I'll wager it concerns Lucinda and Geoffrey. I recall we had some talk of them way back in November, the last time you did me the honor of paying me a private visit." Charlotte maintained a serious expression, though within she felt only amusement at the sluggish pace of her brother's courtship.

"I don't wish to offend you, Mrs. Waverley, and would not trouble you at all about this affair, only Mr. Waverley is detained so long in the capital."

"And?"

"Lucy is not being treated with the respect that is her due. She speaks of Mr. Burnham as her accepted suitor, and I'm sure he has spoken of marriage to her, but he says nothing of it in my presence and he has surely made no formal request to your husband, as her guardian, or Mr. Waverley would have written us about it. Meanwhile he spends hours alone with her--I cannot be always present. I know she would do nothing wrong, much as she dotes on him, but it is not seemly."

"Then why do you not speak to her? She's not a child. Any woman with an ounce of finesse knows how to bring a suitor to declare himself in form."

"I've tried, Mrs. Waverley, but I've only succeeded in getting her back up. She tells me that he thinks it unfair to tie her down when he doesn't yet know the result of his lawsuit, and therefore what sort of situation he can offer her. I argue that since she has enough for both, there is no obstacle. But to her he is all nobility and high-mindedness."

"Then you must speak to <u>him</u>."

"I've tried that too. But he's like a fish just pulled from the stream, and that one can't quite grasp. He wriggled free with great nonsense about his unworthiness, and the extreme respect in which he holds Lucinda and me. When Lucy heard of it, she became quite angry with me. And therefore more stubborn than ever. If only Mr. Waverley were here! Mr. Geoffrey must needs respect his authority, and Lucy would not dare complain of interference."

"Perhaps. I suspect you wish me to scold Geoffrey, and I will do so with pleasure, but he is past master of the deaf ear, which he seems to turn to everything except the flattery of Mme. de Coulanges."

"But that is most troubling, don't you think? I've overheard talk of it even among our servants!"

"I do believe you ladies are sharing a bit of gossip," said the voice of Patrick Levier. He had come over from Old House, clad not very respectably in a rumpled dressing gown and unclean small clothes. "Yes, ladies, the fever has taken pity on me and departed for awhile. So the two of you are discussing our charming French guest?"

"Oh yes, sir," said Charlotte, "she who is making your stay with us so much more agreeable than usual. Her presence, and then the all-too-short refuge that Sophie Meachem found with us a week ago, have quite diverted the old reprobate that you are."

"Yes indeed, fascinating creatures both, yet not half so fascinating as the mistress of the manor." He lifted Charlotte's hand and touched it lightly to his lips.

He emitted the combined smell of quinine and stale sweat. She pulled away and indicated Miss Nelson. You seem unaware that we have a visitor, sir."

"A thousand pardons, Miss Kate! I do hope you and your lovely sister are well? But I intrude. I withdraw upon the instant."

"No, Mr. Levier." Kate spoke gravely, as always. "I would be grateful for a gentleman's opinion, particularly since Mr. Waverley is absent. But perhaps you are too unwell."

"Oh, nothing revives Mr. Levier like gossip. We were discussing my brother's seemingly stagnant courtship of Miss Lucinda. Miss Nelson here has been trying, without success, to bring about a formal engagement. She wishes Mr. Waverley were here to assert his authority as Miss Lucinda's guardian, but what I haven't yet said to her is that if that young lady paid heed to my husband's advice, which I much doubt, she would break with poor Geoffrey."

This was quite true. Matthew took seriously his responsibility for assuring a good establishment for Lucinda and he did not see much chance of that in a marriage to Geoffrey.

"I assure you there is no hope of that," said Kate. "Trying to persuade her even to press him a trifle is like attempting to make water go against the current. A while back, in a moment of exasperation,

I allowed myself to comment on Mr. Burnham's apathy concerning more than the courtship. I suggested that he might well take some interest in the management of Farrington instead of spending his time there in idleness. Lucy was furious, of course, and said not a word to me for the remainder of the day. But since then she is up betimes these forenoons, follows me about and questions me regarding all my duties. She even pays visits to the kitchen, not a fit place for a young lady to be, with Cook using unchristian language and the scullery maid going about her work half-naked in the heat."

"Bless me!" exclaimed Patrick. "What has come over the young lady?"

"Oh clearly," laughed Charlotte, "she thinks she will become competent in all wifely duties, and then perhaps Geoffrey will reform himself."

"But that is not the half of it," continued Kate. "She has taken to finding out Mr. Miles whenever he is about the barns or nearby fields, asking him about crops and livestock, and whatever else is occupying him."

"Oh indeed?" This exceeded all belief. "Does the foolish girl think she will teach my brother how to manage an estate? Has she quite lost her mind? Mr. Miles must be exceedingly annoyed to be interfered with in those tasks he has so kindly undertaken."

"By no means. On the contrary, his spirits have taken wing these last days. He is so fond of her, you know, and I fear he has taken heart and renewed his hopes regarding her."

"We must put a check to this conduct. She is toying with him."

"Pray be easy, Mrs. Waverley," put in Patrick, giving her a penetrating look. "The young lady's object is laudable, however hopeless, and I'll wager that Miles knows what he's about. But why do you not use your interest with Mr. Geoffrey to hasten a marriage?"

"I own I have little influence with Geoffrey these days. A breeze from another direction blows upon him."

"Indeed, Mme. de Coulanges is quite irresistible, in spite of her age--for I suspect she is as old as I--and I understand that Mr. Geoffrey owes much to her and the Marquis' hospitality."

"Would that <u>she</u> gave some heed to what she owes in wifely duties to her husband, and took herself off!" A flush suffused Kate's sallow skin as she said this, and her mouth set tight. "I fear that she will end by breaking poor Lucy's heart."

"I would she were gone quite as much as you," said Charlotte. "Pray be assured that I will needle my brother as vigorously as you would wish to make a formal request for Lucinda's hand and set a date. All he needs is a wife to settle him and make him mindful of his obligations. As for Madame, I will beg her help in pressing Geoffrey into action. And I will begin to take great interest in her plans for the future. She is not obtuse. She will perceive the direction the wind is taking. And now, Miss Nelson, please excuse me. I must look into the state of my household lest the servants dawdle about the whole day."

<hr />

Molly was feeling out of sorts. She'd gone and sprained her right wrist. How that came to happen she could not feature because she was only swinging on the rope over the creek, something she'd done a thousand times. She'd let loose with her left hand to grab hold of a branch of the apple tree on the other side of the creek and somehow the jerk on her right wrist had sprained it. At first she'd enjoyed all the fuss over her, even though Mama had told her crossly that she was too big now to swing on ropes like a boy. They'd put a clumsy old splint on her arm and now she could hardly do a thing, couldn't go out hunting rabbits, couldn't paddle the canoe. Worst of all, she was sternly forbidden to ride even the oldest of nags. The only good thing about it was that she wasn't asked to do any mending or knitting, tasks she'd recently been having more and more trouble avoiding. She could read all she liked, and she liked that a great deal. Papa was home from

Richmond, and had brought her the plays of Mr. Sheridan, which she found quite jolly. But Papa was always busy. She barely caught sight of him at all these days. It seemed long months ago that he'd sat close to her in the bookroom and they'd cried over poor little Edward.

Now she had an idea. She and Sarah had been talking of Madam Marie and her manners that seemed so to shock the ladies, yet did not at all offend the gentlemen, leastways not Mister Patrick or Uncle Geoffrey. They spoke of those French novels in their yellow bindings that the lady had brought with her and kept in a drawer of her steamer trunk. Molly had asked to look at one once when her mother was in the chamber, and the two ladies had exchanged glances. They told her that those books were unsuitable for young eyes. That meant, of course, that they were about secret things that men and women did together in their beds; different, she hoped, from the mating of horses and dogs, because that would be exceedingly disgusting. But still, a girl had to find out, didn't she?

So Molly's splendid idea was to sneak back into her chamber that she shared with Madam Marie, and borrow one of these novels while the lady slept. It would be written in French, of course, but she was making good progress with the language under Lucy's tutelage, so she could probably make some of it out with the help of a dictionary. Madam Marie had given her strict orders not to come back to the chamber and disturb her while she slept--Molly always rose at first light, was dressed in a trice, and was out--but she would be so quiet that the lady wouldn't even stir. Sarah, who was a scaredy-cat through and through, had insisted she mustn't dare do it, but if she, Molly Waverley, didn't have the gumption for a little thing like this, she was indeed a sorry lot!

She turned the knob of the bedchamber ever so slowly and silently, using her left hand and just the fingertips of her right. Thank goodness this particular door did not creak in the least. She pushed the door open very slowly, and took a step into the room.

Glancing immediately at the bed, she saw a man's form kneeling next to it and holding in a close embrace...Madam Marie! The man sprang back as swift as a streak of lightning. It was Uncle Geoffrey, clad only in his small clothes. He and Madam Marie stared at Molly as though she were a charging boar.

It was Madam Marie who found voice first. "Ma foi! What are you doing here? Didn't I tell you not to disturb me in the forenoon?" She paused for a few moments, and then said: "Mr. Burnham was examining my eyes. Yes, all appeared dark to me when I awoke and I cried out so loudly that he heard me and came straight from his bed."

"Quite right," said Uncle Geoffrey, "and you, young lady, have been grossly disobedient. You deserve to be whipped."

"No, no, the child meant no harm. Very well, we will say nothing of your conduct, and you will say nothing either, will you, my dear? It will be our little secret."

For once, Molly scarcely knew what to say, or even to think. She just backed out that door as quick as she could, ran down the stairs taking two at a time, and joined Sarah who was waiting for her in the pantry.

"Sarah! Sarah! What do you think? They were kissing! She and Uncle Geoffrey. And he scarce half dressed. And she in her shift!"

"Oh, I'll not believe it! You must have seen wrong." Sarah sat down with a thump on the pantry stool, her big brown eyes as round as soup ladles.

"Well, I tell you it's true, ninny. Do you take me for a dunce? I know what I saw. Those two are lovebirds."

"But what about Miss Lucy? She does so dote on him, and he's such a fine gentleman. He's got such a sweet temper, and a sweet voice. He wouldn't never..."

"Oh you goose! You fancy him yourself."

Sarah's cheeks turned a deep rose, which made her look positively blooming. The girl grew prettier every day. She was already half a head taller than Molly, and was filling out into a woman. All this irritated Molly, who was still a scrawny, straw-haired child whom no gentleman would ever take a second look at. About that she didn't care the snuff of a candle. Her papa was the only one worth a farthing anyhow.

"The thing we must do, Sarah, is tell Miss Lucy so she can jilt him before he does it to her."

"Oh, but she will cry and cry. Her heart will be so broke she'll die of it, I'll warrant. Let's first tell your mama. She'll know to break it to Miss Lucy gentle-like."

"Not her! My mama's mean as a polecat these days. She'd just hush me up and tell us to mind our own business. We'll go over to Miss Lucy's directly after breakfast."

"But Molly, it's too far to walk, and you're not allowed to ride."

"Oh this blasted wrist! Well, we'll make Pram lend us the dogcart. You're not much of a driver, but even so, it won't take us above an hour."

But they were lucky enough to run into Uncle Miles, who was about to leave to return to Farrington, so he let Sarah ride his horse, a steady nag, and he drove the dogcart for Molly. Of course she was delighted to tell him of her surprising discovery of the morning.

"Good God! What a blockhead!" He laughed most uproariously. "That darling of the ladies has done it this time. It will go hard with him to wriggle out of it. I'll be bound that Miss Lucy will drop him like a bobcat does an unsavory toad." He didn't doubt Molly's word for a moment, which was gratifying because she was beginning to have some doubts about how Miss Lucy might receive her news.

Uncle Miles jumped out of the dogcart at the beginning of the avenue that led to the Farrington Great House, lifted Sarah down from his horse, sprang into the saddle himself with an excuse of some pressing task or other, and was off.

"You'd think he'd want to be here to see Miss Lucy's face when she hears the news," mused Molly.

"Oh no, Mr. Miles is too goodhearted for that," protested Sarah. "I don't know as I want to see it myself. Poor thing."

"Oh pish! We're rescuing her from an unworthy suitor, that's what we're doing. We're heroes."

Lucinda was not to be found in the house, which was empty but for a little servant girl with tiny pigtails bristling out all over her head. She thought Miss Lucy might be in the kitchen. They went around to the back and crossed the kitchen garden, finally locating Lucinda in the laundry. She was wielding a box iron in and out of the ruffles on a puce bodice. She wore a huge white apron over her gown, and a mobcap from which strands of damp hair escaped over her forehead. Her face was flushed and shiny with moisture. At first she seemed none-too-glad to see them, but then she looked relieved and managed a smile.

"Oh thank goodness you're alone, girls. I'd be mortified to have Mr. Miles or Mr. Geoffrey see me like this. Of course they wouldn't come in the forenoon. You are early abroad. I hope nothing is wrong?"

"No...not exactly."

She seemed not to catch the qualification, for she said to Sarah who was standing near the hearth in spite of the heat:

"Be a dear and give me the flatiron you see there. Careful! Use a cloth to lift it. The handle will be hot."

Sarah took the iron from the trivet over the fire, handed it to Lucy, and was given the cooled slug from the box iron to replace on the fire.

"It's hot as blazes in here, Miss Lucy," cried Molly, moving into the doorway to get a little air. "Where's the scullery maid?"

"The careless girl burned herself so bad she can't touch a thing, poor creature, and Sue is down with a spell of the ague. Kate and I have nothing decent to be seen in. But I'm almost finished, and then you two can help me carry our gowns to the house."

There were four gowns to carry, one for each child, and Miss Lucy laid two over her own arms.

"Mind you don't let the sleeves drag on the ground. And watch your step on the stairs."

The clothes press stood in the hall between the two ladies' chambers, and Miss Lucy was most maddeningly slow in laying out each gown on a shelf that pulled out, and smoothing out every fold and ruffle. Then she took her own sweet time in removing her apron and cap and hanging them on a peg in her chamber. Molly could scarce contain the news that was close to bursting within her. But at last they were settled in the parlor, sipping from tumblers of chilled fruit juice. Then she blurted out the whole story, adding a bit of drama by having the guilty ones leap apart and then hang their heads in shame.

She was not disappointed in the effect. Miss Lucy started up in a violent fret, walked away to the front window and paced back and forth several times with her face turned away from the two girls. When she did turn back to them, or rather, squarely to Molly, she looked at her in silence, her face stern, almost angry.

"I knew you'd want to know, Miss Lucy, so as..."

"You'd best hold your tongue, young lady. What age have you now? You're certainly too old for such mischief."

"But Miss Lucy. I truly saw them, just as I said."

"Whatever you saw, it was not what you think. You've always been apt to let your imagination run wild. It will be your undoing, Molly. My gracious! A child like you shouldn't even know of such things to think."

For goodness sake! First she was too old, then too young. Grownups were always telling her such nonsense. And Sarah was no help at all, sitting there with her head ducked down as if she hoped to make herself invisible.

"May one know what brought you to Madame's chamber? Didn't you tell me you were forbidden to go back there in the forenoon after you got up?"

"I wanted to borrow one of her books to read, since I'm hardly allowed to do anything else, with this wrist." Molly spoke up right firmly. She would stand her ground.

"Oh yes, no doubt a book not fit for a Christian to read. Particularly a child. Did you tell your mama or papa this silly story?"

"No ma'am."

"Well, I conjure you not to spread such a vicious tale any further. You don't mean harm, child, and I know you don't want to cause distress to your uncle or to Madame, who is a guest of your family after all. I'm sure I can count on Sarah to hold her tongue as well," and she went over to stroke the bent head. She seemed somewhat mollified, now that she thought no one else had heard of this.

"Now girls, you know that Mme. de Coulanges is Mr. Geoffrey's kin. Only yesterday, as I heard from Kate, Madame received news that her husband is quite ill, far off there in London. She's doubtless exceedingly distraught, and Mr. Geoffrey's kind heart led him to console her, unmindful of propriety."

"You see, Molly," piped up Sarah, "didn't I tell you such a fine gentleman as Mr. Geoffrey would never do anything wrong?"

Oh well, let them get up on their high horses. Molly knew what was what. They wouldn't change her mind one whit. She drew herself up in her chair as tall as she could and tried to imitate that haughty half-smile she'd so often seen on her mother's face. Would that she had her mother's height!

"As you wish," she said. "My lips are sealed." She'd always hoped for an occasion to use this phrase, and here was one quite perfect.

Chapter 18

Another torrid August day was crawling limply toward evening. The air was laden with moisture, but no rain had come for well nigh a fortnight. The sun beat down upon the fields where stalks of corn, tobacco, and flax drooped wearily toward the thirsty earth. One of the Farrington Negroes had suddenly dropped into a furrow while weeding. She claimed to be with child. She probably was, and it might be his, Miles thought with chagrin. It was the first time he had turned to the quarters for solace. Out west there had been a willing white woman, a widow who was glad of the help of a man on her small farm.

Here there was only Sophie, young Meachem's wife, who gave him sidelong glances whenever she spied him on a Sunday in town. But he wasn't such a fool as to go anywhere near that wasp nest. He had had high notions of resisting his urges for love of Lucy, yes, love and hope. But where was that hope now? It had flared bright again when he learned of Geoffrey's utter want of sense, nosing around with the Frenchwoman. The impudence of that idle rogue exceeded all belief! But as far as Miles could see, this had made no difference to Lucy. She had refused to believe it, most likely. God's blood! What gullible creatures women were!

So why deprive himself? The Negro wench had come to his cabin unbidden, not out of fondness for him, of course, but it seemed she was on the outs with her people and hoped he would buy her and take her away when he left. But he couldn't afford such a purchase at this time, and besides, he would never establish a Negro mistress on his estate as long as the barest hope of winning Lucy remained. The girl had said she was with child a bare month after she'd come to him the first time, so of course he had not believed her. After that, he'd thought better about the whole thing, and had not been with her since. He remembered what they used to say of Col. Meachem, that he "couldn't keep his dick out of the nigger gals." Now they said the same of his son, named <u>Dick</u>, the drunken sod. Well, they weren't going to say that about Miles Waverley, devil take them!

But now it seemed that the girl was indeed pregnant. She'd been carried into the shade of a hickory tree, been fanned until she came to, and been given to drink. He would hand her over to Kate for assignment to lighter duties. He would give her a handsome present, beyond what he'd already given, and that would be that.

Absorbed in these thoughts, he arrived at Laurel Hill. Matthew had asked him to come. He'd set out late, hoping thus to avoid attending the family at dinner. But the languor brought by summer heat had slowed the life of the household, as it had the work in the fields, and soon he found himself sitting silently at table while two Negro children wielded big feather fans. He feared that the sweat from his ride was offending the nostrils of his mother and Aunt Abie, who sat one on either side of him. They both wore thin black cotton (to honor the child who had died) and had probably barely moved all the forenoon, whereas he sat at table in his rough worsted coat, straight from field and trail.

Dinner finally ran its course and the cloth was lifted. As claret and brandy were brought in, the ladies withdrew. All but Mrs. Waverley, that is. When Mr. Levier made one of his flattering comments about the honor of her "delightful" presence, she remarked with a laugh that since Mme. de Coulanges, claiming to be completely stripped of strength by the heat, now always retired to her bed as soon as dinner was done, she herself found the company of old ladies and children excessively dull.

When Matthew mildly remarked that she was forgetting Miss Honey who was no longer a child, his wife shrugged those milky-white shoulders of hers, quite bare except for some sort of transparent gauze slung around them. Miles had noted that since the Frenchwoman had come and was wont to display her charms so boldly, Mrs. Waverley had begun to imitate her. About young Honey she commented that the girl could hardly be said to offer lively conversation.

"Besides," she added, "I suspect you mean to discuss with these gentlemen a decision which will have some great effect on me and my children."

"<u>Our</u> children, my dear," he said in a tone Miles had never heard him use to her. Miles had never liked this arrogant and, yes, disturbing woman, but he had always credited her with making the hours his brother spent at Laurel Hill his happiest ones. Of late, however, there were signs that troubled him. Matthew, always so abstemious, was making constant use of his snuff box, and not the delicate silver one given him by Mrs. Waverley, but a rude one made of tin that he had carried long ago while in General Washington's army. What was more, he would linger longer over, and accept more of, the after-dinner spirits. And now here he was unhappy enough with his wife to let it become apparent to others.

"But yes," Matthew continued, "my decision will affect all of you." He spoke gravely now, and the furrow between his eyes grew deeper. "I have given much thought to what course I should take, and have at last firmly determined not to stand for election to the House of Delegates this fall."

"My dear Matthew," said Mr. Levier, "it is in your election, to be sure, to stand or not, but let me conjure you to consider that you are a member of the Public Claims Committee, and likely soon to become its chairman. A most important committee, Matthew, where your wisdom and experience are invaluable."

Matthew made a small bow. "You are good to say so, sir, but I believe I can be of greater benefit to my neighbors right here in the county, as justice of the peace, where I mean to continue. It will give me immense satisfaction to be able to preserve poor Mr. Clancy's livestock and equipment against Col. Meachem's claim for debt recovery, for example. The power to delay hearings can be of great importance, you know. I dislike crossing the Colonel. But he takes too unsympathetic a view toward our struggling farmers."

"That duty you've been fulfilling all along, Matthew. God knows we need men of your moderate views in the House of Delegates, men who support the Constitution and have respect for order. Particularly at this present time when hotheads of the republican persuasion, like this young man here, are in the majority in Virginia."

Miles had to laugh at that. He had expected a shot from his stepfather sooner or later. "Yes indeed, Matthew," he said, "even I, hotheaded as I am, recognize your value and don't wish to see you retire to the county."

No one spoke for a long moment.

"Pardon me, gentlemen, for daring to speak on such a lofty subject in your presence, but will you give up so easily in your efforts to persuade my husband to continue in the public life of Virginia? I agree with you that we need his excellent judgment in the guidance of our Commonwealth."

Miles noted that his brother did not look at her during this speech, and that pain rather than pleasure marked his face. Matthew poured himself a full glass of brandy, and drained it. "I truly regret not having your approbation in this matter," he sighed, "but I am determined on my course. And though this is not my principal consideration, I will add that the very process of standing for office has become distasteful to me."

There ensued a long pause, during which all the others fortified themselves with spirits. Even Mrs. Waverley sipped at a glass of claret.

Then Matthew spoke again. "Please remember that we still have many wise heads in Richmond. And I hope to see my brother's there among them before long."

"Well, he had better throw his hat in directly, for I've been told Will Cracklethorpe is itching to run." This came from Nathan, and all turned their eyes toward him in surprise, for the boy did not often speak up in company, and never in the presence of Mrs. Waverley.

"Ah yes, Miles," laughed Mr. Levier, "your nephew here can serve as an extra pair of ears for you about the county. He's so young and so silent that people talk freely in front of him, forgetting he is there."

"Yes, and I've already heard rumors that you don't mean to stand, Uncle, rumors that must certainly be spread by Mr. Cracklethorpe's friends, for I know you've said nothing of it to anyone but us."

"I dare say there may be two candidates for my seat," said Matthew. "The elder Mr. Appleby has shown some interest."

"Now there's an odd fellow," said Mr. Levier. "He has wit aplenty, but I fear it's too subtle for our simpler folk. Besides, it's been bruited about that he's turned a Methodist."

"That may be. But still and all, I've heard nothing ill of young Mr. Cracklethorpe."

"Come, Matthew," interposed Mrs. Waverley. "He is becoming known as particularly adept at those practices you most abhor. You've been too much absent from the county to notice."

Or rather, thought Miles, too disdainful of gossip to listen. Mrs. Waverley learned of all such things. She'd make a better spy than Nathan because she could cajole information from any man, should she so wish.

"I don't mean," she continued, "only 'merchandizing one's vote for grog,' as you call it. Even you have had to bow to the custom of providing cakes and small beer at election time."

"Yes," sighed Matthew. "I always feel soiled by self-interest at such times, appealing to the gluttony of the voters."

"Well, you are too fastidious by far. I hear that Mr. Cracklethorpe is visiting all the churches, and the militia musters, and talks to everyone with a false smile on his face and inquiries on his lips about each man's wife and children, whom he's never seen and never taken an interest in until now."

"Worse than that," chimed in Miles, who did not stop up his own ears as he rode from this end of the county to the other. (From time to time he visited the Humbolt estate, which he now owned, to give directions and aid to the sick old man and his overseer who were still living there.) "Mr. Cracklethorpe has been quite vociferously holding you responsible for our levies being so high."

"Ah well," sighed Matthew, "that is to be expected. But apart from that, what are his views?"

"He has none, but to get himself positioned among men of influence in Richmond. Oh, and he is the very epitome of the aristocrat. After fawning on ordinary people to their faces, behind their backs he refers to them as 'the common herd,' and abuses them in the grossest terms."

"Yet he is a person of great gentility of manner. And he makes a good figure. But he is aristocratical, as you say, and inclined to indolence as are many of our class." Matthew ran nervous fingers through his thinning hair, took a generous pinch of snuff, and drew a deep breath. "You, my dear Miles, and other young men like you have turned your shoulders to the wheel, carved new land from the wilderness, and made companions of men of all walks of life. You still feel your energy swirling within you, and have the force of character to put it to good use. You will lead us toward a society entirely different from any the world has known until now."

"By God, Matthew, you wish me to run for office when I've not yet even been able to settle on my property?"

"No. You're right to look first to be made justice of the peace, and you will be welcomed among us."

"Indeed, that would be the most conducive to your advancement in the long term," opined Mr. Levier, looking more and more flushed. "Would you permit me to remove my coat and vest, madam, since we are among family only? Thank you, dear lady." Mrs. Waverley graciously helped the old man rid himself of that clothing, and even remove his stock. "But I'll be bound that I'll see you in the running next time around, young man, and the high standing of Matthew here will be enough to assure your election."

"But not, sir, if I don't have the wherewithal to provide plenty of grog," laughed Miles.

At this moment Joan entered the room and spoke in low tones to her mistress. When she left, closing the door behind her, Mr. Levier, who sometimes had a most acute sense of hearing, spoke up.

"Did I perceive correctly, madam, that your charming brother has returned early from his daily visit to Farrington? Will he join us?"

"I think not. I have a few words to say to him in private." Mrs. Waverley drew her brows together in a formidable frown that would have silenced anyone but the irrepressible Mr. Levier.

"Well I'll be bound!" said he. "I do believe poor Mr. Geoffrey is about to receive a dressing down from the lady of the house."

"Mr. Levier, please! Billy, you and Jillie go fan the ladies in the drawing room. Scoot! And close the door behind you." As soon as the black children were gone she expressed the fervent wish that Mr. Levier would learn to hold his tongue in front of the servants.

"A thousand pardons, madam. I shall do my very best to mend. For I quake at the slightest reprimand from you. But I would not be in Mr. Geoffrey's shoes for all the horses in the Waverley stable. Is it his over-assiduous attentions to Mme. de Coulanges that have brought him to this pass?"

The question made Matthew's eyes open wide, and sent young Nathan backing toward the door as though in hopes of creeping out unnoticed. Any sign of trouble for Geoffrey could bring nothing but pleasure to Miles, but what could he hope to gain from it? Best to get himself out of there, so as not to display in front of all the world his feelings on the matter.

"It's time Nathan and I look to the watering of the peach and plum saplings," he said, joining Nathan at the door. "They are surely parched."

"Let Nathan attend to that," came the quiet voice of Matthew. "Whatever is afoot here touches on the welfare of my ward, Miss Lucinda, and that concerns you deeply, Miles."

As Nathan fairly leapt from the room Matthew looked pointedly at Mr. Levier, but of course nothing but a direct command could make the old man miss out on a bit of gossip, and Matthew could hardly issue one to his stepfather.

All were standing now, since the gentlemen had got to their feet when Mrs. Levier rose to leave the room. She now settled back into her chair by the window. She picked up a small, finely carved ivory fan, waved it a couple of times before her face, then motioned to the gentlemen to be seated. As though in response to her husband's gaze still fixed on Mr. Levier, she spoke with a shrug.

"Now that he has brought the matter up, perhaps it's just as well that Mr. Levier remain. He sometimes lacks discretion, but he is, after all, a man of the world."

No one answered, but all seated themselves and waited for her to go on. Matthew in particular fixed upon her a compelling gaze.

"What has happened, Matthew, is that someone discovered Geoffrey and Mme. de Coulanges in a compromising position and went blabbing about it to Lucinda, of all people. Also to Miles, I believe, and of course it got to me as well. I said nothing to you because I knew you were engaged in more weighty affairs after your long absence in Richmond. I was sure, and still am, that the whole matter can be put to rest by the departure of Madame."

"And may one know who made this discovery?" Miles was taken aback by the hostility in his brother's voice.

Mrs. Waverley hesitated, and then shrugged. "It was your daughter, my dear." She glanced toward Mr. Levier and added: "Another one not known for discretion."

"Molly! My God! And you speak lightly of discretion! Yes, of course Mme. de Coulanges must leave, and Geoffrey too, at least for a good long while. But that won't undo the harm. To think that my little girl was exposed to this at her tender years."

"Oh for heaven's sake. For Molly it was a lark. She's quite swelled with her own importance."

"Well then, for Lucinda it is much more serious. She must be quite heartbroken."

"Not at all. Be assured that no harm was done there either. Miss

Nelson tells me that Lucy doesn't credit it, or perhaps forgives him. I don't know which. But once the Frenchwoman is gone, all will blow over."

"No, I will not suffer it. Lucinda will not marry your brother, at least not as long as I am her guardian. And I will do everything I can to prevent it afterward."

"Ah, my dear, what a prig you are! I'm sure that Mr. Levier here agrees with me that men will sometimes do foolish things, but that can't be permitted to interfere with the important affairs of life."

Mr. Levier did not venture an opinion, but was clearly enjoying himself. As for Miles, he heartily wished he'd been allowed to leave.

"My dear, I may be a prig, but I fear you are allowing your desire for your brother to make his fortune to outweigh any concern for Lucinda's well-being." This time he spoke gently, as though this were sufficient excuse for her attitude. "As for Miss Lucinda, she is clearly so attached to Geoffrey that she blinds herself to his faults. As you well know, I already had grave doubts about whether he could become a reasonably good manager of her property and thus offer her the security a woman needs. But now that it's clear he's been playing fast and loose with her affections, I would be derelict in my duty if I let her marry him. Fortunately, this has happened before bans have been published, perhaps even before he has proposed? All the easier to break it off."

"Come, Mr. Levier, do speak up," cried Mrs. Waverley. "Surely you don't think that my brother's prospects for an excellent alliance should be dashed over such a paltry offence?"

A serene smile graced the lips of the older man as he lit his pipe and took the first few draws on it, no doubt relishing the sight of this imperious woman looking to him to back her up. Miles was certain that nothing their stepfather could say would sway Matthew in the least. On this he could rely. He told himself that losing her suitor would never bring Lucy to look with favor upon his own hopes, yet anything was better than seeing her married to such a man.

Having finally got his pipe drawing to his satisfaction, Mr. Levier wiped his perspiring face with his large handkerchief. "You must excuse an old man burning with the ague. Directly I'll be obliged to take to my bed and beg you send a servant to bathe and fan me. But for just a moment I'll say that yes, I do believe that one should not make too much of this little incident. Lay it to proximity, my dear Matthew, proximity to a woman who was doubtless too much of an intimate in the past. If she can be persuaded to leave us--not harshly, of course, and with no hint of scandal--Mr. Geoffrey will soon forget her. And perhaps I should mention that the whole county, this end of it at least, knows of his daily visits to Miss Lucinda and looks upon the pair as affianced. All has been perfectly above board there, certainly, but it would not look well for her reputation to have it broken off."

This long speech caused a fresh profusion of sweat to stream down his cheeks and neck.

"We're obliged to you, sir, but you do indeed belong in your bed," said Matthew. He helped the old man to his feet and assisted him to the door where he called a servant to attend him. Back in the room, his shoulders sagging in apparent fatigue, he said: "I have not changed my mind about the marriage, but since we all seem to be in agreement about Mme. de Coulanges's departure, let us consider that. Where has she to go? Is she entirely without other connections?"

"She has none in Virginia, to my knowledge," said Mrs. Waverley. "She at first intended to go to Philadelphia to stay with a niece, a lady recently widowed. But with the yellow fever rampant there, she was persuaded to stay away. Now it seems that the niece, whose situation in that city was not secure, has elected to remove to Charleston and establish an academy for young ladies. Only sevennight ago Madame received a message saying the niece is already in Charleston and begs her aunt to join her in this endeavor. I need hardly say that I've been doing all I can to encourage her in this direction."

"A female academy? That hardly seems a promising venture," Miles could not resist commenting.

"What do you know of it, sir?" snapped Mrs. Waverley. "I am told they exist in Philadelphia. And did you know that a Mrs. Shelley has written a book on the importance of female education?"

Miles knew nothing of any of this, nor did he like the idea. What's more, it made him uneasy to look into those flashing eyes with their uncanny violet color. Not that her anger intimidated him. But it was disturbing.

"Well," he heard Matthew's voice saying as though from a distance, "we must of course keep her until the heat breaks, especially since it makes her ill. I wonder if anyone has warned her of the climate in Charleston? I suppose I must persuade Mr. Burnham to cease his visits to Farrington."

"Allow me to speak with him first. I've already requested it, and I believe he is expecting me in his chamber at this moment," said Mrs. Waverley. Receiving no word of objection, she quitted the room.

Miles, still discomfited, and wanting no conversation with his brother, bowed wordlessly and left room and house.

Matthew, left alone in the drawing room, stood gazing down at the intricate reds and blues of Charlotte's prize Turkey carpet. The points of its rows of diamonds and octagons were marshaled in warlike formations, cut by four thin lines of sunlight that made it through the shutters of the two west windows. Oppressed by darkness and stale air, he moved to a window and opened a shutter. As though to mock him, the sky suddenly darkened as a purple cloud passed in front of the sun. Four or five such clouds had been hanging promisingly in the western sky for days, but no drop of rain came to relieve the parched earth.

Hearing a step, he turned and saw Geoffrey in the doorway, with Charlotte close behind him.

"Good afternoon, sir," said Geoffrey in his usual sonorous baritone. "I hope the day finds you well?" Matthew could only look at him in disbelief at his calm air. "I met my dear sister on the stair and knew at once that I was in for a reprimand. Of course I guessed the reason for it, and when her first words were that the whole household was up in arms against me, I thought I might as well face the general wrath all at once. Yet I see that only the master of the house remains." This last was said with a graceful shrug and a sigh. "May I sit down?" He did so without awaiting an answer.

Matthew remained standing with his back to the open shutter, glad to think that his face must be in shadow, and determined not to speak until he could get his anger under control.

Of course Charlotte felt no such need and was pacing to and fro, jerking impatiently on her skirt as it impeded her in her changes of direction. "What a fool you are, Geoffrey! What an arrogant fool to carry on like this under our roof and in broad daylight! Do you know how I learned of this incident? Not from my daughter, whose mouth I might possibly have been able to stop in time if only she had come to me. But no, I was informed by a servant! May overheard Molly and Sarah talking, before they went to recount the exciting story to your supposed beloved. I'm sure your little intrigue was already no secret in the quarters, but no one dared speak to me of it. May, however, could not keep silent."

"Yes, my dear sister, you have every right to scold. I was foolish, and weak." The head was bowed; the reddish curls fell over a very white forehead. Shirt, waistcoat, breeches and stockings were all perfectly fresh. He had taken the time to dress after his ride from Farrington. "However, I am sure you will agree that it is beneath any lady or gentleman to pay heed to the gossip of servants. They will talk for a moment, and then it will be forgotten." He had raised his handsome face to his sister's with the hint of a smile upon his lips.

"For the love of heaven, Geoffrey! This is more than gossip. Yours is reckless conduct for a man who is paying court to our neighbor. How long do you think your good looks and pretty manners will prevail over the advice of her sister and my husband?" Both of them turned toward

327

Matthew, but he still did not trust himself to speak.

"Miss Lucy is not tempery like you, dear sister. She will make a sweet, complacent wife." He again looked toward Matthew, and for the first time revealed some unease. He sat up in his chair and began to examine his shapely hands, which he held spread out in front of him. "However, I do begin to doubt that I should make her _my_ wife."

"What on earth?"

"Let me say, first, that whether you believe it or not, up until a few days ago my conduct has been perfectly correct in regard to Mme. de Coulanges. And hers toward me. Having my best interests at heart, she encouraged me in my courtship of Lucy."

"But now she wants you for herself, is that it, and her a married woman?"

"Please allow me to speak. Marie, that is, Mme. de Coulanges, has been a dear friend to me for many, many years. She and the Marquis gave me refuge when you rebellious colonials drove me out of the country. I could scarcely go back to England and ask the aid of our uncle, knowing what I did of his villainy toward you. So surely you can see that..."

"Oh very well, you owe her a debt of gratitude." Charlotte could never hold her tongue when aroused, a trait Matthew deplored. But at present he was glad that her volubility spared him any need, indeed, any possibility, of speaking himself. He leaned back, resting his hands upon the narrow windowsill, and watched his wife pacing angrily like a willow branch whipped by shifting winds. It struck him, not without dismay, that all her emotion, even accompanied by so much beauty, only fatigued him now.

" and what has come of it?" she was saying. "You and she have come close to blighting your prospects for an excellent marriage, and made our household the subject of gossip. You've more than repaid what you owe this Frenchwoman by now. Accompany her to Petersburg, if you must, though it would be better to leave that to Matthew or Miles. Let

328

her take the stage to Charleston, and let that be the end of it."

Charlotte now pulled up a chair opposite her brother and gazed at him as near beseechingly as she could ever do.

"What you fail to understand, Charlotte, is that I can no longer do that. I'm too. . . fond of her. I've persuaded her to let me help her niece and her in their venture. The academy, you know. It's too much for two ladies to attempt alone. Though Marie managed to bring a little money out of France, and the niece has a little, their capital is small. Once my lawsuit is settled, favorably, I am assured, I shall be in a position to help. It will be a modest living, but perhaps in time..."

"Good Lord, Geoffrey, have you taken leave of your senses? You love good company too much ever to subsist on a modest living." She gave a short laugh.

"Who knows?" He laughed too, clearly relieved at the lightening of his sister's mood. "Marie is a more accomplished person than you may think, and a sensible one. She exerts a good influence on your flighty brother. And she thinks I would be a great asset to the academy. I could teach singing and fortepiano to the young ladies."

"You? A singing master? A Burnham? Preposterous. And demeaning."

"In England, yes. But in this country all is different. I shall be a man of business, and if a successful one, not to be sneered at."

"You would not be considered a gentleman, Geoffrey. In marrying Lucinda you will remain one. You will have a large fortune that will allow you to live in the style you are used to. You will have children, Geoffrey, and live a respectable life, worthy of your forbears. Can this old woman you want to tie yourself to, give you children? She can't even marry you."

"Surely you know that she's received word that her husband is ill, gravely ill. If he dies, her financial position will improve, and she will be free."

For a moment Charlotte slumped forward in her chair, appearing deeply dejected, but then she straightened and spoke sharply to her husband.

"I do wish, Matthew, that you could forgo your lofty moral stand and help me make Geoffrey see that he must not throw away his chance of position and wealth."

Matthew wished he could offer her some words of agreement. But he could only speak, now that his anger at Geoffrey had dissipated, gently but reasonably.

"I'm afraid I must support your brother in this, my dear. The venture is chancy, but I've been impressed with Mme. de Coulanges's intelligence and courage. I've been told there is a considerable community of persons of French descent in Charleston. Their forebears, the Huguenots, settled there in the last century. They would surely welcome an academy directed by two French ladies."

"That's as may be, but do you imagine Geoffrey lending his diligent assistance to such an enterprise?"

"I think that Mme. de Coulanges will have a good influence on him. Whereas Lucinda, good young woman as she is, is not one to mold a man's character. And where would her fortune be, after a few years of supporting a lavish style of life? My duty is to protect the interests of my ward."

"Gentlemen, please. This need not be decided today. Geoffrey, do not rush headlong into a decision that you would regret the rest of your life." Charlotte was defeated, however, and surely knew it.

<hr />

Very late that night Charlotte lay awake in the pool of moonlight that bathed their bed. The bed stood in its summer position in a corner between two windows where the slightest breeze from west or north might be felt. At this very moment the thin white gauze of mosquito netting that hung from the canopy stirred a little. But Charlotte, who lay in her thinnest shift, with not even a sheet over her, felt no movement of air on her skin. She tried to make out the hands on the clock on the mantle, but the moonlight caused a glaze over its face. Well past midnight, she was sure.

Matthew had been wakeful, too, but finally lay breathing regularly by her side, inches away yet furlongs distant in sleep. He was to leave in the morning to defend a man accused of manslaughter in Hinton. Things were not well between the two of them. She still felt the blame of everyone, but of Matthew most of all, regarding her lack of devotion to Edward. He denied it, but she knew better.

He had not taken her into his arms, in bed, in the two months since the child's death. This night, at last, he had shown his desire quite clearly, but she had refused him.

Before falling asleep he had been understanding as always, willing to do without, but restless, turning from side to side, giving her a caress from time to time, which one moment would soothe and comfort her, the next would set her nerves on edge. Yet as soon as he fell asleep her mind filled with pictures of disaster: his dogcart overturned and him lying dead in a ditch, or being carried onto the porch of a tavern, hit by a blast of gunfire from drunken brawlers. Then she would never be able to forget that on his last night at home she had refused him, and that they had been at such odds that day over the ridiculous behavior of her brother.

Another worry nagged at her: that of conceiving still another child. The death of Edward had so diminished her milk that she had ceased to suckle the baby. For a month now she had been drinking the tea that Honey made for her from the seeds of Queen Anne's lace. But the girl could not promise her that this would prevent conception for sure.

Finally the pictures of Matthew's face, dead eyes fixed and staring at her in reproach, overcame both distaste and fear. A couple of kisses on the nape of his neck and behind his ear were enough to bring him fully awake.

Soon she was lying on her back like an opened rabbit, with him working eagerly above her. All that excitement seemed far away, barely touching the numbed flatness of her body. Now and then her shoulder or thigh twitched as hair or breath touched them unexpectedly. At times in recent years she had envied that intensity which she could barely remember as ever belonging to her, that mounting excitement and crescendo of pleasure so sharp it sounded like pain. But never before had she experienced this distance and this calm. Tonight she was completely without life.

Scarce a half-hour later she heard slow footsteps on the stair and men's voices that were not loud, but no doubt louder than they thought. It was Nathan with Miles, who would bunk this night in the house before riding the rest of the way to his cabin in the morning. Had they visited the village tavern, or Col. Meachem's whorehouse of light-skinned girls? Men thought that ladies knew nothing of such things. It was no concern of hers, since she was sure that Matthew never went there. Usually the thought of it disgusted her, but tonight it sent a chill, not entirely unpleasant, into the base of her belly.

She had rid herself of the distressing images of Matthew dead, but now another picture filled her mind. It was that of Miles lowering his big, easy-going frame into an armchair, his broad hand slowly unbuttoning his shirt, and his smile at the memory of whatever kind of enjoyment he had indulged in that night. Tears suddenly prickled in her eyes, tears for Matthew. Carefully, without waking him, she drew his long head into the hollow of her neck and gently stroked the thin, limp hair.

Chapter 19

Sitting relaxed upon Bella and lulled by the gentle sway of the mare's walk, Charlotte breathed her deepest breaths in many a day. She felt her waist, in her light summer habit, bend and straighten, bend and straighten, in a slow, steady rhythm. She had mounted at the foot of the front steps, placing the sole of her left boot into Big Moses' laced hands, and swung herself with a tremor of joy into the saddle. She guided Bella along the gravel path to the eastern side of the house, and then turned the animal left, so that they skirted the extensive pleasure garden that offered a formal, balanced vista from the windows of the drawing room and first-floor chamber. Charlotte's eyes skimmed the straight walks, the clipped boxwood hedges, the neat beds of peonies and hollyhocks in bloom. She breathed a small sigh of disdain. In England such formal gardens were long out of fashion. One laid out meandering paths and irregular flowerbeds, so as to make it appear that Nature herself had created one's garden. But Matthew still clung to the squares, oblongs, and ovals of the French tradition. "What do we want with copying Nature?" he would say. "We've worked hard and long in this country to subdue her. And are we not still at it?"

The one plant that Charlotte most loved, clipped or not, was the boxwood. On this day in particular its pungent fragrance filled her nostrils and her heart with throbs of energy.

Beyond the garden their path led them northeast, along the edge of the apple orchard, where Bella stretched out her neck and managed to bite off a small yellow apple, so lax were her mistress's hands on the reins. Charlotte merely smiled, said a quiet "Whoa," and chose for herself the largest, ripest apple she could reach. The sun had just passed its meridian, and beat down hard upon the fruit-laden trees, the parched path, and on Charlotte's head and neck. She gave a sharp kick into Bella's flanks to speed her into the deep shade of the woods that lay only a few yards beyond the orchard.

Charlotte sighed with relief. She took off her bonnet, tied the ribbons in Bella's bridle, and then undid the buttons of her bodice. She was unlikely to meet anyone here, and if she did, what of that? Had she not her shift on underneath? No stays, of course. She wore those only

333

when abroad or when there was company at Laurel Hill.

She was reputedly on an urgent errand. At dawn that morning she'd been awakened by a gunshot, and then had heard loud, angry voices coming from the stable yard. Throwing a cloak over her nightclothes she had run out to find Big Moses clasping Dick Meachem from behind in his thick, black arms. Dick, yelling obscenities, clutched a rifle in his hand but could not move it to do any harm.

"Are you shot, Moses?"

"No, Missus. Massa done missed me. But he got me with the barrel."

A small crowd had quickly gathered. Joan and Honey had drawn close on either side of Charlotte, while others hovered at a safer distance.

"How dare you come on Waverley land, sir, after the orders my husband gave?"

"Hell and the Devil! I've got cause aplenty." He made a sudden, almost successful, effort to shake himself free, and then muttered: "I ain't saying nothing 'til this brute lets go of me." His voice was thick and his bloodshot eyes could not focus on her face.

"I'll have him do so if you will give me your gun and if you'll engage to keep a civil tongue in your head when you talk to me."

"For Christ's sake, take it!" He tossed the gun at her so abruptly that she barely missed receiving it full in the face.

Big Moses was loathe to let go of the man, and leaped back out of reach as soon as he did, at the ready to defend himself.

Then she had dismissed everyone, asking Honey to attend to Moses' wound.

It didn't take her long to learn the cause of the uproar. Dick's wife Sophie had run off and had been gone for two days. He was certain she had taken refuge again at Laurel Hill.

"My whore of a wife," he had dared to yell, "looks at you with your highfalutin ways, and your lily-livered husband letting you get away with 'em. Then the bitch thinks she can do what she damned well pleases."

Charlotte did not deign to dispute with the drunken oaf, but led him personally wherever he cared to look. A search of Great House, Old House, and all the dependencies had found no Sophie. Then she reminded him of some distant kin of his wife who lived in the village.

By good luck Dick took instantly to this suggestion.

His horse, which had not strayed far, was soon caught, his rifle restored to him, and he took off without another word in the direction of Simmons Corners. Charlotte had sent Joe off directly to fetch Miles at Stony Creek Quarter. Someone had already set out to find Nathan, who could not be far. But she had need of more mature counsel and protection than a mere boy could provide. As soon as the crisis was over, her knees had softened to jelly.

At midday Joe had returned alone with the message that Miles would not come until the morrow.

She could scarce contain her anger at this response, but had kept silent and listened to the insufferable fellow's lame explanation. Once at the overseer's cabin where Miles was living, Joe had had to wait a good long while for the man to return from no-one-knew where. When he did appear, he claimed he could not leave. The sheep had just the day before learned to jump over the new fence, so the sinews of their fetlocks must be cut. A delicate job, he claimed, which only he could accomplish. However, he had the effrontery to assure Joe that Dick Meachem would not bother them again at Waverley that day or night.

Nathan, who had ridden up with gun in hand and battle in heart, had missed Dick by half an hour. He then hung about, drooping in disappointment and muttering resentfully because Charlotte had thought it necessary to summon Miles. His complaints, added to the unmitigated gall of Miles' refusal to respond to her summons, were insupportable. She had determined to go to Miles herself, confront him with her thoroughly justified anger, and see how he would dare to answer her. Nothing tempted her so much as an altercation with her arrogant brother-in-law, alone in his sorry little cabin, mooning over his lost love. How she would lambaste him for failing to gallop immediately to her (and the family's) rescue!

So here she was, safe in this dark ocean of trees: oaks, poplars, chestnuts, and she knew not what else. Here, in summer, the sun rarely penetrated the dense vault of branches and leaves. Winds dropped before the legions of sturdy trunks. Here she was free of the prating voices, the unsought advice, the whining complaints, the pleas for this or that decision or favor. Here she heard only the thud of her horse's hooves and the chirping of birds. Matthew and she had taken long rides here in the forest in the months after their marriage, in order to be alone and undisturbed.

How dearly she had loved Matthew then. How filled with gratitude she had been for the haven he had offered her, an orphan thrown upon the mercies of distant cousins after Geoffrey returned to Europe. To them she was a poor relation, treated kindly, but with that patronizing kindness that gave favors that could be returned only by humility, gratitude, and lowly service. Then Matthew had appeared like a burst of sunlight out of a leaden sky. He had bestowed on her more than shelter and position in a family of standing. He had enfolded her in worshipful love. Suddenly, through his love, she had become one of those who confer, rather than receive, favors. That was thirteen years ago. It seemed more like thirty. After the first months of marriage there was no time for rides together in the woods. First the War took him away completely for over a year. Then the local militia claimed him for a while. Then there were law studies, law practice, and the multitude of duties as plantation owner, county magistrate, and state delegate. And as for her, her life became the bearing of babies and the feeding, clothing, and nursing of family, servants, field hands, and visitors. Matthew was absent a great deal of the time, and even during his stays at Laurel Hill she and he were never alone but in their chamber, and not even then, for there was always an infant in the cradle near their bed; or worse, an empty cradle and the memory of a child recently lost.

Now the trail led through a section of forest that belonged to Farrington, Lucinda Ludwell's estate. Would she see anything, perhaps initials on a tree along the path, to tell her she was riding on earth pervaded by Lucinda's spirit? She laughed aloud at the thought. Lucinda's paltry little spirit could scarcely spread farther than the walls of her chamber. Kate's spirit was more likely to dominate the rest of their house. But the land was now in the large, strong, and very capable hands of Miles Waverley. Yes, she did grant him as much ability as he had insolence, and there was an abundance of both. As she scanned the tree trunks for a mark of someone's passage there, she suddenly met shining, yellow eyes that watched her from within the dense foliage of a thicket. For one mad instant she thought they belonged to Miles, fiercely guarding his beloved's territory from intruders. At the same instant Bella shied, no doubt catching wind of the creature in the thicket, and Charlotte grabbed onto her mane to steady herself. It was a wildcat, most likely. Nothing to fear. But the forest was no longer a haven to her. She was no longer welcomed, but suspected, even threatened.

Soon she was back on Waverley land. Of course Miles would not welcome her. He was too busy to come to her, or at least claimed to be so. He would think her foolish to ride all this way to see him. Would he find it questionable, even shocking, for a lady to come all alone to see a gentleman alone in such quarters as were his at present? No, on the contrary, he would hardly give any thought at all to her behavior. He had never liked her; of that she was certain. It was an animal dislike, like a dog's for a cat. And her dislike of him was the same. It would be exciting, and somehow restful at the same time, to find herself alone in the presence of a worthy adversary, rather than in that of a loving, but reproachful, husband.

These thoughts roused in her a delightful sense of danger, the exact nature of which she did not allow her mind to specify. She rode on for another hour, the path now leading her beside a narrow stream flowing in the center of a much wider bed crowded with rocks, most of which were now dry due to the lack of rain. She stopped to give her horse drink, dismounted, and climbed precariously over the sharp rocks to crouch by a tiny, but vigorous waterfall, cup the cold water in her hands to drink, and then pour it over her face, wincing in pure pleasure at the shock of it as it streamed over her hot eyelids, cheeks, and chin.

Despite the deep shade of the forest, her whole body was damp, and when she placed her hand upon Bella's neck to remount, she sniffed deep of the fragrance of the creature's moist neck. She had always liked the smell of horses. It had enveloped her when she took refuge as a girl in her uncle's stables, where he himself never entered because the odor made him wheeze.

Finally she came out of the forest into a vast open area. On her left stretched a field of wheat, its golden blades waving gently in a breeze she could just barely feel on her face. It was deserted, but beyond it she could see a broader field of tobacco, with numbers of white flowers, a little yellowed, still clinging to the plants. At the far end of that field she could make out five or six Negroes, doubtless at work topping and succoring, perhaps also worming, the plants. Beyond them rose an empty tobacco barn. On her right, atop a small hill and sheltered by a grove of poplars, stood a large cabin with wide eaves that shaded a sizeable porch.

Sure that this must be the cabin where Miles was living, she tethered her horse at a post, and approached the open door. From the porch she could see that there was another door in the back wall, open also, no doubt to court as much breeze as possible. For form's sake she rapped her knuckles on the doorframe, but it was obvious that no one was within. She entered the one spacious room and found that in addition to the second door, it had several amenities not usual for an overseer's cabin. There was a window at one end, next to the fireplace, and on the other end a real set of steps, not just a ladder, leading up to the loft. The walls were smoothly chinked and plastered. There was a decent bed, a large table with a water basin and cup set upon it, two chairs, and a wardrobe for clothes and bedding. In the fireplace was a crane with a kettle hanging from it. A toe toaster also graced the hearth, and one of those fry pans called spiders because of their legs. Next to the fireplace stood a bench with a few pewter dishes and tumblers. So Miles was not completely sacrificing his comfort in order to be of service to his brother and also see to the welfare of his ungrateful ladylove. And surely he dined with the ladies of Farrington on most days.

Looking out the window, she could see no sign of Miles with the workers in the field. Down the hill in back could be seen two other cabins, no doubt to house the Negro gang, a small barn, and two other small shacks, probably the necessary and a springhouse. From the barn came the faint sound of voices, and in the paddock could be seen a small flock of sheep. No doubt he was there, attending to the cutting of the sheep.

She closed the window shutters against the hot sun pouring in from the west. She was certainly not going to go looking for Miles in the barn. Soon someone would notice her horse, and he would come. In the meantime she would make herself as comfortable as possible. She dipped herself a drink from the basin that sat on the table, then moistened her handkerchief in the cup and wiped her face and neck. On a shelf were arrayed a number of books, but their subjects were of no interest to her: animal husbandry, winter crops, doctoring, and of course, an almanac. So she sat for a while on the chair, and when that bored her, decided to lie down on the bed, feeling like a Goldilocks who had not found the bowl of porridge but otherwise followed the fairy tale. Would Papa Bear treat her harshly when he returned?

After some time an enormous bear was indeed looming over her, and two smaller ones jumped about barking on either side of the creature.

The growl of the big bear, however, was neither loud nor menacing. The paw it stretched out toward her was devoid of hair and claws. She shrank back against the wall, but the paw grasped hold of her shoulder and shook it.

Suddenly she snapped awake and sprang up, too quick for the hand that Miles now offered her. She felt her blood spring up into her face. Miles spoke sternly to his dogs, who reluctantly withdrew their paws from the bed and ceased their barking. As though being seen flustered and blushing, by Miles of all people, did not enrage Charlotte enough, he proceeded to laugh with an air of the most perfect ease.

"Well, madam, this is the very first time I come home to find a lady in my humble cabin. And indeed, in my bed."

"Not in your bed, sir," she said, attempting an equally light tone but hearing her voice squeakingly high, "merely on it." She smoothed down her riding habit and her hair with all the dignity she could muster.

"There is a glass on the wall by the door if you would like to use it, Mrs. Waverley." What a deep, resonant voice he had. Strange she had not noticed that before. The words and the tone were respectful enough, but she was sure he was laughing at her. At present the reason for her visit seemed far less convincing to her than it had when she set out. She glanced toward the door in a ridiculous impulse to escape, and saw that the afternoon shadows had grown long. It would be time for tea at Laurel Hill. She had expected to be on her way home by now.

"Pray madam, sit down. You must be hungry. I have little to offer, nothing comparable to the cuisine at Laurel Hill. But you are welcome to what I have." He spoke with exaggerated politeness, even ending in a bow, which was of course his way of mocking her.

"Do not trouble yourself. I am not hungry."

"Well, Mrs. Waverly, I have had a long day of painstaking labor. I am famished. And so are Shot and Flint." He crouched at the fireplace to start the logs burning, hooked a pot low over the fire, spread a few chunks of meat from a burlap bag on the hearth for the dogs, and then proceeded to slice great hunks of bread at the table.

She could not leave without making some excuse for her coming. She seated herself, determining to put the best face on the situation possible.

"It was imperative that I see you, sir. Dick Meachem is on the rampage again, and this is truly intolerable."

"Your boy Joe came to me this morning."

"Yes, came to bring you to us, sir."

"Yes, but that was not possible. I could not tell the whole story to Joe, to have it blabbed about everywhere. But to you, madam, I can say that the problem was already on its way to a solution."

"Indeed? And how could you know that, from this distance?"

"If you will but hold your horses--pardon, if you will be patient while I put something to eat on the table for us, I will explain."

He brought a trencher with two bowls of a stew that did not smell unsavory, and produced tumblers of cider. No sense in refusing to eat, since in truth she did feel quite empty inside. The cider, sharp and pungent, must have been sent over from the Waverley Great House. Made from Hewes crabapples, Matthew's favorites for this drink.

He pulled another chair over to the table, and then devoted himself entirely to eating for a maddening time before he spoke again.

"Ah, that's better." He smiled at her with fine white teeth. He must still have all his own, something else she had never noticed; but then, had he ever smiled in her direction?

"Very well. This is how it happened. Dick was on the rampage because his wife was gone. Well, that wife had been here, an earlier surprise guest," (and he had the effrontery to smile at her again) "until I would say two hours before your boy arrived to fetch me."

"What! That strumpet dared to come here?"

"Your language is rather strong, madam. I gather that when she sought refuge with you, some weeks ago, she was not made welcome. Taken in, yes, but not made welcome."

"And of course she was made more than welcome with you!"

"I did not sit in judgment upon her. She made a foolish marriage, but who's to know if she perhaps came from still worse a place?"

Charlotte reflected that she herself had come into marriage from a difficult situation, yet she had not chosen to fling herself into the arms of a surly profligate. "She's pretty enough. Surely she could have done better."

"I gather that her family had neither wealth nor connections. Our young gentlemen seldom make serious offers to such a girl."

"Ah, I see she has won you over. She has played upon your ready sympathy, and you have become her protector." What fools men are, she thought. Particularly this one. First he hangs about like a dog to help a girl who has spurned him, and now he lets a married woman lead him into a reckless liaison. But where is he keeping her, if not here? The thought flickered through her mind that the hussy might be hiding in the loft.

"If I became her protector--momentarily, Mrs. Waverley—it was to shield her from the grave mistake she made in coming here. So I accompanied her back home to the protection of Col. Meachem."

"A great lot of good that will do her," said Charlotte.

"It saved her from being discovered here, and the Colonel sent someone on his swiftest horse to find Dick and tell him his wife was at home. Dick beats her, to be sure, but not to the point of serious injury. Not under his father's roof and in the proximity of his mother and his children. If she must leave him, it should be to someone of her relations, and of course she would have to give up her children. I told her that, but she bridled at the thought. Her best bet is to play the complacent wife, thus minimizing the blows, and hope he breaks his neck on one of his binges. Oh, and we told the Colonel and Mrs. Meachem that the young woman had taken refuge at Farrington. The ladies there have been asked not to say otherwise. That way, since no gentlemen live there, Dick will have no fuel for his jealousy."

By this time both had finished their meal. The breeze had quickened

342

and was blowing briskly from the back door into the room, lifting the damp hair that had escaped from Charlotte's chignon. Her habit was still open a couple of buttons down the front, allowing the cool air to refresh her throat and neck. Miles cleared the table and put out the last embers of the fire. He seated himself on the end of a bench by the fireplace, smoking his pipe and stroking the necks of the two dogs in turn. He looked the picture of complacency. No doubt he was contemplating with supreme self-satisfaction his expeditious dispatch of the affair of Dick Meachem and his wife. And was he studying now how he would send another agitated woman on her way, having calmed her and brought her to his way of thinking by means of his superior reason?

Miles looked perfectly at ease, though he was in shirtsleeves, and except for having dashed a splash of water on hands and face, was still dirty from a day of labor. He would never have dared to appear so in her presence while staying at Waverley. How different he was in every respect from his brother. He was only a little taller, but appeared twice as broad, and had the same thick, coarse black hair that also adorned their mother's head, though mixed, in her case, with strands of gray. That black hair showed itself, though more finely, on his forearms and in the opening of his shirt. Everything about him was broad: his cheekbones (almost like the pictures she had seen of redskins), his neck, and his shoulders. His eyes, a deep brown under black brows, shone in the gathering darkness of the hearthside.

How could she strip that complacent look from his face? The tale he had told regarding Sophie Meachem was almost certainly a lie. Charlotte had observed the little hussy flirting with Miles, more with him than with any other gentleman, at every opportunity that came her way. Was it to be believed that he had ushered her back to Fairhaven, posthaste, without availing himself of the sport so freely offered?

However, even a hint of such a suspicion from Charlotte would only throw an unsavory light upon her own mind. No, it was with respect to Lucinda that he was vulnerable. That is where she would strike.

"I wonder, sir, that you would put abroad an account of the fair and innocent Lucinda receiving a woman of such ill repute into her house. Even if it is only a lie."

"Zounds, woman! Lucy risks nothing from such contact. If I had thought Sophie Meachem had anything serious to fear in returning home I would have indeed taken her to Farrington, and stayed there myself, against the possible coming of Dick. The elder Meachems were away on a visit when Mrs. Sophie fled, but were due to return yesterday."

"Ah yes, little Lucy is quite impervious to taint, pure maiden that she is. Even though my brother, who, I assure you, has as many weaknesses as most men, has been spending countless hours alone with her. And she is so excessively fond of him."

The big man rose then from his bench, slowly, but with clear menace in those eyes that had beamed on her with such self-satisfaction a few moments ago. Good! She had wanted to prick the bubble of his complacency and she had succeeded. She was not in the least afraid of him. The cabin had grown quite rapidly dark, and now she heard the first clicks of raindrops against the window shutters. All the farmers of this land were doubtless rejoicing at that sound, and she was rejoicing that finally she had pierced the shield of her arrogant brother-in-law, so long her enemy.

She rose to face him squarely while he stood without yet saying anything, barely a pace away. Her attack was well launched; she could not but carry it through. "Do not you think it strange that such a pure girl should stay attached and still determined to marry my brother, even though all the world knows of the liaison between him and our French guest? And you wait nearby, like a faithful dog who may yet receive its bone; indeed, I can reassure you that Geoffrey appears more than likely to discard your pretty little Lucy and run off with his doddering mistress."

Miles still stood silent, as though waiting to see just how far she would go. And she, on her part, needed to find out how far she could push him.

"And then, when faithful Fido finally gets his bone, how does he know it hasn't been already chewed upon?"

Now he stepped still closer, not touching her, but so close that she, a tall woman, had to bend her head well back to keep looking him in the eye.

"You had better leave. Now."

She reached up and grabbed hold of the lapels of his shirt, bringing his face still closer to hers. Then she stepped off the last wobbly rock into the rushing stream. "And what will you do if I won't?"

What happened then was no surprise to her, and she was sure not to him either. It was like being run away with by a spirited horse, something she had long feared and long expected, something that had played itself out in her imagination many a time. This was the third man who had possessed her. The first, her uncle, had forced her and she had been drowned in a deluge of helpless fear and rage. With the second, Matthew, who had been unceasingly kind and considerate, she had always floated safely on the surface of the water, often following swells of delight, sometimes bobbing about in irritation, but always in perfect control of herself and him. And now here was the deluge and the helplessness again, but also pleasure so strong it resembled pain. To find herself powerless, and delighting in that very weakness, was a sensation she had never felt in any other circumstance of her life.

Afterward, when their breaths finally came slow and even again, he asked her in a whisper, his lips close to her ear, if he should take her back to Waverley. For an instant the risks of remaining here longer swam into the backwaters of her mind, but she let those thoughts sink into muddy darkness, and snuggled closer into his arms. She shivered in a fresh rush of cool air brought by the rain in from the back doorway, and he pulled a coverlet over them.

It was still dark when she awoke, feeling him stirring beside her. For an instant she thought herself at home, with Matthew in the bed with her, but quickly the full memory of what had happened came to her. Joy flooded into her, unclouded by even a trickle of fear or remorse.

She had paid for this freedom, this pleasure, with all the annoyance and drudgery and loss that life had brought her so far. She would somehow brazen out whatever befell her as a consequence.

The hand that was slowly caressing her belly and hip chased away these thoughts. She raised it to her breast, rejoicing that since she had ceased suckling Charles, her nipples, deadened by suckling, had again grown sensitive to the touch. She raised herself and sank onto him. This time their lovemaking was slow, with time to savor each separate sensation. Later, as she lay still under the weight of his thick arm lying across her waist, she reveled again, again to her surprise, in feeling small, weak, and helpless. She had never known what repose could come from being freed of all choosing.

They arose at the first faint light in the east. Their bare feet soon told them that a third of the floorboards were wet with the rain against which neither had thought to close the door. Miles made coffee and cornmeal mush by candlelight. He fried thick slabs of bacon over the fire, while he kicked the toaster with a practiced foot to produce evenly browned slices of bread. The bacon she ate with her fingers, and then gave her hands to the dogs to lick, enjoying the feel of their rough tongues on her skin. She laughed at the gurgle of the molasses as Miles poured it from a jug onto her mush. She smiled at him over the rim of her mug of coffee. They were rebels, pirates, conspirators, everything reckless, dangerous, outside every law of decency. Only after they had eaten did they speak seriously of what they must do.

"We must spare Matthew," was the first thing he said.

"You do not speak, sir, of sparing my good name." But she laughed as she said it. "In truth I care little for that myself. What has it brought me but tedium?"

"Matthew cares for it, I'm sure. But more, he cares for you."

"Matthew will believe whatever I tell him. And will give credence to nothing anyone might say against me." She spoke with confidence, yet was not unmindful of the low ebb in the relations between herself and her husband. Still, he would never believe this of her. And yes, he must never be obliged to believe it. Miles was right about that.

"I will take you home. The rain was a fortunate thing, for us as well as for the crops. You could not be expected to ride home in such a storm."

"Yes, we will arrive, I perfectly at ease, and you a bit disgruntled because accompanying me home has interfered with your work." She wanted to prolong this delightful sense of conspiracy. "Your mother will think the worst, no doubt of that, because she delights in thinking the worst of me at all times."

She was glad to see him nod. Matthew would have frowned and maintained that she was imagining ill will on the part of Mrs. Levier. Miles' fondness for his mother was of the easy kind that could concede that she had her weaknesses, whereas Matthew, her least-loved son, felt impelled to hide from all, himself above all, any awareness of her faults.

"The sooner we leave, the better," he said. His manner had become withdrawn. That did not disturb her. After the pleasure, ferocious, then leisurely, that they had known together, he would never be able to hold off from her. Despite her delight in the helplessness she had experienced in his arms, she would always have sufficient power to make him open them to her.

Chapter 20

Honey always rose before dawn these summer mornings. Only then could she walk out in air still unheated by the sun. She took this time to go over in her mind the lessons she had learned the day before, reading the Pilgrim book with Mrs. Levier and reading the *Spectator* to herself as counseled by Mr. Waverley. Both he and Mrs. Waverley insisted she do no housewifery after dinner. From three o'clock on, she must mind her book and her ciphering, and practice her drawing. Thank goodness the dancing master had put off his visit until the fall. She dreaded his coming, for surely Mrs. Waverley would order her to join in the lessons.

This morning she was abroad even earlier than usual, drawn by the fresh, damp smell of earth brought by last night's rain. At this hour only a handful of Negroes were stirring; they were in the barn at their milking or in the kitchen starting the fire. Ladies and gentlemen were still in their beds. Honey had orchard, gardens, fields, and woods all to herself, and could for an hour drink in the peace of solitude that had been an unnoticed gift of her life back home, but was a precious rarity in this crowded, busy place where the constant coming and going, talking and shouting, still sometimes muddled her head.

She had put on the clogs that Noah, the carpenter, had made for her, and made her way around the cabinet and pantry side of the house, where the vegetable garden and the peach and nectarine orchard were found. Ripe melons and tree fruit glowed faintly in the dark. Right pleasant to her was the sucking sound made by her clogs in the sand of the path. She heard the throaty hoot of an owl, who would soon drop off to sleep, and the plaintive voices of the mourning doves saying sad greetings to the day.

As she sloshed along the side of the pasture she could just make out the dark outlines of four horses, one lying in the grass, one leaning against a chestnut tree, two already grazing. Four heads turned with placid curiosity to see who might be abroad at this hour. When she came to the pond she paused for a few minutes, straining her eyes to see if she could make out the shapes of the carp, chub, and eels that she knew to be there. But the water was still quite black. As she passed the stallion's special high-fenced pasture she was startled to see him standing on his hind legs, his head over the rail, and his wild, bloodshot eyes staring at her.

Now she entered the woods, where the thick canopy of oaks, elms, and chestnuts had caught and held many of the raindrops, leaving the path below damp, but not muddy. Sometimes the dark and silence of the woods brought back to her the peace she had known at Granny Harriet's cabin, or she would recall the happy times at home: picking bluebells with little Sarah on Fox Bald, or singing hymns and ballads with Mama as they shelled peas or shucked corn.

These days the old bad memories plagued her less and less, giving way to the good ones. There were even some quite happy moments, like the kindly words Mr. Waverley had said to her a fortnight ago. Whenever he left Laurel Hill he spoke to the overseers, to the most trusted servants, and to every person in the family, one by one, to make sure they knew what was wanted of them whilst he was gone. He appeared to have forgotten her, this time, until the very last moment. His dogcart was at the front portico; the baggage was strapped on, and Stove was standing by the horse's head. Yet Mr. Waverley guided her into the drawing room and sat her down in his usual deliberate way.

He had assigned her no particular tasks, but had repeated once again that she busied herself too much with household work. She must not neglect her studies. She'd been right proud to tell him how she could now comprehend most parts of the *Spectator* articles, and how she now read the Gospels to Mrs. Levier so the lady needn't tire her poor eyes, and how Mr. Jenkins asked her to read a prayer at Methodist Class just about every Wednesday.

"My dear child, I hope these people are not burdening you with thoughts of sin. That they help you know yourself a thoroughly good young woman."

Despite these kind words, fear had flared up in her belly. Had Mrs. Waverley told him the terrible things Honey had confessed to her?

"I seem to recall," he continued, "that at the barbecue last spring you feared a little dance might start you sliding down the slippery slope into sin. You spoke of yourself as already a sinner. At your tender years! I must avow that I think these New Light people much too stern."

His words damped the fire in Honey's stomach. Of course Mrs. Waverley had far more important things to talk with her husband

349

about than a poor relation's past deeds, which after all were not so sinful, since they'd been forced upon her.

He was patting her hand then, and smiling at her. Some of its natural ruddiness, gone these last months since Edward's death, had returned to his face. Even its deep-etched lines seemed a little shallower. He almost looked a happy man, and that happiness so warmed her that she felt she must explain how she had indeed done some wrong.

So she told him how she'd run away from home, years before Papa was killed, and taken Sarah with her. And how if she'd only stayed, she likely could have kept things from getting so bad, what with drink and the one-eared red Indian, and then her papa and her brothers would not be in the cold earth this day.

He looked at her for a time so long that she feared he would never warm her with his smile again. But his hand still lay upon hers. He hadn't taken it away.

"I do not doubt you had good reason to leave your home, my dear girl. But tell me, is not your God an all-seeing God who knows the truth of your good heart?"

"I do trust in His forgiveness, sir. But sir?" She hesitated, then said: "Isn't He your God too, sir?"

"Ah," and he laughed a little sadly, "my God is not so active as yours. I do believe He made this great and admirably fashioned world of ours with all its wonders and its laws, but since then He has let it run its course unhindered by any interference from Him. That is my view, and that of some others. But my God is of little use in times of trouble, I fear."

Now he did remove his hand from hers and for a moment his sorrowful face of recent months returned. He raised his long, thin hand to his forehead and passed it down over his face to form a V around his chin and jaw, which he slowly rubbed. Then he shook himself slightly. "My dear, I beg you to hold firmly to your God. He must surely forgive those peccadilloes of which you accuse yourself, and must see what a great blessing you are to us all. I agree with Mr. Pope who wrote:

"For modes of faith let graceless zealots fight,

His can't be wrong whose life is in the right."

"I think you might benefit from reading his great poem, the 'Essay on Man.' It will introduce you to the pleasures of rhyme, and add to your vocabulary."

"Oh yes, sir. Perhaps Mrs. Waverley will kindly show me where to find it." Her utmost wish was ever to please him.

He had risen, kissed her on the forehead, and was gone.

For sure and certain Mr. Waverley didn't think much of Mr. Jenkins and his Methodist class. To tell the honest truth, Mr. Jenkins scared her right much, with his shiny black eyes that seemed to peer deep into you for any sign of sin. His voice was harsh, like a crow's, and his beard bristled like a boar's hair. There was naught gentle about that man. He appeared so certain about what's right and wrong. Yet Mr. Waverley, though he wasn't so sure of everything, seemed wise beyond all that sureness. And wasn't he just as righteous a man as Mr. Jenkins?

But you couldn't say that of some other folk at Laurel Hill. First there had been Mr. Geoffrey and Madam Marie. Both great sinners, if Molly was to be believed. But Honey didn't need to take Molly's word for that, for she herself had seen things going on between those two that gave her no great opinion of them. Worse than that, Sarah was bewitched by that lady and gentleman. To her, fancy clothes and fine manners covered over every fault. She refused to go to Methodist class. She said the folks there were ugly and bad-tempered. Of course Honey couldn't insist because then the Waverley people would think she didn't believe their church was good enough. Still, Sarah was gentle and good. Honey would just have to keep a constant eye on her.

Mr. Geoffrey was gentle, too. And he sang like an angel in Heaven. Madam Marie was kindly when in a good humor, and when she was snappish you could see she was feeling poorly. Wasn't she much more alone than Honey had ever been, for Honey had always had Sarah.

She was far from her husband and son, and had no real kin in this country. She had no religion, either, for she didn't go to church with the Waverleys. Mrs. Levier said she was a Papist, and what could you expect of folks of that persuasion?

Mrs. Waverley hadn't that excuse; yet she was behaving quite shamefully. A fortnight ago Honey had spied her close to this very spot, kissing Mr. Miles in a way you could not mistake. Since then she had seen her return more than once to Great House from the path that led to the home quarter where Mr. Miles was living. Yet Mrs. Waverley strode about, assured as ever. She beat the house servants when she was in a passion, and had hard words for everybody that couldn't stay out of her way. But the lady had such a heap of things to attend to, and Mr. Waverley was from home so often. Hadn't she been a comfort to Honey, telling her that her badness wasn't her fault, and making her believe it?

You would not think that gentlefolk could behave so. "Worldly people," Mr. Jenkins called them. Now Mrs. Levier surely was not worldly. She was a God-fearing woman, for sure and certain. Yet she said such mean things of Mrs. Waverley, behind her back and even to her face. She spoke near as bad of Mr. Waverley, her own flesh and blood. Mrs. Waverley paid her no mind at all. She appeared hardly to hear, or would sometimes even answer back. Not Mr. Waverley, of course. He minded, you could tell. But he was always quiet and respectful.

And that Mr. Miles! His sounding voice and strong arms filled her with awe. He'd been so kind about her running away that time. How could he do such a bad thing as steal his brother's wife? All these ladies and gentlemen talked so fine and smiled so sweetly and dressed so neat and pretty that you couldn't guess that sin was still there, only hidden.

Well, she couldn't stand out here cogitating forever. She'd be wanted in the infirmary, and at lessons, and there was work to do on the loom. She must take off her wet gown and shift, and put on dry things.

Unwillingly giving up the peace of solitude, Honey tried to sneak in the pantry door and up the back stairs, but was spied by Mrs. Waverley.

"There you are! What on earth are you doing with your skirt all wet around the bottom? Do dry yourself, and when you're presentable, please go to Mrs. Levier. Joan says she's complaining of something or other."

She mounted the stairs to the loft room and spread her damp gown and shift over the chest near the small window. The shutter was open and the air that filled the room was already heating up. Her eyes followed the sloping lawn, small because lawns took too much work to keep, to the copse of willows and reeds, the rocky reach of shallow water, and finally to the deep channel in the middle of the river. Far down to the south, smoky billows of clouds threatened a more violent storm to come.

She might as well stop trying to figure these gentlefolk out. She was too young, and not smart enough either. Likely she never would comprehend any better than she did right now.

The usual bustle surrounded Great House at Laurel Hill as Miles rode up to the pantry door in early October. He succeeded in dismounting directly onto the stoop so as not to be obliged to clean his boots before entering. The last six weeks, since Charlotte's first visit to his cabin, had continued dark and gloomy, with storms passing through every two or three days. At first he had promised himself not to allow his lust to sweep him into such disloyalty again. Then, when Charlotte visited him a second time and he again succumbed to temptation, he determined to depart for the Humbolt plantation, finding some excuse to take up his abode there, even though old man Humbolt still lived. Yet here he lingered still. And there had been more visits, even though Matthew had returned from his court duties.

Then, as though fate had determined to force his hand, he received word from Mrs. Humbolt that her husband was no more. His will was already proved, and inventory about to begin. She wished to leave the place as soon as she and Miles could settle all the necessary business of what stock, equipment, and furniture he intended to buy, so that she might sell the rest elsewhere before she left.

Miles was surprised at the enormity of the weight he felt lifted from his shoulders. After each visit from Charlotte he truly wished it might be the last. Not for a moment did he long for her return. He was no longer a boy, constantly dreaming of petticoats and bodices. Yet he had not the strength to refuse when she, in all her brazen assurance, offered herself. But indeed, she did not offer <u>herself</u>, but rather, she demanded <u>him</u>.

He had not set foot on the home quarter at Laurel Hill since the morning he had accompanied Charlotte home. After her subsequent visits she rode back alone, never staying the night again, confident that no one, and certainly not her husband, would question her taking such long rides in the forest. On one occasion, Matthew had come to see him, arriving while he was talking with the gang in the tobacco fields, reproaching him for not responding to his and Charlotte's invitations. That morning Miles' discomfort was almost beyond bearing. He was certain that every one of the Negroes knew his secret and was watching the two brothers with contempt. It took a long while before he could turn his mind to the problem Matthew wished to discuss, that of harvesting the tobacco this year, the season being so damp. He could not, even once, lift his eyes and look into his older brother's trusting face.

Now, as he entered the pantry and then strode into the hall and peered into the parlor, he found no one. He had counted on not finding Matthew at home (knowing he would be in the village for the election and court days) and he hoped to avoid Charlotte as well. It was someone else he wished to see, someone who kept late to his bed. Finally he spied May skipping down the back stair, her black arms full of white laces and many-colored ribbons.

"Just a moment, girl. Tell me, is Mr. Geoffrey awake? I must have a word with him."

"Oh yessuh. He be up and off to Missus Marie's chamber. But you can go wait for him in the front chamber   at the top of this here stair."

He mounted the narrow back staircase where his sleeves brushed the rough walls on either side and his head cracked smartly against the turn of the ceiling. He paused at the top, cursing aloud. The door to the gentlemen's guest chamber was open. In it he found a Negro woman on her knees by the bed, examining closely a man's waistcoat that lay there among numerous shirts and smallclothes. She started at his step, and scrambled to her feet, bobbing a curtsey, but saying nothing. It was Maudy, he was sure, but sadly changed from the pretty girl who used to gaze back at one quite directly, as though defying you to give her an order. That had long irritated Charlotte, and secretly pleased Miles, who liked to observe any resistance to her imperious airs. Now the poor girl kept her head bent, but he could see all too clearly the ugly white line that stretched from temple to jaw. That Meachem rogue deserved to be horsewhipped. Of course, nothing could be done about any sort of brutality to a runaway slave, unless it lessened his capacity for work. But one day that ruffian would go too far.

He brought his mind back to the task at hand. "Good morning, Maudy. It appears that Mr. Geoffrey requires much attention to his wardrobe at present?"

"Yes, sir. He goes away soon, and must have everything in order."

A huge portmanteau stood open at the foot of the bed, nearly full of hanging waistcoats and carefully folded linens. Another smaller case sat upon a straight chair, showing an assortment of stocks, gloves, and hats. A finely dressed wig hung upon a post of the chair back. The coxcomb! A veritable macaroni, if ever there was one. The impending departure of Geoffrey was not a surprise to Miles. Charlotte had told him that her brother would accompany Mme. de Coulanges to Charleston, and that there was some doubt as to whether he would return. That was exactly why Miles had come to Laurel Hill this day.

"I wish to speak with Mr. Geoffrey in private, Maudy. So when he comes back, be pleased to gather up what you need, and leave us."

The girl laid several garments over her arm, and left forthwith.

Miles knew well enough that Matthew would speak to Geoffrey about his conduct toward Lucy, or perhaps had already done so. But he would not have spoken forcibly enough. And Miles certainly did not wish to discuss this, or anything else of a personal nature, with Matthew. So he himself would speak to Geoffrey. If there was one good deed he could do before he left this place, it was to insist that Geoffrey do the right thing concerning Lucy. Even if he had to stand in front of the dogcart and block Geoffrey's departure until he did so. He himself would cut a ridiculous figure, but he cared nothing for that. He had sunk too low to trouble himself about appearances. If he had anything to say of it--and he would have his say--the aging coxcomb would either betroth himself to Lucy formally, before all the world, or he would let her know in perfect clarity, as any honest fellow would do, that he did not intend to become her husband.

Miles stood for what seemed an interminable time gazing out the window at the soggy pleasure garden below, looking at the heads of hollyhocks and daisies bent low from last night's hard rain, and trying to fend off thoughts of his own wretched weakness and dishonesty. From time to time the peal of feminine laughter, not Charlotte's, thank God, came from the chamber down the passageway, interspersed with the resonant male voice of Miles' enemy.

Finally Geoffrey sauntered into the room, betraying only by the lift of an exquisitely shaped eyebrow his surprise at finding Miles there. In his embarrassment Miles bobbed the most awkward of bows, to which Mr. Burnham responded with his infinitely graceful one.

"What a pleasant surprise, Mr. Miles. You have not recently graced us with your presence. And today I would have thought you most surely in town with the other gentlemen."

Miles murmured something about being too much occupied with his preparations for departure to his new plantation at the other end of the county.

"Ah, and you will leave the ladies at Farrington quite abandoned, with no one to manage the estate for them properly? No one even to keep an eye on things once Mr. Waverley departs again for Richmond?" What gall the fellow had! He himself should long ago have taken up these duties. If he intended to marry Lucy, that is.

Miles took a few moments to master his temper before addressing this subject. He was determined to discuss it calmly and reasonably, so as to bring about consequences the most favorable to Lucy's happiness.

"I've been training Crick, Jed's son, who will do a tolerable job. He's nearly forty now, and ambitious. Some of the old man's authority appears to have rubbed off on him. Besides, Nathan will be here yet awhile, and he improves in competence by the day."

"Ah well, then. So you are about to take up a new life. I too. My documents have finally arrived from London, and my case will come before the General Court in a fortnight. First I will accompany Mme. de Coulanges to Charleston, then go to Richmond where I have every confidence that the Court will decide in my favor. I will be a landowner! Oh, on a modest scale, to be sure. But to one so unfairly maligned as a Tory, it will bring some modicum of the respect that I merit." The fellow laughed, a quite easy laugh, and smoothed his well-dressed hair with his well-manicured hand. He appeared to have no shame about being called a Tory, an appellation that he certainly deserved.

The reminder that Geoffrey would never be truly accepted as a Virginia gentleman was comforting to Miles. He was ready to bring up the matter that was so close to his heart.

"Allow me to speak to you about a personal matter, sir. It is more in the province of my brother, who is Miss Ludwell's guardian, but Matthew can be overly polite, overly lenient, particularly where it involves his wife's brother."

If Geoffrey was annoyed by this overture he did not betray it. He gestured gracefully toward a chair, and seated himself upon the bed, carefully avoiding doing damage to the clothing spread out upon it.

"I would ask, indeed I would require, that before you leave us you make your intentions concerning Miss Ludwell quite, quite clear. If you intend marriage--and we won't pretend that her consent is in question--then have the banns published and set a date." Miles paused, determined to get an answer. He was pleased with himself. His voice was low and steady. He might have been doing business with a merchant, rather than discussing the future of the girl he loved with a man he hated.

Geoffrey took his own good time to answer, examining the smooth palms of his hands, then turning and polishing the large gold ring he wore on his left index finger. Miles was certain that the man was discomfited, little as he betrayed it. Finally Geoffrey raised and lowered his shoulders with a great sigh.

"It is indeed good of you, sir, to take such interest in the welfare of Miss Ludwell. Of course all the world knows why you take such interest." This was said with a mocking glance from under the heavy-lidded eyes.

Miles had prepared himself for anything: anger, evasion, or just such derision. He remained silent, breathing deeply and keeping his eyes on the man's face.

"Well, that is neither here nor there," Geoffrey continued. "While I am filled with the utmost respect and affection for the lady in question, another obligation has pressed itself upon me. The Marquis de Coulanges and his lady gave me refuge during the recent troubles in this country. Now that I am in a position to offer her aid, could I in all honor refuse it? Mme. de Coulanges and a female relation intend to establish an academy for the education of young ladies in Charleston. They will need my helping hand, so I will return to Charleston as soon as my case is decided. For how long I do not know. Of course it would be unfair to expect Miss Ludwell to wait for me."

What a quantity of high-sounding phrases to mask a simple case of attachment to a married woman! But there was nothing to be gained in pointing this out. And Miles, regrettably, no longer stood on the lofty moral ground from which to make such a comment. Why, perhaps this idle and extravagant brother of Charlotte was also her confidant! Miles must keep his object, Lucy's welfare, firmly in mind.

"Then the manly thing for you to do, sir, is to go to Miss Ludwell and tell her that you have no pretensions to her hand."

"Ah no. That I cannot do." For once the man appeared to speak from the heart.

"You must. Else she will continue to hope for your return."

"Could not you speak to her?"

"Certainly not! I wonder you would suggest it. In any case, she will not believe it if not from your own lips."

"Ah, I see." All its usual arrogance returned to the hated face. "Only when she truly believes me gone for good will the way be open to you."

The man's conceit, the man's disdain, were past all bearing. But they must be borne. Miles again breathed deeply and summoned the steadiest voice he could muster. "You are mistaken, sir. She would never accept me, and rightly so. I am as unworthy of her as you. I will soon be fully occupied at the other end of the county, and she will be free to listen to the addresses of other suitors. They will not be lacking." He realized how bitter these last words sounded before they were out of his mouth. But what matter? This arrogant fop would soon be far away. Never would Miles have to see a complacently smiling Lucy hanging on his arm as his wife.

"If you have not the courage to tell her your truth in person, you will have the goodness to write her. Now, before you leave. I will wait whilst you do so." Miles gestured toward the small secretary that stood between the windows.

"Ah well. Why should I not indulge you in this? I am sure I may count on you to deliver the note in person."

Miles merely bowed. Of course he wouldn't dream of delivering with his own hand such a message to Lucy.

Geoffrey had scarcely seated himself and dipped his quill in the inkpot when the Frenchwoman appeared in the doorway. A plump and very white little hand flew to her throat.

"Why Mr. Miles, such an unexpected surprise. <u>Mon Dieu</u>! We never see you anymore. And your absence is so much regretted."

"Very kind of you, madam." To his surprise, Miles felt a surge of warmth toward the lady. Was it not to her that he owed this hoped-for renunciation of Lucy by Geoffrey Burnham? She was dressed in what he supposed was called a negligee, fastened so carelessly in front that almost the whole of her breasts could be seen. She appeared suffused with energy and her color was much improved over the last time he had seen her.

She glanced at Geoffrey who was still seated at the secretary. "Pray excuse me, gentlemen. I do not wish to disturb you."

"My dear," said Geoffrey, "it seems I must write an important message. Do entertain Mr. Miles for a few minutes, perhaps in your own chamber, while I concentrate my thoughts on my task."

The lady led Miles down the hallway to a chamber even more in the disarray of packing than was Geoffrey's. Miles had been told that French ladies habitually entertained visitors in their bedchambers, but still he was ill at ease, and was glad to find Sarah and May occupied there with some sort of needlework.

Mme. de Coulanges cleared a space for the two of them to seat themselves. "You, my dear sir, with your radical ideas (ideas that spring from the idealism of youth, to be sure) must be pleased with the latest events in my country. Indeed, I am told that your countrymen in the great cities of the North are quite wild with enthusiasm over the recent victory of the revolutionary army at Valmy."

"Madam, I know nothing of this."

"Oh yes, sir. But you will see. This frightful republic that the bourgeoisie and their puppets among the rabble have declared will go too far. <u>Parbleu!</u> Have already gone too far. Our poor king and his queen imprisoned! Some of the finest of our nobility put to death! Even your dear friend, and traitor to his own friends, M. de Lafayette, forced to flee for his life."

She was fanning herself now, in the heat of her agitation. Then she stopped suddenly, snapped her fan shut, and tapped him with it on the arm. "My dear sir, forgive me. Sometimes I am quite carried off. May you be fortunate enough, here so far from the evils of Europe, to continue in your innocence."

"Madam, I do sympathize with the grievous disturbances, and losses, that you have suffered."

"<u>Eh bien</u>, perhaps it is as well things are come to such a pass in France that I assure myself there is no chance of my return. Nor can I join my husband, who in any case is not expected to live long. So I begin a new life, in Charleston, which they tell me is truly a city. For I must confess that this country life is not to my liking."

He smiled at her. Remarkable how much the impending departure of a person one had quite thoroughly ignored could make her appear suddenly appealing.

It was not long before Geoffrey appeared in the doorway, a sealed note in his hand.

"Here you are, sir. I believe this will satisfy you. Despite what you say of your prospects, I wish you the greatest happiness from the consequences of this painful duty I have performed." This was said with an air of great dignity and even heroism.

Miles could not trust himself to reply. He slipped the precious paper inside his waistcoat, bowed first to the lady and then to the gentleman, and briskly got himself out of the room and the house.

Chapter 21

E lection Day had dawned bright and clear, with the last of the gray clouds slowly blowing away to the east. No rain had fallen for the last two days. Restless breezes had dried the ruts in the roads and the puddles on the town green, but with every footstep one sank into the damp earth, and among all those gathered in the open in front of the courthouse, not one pair of boots or breeches, from potboy to gentleman, but was smeared or spotted with mud.

Simmons Corners, where Solway County's courthouse was located, was ordinarily a quiet little knot of nondescript structures, the most impressive of which was the Silver Stallion tavern. This was a long, low building of close-fitting, squared-off logs, with a roof of cedar shingles. Above the door was a large square of wood on which was painted the form of an animal somewhat resembling a rearing horse. Across the front ran a spacious porch with a row of worn, wooden armchairs. In back could be found the tavern's kitchen, and to the side a stable which could accommodate a dozen horses. Next to this relatively imposing structure, the church and the courthouse appeared paltry indeed to those entering town. The small clapboard church had no steeple, and badly needed a coat of paint. The sag of the floorboards could be seen from outside between the piles of stones on which its corners sat. Though also very small and plain, the general store was in good condition. Mr. Jenkins, its proprietor, saw to that. But one could barely move about inside, so crammed was it with all the necessities, comforts, and even some small luxuries that the county inhabitants might seek there. As for the lockup, a mere shack served that purpose.

The courthouse was a simple, one-room structure, with a tiny alcove that served as office of the county clerk. Its only claim to grandeur was a broad door with a triangular frame above it that enclosed a decently carved eagle in low relief. Mr. Ludwell, Lucinda's father and a man of public spirit, had contributed the door to the county shortly before his death. Before this door spread a wide stone stoop, with two steps that led down onto the village green.

Matthew had driven into town, with Mr. Levier sitting next to him on the chaise and Nathan riding ahead of them on his new chestnut, a gift from Matthew and Charlotte upon his eighteenth birthday. She was a swift little mare that Nathan was bursting to race that day against anyone who would accept his challenge. Pleased to journey on such a fine day, Matthew had let Boston take a slow pace. He breathed deep of the light, dry air, finally freed of the damp of summer dog days. An occasional breeze sent a shower of red and gold leaves sparkling down in the sunshine. The gentle scent of honeysuckle sweetened his spirit. Yes, he would gladly ride on forever, never joining the contentious bustle of Election Day.

Somnolent Simmons Corners, which merely tossed about and talked in its sleep of a Sunday morning, awoke to lively activity once a month on court days, and reached a pinnacle of exuberance on the yearly day of election for the two county delegates to the Richmond Assembly. On the river road, as it approached the ferry, peddlers had aligned their carts and loudly extolled their fish, corn cakes, buttons, hay, and so forth. On the far side of the courthouse green a young officer was exercising the militia. Nathan, not being of an age to vote, was obliged to leave his companions and join the muster. This was not an unwelcome duty, since the young men found great delight in marching about, their guns on their shoulders, joking, boasting, challenging each other to contests of strength or skill. Sometimes they were fortunate enough to find themselves the spectators of a fistfight.

Down by the river, behind the tavern, penned horses, cattle, hogs, and sheep waited to be sold. Participating in, or just listening to, the dickering always held interest. At night there would be cockfighting behind the lockup, and tomorrow would bring whatever horse races had been arranged, as well as the usual activities of a court day. In short, thought Matthew, these gatherings offered entertainment that went far beyond the interest of choosing delegates and trying those cases that came before the local justices. These were innocent pastimes to work off the excess humors in the blood of young and not-so-young manhood. Since the day was fine, votes were being cast out of doors. A long table had been set up at the foot of the courthouse steps. At it sat the three candidates for the two seats in the House of Delegates.

Col. Meachem had been representing the county for more than twenty years. Twenty stone of arrogance and complacency, he was the largest landowner in the county and commanded the votes of many who disliked his lordly manner, but could not afford to antagonize such a man. His son Dick was sprawled indecorously on the chair next to him, holding a hornbook on which to record the Colonel's votes.

Now that Matthew had declined to run again, two gentlemen had offered themselves to the voters of Solway County.

The first of these was Mr. Appleby. He had long served as justice of the peace, and since the Revolution had been an active rider of the court circuit, but had never sought elective office. Perhaps the daughter of a Richmond merchant, who had lately become affianced to Appleby, wished to see her future husband in a more exalted position. A man in his fifties, Mr. Appleby was not exceedingly rich in lands or connections. His short, thin frame stooped forward so that he had to look up even to most women, and the face he turned up to you was pale as skimmed milk. He was said to guard his complexion as anxiously as if he were a lady, never going abroad without hat and gloves. Yet this was a popular man, a man of principle and of delectable wit. As a justice of the peace, he could be counted upon to send the courtroom into frequent ripples of laughter. Because of his thin voice, hardly louder than the mew of a cat, those in attendance would scarcely draw breath whenever Mr. Appleby chose to speak, for fear of missing one of his sallies.

364

Next to him sat his polltaker, Mr. Higgens, the Anglican minister, stiff in the aura of his dignity. Then came Will Cracklethorpe, that assiduous campaigner who had cultivated both rich and poor with considerable shrewdness. With the money of his new wife, he had been able to offer by far the most sumptuous of the treats spread out on tables by all three candidates, each at a different corner of the green. Some considered that the perpetual squint of Will's eyes represented all too well his character, but this was perhaps unfair. Seated next him to record his votes was young Ned Crawford, shifting about in evident discomfort at this unwonted importance.

As Matthew and Mr. Levier, after leaving horse and chaise with the potboy at the tavern, were walking slowly up the village green toward the courthouse and the candidates' table, they were waylaid by the elder Mr. Crawford, bustling up in a manner quite foreign to his usual slouch. His thin hair and tobacco-stained beard looked as though an unsteady hand had trimmed them.

"Good day to you, Mr. Waverley and Mr. Waverley's father." (Mr. Crawford was not one to bother with more knowledge of his neighbors than necessary.) He had stopped them at several paces from the table, and keeping his voice low, addressed Matthew.

"I'm right aggravated, sir, not seeing you up there with the other gentlemen. Nobody warned me you wasn't to be running. Whatever your reason, sir—and I'm bound it's a damned good one—you mustn't desert us this here way."

While he listened politely to this appeal, Matthew noticed that Mr. Clancy, his other impoverished neighbor, was slowly limping his way toward them. He had been startled to find himself so abruptly addressed by Mr. Crawford. He disliked the necessity of once again explaining his decision not to run. He knew that certain gentlemen, even the most desirous of honor and advancement, were wont to show great reluctance to stand for office or even accept an appointment. So it was not surprising that some people doubted the sincerity of his refusal.

So far it appeared that Col. Meachem and Mr. Appleby were going to carry the day. Most of the gentlemen and farmers of the eastern part of the county, which was closest to Simmons Corners, had come forward, one by one, to announce their votes and be graciously thanked by the favored candidates. Now that the result looked certain, most of the men had wandered off to the tavern or some other more interesting area of the village. A couple of justices remained close to the candidates, and of course the sheriff, who took charge of the whole procedure, remained at his post at the center of the candidates' table.

The sheriff was grumbling about the small number of votes so far cast, and was beginning to threaten to close the polls. But Will Cracklethorpe objected most vociferously, claiming that the main body of his supporters from the west side of the county had of a certainty been delayed, or perhaps were detained at the cattle sales. Jake Crawford had been sent down to the pens to round up whomever he could.

Now poor Mr. Clancy had finally reached the place where Matthew stood. They exchanged the usual niceties.

"Oh, we are well enough, sir. Can't complain." In truth, the poor fellow always carried a plaintive expression on his deeply lined face. He ducked his head obsequiously at every inquiry he made. When all the proprieties were fulfilled, Matthew turned back to Mr. Crawford.

"Indeed, sir, I firmly believe that I have served long enough. Fortunately, Col. Meachem is willing to continue, and either Mr. Appleby or Mr. Cracklethorpe will represent the county admirably in Richmond. New blood is needed. New ideas."

"I say naught of Mr. Appleby, sir," cried Mr. Crawford, "except that mayhap that gentleman's a bit too clever for plain folk to know what he's about. But that young Mr. Cracklethorpe, devil take him! He only knows poor folks at election time." A thickness in the man's voice indicated that he'd already paid a lengthy visit to the tavern.

"We truly do need you in Richmond, sir," said Mr. Clancy. "Them others are fine gentlemen, but just you can we trust. You're a right up and down honest man."

"Hear! Hear!" yelled Mr. Crawford. "Tell 'em, Jim. Me, my throat's dry and I've got to pee." And off he took himself toward a laurel bush behind Mr. Cracklethorpe's refreshment table. His scorn of that gentleman did not extend to his corn liquor.

"No, Mr. Clancy. You do me honor but it is impossible. And I must hasten to cast my own vote." Matthew strode briskly over the soft grass, announced his votes for Mr. Appleby and Col. Meachem, and duly received their thanks. Chairs were brought for him and Mr. Levier at the end of the table, near where the Colonel was seated. After the flurry of greetings subsided, the Colonel continued a conversation punctuated with laughter with the witty Mr. Appleby. Mr. Clancy edged up close to Matthew.

"Begging your pardon, sir, but will the Assembly decide to sell off glebe lands in Solway County? The Church, it's been good to us. Gives us a bit of corn when things is bad. A few seeds, even a calf one year, though it was puny. How can the Parish help us, with their lands all gone?"

"Overseers of the poor will be appointed, Mr. Clancy. It will be their task to assist those in need."

"But who may they be, Mr. Waverley? Will they know what I need, or care? That suit for debt that the Colonel's brought against me--would to God I never asked him for naught!--he'll take my beasts, my tools! Where will I be?"

Matthew took a deep breath and tried to quell his rising irritation. The man was needy, and through no fault of his own, but why must he badger him here, instead of going quietly to see him in his cabinet? "I will surely be able to get your hearing for debt postponed again at tomorrow's court session," he said. "And if it should ever come to your property being seized and put to auction, you may be sure that I will be the highest bidder. Then I will put them back into your hands. Now please take advantage of the largess of our candidates, and stuff your pockets with cakes for your girls."

This suggestion got the man moving. Matthew sighed in relief, and looked at Mr. Levier, hoping to get some acknowledgement of his great patience.

Instead, the older man pursed his lips and shook his head. "My dear Matthew, you should have given way to our persuasion and continued in your post. You see how popular you are. How the people count on you."

"They flatter me because my good will is useful to them. In truth, I'll be more useful here than off in Richmond. I pity Mr. Clancy, lame as he is and with no sons to help him. Mr. Crawford is another tale. I've been too indulgent with him. In any case..."

He was interrupted by the booming voice of the sheriff, who had mounted the steps of the courthouse. "Silence! Silence! Will you stop your gabbling for one moment?" Then, when the laughter, bickering, and cursing had subsided just a little: "Gentlemen freeholders! If any one of you has not yet cast his vote, come forward. For I am about to close the poll."

Matthew had watched a good number of men of the county, mostly the western half, come announce their votes, and noticed that Mr. Cracklethorpe had done a good deal of bobbing up and down, giving thanks and shaking hands. So when the poll was now closed and each of the recorders announced the number of votes cast for his candidate, he was not surprised to hear that Col. Meachem and Mr. Cracklethorpe were to be the Solway delegates, come spring.

"A dismal outcome," murmured Mr. Levier. Matthew was of the same mind, but did not say so.

Most of the county's freeholders had dragged themselves back from cattle sales, betting, and drinking, to learn the outcome of the election. Now they moved in two separate waves, one to the treats offered by Col. Meachem, the other to those brought by Mr. Cracklethorpe, to congratulate and imbibe. A few drifted toward Mr. Appleby's table, to condole with that gentleman.

Those whose love of gaming triumphed over all other pleasures lingered only long enough to settle their election wagers, a few with cash, most with arrangements for payment in ham, corn, or tobacco; then they were off to cards, dice, or billiards at the tavern. Others had to return to the business of buying and selling. Those whose passions, or necessities, did not draw them away, remained on the green in front of the courthouse. Soon they all drifted to Mr. Cracklethorpe's table. Col. Meachem's reelection had been taken for granted. Mr. Cracklethorpe was the new man, of whom it was best to make a friend by the warmth of one's congratulations.

Once compliments, good wishes, invitations, and hints at personal wishes regarding upcoming bills were exhausted, the reigning monarch of topics of conversation was introduced.

"My dear Colonel," said Mr. Appleby, apparently in no way cast down by his recent electoral defeat, "I hear all manner of good things about your new yearling."

The Colonel nodded complacently. "Prideful will do me credit, without a doubt. He's shaping up well, thanks to Mr. Waverley's nephew. He's been filling in as trainer, since I lost my groom. But now I hear that the young gentleman has a swift filly of his own. Perhaps he even has the effrontery to suppose she can outrun my Prideful."

All eyes turned to the back of the knot of men, where Nathan had joined them. The poor fellow flushed and bit his lip. Matthew thought best to speak up for him, since it didn't look as though the boy would find his tongue.

"I'm sure Nathan thinks his little Sprightly can make a fair show against the best of them. With a sire like Fearnought, and out of Mr. Humbolt's Nancy, you know." Matthew could hear the pride in his own voice, but why shouldn't he be proud to be the owner of such a horse?

"Well, I believe that Dick intends to issue a challenge to young Nathan tomorrow. Just a quarter run, but it will be good experience before a crowd, so I expect a goodly number of you to attend." The Colonel's florid face, with those eyes that protruded like marbles about to be thumbed, traveled slowly from man to man. "Indeed, we'll give Waverley the advantage, since Dick carries twice the weight of his little whippet of a nephew."

"To be sure, every man will attend, Colonel." Mr. Cracklethorpe followed the Colonel's stern look-round with his own would-be commanding squint. It looked as though the Colonel had acquired a reliable subordinate in the county and in the Assembly.

A great blanket of weariness settled over Matthew's shoulders. He walked over to join Mr. Levier who had had a chair placed under one of the venerable oak trees lining the green and was enjoying a slab of pork well soaked in sauce and a cup of cider, compliments of Will Cracklethorpe. Matthew leaned his back against the furrowed tree trunk and rested his gaze upon the thick curtain of leaves, some still in the green of summer, others already turned red. Fortunately, Mr. Levier was too engrossed in his succulent meal to engage in conversation.

He tried to attach his thoughts to the outcome of the election. What would young Cracklethorpe's presence among the delegates portend for Solway County? But such thoughts could not hold him. His mind flew back to Laurel Hill, and his mind was far from easy. Most disturbing was the fact that he could not attribute his unease to anything definite. Not to any action or even word of Charlotte's. And yet Charlotte was at the center of his misery. It was indeed misery. Bad enough to feel it at all, but far worse to find himself helplessly drawn back, again and again, into such baseless, inexplicable emotion, he who prided himself always on the clarity of his mind and its ability to overcome even the most blatant provocation or grievous loss. Had he not conquered the temper that had plagued him in youth? Had he not brought himself to accept, last spring, the terrible loss of little Edward, teaching himself that longer life would only have brought more suffering to the frail body that somehow could not be toughened against the buffeting life inevitably brought? But why now this persistent, causeless malaise?

Since his return from Richmond at the end of the spring session the breach between him and Charlotte had been mended. Particularly of late she had been unusually compliant, scarcely resisting him in anything, leaving off even her habitual jesting at his expense. She agreed with his opinions, assented to his requests, all the time wrapped in an invisible shawl that hid her true thoughts and feelings. He heaved a great sigh, and slid down to sit upon the ground. Now that he was released from his position of delegate, why shouldn't he also release himself from his usual pretense to a dignity he had never felt?

"My dear Matthew," said Mr. Levier, wiping red sauce from his mouth with the back of his hand and staring at him with those furry gray eyebrows raised, "I must confess that you worry me. You appear exceedingly somber. I'll wager that you now heartily regret giving up your place and letting that unprincipled young whippersnapper take possession of it. But take heart, Matthew. In two or three years, when Miles has become quite settled on his own land and the growing steadiness of his character is known throughout the county, he will readily defeat Cracklethorpe. You will have a worthy successor. If truth be told, I wonder at his absence here today. I've never known him to miss our court days when he's in the county."

"I too wonder at his absence. I've seen almost nothing of him since I returned from pleading that case in Yorktown. He's not come once to dine with us, and I've been told he still avoids Farrington because he does not care to see Mr. Burnham there. It appears he's become a veritable hermit."

"Ah, 'tis tragic what disappointment in love will do to a man," cried Mr. Levier with a hearty laugh. He had doubtless never truly loved a woman in his life. So thought Matthew, with not a little bitterness, because of his mother who had certainly much to complain of in this husband.

Mr. Levier heaved his round body out of the chair and returned to the table for more refreshment. Matthew sighed. When he had complained to Charlotte about Miles never coming near them, she had told him not to be a fool. Indeed, this was the only lively comment he'd heard from her in weeks, and not one to encourage any further confidences. Well, so be it. He would keep his own counsel. Yet there was one, and such a young girl too, who was in her quiet way a comfort to him. He would not burden her with any confidences, of course. She was hardly more than a child. Was she yet twenty? Still, in the year, or almost a year, since she had come to them, she had changed from a frightened child to a young woman who always seemed to be where she was needed. He'd noticed that Nathan, the children, even his mother, and all the servants, came to her quite frequently with their questions. Charlotte, who had complained at first of Honey's being so irritatingly meek, and suggested more than once that they might marry her off to Ned Crawford, of all men, now spoke of her as someone she expected to be with them forever.

As Matthew was resting his mind with thoughts of Honey, he was startled by a loud curse coming from Col. Meachem's table where a few men still lingered. Dick Meachem threw something down, perhaps a cup or a tumbler, and strode off toward the tavern.

He had not spoken more than two words to Dick, nor Dick to him, since that day he returned from Richmond and learned of the man's violent intrusion upon his land, and confrontation with his wife. Charlotte had quite proudly spoken of how she had "put the rascal in his place and let him know with whom he was dealing." In speaking so she had frightened Matthew more than had the actions of Dick, disturbing as these were. Her imperious manner was effective in quelling any impertinence from the family or house servants, but Dick was quite a different animal. He was a danger, and Charlotte made it a point of honor to retreat before no danger. Ah, Miles had been right when he remarked, long ago when first meeting his brother's bride, that she should have been born of the male sex. The same could be said of Molly, alas.

On the very day he learned of that incident he had sent a blunt, unequivocal message to Dick threatening to have the sheriff arrest him for willful trespass if he ever showed himself at Laurel Hill again. He could only hope that the warning would scare the fellow enough to keep him away. All Matthew's people, servants and field hands, had orders to intercept and delay the man, should he appear at Laurel Hill. And of course Nathan, Big Moses, and he himself were to be instantly summoned. What more could he do?

Trying to shake off his fears, Matthew made his way to the Silver Stallion, where he hoped to dine quietly in a small area set apart from the raucous shouts and laughter of the taproom.

Nathan was in the best of humors. Indeed, he could not remember a time when he had felt better than at this very moment. He was walking slowly through the knee-high weeds of Foster's Field, leading Sprightly, his new chestnut filly, to cool her down after the first race of the afternoon.

As he neared the edge of the woods he began to feel the crunch and hear the swish of fallen leaves under his feet. He raised his eyes and followed the oblique line of a reddish leaf sailing gently to the ground. A secret contentment, quite apart from his win in the race, pervaded his being.

It was Saturday, the day following the election of delegates. A long court session had been held in the forenoon, and after that, the flogging of one of Col. Meachem's Negroes for thievery, an event that no one but the Methodist parson and Uncle Matthew (who had a distaste for such things) could possibly consent to miss. So the races had not begun until four.

Mr. Cracklethorpe had bet Nathan ten shillings that his bay mare could beat Sprightly by a rod at the least, and Sprightly had won quite handily! It was a fair and clean race, too. Mr. Cracklethorpe's boy Sims, scarce more than a child, had clearly feared to do the usual kneeing and elbowing, so Nathan had done none of that either. The horses were close in size, and though but half-grown, Sims was stocky and nearly matched Nathan in weight.

Nathan slowed to a stop and plunged his hand into the deep pocket of his breeches. He pulled out a large cloth which he hung over Sprightly's back, then stuck his hand back down in the pocket to feel the coolness of the ten coins and toss them gently in his palm. Real metal money being so scarce, one never had enough of it. Even when worth far less, it was so much more pleasant to the touch than dirty, crumpled tobacco notes.

Yet money was only a small part of his pleasure. This was Sprightly's first win. Nathan let go the coins and ran his hand lovingly over the damp sinews of the filly's neck, then laid his cheek against the velvety hair on her muzzle. She was a gift from Uncle Matthew and Mrs. Waverley in honor of his eighteenth birthday. A lovely little creature she was, with her unusually light chestnut coat and her white mane and tail. Nathan's aunt in Richmond had purchased the horse for her son, but the young man, already hefty, had grown more so by the month, and the animal soon proved to be too small for him. So uncle Matthew bought her, and a more precious gift Nathan had never received.

She was the perfect quarter horse. She could spring into a full gallop from a standing start, and from that gallop pull up to a sudden stop on the instant. For the fortieth time he caressed the fine creature with his eyes, from her foxy little ears to her full jaw, her deep chest with its well-sprung ribs, and on to those powerful hindquarters, the source of all that winning speed. He took the cloth from her back and began to rub her down, murmuring her name softly to himself: "Sprightly, my love, you did me proud."

This led to other thoughts, equally gratifying. It was Honey who had given the filly her name. "Right sprightly she is, Mr. Nathan," she had exclaimed when he paraded the animal back and forth in front of the door for all the family and servants to see. Honey was quite taken with the little creature, who was, after all, so like herself: small, graceful, and gentle. Honey would be delighted when he told her of Sprightly's win. Nathan now felt quite at ease with his cousin, well, first cousin once removed. Ever since she found out that it was Molly, not he, who had put the snake in her bed, and had shyly begged his pardon for having thought ill of him. Yes, he was impatient to tell her of his win, and also of the good prices he had got for the Waverley stock, and for the Ludwell stock as well. For he had been entrusted with all the sales, and a purchase or two as well, while Uncle Matthew was busy with the election.

As he led Sprightly back toward the track where it looked like another race was about to begin, he noticed, with chagrin, that Dick Meachem was riding briskly toward him on that big blooded horse of his father's.

Prideful was his name, Nathan remembered, a descendent of the famous Godolphin, and therefore a horse that both Meachems preened themselves upon before the whole county. And beyond the county as well.

Dick was now towering above Nathan, for of course the fellow had not the courtesy to dismount. Nathan thought of springing into Sprightly's saddle, but that wouldn't answer, for the horse must be nearly two hands taller than the mare. So he endeavored to lean nonchalantly against Sprightly's flank, while feeling like a half-grown cat approached by a husky cur.

"Mighty cocky about your little win, aren't you, Nathan Waverley. I think we need to take you down a notch. A swelled head might overbalance that meager body of yours. I'll wager you a pound I'll see your little filly outrun by three yards."

"You wish to run your Prideful against Sprightly?" asked Nathan with a leap of hope in his heart, for in a quarter race Sprightly had a very good chance of winning. A pound was more than he should bet, but he'd already won ten shillings, so he stood to lose only six.

Dick laughed. "A fine blooded animal like Prideful against your measly little sprinter? I'll warrant she's not even fourteen hands."

Only by reminding himself of what a coward the man was, and more to the point, that everyone knew it, could Nathan keep his lips clamped together.

"Do you imagine I'd allow Prideful to be demeaned by running in a rustic quarter-mile like this? No, I'll pit my little Dundee against your Sprightly."

"Will you ride him?" asked Nathan, as evenly as he could.

"Are you daft? He's almost as small as your weasel there. He'd cave in under me. No, I'll get Jake Crawford to ride him. He's about your size. And let's raise the stakes to two pounds. If you can afford it, that is."

Damned lucky that several other young men, those dregs of the county populace that were wont to fawn upon Dick, straggled over to the two of them at that point, for Nathan's growing rage was close to mastering him. They were full of their pleasure in watching the flogging, an enjoyment Nathan had missed in his zeal to exercise Sprightly properly before the earlier race.

"Tore up that nigger's back damn good!" exulted one whose thick red mouth was ever inclined to drip saliva.

"Insolent cuss! They say he stole fifty pounds worth of beef. And leather and clothes besides." This came from one whose oily hair competed with the grease on his shirt and whose fingers were known to cut a pouch of tobacco from his neighbor's belt at the tavern.

"Aye. An incorrigible bastard," said Dick. "The fucking good beating I gave him for running away, with a wench of Waverley's in tow, wasn't enough for him. If he wasn't such a damn good workhorse-

-when he's around to work--I'd finish him off."

"Don't you think you could stand us all to another round at the taproom, Dick, in honor of such a fine flogging?" said one who conveniently never had cash on his person and whose credit at the tavern had long ago been exhausted. "Or how about you, Nat? You got good revenge for the cur's taking off with your uncle's wench."

"Shut it, Jim. Nat and I are going to have a little race. Dundee is going to whip the tail off what's-her-name and win me two pounds. And just maybe you'll guzzle some of that in small beer."

Nathan despised being called "Nat," and indeed despised this clump of riff-raff that Dick was pleased to call his pals. He knew that he had no business risking two pounds, either, but Ned and Jake Crawford, Mr. Crawford, and more important, Mr. Appleby and Will Cracklethorpe had strolled close enough to hear this last, so pride would not allow him to refuse. He could see his uncle, who had congratulated him most heartily upon his earlier win, standing with Mr. Levier and Col. Meachem by the track waiting for the next race to begin, but fortunately too far away to hear the amount of the wager between him and Dick.

As soon as the next race was run Nathan led Sprightly toward the starting clearing, and was soon joined there by Jake Crawford already mounted on Dundee, a gray roan horse with much experience on the quarter-mile track. Still, Nathan had good hopes for Sprightly, who was young and fairly bursting with energy.

The crowd had surged forward onto the track to voice their satisfaction or chagrin about the race just run, but Jake and Nathan now rode slowly down the field to clear space for the next one. Dick Meachern still sat high on Prideful, behind the crowd and with a good view of the track.

Col. Meachem, as the highest ranking military man, gave the riders instructions on how much liberty he would allow them in their efforts to unseat their opponent or run his horse off the track: namely, that they might of course use knees and elbows, but whips only on each other's horse, not on his person. As the tavern keeper's boy waited with his drum to give the signal to start, Nathan and Jake jostled each other vigorously for a favorable position on the smoother side of the track. Nathan managed to win this struggle just an instant before the drumbeat, and was off to an excellent start.

It gave him a surge of joy to feel Sprightly spring instantly into her leaping gallop. Never would he have to apply the whip to her. No, his main endeavor was simply to keep his seat.

But the Colonel's horse was no sluggard, and Nathan soon heard the crack of Jake's whip on Sprightly's rump. She shied ever so slightly, but did not break her pace. Dundee was crowding him so powerfully that Nathan felt a piercing pain from Jake's knee digging into his calf. He tried to thrust his elbow into the fellow's neck, but couldn't quite reach. As he kept leaning out from the saddle, he suddenly took a stunning blow across the shoulder and went flying off into the crowd, hitting his head on Mr. Higgens' chest (so he was later told) and hearing with a stroke of panic an ominous crack as his right leg bent under him and took the force of his whole body upon it as he struck the ground. Then all was darkness.

He came to his senses on a bed upstairs in the tavern, with a pulsing ache in his right leg. As he carefully opened his eyes he heard Mr. Jenkins say, with a puff of exasperation:

"Pity he's coming to. I might have set it while he was insensible."

The man, who had a vise-like grip on his right ankle, suddenly jerked it and sent Nathan's leg into such searing pain that again, mercifully, he sank back into darkness.

When he once again came to, he looked up into coal-black eyes overhung with thick, tangled brows. "Hold him firm, gentlemen," said Mr. Jenkins, "lest the work be undone."

Indeed, Uncle Matthew held down his leg at thigh and knee, but it throbbed so bad that Nathan had no wish to move it. Tim, the potboy, had him pinned down by both shoulders. He tried to squirm away from those rough hands, but the pain that shot down his chest put an end to that.

"Lie still!" barked Mr. Jenkins. "Your foolishness has broke your leg for you, and cracked some ribs as well, I'll warrant. This is what comes of your wicked boasting and betting. Rather than throwing yourselves on the mercy of the Lord and learning to mend your ways, you young men are bent on killing yourselves and each other on the track."

"Indeed, sir," said Uncle Matthew, his quiet voice in marked contrast to the fierce rasp of Mr. Jenkins, "I grant you that the present circumstances provide you with excellent material for a sermon, but forgive me for saying that this is not the proper time to deliver it. My young nephew is suffering enough in his body without having his mind battered as well."

"That salutary lesson will never, then, be delivered, sir. Not in your English Church, not by your Reverend Mr. Higgens, so indulgent toward the gaming, fighting, and fornication rampant in this country."

It was fortunate that Mrs. Hanna arrived at that moment with the wooden slats and strips of cloth needed to bind the injured leg. The process was painful, and three or four times Nathan needed all his will to suppress a cry.

When all was done Uncle Matthew paid Mr. Jenkins his fee and descended for a few minutes to the ground floor to speak, he said, to those gathered to learn of the injured man's condition. Nathan's thoughts turned to two female creatures: Sprightly, of course, and the young lady who had given Sprightly her name.

The first thing he asked when his uncle returned was whether his little filly was injured. Reassured on that score, he wanted to know when he could return to Laurel Hill.

"You must remain here for the next few days at least. I would not have you jostled in our phaeton, but Col. Meachem insists upon sending his carriage for you on Wednesday."

"Why could I not go back with him today, Uncle?"

"No. You must rest and begin to mend first. I'll send Joe with a couple of books for you to study, so you will not lose your time. And perhaps I can persuade Mr. Jenkins to come read you a sermon or two. That would delight you, eh?"

Nathan groaned. His uncle took it lightly, but he was a bookish man who might actually enjoy being confined to bed and books for a few days. To Nathan, who cared nothing for reading, it offered only boredom. He'd spent many a night in taverns out west with Uncle Miles, and that life was agreeable enough, listening to the rough jests of ordinary men with no pretension to rank or learning. But lying up here and hearing their laughter without understanding it would be tormenting. For of course Uncle Matthew had hired for him the private room, where ordinarily only a gentleman traveling through and having no acquaintance in the region, or more rarely, a lady in the same situation, would sleep. Well, he must make the best of it. Meantime, he could console himself with thoughts of how pleasant life might be, once he was back at Laurel Hill. Doubtless Honey would take charge of him, would take pity on his sad state, would bring him extra fine food and drink, might even help him dress, and if he must be read to, he would gladly listen for hours to her lilting little voice.

Chapter 22

Another splendid October day greeted Charlotte as she stepped out into the kitchen yard after taking a meager breakfast alone in her chamber. The sun shone serenely down upon the gold of maple leaves and the red of oaks. The trees were alive with the chirping of birds and the flash of their wings. Indeed, the whole world seemed to mock the cloudy turmoil within Charlotte's breast.

The kitchen yard was just as alive with sound and motion as the branches that shaded it. All the household carpets were hanging on ropes strung from branch to branch, and two young women were beating upon them as ferociously as though they were evil spirits rendered helpless by some kind of magic. An older woman sat with Joan and May plucking feathers from several freshly killed geese. Near them Charlie crawled about among the wisps of down, becoming an increasingly fluffy baby. The five women were tossing joking remarks back and forth, no doubt glad to be out in the fresh, dry air. This would be especially true for the three women of the crop who were ordinarily never excused from fieldwork except on rainy days or for sickness.

But extra hands were needed at the house, and with Matthew gone to Richmond and Miles to his distant plantation, there was no one to argue the point with Charlotte, something that Amos would never dare to do. Nor would Nathan, but he was in any case laid up with his leg broken. This year Charlotte was determined to replace all the pillow feathers, and the bed feathers in half the beds, so she had bought several extra geese from Joan, who with her husband Stove tended a gaggle of them behind their cabin. The household would have an abundant supply of quills for their pens, as well.

"Girls! For heaven's sake, that's enough! Those carpets are thin enough as it is, without you beating holes in them. Joan, direct the girls where to lay them. I want all the carpets put down by this noonday. Who do you have churning the butter? Whoever it is, you know how they take their ease as soon as no one is watching."

Joan, who had always maintained an air of equality with her mistress, an air that Charlotte tolerated because of the reliance she placed on the woman and even the fondness she had for her, had lately appeared to hold herself above her mistress and look upon her with disapproval. She did not interrupt for a moment the rhythm of her plucking.

"I got a good girl churning, missus, and Charlie and me, we takes a turn down there ever now and then. Don't you worry your head. You got other things to think on." This last was said with a certain emphasis, which startled Charlotte. The woman had the eyes of a ferret. Did she suspect something?

"Very well then, but see that you get those carpets laid today."

Knowing how touchy Joan was, Charlotte regretted repeating the order to her even as it came from her lips. But she couldn't help herself. These days she was nervous as a cat. She had to keep herself busy somehow or else she'd go as mad as Crazy Mary. Old Sukey had died suddenly the month before. Such a shock it was, since everyone was used to her complaints of rheumatism and indigestion and who knows what, but she kept going and going. Matthew took it hard, of course, wringing his hands like an old woman and saying that Sukey had been more of a mother than a servant to him--for indeed, she had suckled him--and that they should have retired the poor soul long ago and let her take her ease for a few years. Charlotte keenly felt the loss. It was like having a leg of her chair knocked out from under her.

Well, she'd leave Joan alone and look to the kitchen, where there was good reason for vigilance. A new cook, a plump, maple-colored woman named Jess, had been brought from Matthew's sister's place near Richmond. The woman had little experience in the kitchen, but she seemed eager to learn and was properly respectful. Still, she must be trained, and that meant much added work for Charlotte. What a prodigious pain in the neck it all was. And doubtless Matthew and the other gentlemen were lolling in the tavern at this very moment, sipping their morning chocolate, smoking their pipes, and making themselves important with talking of the laws they would pass and the orders they would send out. While she, once she got through the interminable checking into the work that must be done, must seat herself somewhere, thrust her glass darner into the toe of a stocking, and be forced to hear the tedious chatter of mindless women and girls.

She now entered the kitchen, a place where she never used to set foot, relying completely on Old Sukey, once she'd dispensed the foodstuffs for the day, relying on her even for planning the meals on ordinary days, conferring with her only when guests were expected. But now, with the new woman, all that had changed.

"Good morning, Jess." The woman rose from where she crouched by the trammel that she had just pulled from the fire. She had been examining the contents of a large iron pot.

"Morning, missus," she said in a soft purring voice, and bobbed a curtsey. She was a tall, sturdy woman with a pleasant, round face that glowed from the heat of the fire. A healthy, good-natured wench. No wonder Stove had taken a fancy to her. But Charlotte noticed an ugly-looking burn on her left forearm.

"For heavens' sake, Jess, get that burn attended to. Miss Honey will put her ointment on it, and wrap it for you."

"If you say so, missus, but it ain't much. I got this here broth ready for you, like you said."

"I'll send Joe to get it. Just set it farther from the fire, to cool a bit."

Jess stood silently before her, rubbing her plump brown hands on her apron, her head bent, but glancing up from time to time with those soft black eyes. So respectful and innocent looking. Joan hated her, of course, yet how was Jess to blame if Stove preferred her comely, gentle face to Joan's stern, worn countenance?

"All right, Jess. You have the recipe for the succotash by heart, now?" Getting a nod, she went on. "I have another recipe for you to learn. She drew a paper from her pocket, looked around for a reasonably clean spot on the bench by the worktable, and read aloud, very slowly, the ingredients and the simple steps for a peach cobbler. "Now I want you to start directly on the crust. It appears you have the fire hot enough, and you know to use the Dutch oven. If you forget something I've read to you, or even if you're not quite sure--you hear, girl? Send Jillie for me or Miss Honey to read it to you again. Do you understand? It's Mr. Nathan's favorite dessert, and it must be done right. I'd prepare it myself but I swear I don't have the time."

"Yes, missus. I does it just right. For sure."

Of course her assurances meant nothing. Only two days ago she'd put too much salt in a lamb stew and the whole thing was ruined.

That was all Charlotte could do for now. Besides, the sun was warming the air outside, and the heat from the hearth was producing beads of moisture on the nape of her neck and between her breasts. She stepped out into the open, taking a deep breath and walking slowly toward the house. A breeze cooled her neck and throat. She would have the house to herself for a little while, and could write down her orders for supplies in the cool peace of her chamber.

Once seated at her secretary she dipped her quill into the inkpot and quickly wrote down those items that were already fixed in her mind: three barrels of flour (the wheat crop had not been good this year), two hogsheads of plain sugar and three loaves of the fancy kind, three sacks of coffee. Hogsheads reminded her of something. What was it? Ah yes, she had to tell Noah to make at least a dozen more hogsheads for the tobacco.

In the midst of her work she failed to notice that Honey had crept in--always so damnably quiet!--until the girl's foot made a floorboard squeak.

"Well, what is it, Honey?"

"Pardon me, ma'am. If I could just speak to you for a minute?"

"I'm in the midst of ordering supplies, and I'll forget something if I don't go ahead and finish. Just seat yourself and be quiet for a few minutes."

The supplies were an excuse. The girl looked anxious and determined. She had gained such a place in the household that even Charlotte had to take her quite seriously. She needed time to think. Surely Honey would not dare reproach her concerning Miles. Doubtless the girl knew what had been going on. She had dogged Charlotte's footsteps right up until Miles' departure. She would find something that needed Charlotte's attention just after dinner, the time she would leave the house if she intended to visit Miles. Doubtless the foolish girl hoped to prevent Charlotte from leaving. She would not have spoken a word of this to anyone. And she would certainly not be a bearer of tales to Matthew. Charlotte was sure of that. Still, she was a living reproach. It was bad enough that Sarah had been sewn to Charlotte's skirts for months. But that one was such a simple creature, and so devoted to Charlotte, that she would not see a wrong even it were dangled in front of her face. Besides, Sarah could always be sent off for a while, to Matthew's sister Millie in Richmond to help with the new baby, or even just to Kate and Lucinda, who were hard-pressed these days. But Charlotte was not about to deprive herself of Honey. In addition to all the other help she gave, she was having an invaluable influence on Molly, on Nathan, on the servants, even Maudy. But why must she be such an insufferable little saint?

How fortunate it was that Mrs. Levier had insisted upon having the injured Nathan moved into Old House with her. It made much sense, for she'd had a bed for him installed in her dining room, which had been used only as a second parlor for many years. There he could hobble about on his crutch, even go out of doors without stairs to contend with. This arrangement meant that Honey could conveniently nurse him and his grandmother both. They had even had her loom placed in the parlor, so between Honey's weaving and nursing, in Old House and in the sick cabin, she was seldom seen in Great House other than for dinner.

Well, if the young woman did dare to utter a reproach, she, Charlotte, would simply recall to her mind who was mistress here at Laurel Hill.

"All right, Honey, what have you to say? Pray make it short, for I've a mountain of things to attend to."

The girl started, sat up straight in her clean white apron and mobcap that almost completely hid her gray work gown and all but a few wisps of corn-yellow hair. "I wouldn't bother you, ma'am, only it worries me so and I don't know what to do."

"Well, out with it. What's so troublesome to you?"

"It's Mr. Nathan, ma'am. He's been talking to me."

"Good heavens, Honey, why shouldn't he talk to you? Haven't you been over there nursing him every day?"

"He's been...courting me, ma'am." Here the girl flushed deeply, and one had to admit it became her. She had such sallow skin--although in truth her color had improved over the months, and now one noticed the grace of her movements more than the meagerness of her figure. "I've told him how as I'm not good enough for him, and that you and Mr. Waverley for sure want him to marry a real lady. From good family, I mean, with education and fine manners." Her voice trailed off. She really looked quite wretched.

"I assume you were not able to discourage him," said Charlotte, trying to maintain a serious expression.

"Oh no, he says he don't, doesn't want somebody like that. He says Mr. Waverley will be glad of whoever he wants. Maybe that's right because Mr. Waverley is so kind. But I reckon <u>you</u> would never..." She broke off, realizing, no doubt, what she'd implied.

Here Charlotte couldn't help giving way to laughter. How long it had been since she'd enjoyed a hearty laugh. "My dear child, I may not be kind, but I see no objection to such a marriage. You are a Waverley, after all. It must not be soon, of course. You are both too young."

"But there is a great objection, ma'am. You see, after all that happened back there--you know about it--I can't have babies. Granny Harriet said so. So I can never marry."

"Oh nonsense. There's always a relation with too many children. Your own sister, most likely. She looks the fertile kind to me. You've only to wait a few years. Believe me, you can thank God to be relieved of childbearing."

"But for sure and certain Mr. Nathan wouldn't like it."

"Of course you'll say nothing to him. You'll adopt a couple of strapping boys from someone else's litter, and Nathan will be proud as a lord. Now run along and leave me in peace."

After the girl left Charlotte leaned back in her chair and let her arms fall limp at her sides. She gazed up at the delicate scrollwork that ran along the top of her walls and slowly dismissed, one by one, every task, every decision, every problem, from her mind.

As though in answer to her desire for some distraction, she heard a soft swish of cloth at the door left open by Honey, and turned to see Sophie Meachem glide in. She had seen quite a bit of Sophie of late. What pleasure this spirited young woman brought her! What a delightful contrast to the priggish moralizing of Honey, Mrs. Levier, Matthew, yes, and even Miles.

"Why Sophie, how early you are today! Are you not wont to be deep in your dreams at this hour?"

"Ah, would that I were, Mrs. Charlotte," sighed the young woman as she embraced Charlotte in a puff of rosewater scent. She abandoned herself to the wing chair by the window, removing her bonnet to let a cluster of nearly black curls settle about her shoulders. What an attractive little creature she was, with her olive skin that fitted so smoothly over her heart-shaped face and her perfectly rounded neck and arms. She was dressed in deep rose muslin (a color that Charlotte could not wear), with a virginal pink fichu that belied her true character. Charlotte looked questioningly at her stocking feet.

"I left my boots at your door, dear Mrs. Charlotte. I could see no sign of a servant to wipe them, and I didn't wish to track dirt on your nicely polished floor." She smiled that winsome smile of hers, and Charlotte thought once more that she well understood why Dick Meachem had defied his father to marry this girl.

"I hope you were not chased out of your home again?" said Charlotte.

"Dick was still sleeping off his carousing in the village last night. As you know, most mornings find him in a waking coma. He took me to the ball at the tavern, but I came home alone in the carriage because of course he had to stay on with the worst of his rowdy companions. I knew I should be in for it when he woke up, particularly since Mrs. Meachem has gone to visit her sister, and the Colonel is in Richmond."

"I hope you gave him no excuse for mistreating you," said Charlotte, putting on a severe face.

But Sophie knew her neighbor too well by now to be fooled by it. She laughed. "Oh my dear friend, if I gave him no excuse (and he needs almost none) I should die of boredom. There were a couple of pretty young gentlemen there for the dancing, guests of Mr. and Mrs. Cracklethorpe. I avow that they paid me more attention than to Miss Cracklethorpe or to any of the other hopeful young ladies. Of course Dick spent most of his time down in the taproom, but I don't doubt he mounted the stairs a time or two to spy on me."

"Ah Sophie, Sophie, you are a wicked, wicked woman." Before this past summer Charlotte would have seriously admonished the young woman, not out of any real disapproval, but simply for the sake of her welfare. Now the words she spoke were in jest, and Sophie knew it. Now Sophie's recklessness seemed no more extreme than her own. Although in truth the risks she had taken after the unthinking abandon of that first night with Miles were calculated ones. She had been careful. She had made sure that should there be a consequence, it would be assumed to come from the matrimonial bed. And more than that, she knew, deep down, that if Matthew ever should learn the truth, he would forgive her.

"I may be wicked, dear Mrs. Charlotte, but I am determined to snatch what pleasures I can as they are offered me. What a shame that Miles, Mr. Miles, that is, has left us. Now there is a manly fellow! And living all alone there in the forest. I paid him a visit once. Did you know that, Mrs. Charlotte? He played Master Honorable and took me home, but I am sure that in time...don't you think?" She gave Charlotte a meaningful glance.

Little hussy! Did she suspect anything about her and Miles? Well, and what if she did? The principal thing was that Miles had spurned her. That thought brought a smile to Charlotte's lips.

"I can only bide my time," Sophie continued, "until the Colonel dies. When Dick comes into the property, I trust I'll be able to wheedle him into spending the winters in Richmond, perhaps even Charleston. Meanwhile, things aren't so bad when the senior Mrs. Meachem is in residence. Dick is a little restrained by the presence of his mother. Oh, by the by, dear friend, I would be ever so grateful if you would let me spend a few nights at Laurel Hill. Until Mrs. Meachem returns." She had risen quickly and come to kneel by Charlotte's chair, taken her hand and squeezed it.

"But won't Dick come after you?"

"Oh no. As you know, Mr. Waverley has quite formally forbidden him from setting foot on your property."

"Very well, my dear. Of course you may stay at Laurel Hill. Matthew will be delighted when he learns that we have given haven to a lady in distress. Shall I send the dogcart for your things?"

"No, dear Mrs. Charlotte. Forgive me, but I counted on your good heart and had myself driven here in the carriage. I'll just have Abram unload my little case."

Charlotte had to laugh. "You're a sly minx, Sophie, but you do me good. I've too many pious souls about me. I'll have you put in Molly's chamber. Mme. de Coulanges has only just left it. They got along famously, and so shall you and Molly, who dearly loves a change. Now go along and get yourself settled. They'll be calling us in an hour for dinner."

She ushered Sophie out of the room and then, feeling a sudden drop in her spirits, crossed to her dressing table and sank down heavily on the chair facing the glass. Her reflection made an unpleasing contrast to the pretty young woman she had been gazing upon. The line from jaw to chin was no longer straight, her eyelids drooped, and the skin under her eyes puffed out ever so slightly. Her figure was still good, her hair still thick, and no wrinkles threatened as yet. But clearly, her beauty was on the wane. Patrick Levier still flirted with her, but then, what could his old eyes see, even through those spectacles? Matthew again looked upon her with nothing but love, since their reconciliation, but he no longer really looked at her. He merely carried the memory of her beauty in his head.

And Miles? She knew well that he had long been drawn to her, as she to him. They had both hidden it, and nourished it with their mutual taunts and pretended dislike. So of course when opportunity arose he succumbed in spite of his high-minded love for that insipid little Ludwell girl. Oh Miles, you fool! You coward! That glorious bonfire we ignited would have burned itself out. No harm done. Why in God's name did you run away?

She bent her head forward onto the cold surface of the dressing table. She could not recall a time when she had felt so miserable. She was not inclined to self-pity. Indeed, she despised it. She had been deserted by a most ordinary man. For who was more ordinary, more mediocre, than Miles Waverley? He had nothing of Matthew's refinement, manners, learning, and reputation. All he had was raw energy, strength, youth. She raised her head and gave a rueful laugh, for after all, that was exactly what she wanted. Somehow she would have her revenge. She would treat him with icy indifference when next he dared show his face at Laurel Hill. She would support Lucinda's resolve to remain loyal to Geoffrey, assuring her that he would surely return to her one day. And she would meanwhile amuse herself with that fascinating little Sophie.

Late that same afternoon as clouds moved over the sun and a chill crept into the dining room of Old House, Elizabeth rocked in quick staccato rhythm in her chair close by the hearth as Cyrus laid logs to start a fire. Her rheumatism always returned with the first cold nights of autumn, and this year it threatened to be worse than ever before. She watched as Cyrus struck flint against metal, and was heartened to see the tiny sparks incite the punk into flame. Cyrus was a good man. A shame that either he or Juno must be constantly in attendance upstairs now that poor Mary had returned. She too grew worse in the first chills of autumn and paced relentlessly on the floorboards of the second story.

"All right, Cyrus, you'd best relieve Juno upstairs so she can go help that new cook prepare us some supper." Ah, how her hips ached! And her legs too. Would that Honey come soon with her liniment. She could hear the clack of the loom in the parlor where Maudy had been at work for the past hour. It was a pleasant, steady sound, the sound of useful work. But the high-pitched, excited voice of Molly was beginning to get on her nerves. The child was lying on the rag rug next the bed reading aloud to Nathan who lay stretched upon his back, his hands cradling his head, and his eyes closed so you couldn't tell if he were awake or asleep. Molly wouldn't notice anyway, for she was quite carried away with the story of someone cast away on a desert island. What good such a tale could do either of them Elizabeth did not know. When she was growing up in that good Quaker household in Philadelphia, no frivolous book ever crossed the threshold.

At least the reading distracted Nathan from the pacing overhead, which drove the poor boy quite wild, that and the lack of movement and occupation that his broken leg had caused. Honey was the only one who could truly calm Nathan, and even his poor crazy mother for a short while at least. Honey never failed to ascend the stairs every morning as soon as she entered the door of Old House. She would brush Mary's thin, graying hair that hung to her waist, and sing her old songs in a sweet voice. Mary would sit so stiff and so still you almost believed she had turned into a statue, and Juno said she would stay that way as though still hearing the song for a while after Honey left.

Then the dear girl would come down, and drawing the screen in front of Elizabeth, would raise her skirt and petticoat and rub the liniment that smelled of lemon balm on her legs and hips. After that she would tend to Nathan, bathe him, help him up, and walk close to him as he hopped about on his crutch.

All that she would do on her morning visit. In late afternoon she would return to work with her needle in the main parlor and direct Maudy at the loom. But first she would read to Nathan from the law books Matthew had directed him to study. Poor Nathan struggled so laboriously to read for himself, and was so slow. Why Honey could read a whole page aloud in the time it took the poor boy to make out three lines. Yet he was no dunce. He remembered well what was read to him. Honey was a good reader now, could sound out big words, even the Latin ones, without a notion of their meaning, of course. Molly, that sharp little minx, could have done the same for him, but she had no patience and would start grumbling about how tedious it was, and soon jump up and run out of the room.

Now Nathan rolled over with a groan and muttered, half-asleep, something about Miss Honey, to which Molly responded by poking him in the shoulder and singing: "Nathan's got a sweetheart, Nathan's got a sweetheart." A silly smile spread over the boy's face.

Well, why not? He would be lucky if he got Honey for a wife. Salt of the earth was that girl. Of course Matthew and Charlotte would not allow their nephew to marry a poor relation from the backcountry. Charlotte in particular, with her highfalutin ways, would oppose it. To be sure, her pride had been chastened by the scandalous behavior of her brother, running off with that shameless woman, a married woman at that, and ruining his chances of marrying into the Ludwell family.

She was jolted out of these thoughts by Molly's hand shaking her knee.

"Nathan's fallen asleep again, Grandmama. I can't imagine why, seeing as how the part I'm reading him is quite astounding. But my voice is tired anyhow."

She smiled at her granddaughter, of whom she was really very fond despite the child's wild ways. "You're here at Old House so much more these days, child. I'm glad to see it."

"I like it better here with you and Nathan and Honey. Great House is dreary these days, with Papa and Grandpapa Patrick gone, and Uncle Geoffrey and Madam Marie, too. She was such great fun. Uncle Miles is gone as well, though he never came to see us anymore. And Mama's even more cross than ever. With the Meachems away and Miss Kate and Miss Lucy so busy, no one comes to visit. I vow, it's like a graveyard over there. Except when that Mrs. Sophie comes. I do so like listening to what she and Mama talk about. But then Mama sees me and shoos me away. Not that I care a fig for Mrs. Sophie. She treats me like I'm a fly on her teacake."

Elizabeth was gathering her thoughts so as to say something edifying to the child, when Honey finally came in, a little breathless and with tired eyes, but still with her shy smile upon her lips. She kissed Elizabeth and the child.

"Guess what, Miss Honey! I shot two squirrels and a hare this morning. I gave them to Joan to cook for May and Maudy and herself."

"Why that's mighty fine, Molly. I'm sure Joan was pleased."

"You bet Joan was pleased! And guess what else. Whilst I was checking my traps I came into that clearing where the creek widens out, and there, not a stone's throw from me, was a boar! A big one, too. Came up to my chest. I shot it too. Hit him in the rump, but only grazed him, I think. Before he could turn to charge me I lit out of there lickety-split. What do you think of that?"

"Oh Molly, Molly. I don't think well of that at all. You could have been killed! You must promise me never, never to do such a thing again. I'm sure your uncle Miles taught you to run away fast as ever you can if you come upon a boar."

"Oh all right, all right. Don't make such a fuss. Fess and Carter had good fun with a boar only last week."

"And Fess got a wicked gash in his leg from fooling with that boar. His wound needs dressing, but I've so much else to attend to. Would you run over to the infirmary and clean it and change the bandage?"

"Oh goody! Shall I put a leach on it?" The child was jumping with delight, all her annoyance at being scolded dispelled.

"No, just clean it with tincture of arnica. It's the brown bottle. And add more foxglove to the compress. The leaves are in the large tin box. Mind you bruise them well. Fess will be glad to see you. You're such a favorite of his."

Molly was off like a quarter horse at the gun. Would that Honey, with her gentle ways, might in time have a good influence on that child. Would that she not turn out as arrogant and self-willed as her mother. In any case, what could a weak woman, whose son ignored her and whose daughter-in-law despised her, do to better anything in this household? Elizabeth sighed.

Meanwhile Honey had roused Nathan from his slumber. She pulled a heavy book with a worm-eaten black binding from under the bed, seated herself on a straight chair, and began, slowly and hesitantly, to read aloud as Nathan gazed upon her steadily with those deep-sunk dark eyes of his.

Less than an hour later Molly was skipping over the dry earth, raising a tide of dust on her way back to Old House from her errand of mercy at the infirmary cabin. She was quite puffed up with pride over the perfectly neat bandage she had applied to Fess's almost-closed wound, and over the humble and respectful eyes the boy kept fixed upon her. She hadn't minded at all making him groan from the pain of the arnica because that was all for his own good, wasn't it? She might even have lingered a bit longer than necessary over that painful part of the task. But she was indeed thorough and efficient!

She found Nathan sitting in a rocking chair on the verandah with his splinted leg propped up on a stool. He was gazing off toward the sun that glowed a golden red in the west, and did not even turn his head toward Molly as she passed. He certainly wasn't much fun these days. But how could he be, laid up so he had to lie around all the day long, or hobble about a little, which wasn't much better. Being daft over Honey didn't improve his wits either.

She entered the main parlor and found Maudy still peddling away at the loom, working on a cover for one of Mama's chairs. Honey was on her knees by a chair she'd brought from Big House, pulling and pinning a finished cover on it. Grandmama was sitting in her wing chair close up to a lively fire. Molly strode proudly to the center of the parlor and announced the excessively successful completion of her mission in a loud voice.

"Hush, child," said her grandmother. "Where are your manners? Now, what was I saying? Oh yes, bring your work closer to the fire, Honey. And Molly, light two more candles here on the mantle." Grandmama was allowed all the candles she wanted, and wax ones at that. Whereas if she, Molly, burned a plain old smelly tallow one to read at night, Mama snapped at her.

Molly did as she was told, heaving a great sigh to let everyone know how she disliked being ordered about. Grandmama kept her moving the candles about, so as to throw equal light on loom and chair. The heat of the fire, up close like that, was well nigh unbearable. How much more comfortable she would be in the cool of the outdoors, with no one telling her what to do. But then, of course, she might miss something interesting in the grown-ups' talk.

"Honey," Grandmama was saying, "you missed prayers this morning. We had to have Molly read them, and she dashes through like her tongue was on fire. And you weren't at the dinner table more than ten minutes."

"I'm sorry, ma'am. I've spent too much time working at these chair covers, so as Mrs. Waverley can have them for the holiday season. When

Maudy can do them much faster than me, and neater too. So now I've taught her the pattern, she can do the rest. Mrs. Waverley has promised, if Maudy finishes right soon, to let her have more time to work on the Queen's Fancy coverlet. She means to sell it so she can make some money for herself and buy her freedom one of these days. It was so kind and generous of your grandmama to let us move the loom into her house, with her fire and her candles, so we can have the light."

"Oh my goodness, Mama will never allow Maudy to buy her freedom. She needs her here."

"Sh! Don't say that!" Honey sounded angry, which didn't happen very often, and when it did it made Molly feel almost as bad as when Papa was mad at her.

"Why should Maudy want to buy her freedom? She's well enough treated here."

Everybody was quiet now and looking at Maudy, so she must have thought she was supposed to say something.

"You know I needs to get away from here, missie. My man Quash, he don't care for me no more since I got ugly, and those other niggers, they spit on me."

"It's all because you gave yourself airs, girl," said Grandmama. "Set yourself above the rest of them. Just because of your pretty face. And I'd be surprised if you didn't brag about how you were going to run away and live in a town with a house and a man to take care of you. Goodness knows why that man Quash came here looking for a woman. Aren't there good women there on Col. Meachem's place?"

"That's 'cause he don't like to see his woman worked hard and whipped, while he got to stand by and do nothing."

"All I can say is 'pretty is as pretty does.' You've acted high and mighty and now the others have their chance to get back at you. Well, well, don't cry, Maudy. I have a little bit of money to help you buy your freedom, and Mr. Levier will find work for you in Richmond."

Then Joan's voice came from the doorway, which caused everyone to start, since nobody had noticed her coming. "You'll be sorry, gal, if ever you goes free. Who'll look after you then when you is sick or in trouble? You won't have your mammy, or Missie Honey, or Missus Charlotte. Cross as she be, she takes care of you."

"Humph! What do you know, Mammy? You ain't never been off this place. Not since you came, and that be long ago. I'd rather be free than anything. Besides, folks take care of other folks there, in town. Black folks, I mean, just like here."

"What can them town niggers, even if they be free, do when things is real bad? They's at bottom of the heap there just like here. If I knows anything, I knows that."

At this point Nathan limped into the room. He refused to let them settle him into a chair.

"Damned sick of sitting and lying," he growled, but then apologized for speaking so in front of Grandmama. He began to hobble back and forth, back and forth, on the bare boards beyond the carpet. Joan still leaned against the doorjamb, in spite of all the work she probably had to do. Honey and Maudy had resumed their tasks.

"Mayhap you won't have to buy your freedom, Maudy," said Grandmama. "Perhaps Virginia will finally abolish slavery, like they've done up north."

"Fat chance of that," Nathan snorted. "Where do you think folks hereabouts would be without their Negroes? My uncles, for example."

Nathan had grown soft and fat, with all his lying about. Well, not fat, but not so bony anymore. He'd grown bossy and talkative, too, at least when no one but Grandmama and Honey and the servants were about. He thought he knew more than any female, even Mama. He was like all men. That is why she, Molly, wasn't ever going to get married and have some man lord it over her.

"Perhaps we shouldn't speak of such things right at present," said Honey to Nathan.

"Why not? Joan and Maudy might as well not get their hopes up.

Uncle Matthew says the tide is turning against emancipation. He thinks the whole system is evil, but he knows no way out for Virginia."

"I suppose you're right, dear boy," sighed Grandmama. She never disputed with Nathan, her great favorite. "Honey tells me that even at Methodist class, where they used to have such high principles regarding slavery, just like us good Quakers, now they are telling folks that the spiritual liberation of our Negroes is what's most important."

"That's what Mr. Jenkins reads in letters from other Methodist preachers, ma'am," said Honey, "but he himself is still a staunch abolition man. But I didn't ask if you wanted something, Joan."

"Yes, Miss Honey, I come to ask you something." She moved up close to Honey and spoke in a whisper, but Molly's sharp ears caught it all.

"Did you know that Mrs. Meachem, the young one, is come to stay at Great House? Yes, missie, this very morning. Look like she mean to stay a good spell. She brung her little trunk along. That crazy mad husband of hers is sure to come after her, Master's orders or no. I is worried, Miss Honey."

"What are you saying, Joan? Speak up, woman," said Grandmama. "Something about Sophie Meachem? That baggage prowls about here like a hungry cat at butchering time."

"Seems like young Mrs. Meachem has come to visit for a while, ma'am," said Honey, "and Joan here is afeared--uh, afraid. I mean on account of Mr. Dick Meachem. Did you say something to Mrs. Waverley, Joan? She listens to you."

"Not no more she don't. She done told me with that voice of hers that means 'Don't you open your black mouth!' to make up the bed in Miss Molly's chamber for Mrs. Sophie."

"I reckon Mrs. Waverley knows best," said Honey, but Molly didn't think it sounded like she believed her own words. "We must all keep watch, though, so as we can call Big Moses if need be--oh, and Mr. Nathan here, too." (For a fearful oath had burst from Nathan's lips.) "He'll be walking just fine again in no time. Now I must go to the kitchen and make some of my chamomile tea for your stomach, ma'am. You said it does you more good than the wine the doctor told you to drink. And Joan, I'll bring more salve for you to rub into Maudy's scar. Truly it won't show so much in time, Maudy dear."

Molly saw, yes, in truth, she saw a little smile turn up the corners of Joan's lips. She couldn't remember ever seeing one there before, except when the Negroes were off by themselves having their fun, and she'd been allowed to watch.

"You're a good lady, Miss Honey." Honey ducked her head and colored, reminding Molly of the awkward little backcountry girl that had fallen asleep on the kitchen hearth that first day Molly had seen her a year ago.

"Oh Maudy, do stop your work now. Don't you see it's too dark, even with the candles? You'll plumb ruin your eyes." Molly knew that compliments always fretted Honey, so she would be quick to change the subject. "Now, don't anybody worry. We're all going to be good and careful, and everything will be all right."

Molly would long remember those words, and how Honey gave to each in turn her comforting little smile that made it seem like a candle had been lighted next to her faintly freckled face. Afterward, Molly was to grit her teeth in bitterness every time she remembered how easily she'd been reassured. Joan, always so stony-faced and silent, didn't get herself worked up over nothing. But what could anybody have done to ward off the cruel blow that was to strike Laurel Hill?

Chapter 23

As it turned out, Joan had been only too right to fear the coming of Mr. Meachem. And Honey had spoken to the people gathered in Old House with an assurance she did not feel. She awoke before dawn as always she did, and walked out far beyond the orchard, under the weight of glowering clouds and air so heavy with moisture that the very drawing of breath required great effort.

Day had fully dawned by the time she returned to Great House. It was just as she approached the front steps that there came to her ears the somber hoot of an owl, a sound that, heard in daytime, foretold misfortune to come. She stopped, shivering, and pulled her shawl closer about her shoulders. Then she recalled the scornful laughter of Mrs. Waverley at what that lady called foolish backcountry superstitions, and pushed herself quickly up the steps.

She took her breakfast with Aunt Abie in the otherwise empty dining room. Aunt Abie slept poorly, and was usually pacing to and fro in her chamber by the time a sleepy May came to dress her. Honey sat patiently with the poor addled old lady, persuading her to eat a few spoonfuls of hominy so that May might be off to help Jess in the kitchen, and then carry their breakfast to the folks in Old House.

Honey's next duty was to look in on the sick servants and field hands in the infirmary. Her task there was lighter than usual that morning. The cool of autumn meant fewer cases of ague, and not yet the pleurisies and fevers of winter. But all the time, out-of-doors, in the dining room, in the infirmary, unease clung to her close as a shadow.

Other than the soft voices of May and Aunt Abie, she had heard no sound of life in Great House. That was only to be expected. Molly and Sarah had gone to stay a few days at Farrington with Miss Kate and Miss Lucinda. This was at Honey's own suggestion, since the girls irritated Mrs. Waverley so very much these days. They would be good for Miss Lucinda, who loved them well and was grieving so bad over Mr. Geoffrey's leaving. It might have helped if Mr. Miles, that she was so fond of, was nearby to console the poor lady, but he'd gone off to the other end of the county to settle himself on his new estate.

To speak the truth, Mrs. Waverley, ever a spirit not over patient, had been more than usually ill-natured these last days, cuffing the servants about right cruelly. Honey knew perfectly well why she was acting up so. It was over Mr. Miles. Never would Honey have believed that a married lady, especially one with such a good, kind husband as was Mr. Waverley, could fall so deep in sin.

So small wonder that the house was silent at eight of the morning. Mrs. Waverley had taken to rising late these last weeks, and Mrs. Sophie was certainly a lie-abed kind of lady. Joan would be in the cellar or the smokehouse giving out vegetables and meat for the family and servants, now that Mrs. Waverley no longer tended to that herself. Joan would have Charlie on her hip, having already fed and dressed the baby.

After the infirmary Honey always went to Old House to see to the needs of Mrs. Levier, Mr. Nathan, and poor Mary. But this morning, all because of that scary shadow that still followed close on her heels, she turned first to Great House. Just as she came through the opening in the boxwood hedge and smelled that pungent scent that she would never again breathe in without a quake in her heart, Joan burst out the front door, clutching Charlie tight to her bosom. She ran straight to Honey as soon as she caught sight of her.

"Oh Miss Honey, quick take this baby. I got to run for Big Moses. Mr. Dick here, and he yelling something awful."

She pushed Charlie so hard against Honey's chest that she staggered and nearly fell. As soon as she righted herself she ran fast to the house, murmuring to the crying baby and patting him as she ran. Even before she reached the door she could hear a roaring voice coming from the direction of Mrs. Waverley's chamber on the ground floor.

There she ran, and the first thing she spied was Dick Meachem's broad back looming just inside the doorway.

"You're a pretty pair of hussies," he was barking in a voice thick with drink. "Dolling yourself up for visitors tonight, slut?" He took a couple of steps further into the room, so that now Honey could see that Sophie Meachem had been sitting at the dressing table tying a bright red ribbon in her dark hair. She'd turned round and got half up,

401

with her arms still raised to her head and her eyes wide open in fright. Mrs. Waverley was sitting straight up in her bed, her eyebrows almost meeting over her nose and her elbows poking out the sleeves of her lacy white nightshift. She looked like an angry hen with her feathers all ruffled up.

"D'ya think I ain't heard how you'll have all the bastards in the county here tonight to service you, you damned whore? And you, Madam High and Mighty, you're nothing but a bawdyhouse keeper, getting men here to fuck this whore." He gripped a shotgun in his hand and was waving it first at one lady and then at the other.

Right then he fell into a fit of coughing, and that gave Mrs. Waverley the chance to speak.

"Mr. Meachem, you are an unspeakable scoundrel. I owe you no explanation, but for Sophie's sake I will tell you that a few neighbors are invited to dine and dance this evening, ladies as well as gentlemen. If you were, by any stretch of the imagination, a gentleman, you would have been invited too."

Mr. Meachem had turned to spit his phlegm upon the carpet, and noticed Honey in the doorway.

"What in Satan's name are you staring at, you scrawny little chicken? Get out of here with that screaming brat or I'll shut him up right enough."

Charlie was indeed screaming and Mr. Meachem was turning the gun toward him. Honey backed off quick and ran with him to the parlor where she knew there would be no fire burning at this hour. She set him down on the carpet and shut both doors. He would be safe there. She then hurried softly back down the hall, hoping not to be noticed and thinking fast on what she should do.

When she got back to the chamber Mrs. Waverley was standing at the far side of the bed, blocking Mr. Meachem's view of the dressing table. He had the gun pointed right at her. At first it seemed like Mrs. Sophie had disappeared, but then Honey caught a glimpse of the tip of that red ribbon. The lady was crouching low behind the bed.

"Get out of my way or I'll blast the both of you. Fact is, you deserve it more, you she-devil."

"Please sir, Mr. Meachem. You feel real bad, I know." Honey spoke in the sweetest tone she could muster, but she could hear her voice squeaking like she was a scared piglet.

He turned his head just a little, but kept the gun aimed at Mrs. Waverley. "Didn't I tell you to get out of here, brat?" Yet his voice wasn't quite so loud as before.

"Folks are mean to you, ain't they, sir? They worry and fret you, and don't pay no mind to you at all. A fellow feels mad to bursting." Honey was talking to her papa now, like she ought to have done all those years ago. Like Mama used to.

"What to you know about it, a meek little rabbit like you?"

"I rightly don't know much, sir, but if you'll just take my hand, we can go out in the fresh air--it's so close in here--and you can tell me all about it."

She really did feel sorry for him then. He turned around to face her and let the barrel of the gun sink toward the floor. But he was staring out over her shoulder, like he didn't see her at all. His lips were quivering like he was a child getting ready to cry.

"It hurts real bad when somebody's mean to you. I know how it is, I surely do. Won't you let me take your hand?"

He hesitated, letting the barrel of the gun sink still further toward the floor.

It was so quiet Honey could hear the man's breath catching as he let it out. She hardly dared breathe at all herself.

But she had to do something. She slowly reached out her hand toward his. Just as she touched it she started back like it was on fire. But it wasn't fire. It was the voice of Mrs. Waverley ringing out loud as a church bell.

"Well that's better! Remember where you are, sir, and leave this chamber directly. And don't you ever show your churlish face on our property again!"

Oh, she looked so grand with her eyes darting lightning and that dark red hair streaming over the shoulders of her snowy-white nightshift. For a moment Mr. Meachem stood frozen quite still. Honey's heart beat like the great drum at muster time, faster and faster as she felt the gun swing round and graze her belly, saw it raised and fired straight into that beautiful face just as it took on a look of utter amazement. Then something crashed into Honey and she fell to the floor.

Next thing she knew, Maudy was feeling her arms and legs, asking if anything was broke. Hurting all over and clinging to Maudy, she managed to get to her feet. (They told her later that Mr. Meachem's gun had smacked into her when he burst out of the room. Big Moses had got there just then and run after him, but Mr. Meachem had his horse nearby, so he got clean away in no time.)

She looked across the bed and surely would have fallen again if Maudy hadn't been holding her up. Mrs. Waverley had sunk to her knees, and lay back against the dressing table, her face nothing but bloody pulp, and the front of her nightshift speckled with spots of blood. Her hands, raised against her bosom, were covered with small wounds. On her knees as she was, she looked like she was begging for mercy. That thought shocked Honey more than all the rest. That Mrs. Waverley, who had surely never knelt to anyone in her life, should be seen like this!

Joan was there now too, bent low over Mrs. Waverley and moaning: "She gone. She all gone." Mrs. Sophie was sitting on the floor behind them, leaning against the wall with her eyes closed. Blood had spattered over her face and bosom. But it transpired that she was not hurt one bit.

Big Moses came back then, his head bowed and his big black hands hanging limp and useless at his side.

Honey dragged her eyes away from that terrible sight. She got herself free of Maudy's grip on her shoulder, which was hurting her bad, for that was where she'd been hit. She had to see to what must be done. It was her place. There was no one else.

Through all the orders that she was finally able to give, about tying many layers of linen around the poor lady's head and then washing and dressing her, about tending to the baby in the parlor, about sending word to the neighbors, the village, and the county, and saddest of all, to Mr. Waverley in Richmond, her one consoling thought was that Mr. Waverley was not here to see his wife like this. God had granted that he, and everybody except the five of them in that bedchamber, would be allowed to remember her in all her proud beauty.

———⟞◦◦◦⟝———

Many days later Honey sat deep in the long, browning grass atop a low ridge above the Solway. Her skirt that curved in a blue calico circle around her was slowly soaking up the morning dew. She waved once more toward the two large rafts floating in the slow current at the center of the river. They were heavily charged with hogsheads of Laurel Hill tobacco, and were piloted by Nathan on the smaller one and Stove on the other.

Now that the heavy rains of early autumn had subsided, the Solway would carry the men safely to the Appomattox, and from there they would float on to Petersburg.

Honey sighed and let her shoulders and arms hang loose. She breathed in the clear, cool air, delighting in the thousands of dancing silver patches of sunlight on the dark green water, and on the rocks and tiny transparent waterfalls near the bank. She tilted her head back and watched the soft clouds, some gray, others the color of cream, drift lazily toward the east. To her right the tops of a couple of longleaf pines rose into the sky, their pale green needles glistening in the sunshine. To her left, along the horizon, huddled long, scraggly clouds, flushed with gold by the rising sun.

She was allowing herself these few minutes of rest at the dawn of day because she knew it would hearten Nathan to have her watch him off. He had been reluctant to leave Laurel Hill even for a few days.

She sorely needed to rest a spell. In the four weeks since that cruel deed had struck Laurel Hill like a great boulder falling from a cliff where it had been balancing a long time, she had been in almost constant motion, scarcely taking a few hours sleep at night. Now that old pain in her leg had returned, the one from the time Papa had thrown her against the porch rail, in a rage because she had hidden from him when he wanted her. For months the pain had felt like a knife was turning in her leg with every step. Then time had pretty well healed it. Yet once in a great while, when she was on her feet too long, the pain came back, only never so bad as the first time. After looking about to make sure no one was near, she pulled up her skirt and petticoat and rubbed hard along the side of her leg, noticing that her stocking needed washing and darning too.

There was such a sight of chores to see to, now that she must attend to all that was once the charge of Mrs. Waverley. Mrs. Levier had thought it her duty to make herself mistress of Laurel Hill. But truth to tell, she had only taken on the name. What had surprised everybody was that the lady's health had miraculously improved. Or else she bravely made like it had. She, who had been spending her days rocking by the hearth and showing Honey just where her aches and stiffness were the worst, now bustled about into every corner of both houses and into every dependency, whipping out orders to anyone in sight. But her orders, most times, just made trouble for everybody. Like when she lengthened the daily prayers to twice the time they used to take, and kept pestering Mr. Nathan and Mr. Miles, and even Mr. Waverley (calling to him through the door of his chamber), to attend them. Those gentlemen would not come, and then there was no end of complaining on the lady's part, and black silence on theirs. She refused to order the usual special treats for the Christmas season, calling them extravagances, but Honey had noticed that the least change in the way Mrs. Waverley used to manage things threw Mr. Waverley's spirits into still deeper gloom. You might think his mind was so far away from all household affairs that he noticed nothing. Honey knew better.

So she must do her best to console Mrs. Levier for the missed prayers. She must order the holly and the Yule log and the puddings and the music just like it was done every year, and then listen patiently, over and over again, to Mrs. Levier's complaints.

Sarah was a good girl and truly tried to help. But she was fast blossoming into a very pretty young lady, with her head full of flounces and curls and the young gentlemen she hoped soon to see at church. She could not keep her mind long on a simple household task to be performed. And Molly, when she wasn't with her papa, kept herself outdoors and out of sight.

Honey's true helper was Joan, just as she had been for Mrs. Waverley. Joan thought she was far too easy on the other servants, and would often chide her for that. But wasn't Honey just a backcountry girl who had never even seen a Negro until she came here? How was she supposed to lord it over these poor souls just as sternly as Mrs. Waverley had done? Joan appeared only too glad to act the strict mistress herself and fault them at their every move.

All the family had come for the funeral service. They had crowded into the parlor and the dining room, with the double doors wide open between them, just like after the barbecue last spring, when all were gathered for merrymaking and she, Honey, had got scolded for refusing to dance.

Mr. Geoffrey Burnham came from Charleston, in a suit of such fine black satin that it must have been bought for the occasion. And such curls and such lace and such great gold buckles on his shoes! He had finally won his lawsuit, so they said, and now owned a goodly estate near Norfolk. But once he'd seen Charleston, he announced to everyone, "no question of any genteel person living elsewhere on this continent." He had written to Miss Lucinda before ever he left Laurel Hill, so Kate had told Honey. He'd claimed he could not think of marriage for a long time to come, perhaps never. Poor Miss Lucy had borne this in silence and sorrow. At the funeral supper Honey had noticed her gazing at that gentleman in his finery like he was a visitor from across the seas. As for him, he hardly looked at her, and hardly even seemed sad about his sister's death. Right after the funeral he'd taken his foot in his hand and lit out, as folks said back home. For sure he was itching to get back to "genteel life."

Mr. Miles had come too, of course, and some folks remarked on him seeming more cast down than one would expect, seeing as how he and Mrs. Waverley "had little use for each other." Of course Honey kept her own counsel on that subject. Mr. Miles had stayed on at Laurel Hill, and being an active, manly sort, his spirits were soon lifted. He made himself useful at Farrington as well as Laurel Hill. Honey's heart was always gladdened by the sound of his boots on the gravel and the excited barking of his dogs as he strode right smartly up to the dairy or the smokehouse or the kitchen garden. He would bring news of Miss Kate and Miss Lucy, of work progressing at Farrington, of field hands and their sicknesses, of carts and horses available if they at the house needed them. She would see him chatting with Mr. Nathan, his big, broad form towering over the slight figure of the younger man, both leaning in loose, friendly fashion over the crossbar of a fence.

Now Mr. Nathan, he gave her worries aplenty. At first he was beside himself because he hadn't got there to that room to prevent the terrible killing. "Why wasn't I called?" (He'd been walking with his crutch in the orchard and no one knew where he was.) "How could that crazed bastard of a Dick Meachem ever have set foot on Laurel Hill at all?" He was up in arms against everybody. Honey thought she knew who he truly blamed, deep down inside, and she had tried to persuade him that he couldn't have done anything, as he was still just able to hobble about at the time. Yet as soon as he had heard what happened he'd lit right out after Dick Meachem, mounted with his poor leg still in the splint. By good fortune the Sheriff had caught up with Mr. Meachem before he ever reached Petersburg, and shut him up safe in the town jail before Mr. Nathan could get to him. So the still-raging boy, for he <u>was</u> still but a boy, came home to stamp his foot and shout at everybody. After a while he quieted down and just glowered at all he met. But work is always a savior. Soon his leg was freed of the splint and he could help out at the tobacco barns for the stripping, rolling and packing. He was useful, too, for the fencing of certain tobacco fields, so as to pen in animals to fertilize the soil.

But then, with his mind more at ease, he'd begun to pester Honey about wedding him, or at the least, giving him her promise. She did what she could to keep from letting him find her alone.

Honey peered far down the river to where it bent off toward the north. But the sun dazzled her eyes, and she could see nothing of man or barge. She was glad to have Stove, Mr. Waverley's man, leave Laurel Hill for a while. He only vexed his master in trying to serve him, and he was not much use in other household tasks. She was even happier to see Mr. Nathan leave. She was right fond of him, but how could she explain why she could not marry? She would have to tell him she couldn't have babies. He would ask her how she knew! Yet mayhap he loved her so dearly that he would not mind, seeing as how it wasn't her fault.

She truly could not figure how a girl could like being with a man the way a wife must. To be held, just held, in the arms of a gentle loving man like Mr. Waverley...ah, that would be like going to heaven! But such a thought was terribly wrong. Nathan was a good-hearted boy, after all. Too easily wrought up, but time and age would calm him down. She could be a help to him.

Come to think on it, Papa had done her and Sarah a truly good turn when he made them take the far journey to Laurel Hill. Just about this time of year it was when they arrived, with the sweet gum trees bright yellow and the oaks deep red, but all dusted with snow. The ground and all the outbuildings were pure white, as if a river of skimmed milk had been poured over them, but the dark sky frowned on them, two wretched orphans trudging knee-deep in snow.

Today everything was different. The red and yellow leaves shone bright against the sky and only a few patches of snow from yesterday's little sprinkle lingered in the shaded hollows of the ground. Laurel Hill was truly home to her and Sarah now. That was another reason why she could not think of marrying Nathan. He would take her out west where he aimed to settle, and then who would take care of things at Laurel Hill? Poor Mr. Waverley. Heaven knew when he would recover his spirits. He would never marry again, for sure. When his sister from Richmond, home for the funeral, had thought to console him by saying his heart would heal and someday someone would fill it more kindly than Mrs. Waverley--you could tell she hadn't cared for her sister-in-law--his face had gone so black you'd have thought he'd throw her from the room.

If truth be told, Mr. Waverley worried her more than Nathan. For a fortnight after the funeral he had refused to leave his chamber, their chamber. He suffered only Molly to bide with him there. She it was who carried him broth, the only thing he would eat. He'd found a small kerchief Mrs. Waverley had had in her bosom that day, one stained with blood, that had somehow been dropped unnoticed on the floor. Molly said he kept it inside his shirt. Oh, it surely was not right.

On the third day she had got Molly to persuade him to let her, Honey, bring him his broth. The child was growing restive, torn between her papa's grief and a child's need to be off and about. Nowadays Molly took only her dinner with her papa. Honey would bring it to them without a word (for he clearly did not wish to hear any) and then promptly leave, letting Molly carry away the tray afterward.

One day Honey asked him to let her have the kerchief, to be washed. He just turned away. Of course she comprehended. For when she and Sarah had come home to their dying father and the graves of their already-buried brothers, she had found little Josh's nightshirt thrown into a dark corner of the loft where no one had noticed it. She had slept with that crumpled shirt of his for the whole time she was home, breathing in the smell of him, all she had left of Josh.

How gaunt Mr. Waverley looked these days! A man of fair skin, his face always used to be burned brick red by the sun. Now it was the color of yellowed paper. He did go out of doors again now, but only in the evening, riding his favorite, old Dauntless, alone through the woods where he could be sure of meeting no one. Seeing as how he ate so little, leaving half the bowl of gruel, it was a wonder he had the strength to mount his horse.

Once, when she brought their dinner to him and Molly, he had the child on his lap. Her head lay against his breast and his own head with its thin sandy-colored hair only a shade darker than Molly's was bent forward and resting on top of the child's. How Honey's throat tightened then! She could scarce get back out of the chamber before the tears that she hadn't yet shed for Mrs. Waverley finally gushed right out. Only they were for him.

She knew well enough that grief, even as sharp as his, doesn't last forever. Yesterday she had found him gazing out his window at the men repairing the roof on the dairy, with Mr. Miles calling out this and that direction and lending a hand to show them what to do. Mr. Waverley's conscience would not let him stay idle forever.

And what about her? Why, she had a sight of chores to attend to! She gave a last hard rub to her sore leg and pulled herself to her feet. She took a last look at the smooth-flowing Solway and at the tall grass bending in the breeze along its banks. Then she turned to admire Great House with its proud pillars and neatly patterned bricks. She would be needed here, sorely needed, for a long time to come. She raised her damp skirt and scurried up the bank.